A LIFE OF BLISS

DON BUTLER

a life of bliss

Don Butler

OTTAWA PRESS
AND PUBLISHING
MYSTERY

Ottawa Press and Publishing Mystery (OPP Mystery)
ottawapressandpublishing.com

ISBN 978-1-988437-70-5 (softcover)
ISBN 978-1-988437-72-9 (epub)
ISBN 978-1-988437-71-2 (mobi)

Cover Design: Joanna D'Angelo

Interior Book Design/Formatting: Indie Book Designer

Published in Canada

Dedicated to my mother, Peggy Butler (1924-2021).

CONTENTS

ACKNOWLEDGMENTS

I wrote my first draft of *A Life of Bliss* some years ago, drawing on numerous trips to Greece. I then set it aside while I focused on my newspaper job, and returned to it when I retired. During this time, my wife Christina Spencer—a terrific writer and editor in her own right —has been invaluable, pointing out plot flaws, critiquing my writing and pushing me relentlessly to get the novel published. I doubt this book would exist without her.

I'd like to thank friends and family members who read my manuscript and offered encouragement, especially my sister-in-law Joy Ferguson. Joy edits books and magazines for a living—and writes fiction to boot —and kindly read my manuscript, offering insightful comments that improved it. Alex Zych did a thorough line edit that caught and fixed a number of style errors, and endeared herself to me by loving my book. Thanks Alex! And Joanna D'Angelo designed a lovely cover that should make my book irresistible to readers.

Finally, I'd like to thank Ron Corbett, owner of Ottawa Press and Publishing, for agreeing to publish my novel despite an ongoing pandemic, and Teri Barnett of Indie Book Designer for the formatting.

PART I

"To fear love is to fear life, and those who fear life are already three parts dead."

- Bertrand Russell

CHAPTER 1

Bliss Browning glanced down furtively. What ought to have been the robust symbol of his manhood had nearly vanished, withered by 40 minutes immersion in the chill waters of the health club swimming pool. Discreetly turning away from the strangers in the shower room, he tugged at his shrunken shaft as jets of water drummed on his abdomen. This stretching exercise was something of a ritual for Browning, who had a pathological fear of ridicule from the better-endowed men with whom he shared his nakedness. He could have eliminated this risk by leaving his bathing suit on while he showered, or by dispensing with a shower entirely. But at the health club, this behaviour would have been seen as abnormal. With the peculiar logic of the truly obsessive, Browning reasoned that he stood a better chance of avoiding attention if he blended in with the prevailing culture, even if it meant baring his privates to the judgment of others.

Admittedly, the dimensions of male members vary widely. But relatively few men are cursed with the cocktail sausage that dangled between Browning's legs, whose inadequacy, he imagined, symbolized his own unmemorable life – his fleeting marriage, mediocre career and paucity of true friends.

Yet he clung to a thin hope that things could be different. The feeling was little more than an intuition that fate would eventually reward him for whatever virtues he possessed. Armed with that uncertain belief, he steeled himself to partake of life.

The lane swimming was part of that discipline. Three times a week, Browning trekked to the health club to grind through grim, endless laps in a Sisyphean effort to transform his flabby body into something worthy of admiration. Three times a week, he was forced to acknowledge that no amount of front crawl could overturn nature. Yet he dutifully returned every Monday, Wednesday and Saturday, because the alternative — withdrawal, solitude, decay — was unthinkable.

The health club visits were among Browning's few regular sources of social connection. Not that he actually interacted with his fellow club members. He visited alone, churned through his swim, showered and dressed in silence. While others chatted with friends or genial strangers, Browning avoided eye contact and was rarely approached. He told himself he preferred it that way.

"Keep yanking on that thing and it might come off."

The words cut through the shower room like a fart at a funeral. With sudden horror, Browning realized that his right hand was absently plucking at his penis, and that the beefy, red-faced man to his left was gazing at him with a mixture of bemusement and contempt. Quickly, he released his prey.

"Beg pardon?" he stammered stupidly.

"Yer dick," roared the stranger, his loathsome voice rising above the water's hiss and echoing off the tile walls. A few fellow bathers glanced curiously in Browning's direction. "You're likely to do yourself an injury, tuggin' on the poor little feller like that."

Synapses misfiring in the sudden stress of this long-feared humiliation, Browning blurted the first thought that came to mind. "It wasn't me," he babbled. "You must have me mixed up with someone else." He instantly realized this was not only unconvincing, but farcical. He shifted swiftly to a strategy of total capitulation. "No, no, it was me all right, is what I meant to say," he amended, with a wild-eyed grin.

Everyone in the steaming shower room was watching now. Like passers-by at the scene of a grisly accident, they were drawn, almost against their will, to witness Browning's self-immolation. He could feel the eyes of a dozen strangers assessing his sex organs, which reflexively shrivelled further.

Browning seemed incapable of speech. He stared helplessly at his tormentor. The red-faced man returned his gaze for a moment, then turned away with a short shake of his head. Heart pounding like a rabbit hotly pursued by wolves, Browning grabbed his shampoo bottle and scampered toward the shower room exit. In his haste, his right foot skidded in a pool of water. Almost gracefully, he did the splits, landing ignominiously on the tile floor.

He sprawled there for a few seconds, too stunned to move. Then an uncontrollable laugh, fueled by a recognition of his own absurdity, began to build. The laugh put final rout to what remained of his dignity. As naked men watched in astonishment, Bliss Browning rolled around on the shower room floor, wracked by choking laughter that rose like magma from within him.

~

THE OFFICES of the *Daily Advocate* consumed half a city block in the somnolent heart of Canada's capital city, Ottawa. The newspaper, the city's only broadsheet, had occupied its present quarters, a gloomy four-storey red brick building topped with gargoyles representing Liberty, Truth and Courage, for more than a century.

Typical of its dying breed, the *Advocate* had been slow to embrace change, keeping computers at bay until the early 1980s. For years after that, it opted to employ a small army of compositors to paste up its columns of type rather than shift to a desktop publishing system.

As long as the *Advocate* was earning outsized profits, its Toronto-based owner, Medialand Corp., had tolerated this Luddite predilection. But now, a few years into the new millennium, the newspaper's fortunes were in steady decline. Circulation was down a third from its peak. Advertising lineage was half what it used to be. Profits were evaporating. Last year, the paper had, for the first time, laid off employees.

But it wasn't enough. Medialand's bean-counters were losing patience. So far, Reid Hartley, the *Advocate*'s legendary publisher, had been able to keep the corporate vultures off the carcass. But Hartley was 67, closing in on retirement, and pessimism about the future was rife among *Advocate* staff.

Bliss Browning's piece of this troubled universe was a pale green, vinyl-clad desk in the least accessible corner of the congested second-floor newsroom, piled high with yellowing newspapers, press releases well past their expiry date and glossy travel magazines. A lumpy blue upholstered chair, with the words "Property of Bliss Browning — piss off!" scrawled in red grease pencil on the back, was sometimes tucked under the desk when he arrived for work at 9 a.m. More often, a night shift worker had appropriated it, forcing Browning to scour the newsroom for retrieval.

There were a few personal touches, of course. On his desk, Browning kept a stained ceramic mug that boasted, over an image of an impossibly proportioned woman in a thong bikini, "It's Better in the Bahamas." A calendar from the embassy of Greece dazzled the eye with scenes of Santorini and other Greek islands. Taped to the side of the desk was a prized poster of the legendary diva, Maria Callas, playing the role of Floria Tosca in the 1964 Zeffirelli production at London's Covent Garden. Browning had acquired it at a garage sale for $1.50 from someone sadly ignorant of its historical significance. And tucked away on a corner of the desk, obscured by his computer terminal and the rising piles of detritus, was a five-by-seven framed portrait of his younger self with his arms wrapped self-consciously around the narrow waist of the flaxen-haired woman who was, very briefly, his wife.

Browning, who joined the *Advocate* just as its fortunes began to wane (a coincidence, he told himself, without conviction), had called this desk home since becoming travel editor four years earlier. The appointment had mystified him. Not only had Browning never travelled (except to Lake Placid, New York for a ski weekend six years ago, during which he had fractured his fibula on a beginner's slope), he actively disliked travel. His antipathy was fueled by an impressive collection of phobias. He was convinced that any airplane he boarded would plummet from the sky, suitcases he packed would be irretrievably lost, automobiles he rented would suffer brake failure on winding mountain roads, hotels he booked into would explode in flames while he slept.

But Norman Pugsley, the *Advocate*'s irascible managing editor, had waved off Browning's objections. "Christ on a bicycle, man, we don't need some adventurer with itchy feet for this job," Pugsley had exclaimed. "How many of our readers do you think sail off to fuckin' Fiji for their vacation?"

Browning had said nothing. He could recognize a rhetorical question when he heard one. "Most don't get more than a few hundred miles down the highway," Pugsley continued, "We need someone who can relate to them, not some globe-trotting dilettante.

"Besides," he had added triumphantly, "the travel section has no budget, so you couldn't go anywhere even if you wanted to. You're perfect for the job, Browning. All you have to do is sit here at your desk, check the wires and pick out a few wind-in-your-hair reads. Even you should be able to handle that."

Pugsley, who had been managing editor for a dozen years, had scant use for contemporary management theories. He favoured authoritarian rule leavened by occasional moments of magnanimity. If Pugsley had decided that Browning would be travel editor, then that's what he would be. And Pugsley had so decided, more out of necessity than enthusiasm. The previous travel editor had stepped on an unexploded land mine while hiking in Sicily, reinforcing Browning's apprehension about the perils of travel. He survived, minus both legs and half his right arm, and had retired on a disability pension.

The *Advocate*'s travel section was not a journalistic priority. Indeed, it was little more than a vehicle for advertising. But someone had to fill the space between the ads. Browning, whose modest talents wouldn't be missed by his fellow editors on the news desk, was deemed expendable. Like it or not, the travel editorship was his.

And, truth be told, Browning had slowly come to enjoy his job. It had several qualities that appealed to him. Because he had no staff and his superiors evinced little interest in what he did, contact with other humans, with its ever-present potential for trauma, was minimal. The section was published just once a week, so both the pace and the hours were congenial, a rarity in the frenetic world of daily journalism. And because the travel articles he selected and edited permitted him to "visit" exotic destinations without the fuss and bother of actual travel, Browning had developed an interest in faraway lands that surprised even him.

The arcane bits of knowledge he was accumulating were impressive, if of little practical value. He knew, for instance, that Portugal has about 61,000 kilometres of paved roads and 2.6 million registered cars; that the highest mean annual rainfall in Italy, about 60 inches, occurs in the province of Udine; that a popular form of entertainment in Burma is the pwe, a type of folk opera incorporating music and dance. There were times when, stuffed with this useless knowledge, Browning actually felt like something of a world traveler, a Columbus of the cerebellum, roaming the Earth from the security of his office chair (when available), peering into the magical maw of the computer screen that brought the world safely and expediently to him.

~

BROWNING LIVED ALONE in a one-bedroom apartment on the fifth floor of a nondescript high-rise on Laurier Avenue West, just blocks from the *Advocate*'s offices. Its narrow kitchen, barely large enough to accommodate a two-person table, came with all the usual accoutrements of bachelorhood: a refrigerator containing half a litre of souring milk, three beers, a pizza slice, a jar of Jamaican pepper sauce, six processed cheese slices and some unidentifiable organic matter; a stove splattered with crusted tomato sauce; a microwave oven, flashing "pause" in fluorescent green; an electric frying pan, half-filled with water in a vain attempt to soak off the remnants of an ancient dinner; a toaster oven, at risk of being overwhelmed by crumbs.

A plastic cutting board, scored by sharp edges and breeding unimaginable bacteria, lay on the counter, next to a sink piled high with the week's unwashed dishes and a wok, still betraying evidence of the previous night's tofu-and-vegetable stir-fry. An odiferous garbage can, originally white, a bag of pretzels, largely consumed, an empty pizza box, size large, and a message board bearing a three-month old reminder to pick up the dry-cleaning completed the kitchen's decor.

The living room was sparsely furnished with assembly-kit furniture from a local Scandinavian outlet. A grey hide-a-bed crouched uneasily in the box-like room, next to a low pine coffee table, a folding chair and a flat-screen TV. Opposite the hide-a-bed, red display lights flashing like the eyes of jungle cats caught in a searchlight, was one of the few pleasures of Browning's lackluster life: his audiophile-edition stereo system. Much of his disposable income had vanished into this and earlier systems in search of the best possible reproduction of the music embedded in the racks of vinyl albums and CDs that filled the living room's remaining wall space. The collection was weighted heavily toward opera, including virtually every known work by Browning's obsession, La Divina, the great Maria Callas, whose musical output was displayed, shrine-like, in a special teak cabinet of its own.

The walls were bare except for a huge framed black-and-white portrait of Callas as Violetta in Visconti's 1955 production of *La Traviata* at La Scala. Callas's courtesan, bare-shouldered in a black evening gown, had an expression of patient suffering on her face. Her hands were clasped at her throat, in a gesture mid-way between prayer and supplication, and the yearning on her face was palpable. Browning had spent hours gazing at this portrait, as Callas's unforgettable voice filled the small room.

Browning's bedroom held another great attraction: his laptop, which connected him to the wider world with none of the risks that made his other contacts so unpredictably perilous. Not a day passed that he didn't spend hours trading ideas with strangers. It was as addictive as cocaine, as thrilling as a Callas high C.

And — this had been his most exciting discovery — the Internet linked him with people who shared his passion for Maria Callas. Browning had stumbled on the chat group by accident, astonished and gratified to find others who felt as he did about the great diva. Like a starving man at an all-you-can-eat buffet, he devoured their comments, analysis and arguments. To his surprise, he found that he possessed sounder knowledge of Callas's life and career than many who contributed to the group. Emboldened, he entered the debate, politely but firmly correcting the ignorant and explaining his favourite Callas theories with quiet authority to his unseen colleagues.

When someone asserted that Giovanni Battista Meneghini, the Verona industrialist whom Callas married in 1949, was 25 years her senior, Browning pointed out that the true age discrepancy was just under 30 years. When another said Callas sang her first "Norma" in Buenos Aires in 1949, Browning informed all that she had first performed the role in the Teatro Communale in Florence the previous year, under the baton of the distinguished maestro, Tulio Sarafin. And when a third insisted that no recording existed of Callas's towering performances in Cherubini's Medea, Browning was able to report that she could be heard in the role on a hard-to-find 1957 recording on the Ricordi label.

To Browning, the Callas group was a delightful revelation, where all that mattered was the depth of your knowledge and the strength of your ideas. The cut of your clothes, the status of your profession or the thickness of your wallet, all so important elsewhere, were meaningless. It was also anarchic, male-dominated and alarmingly uncivil, but Browning saw only its liberating qualities. The Internet freed him from limiting preoccupations (penis size was irrelevant) and let him meet the world as an equal. Others in the Callas group quickly acknowledged his expertise and treated his opinions with deference. On the Internet, if nowhere else, Bliss Browning was respected.

It was a strange sensation for one conditioned to expect indifference or even contempt. It was disorienting, but Browning liked the novelty of the emotion. He would labour late into the night, sacrificing sleep, to trigger those pleasing feelings. He might even have said the Internet was better than sex, except that Bliss Browning could barely remember what sex felt like.

CHAPTER 2

AS USUAL, SOME DEGENERATE ON THE *ADVOCATE*'S NIGHT SHIFT HAD pinched his chair. Worse, the culprit (may he spend eternity standing in a chairless section of Hell, Browning thought bitterly) had hidden it so cunningly that he couldn't find it. Ten minutes of peering at chair backs all over the newsroom had failed to locate it, and Browning's patience was wearing thin.

"Dammit Harry," he fumed to the slim, sardonic man at the next desk. "This chair theft problem is out of control. I spend more time looking for a place to park my butt than I do editing copy."

Harrison Howard, the *Advocate*'s books editor and Browning's only close friend at the paper, glanced up from the pile of new releases that had arrived in the morning mail. He nodded sympathetically. "The death penalty for chair theft, I say. The electric chair would be appropriate."

A ringing telephone interrupted these meditations on judicial reform. Browning winced and picked up the receiver.

"Hi, is that Bliss? It's Judy. If you're looking for your chair, it's in Renata's office."

Renata Richter was the *Advocate's* erudite but erratic editor. Recruited by publisher Reid Hartley two years earlier from a high-profile post in academia in an effort to raise the foundering newspaper's tone, she drove her editors mad with a ceaseless stream of brilliantly impractical ideas. It was her idea, for example, to publish special monthly sections examining the historical context of present-day world problems. So far, bewildered *Advocate* readers had been subjected to 20-page supplements on 18th-century clan conflicts in Somalia, the colonial roots of economic crisis in Zaire, the Mogul era in India and philosophical thought in Czarist Russia. It was, *Advocate* editors thought, as removed from readers' interests as the price of turnips in Tashkent, but Richter would not be deterred.

"Christ, Harry," said Browning, dropping the receiver into its cradle, "Richter's got my chair!"

"Whoop-whoop-whoop, danger, danger," sang out Howard. "Just make sure she doesn't spot you when you retrieve it. God knows what mad-assed scheme she might lay on you."

Browning laughed mirthlessly. Howard spoke from bitter experience. Soon after her arrival at the paper, Richter had called the books editor into her office and informed him his section was badly in need of an overhaul. Henceforth, she instructed, the weekly books section would be 16 pages instead of three, the reviewers all distinguished authors (preferably Nobel Prize winners), and the content heavily skewed toward literary fiction, poetry and obscure works of history. Popular books would be noted briefly or ignored altogether. These lunatic orders had actually been implemented until reader complaints and the ruinous cost of producing the section prompted Reid Hartley to intervene and restore sanity. So far, the travel section had escaped the editor's rarefied attentions, but Browning feared it was only a matter of time before her restless intellect would alight, however briefly, leaving carnage in its wake.

Warily, he approached the editor's office. Judy Rendell, Richter's executive secretary, waved him over. "Your chair's in her office," she said. "She needed it last night for a meeting on the supplement on Iran. Big, big crowd at that one. Standing room only." She gave him a conspiratorial smile. "Go on in and get it — she's not there."

With a grateful nod, Browning entered the august sanctum. Books filled one wall, a veritable library of deep thinking on philosophy, history, literature, economics and the arts. A couple of journalism tomes, recent additions to her collection, were wedged in among well-thumbed volumes of history. A laptop computer, loaded with all the latest software, perched on a credenza next to Richter's desk. (Rumor had it she was hopeless with technology and needed instruction every time she wanted to write a memo.)

Her desk was clear except for a foot-thick pile of mail and memos in her in-basket. Richter, whose relentless creativity was coupled with the attention span of a senile newt, was notorious for never reading anything in her in-basket, though she asked for memos incessantly from her underlings. Those who dealt with her regularly understood that the only way to get a decision was to confront her (quickly, before her mind wandered) and demand a judgment on the spot.

Browning spotted his delinquent chair. "Ah, there you are, you rascal," he scolded the innocent piece of furniture. "Come to papa."

Quickly, he began to roll the chair toward the newsroom, nearly bowling over someone striding obliviously into the office. It was, he realized with a heart-sinking start, Renata Richter.

"Sorry, sorry," she said, looking up. "Clumsy of me. Just not looking where I'm going." Richter focused on Browning's face.

"Oh, it's you." After two years as editor, Richter still didn't know Browning's name, though he seemed familiar. "You're in travel, aren't you?"

Browning nodded unhappily. "Bliss Browning," he offered.

"Of course, of course, Browning, Browning. Actually, I've been meaning to talk to you about something. Do you have 30 seconds?"

Like a man trudging to the gallows, Browning followed Richter back into her office.

"I've been thinking about our travel section," Richter began. "It's very good, of course — brilliant, actually. I'm a very big fan of your work. But I think with just a bit of fine-tuning, we could elevate it into something truly remarkable, something people would feel obliged to consult before making their travel plans."

Browning braced for the worst.

"You'll have your own ideas, of course, but if you'll permit me, I have a humble suggestion. I notice that you never write for the section. I think we should tap into your own travel experiences; I'm sure readers would enjoy your insights into the perils and rewards of travel in distant lands."

Startled by this bizarre proposal, Browning tried to speak. But Richter, heedless, carried on.

"I'm not sure what's in your travel budget this year, but I'd strongly suggest a visit to an African country — Botswana, perhaps. I was there a few years ago, and it's just taking off as a tourist destination. I'm sure you could pull together a 10-part series that would be of great interest to our readers. You might have to shuffle your budget priorities, but I'm sure it can be done. Anyway, let it marinate for a while and maybe you can lay out the modalities in a memo."

Richter smiled brightly at Browning, but he clearly had been dismissed. She picked up the phone. "Judy," she said. "Could you give me a hand? I need to write a memo to Reid, and you know me and computers."

Browning backed out of the office. He felt like Dorothy in *The Wizard of Oz*, scooped up by a freak tornado and deposited in an alien land. He slumped into his chair — the same chair whose wandering ways were responsible for this debacle. Next time, he thought, I'll stand.

"WHAT ARE YOU GOING TO DO?" Harrison Howard tried to sound concerned, but he was unable to fully suppress his amusement. Though *Advocate* staffers lived in terror of Richter's attentions, they took malicious glee in the headaches she caused their colleagues. It was only because Browning was a friend that Howard's response was as sympathetic as it was.

"I don't know, Harry, I don't know. Jesus, Botswana!" Browning moaned. "I'll be gored to death by warthogs!"

"Maybe she'll forget about it," Howard suggested, though he didn't actually believe that she would. "You know what her attention span is like."

"You think so?" Browning asked, too eagerly. "Maybe my best strategy is just to lie low and hope she never thinks of me again. I mean, she managed to ignore me for nearly two years. It's not like I'm very visible around here."

Howard nodded. "That's what I'd do. Just stay out of her line of fire for a month or two, and it will be as if your nasty little encounter never happened."

"Ah, there you are, Blissy boy." The florid face of Ryan Young, the *Advocate*'s news editor, loomed over Browning's cringing form. "Afraid I've got a piss-cutter for you here," he chortled, not sounding sorry at all. A piss-cutter was the colloquial term for one of Reid Hartley's scathing memos, so named because a recipient once reported that his water dried to a trickle while reading the publisher's critique at a urinal. Given the name, it was oddly appropriate that Hartley's piss-cutters were invariably written on lurid yellow notepaper.

"The old man's in a fury because you ran an article on the weekend about antidotes to air-sickness right next to a big Air Canada ad. Air Canada complained, and now we have to run a make-good to get them off our backs. Cost us a cool five grand!"

With a smirk, Young handed Browning the publisher's rant. It was vintage Hartley, opening with a belligerent question — "What gormless nitwit do we have working on the travel section?" — and ending with a vow to personally end the offender's career in journalism if he made a similar blunder again.

Browning rubbed his eyes morosely. What next, he thought. First the editor hatches a plan to kill me, now the publisher wants to fire me. "Do you think this is fair?" he asked Young. "I mean, do you think Air Canada has a legitimate gripe here? After all, the story was about ways of preventing air-sickness. You'd think an airline would welcome that."

"Well, that just shows what you know about the world of business, Blissy boy." Browning hated being called Blissy boy, a fact that Young, a natural bully, used to ruthless advantage. "D'ya think airlines want us to remind people they might puke if they fly? No fuckin' way they do. I don't blame them for being upset, a story like that right next to their nice, expensive ad."

"This is all bullshit." Harrison Howard had been listening with growing agitation. "Are we supposed to let advertisers dictate what we can run in our newspaper now?"

Young fixed a rheumy eye on the books editor. "First of all, Harry, we're not talking about the newspaper, just the travel section, which is practically an advertising supplement anyway. Second, those advertisers you're so pleased to scorn pay your salary and mine, so yes, you're damn right we listen to them."

Browning and Howard lapsed into sullen silence. "I want a memo from you by 3 p.m., Blissy boy, explaining exactly how this clusterfuck happened and outlining how you'll ensure it never happens again." Young glanced at his watch and yawned. "Damn near time for lunch. Couple of brewskies will go down well today, I think." He shuffled off in the general direction of Sassy's Bar and Grill, the newsroom's favourite watering hole.

"Charming as usual," Howard said sourly. Browning grimaced. "Goddamn, Harry, this has been one pisser of a day. And it's not even noon yet."

He raised his eyes toward the newsroom's stained ceiling tiles. "Oh Lord," he intoned, "why have you forsaken me?" But except for a snort of laughter from Howard, there was no answer. If the Lord knew, he wasn't telling.

THAT EVENING, Bliss Browning hunched over his laptop, seeking solace after the bruising events of the day from the like-minded in the Maria Callas newsgroup. From the stereo, Callas's fluid voice glided over the notes of one of his favourite arias, the famous "Casta Diva" from Bellini's *Norma,* a role that Callas performed more than any other in her repertoire. *Norma* tells the story of a Druid High Priestess who willingly mounts a funeral pyre to save her unfaithful Roman lover, only to have him, moved by her sacrifice, join her in the flames. It was, Callas had confided to interviewers not long before her death in 1977, the opera character most like herself. As he scanned the latest entries, Browning was distressed to find a posting that attacked Callas's voice for "tonal deficiencies" and insisted that her fame owed more to her extravagant personal life than her musical gifts. Browning had heard the criticism before and had little patience for it.

Typing with concentrated fury, he composed his reply. "What you don't seem to grasp is that Callas was much more than just opera singer. She was a once-in-a-generation genius who redefined her entire art during her all-too-short lifetime. Consider her achievements: she almost single-handedly revitalized and expanded the *bel canto* repertoire, giving instant credibility to previously undervalued operas by Bellini, Donizetti and Spontini; through her dramatic gestures and expressiveness, she married dramatic acting to music, and so rescued a moribund genre from its own stifling conventions; she inspired Visconti and Zeffirelli, whose own directing genius raised operatic productions to a new level. No diva, before or since, has mastered so many roles so quickly. No diva ever demanded more of herself or sought excellence with such single-minded force of will. No diva ever drove her voice, her most precious instrument, so mercilessly, and at such cost.

"Callas's voice may not have had the sterile beauty prized by purists, but it had a passion and power that won opera a huge new audience and revealed the full meaning of librettos that had long been dismissed as vacuous or silly. If the price of that passion and commitment was an occasional unsteady note, surely that was little enough for such genius. Even now, nearly three decades after her death, Callas's voice can move me to tears; the few films that survive of her performances only hint at the grandeur of Callas on the stage. If you cannot grasp her importance to the art that you claim to appreciate, then I beg you to turn your attention to heavy metal, country music or some other genre more suited to your coarse sensibility."

Browning felt a pang of guilt at this uncharacteristically harsh last sentence. But his irritation with the Callas critic, coupled with the stresses of the day just passed, had shortened his fuse. He posted the message with a flourish of key strokes.

He wandered into the kitchen and cracked a beer. When I finish this, he thought, I'll sign off for the night. He'd been spending far too much late-night time online recently, and fatigue was dulling his judgment and fraying his nerves.

Browning took a long pull from the slender-necked bottle and, wandering back to his computer, called up the Callas newsgroup to double-check his posting. To his surprise, he saw that it had already attracted a reply. It must be someone objecting to my flame, he thought, regretting anew the intemperate tone of his missive. Tentatively, he opened the file.

"My dear Browning," it began. "I've been reading your contributions to this newsgroup for some time now, and it's clear that when it comes to Callas, you are what they call a True Believer. You know her work well and you defend her artistry with passion. She was, as you say, a genius of her art. But this is commonplace wisdom; many people, some of them far greater authorities on opera than yourself, have said as much.

"I'm looking for evidence that you understand her as a woman, or even as a human being. Granted, she was complex, her motives often hard to fathom, her psychology elusive. But if you really want to know Callas, you have to get past the public persona, past La Divina, to the real, flesh-and-blood woman who created these legends.

"By that, I don't mean merely the temperamental-diva image that Callas acquired in life, which has grown even more exaggerated in death. I mean truly understanding the woman who transformed herself from an overstuffed blimp into a slender beauty almost overnight; who sang to German and Italian soldiers as a teenager to help her family survive in occupied Athens, then, as a woman, cut off her mother and sister without a word; who married a man her father's age; who, while still married to this father-figure, fell in love with Aristotle Onassis, and remained in love with him even after he jilted her in favour of Jacqueline Kennedy; a woman who won the world's adulation, but couldn't win the only man she ever loved.

"What made her what she was? Do you know? Do you care? Or do you only care about her artistry, the virtuosity of her voice, how she could break your heart with a gesture? These things are wondrous, to be sure, but they are not real life. They are not Callas. Would you want people to judge you solely by the travel section you edit? Of course not; that is but one facet of your existence. No more would Callas want to be understood only through her music. A voice, even a great voice, is not a person. It's not even tangible, like an earlobe or a finger. I get tired of people knowing Callas only through her voice; it is so . . . incomplete.

"So, my dear Browning, my question to you is this: Are you ready to really know Callas? Are you ready to know her like nobody else alive today? I ask you alone this question because I believe you can handle the answers. I believe that you see qualities in Callas that inspire you, that make you struggle to be better. But understand that saying yes carries a price. You may question your own sanity; it's certain that others will. I will expect you to undertake difficult and, for you, terrifying tasks. The rewards for this are uncertain — there may be none. I know all this will seem strange to you. You needn't answer right away. I'll give you two days to think about it, and then you must reply. I have faith in you, my dear Browning. I hope you can find as much faith in me."

To Browning's consternation, this extraordinary missive was signed: Cecilia Sophia Anna Maria Kalogeropoulos (Maria Callas).

CHAPTER 3

COMPARED TO MOST CITIES ITS SIZE, OTTAWA IS UNUSUALLY SAFE. Though the incidence of break-in and car theft is on the rise, violent crime is still relatively rare in the nation's capital. Murder is uncommon enough to warrant banner headlines on the *Advocate*'s front page; even common assaults often rate a few paragraphs inside the newspaper.

So, though it was nearing midnight, Bliss Browning felt comfortable leaving the security of his urban bunker to walk the downtown streets. The message from the Callas impostor (for surely this was someone's bizarre practical joke) had rattled him, and he needed some crisp night air to clear his head.

What sort of person would post such a message? What possible motive could he have? Was it an attempt to humiliate him, to discredit him with the newsgroup contributors, the only people in an indifferent world who appeared to value him? Was the culprit someone Browning had unwittingly offended? Yet aside from that night's snippy rejoinder to the Callas critic, he could think of nothing under his name that could cause offence. Indeed, the tone of his past messages had been unfailingly polite and respectful — a bit pedantic at times, perhaps, but certainly not nasty or hurtful. It made no sense.

Browning turned onto Bank Street, the city's scruffy commercial artery. At this hour, little was open but a handful of bars and clubs and a few garishly lit shops selling pizza by the slice to young men redolent of brewer's yeast. The earthy twang of a country-and-western band leaked out of one establishment as Browning passed. Three shimmying, braying men in dark leather reeled out the door and fell in unsteadily behind him.

"Bruno!" cried one of the inebriates. "That blond bitch had the hots for you, you bastard!"

"Too bad she looked like the inside of my dog's ass!" replied the one called Bruno, whose patchy complexion and greasy, unshaven face made him less than a prize himself. His companions, defenceless in the face of such repartee, surrendered to helpless laughter. Before they could recover, Bruno farted lustily, triggering another round of hoots.

Browning, deep in thought, was only vaguely aware of his obnoxious fellow travellers, and they had been even more oblivious to his presence. But now Bruno, goaded by his buddies' febrile appreciation, spotted him on the sidewalk ahead.

"Hey, faggot!" he screeched at Browning. "Yo, bum-blaster!"

These bon mots had the desired effect on his sodden pals, who sniggered loudly. His reverie rudely shattered, Browning took a fast look over his shoulder and quickened his pace. The drunkards soon fell behind, with only the occasional incoherent bellow testifying to their loutish presence.

Browning resumed his brooding. If only, he thought, momentarily succumbing to fantasy. If only it really had been from Maria Callas instead of some twisted jokester. Imagine the great Callas, choosing Bliss Browning, nonentity nonpareil, as her earthly go-between! Browning's lips curled in an involuntary smile, lost in the absurd thought. Then the moment passed and Browning began to fret anew about the agenda of his unknown correspondent. One thing's certain, he promised himself grimly, he wouldn't allow this clown to make a fool of him.

Browning turned onto the Sparks Street Mall, looping back

toward home. The Mall was once the city core's shopping showplace. But it had fallen on evil days, drained of shoppers by suburban malls. At night it was a sterile place, eerily deserted and pock-marked by vacant storefronts, the ghosts of retailers past. Browning's leather-soled shoes echoed off the empty pavement like small-arms fire.

As he neared Lyon Street, a shabby figure, belly inadequately constrained by low-riding corduroy pants, lurched out of the shadow of a high-rise hotel. Browning recoiled, his brief but unpleasant encounter with Bruno and his pals still fresh in his mind. But it quickly became apparent that this man, who appeared to be about 60, presented little risk. Fully six inches shorter than the six-foot Browning, he clearly favoured his right leg, which he held ramrod straight as he approached.

"Good evening, monsieur," he began civilly, speaking heavily-accented English interspersed with random bits of French. "My nom est Joseph Louis Bergeron." He stuck out a hand and looked expectantly at Browning.

Browning, nonplussed, shook his hand. "Pleased to meetcha," he mumbled.

"Mitchell?" replied Bergeron. "Your name, it is Mitchell?"

"No, no, I said I'm pleased to meetcha."

Bergeron appeared to take this as confirmation. "Ecoutez, Mitchell," he said, grabbing Browning by the left arm, "I 'ave to go to Toronto. I need un operation on dis bum jambe. Hurt it in an accident two years ago, and da bastard's getting worse and worse. Ma fille, she lives in Toronto, she's got t'ings fixed avec l'hôpital. I was set to go dere tonight sur l'autobus, but some cochon picked my pocket at da terminal, tabernacle!!" Bergeron spat noisily on the sidewalk, expelling a great phlegmy gob of mucus. His sour breath was in Browning's face. "If you would lend me $20, Mitchell, I could buy le billet and get my leg fixed finalement. It would make un gros difference to me, Mitchell. Please, will you aidez-moi?"

Browning didn't know whether he was bemused or exasperated by this unlikely tale, but decided the bum deserved something for originality. He reached for his wallet.

"Merci, merci, Mitchell," Bergeron blubbered, kissing his benefactor lightly on the upper chest. Embarrassed by these sloppy attentions, Browning picked out the first bill he could find in his wallet, a twenty, and handed it over.

"Bless you, Mitchell, bless you!" cried Browning's new friend, eyes wide with surprise and delight. "You are un bon homme, Mitchell." He pronounced the name lovingly, like an incantation, as if the syllables themselves were holy. Browning disengaged from the grateful man's embrace. "Merci, Mitchell, thank you!" Bergeron cried again, fingering the $20 bill as if to assure himself that it was real. "I pay you back, Mitchell, c'est un promis."

With a quick nod and tight smile, Browning turned away. The day had been quite eventful enough, he decided; he walked directly back to his apartment, undressed and fell into a restless sleep.

~

AS SOON AS he awoke the next morning, Browning knew he had to make a public reply to the prankster. His news group would be expecting it, and Callas, were she alive, would not want this brazen deception to go unanswered. He chose the words carefully, re-writing each sentence until he was satisfied that the message had just the right balance of indignation and affronted dignity. Then he posted it to the Callas group and hurried off to the office. This is what he wrote:

"To 'Maria Callas': I don't know who you are, or why you have chosen me to torment, but I'm neither fooled nor amused by your pathetic prank. You dishonour the memory of the great Callas with this sort of escapade; a woman of her stature, nearly 30 years in the grave now, deserves better. Since she can't be here to defend herself, I object on her behalf to your appropriation of her name and thoughts. I don't know what your game is, but that is of little consequence. My only concern is that you not sully the memory of a great woman. If you have an ounce of decency, you will desist at once."

That evening, Browning, having successfully evaded the attentions of Renata Richter at the office, eagerly logged onto the Callas group to see if his missive had attracted a response. To his surprise, there were no fewer than a dozen replies. He opened the first one.

"Re Bliss Browning message to 'Maria Callas.' Bliss, what's this all about? I don't understand." The message was signed by Antonio Scarfino, a regular chat group contributor from Milan.

Puzzled, Browning selected the next response. "Huh????" it began. "Message from Bliss Browning to 'Maria Callas' makes no sense. Are you all right, Bliss?"

With a sinking heart, Browning called up the next message. It was similar to the first two, but with a nastier edge: "Who is this Browning, some sort of lunatic? Sounds as if he needs a long rest, preferably under close supervision."

Browning quickly scrolled through the remaining messages. All expressed puzzlement about the meaning of his morning posting. All, that is, except the last one.

"My dear Browning. I see you lack faith. I'm disappointed — I really thought you had more imagination than that. But as you can see, your colleagues in this group are mystified by your message. That's because they cannot read my words; only you can do that, because I choose to let you. Does this not prove, since you seem to need proof, that I am really Callas? I hope you will not need further evidence. Neither my supply of miracles nor my patience is limitless. As one of your baseball players once put it, 'you gotta believe.' I'm waiting, my dear Browning."

This message, like the first, was signed with Maria Callas's birth name, Cecilia Sophia Anna Maria Kalogeropoulos. Browning stared at the words on his computer screen. Finally, he roused himself and rapidly typed a new message.

"Colleagues," he wrote. "I am sorry I confused you with my last posting. But someone, I don't know who, is writing under the name of Maria Callas and sending me messages through this news group. One was posted last night at 2245 hours Eastern Daylight Time. A second appeared just a short time ago, at 1750 hours. Both are still listed and can be read by any of you. Would anyone reading this message please let me know ASAP if you can locate these postings by someone claiming to be Callas? It is urgent that I hear from you as soon as possible."

Browning looked at his watch. It was 7 p.m. He needed to kill some time, to give other group contributors a chance to respond. First, he thought, I'll have a swim; despite the humiliation of his last visit to the health club, exercise always burned off the day's tension, and he badly needed to calm down. Then, maybe a pizza at the Impresario (best in town, by general agreement), followed by whatever's showing at the Uptowne, the city's main repertory cinema. That should allow enough time for people to answer. Grabbing his gym bag and slipping on a light jacket to ward off the spring evening chill, he set off for the health club, wondering whether his predictable world would still be there when he returned.

~

IT WAS NEARLY midnight when Browning unlocked his front door and kicked off his shoes. His evening had unfolded as planned: a kilometre in the pool (and mercifully, no unpleasant encounters in the shower room afterwards), a gooey Impresario pizza with double cheese and anchovies, a depressing German film wallowing in post-Nazi angst and existential maunderings.

Browning signed back onto the Internet and carefully selected the Callas group. He was pleased to see half a dozen responses to his last message already posted. Almost timidly, he opened them, one by one. He read the replies with a growing sense of alarm. The message in each was essentially the same: Can find no messages from Callas impersonator. Not sure what you're trying to pull. Is this some sort of joke?

Browning realized he was hyperventilating. Relax, he told himself. There must be a rational explanation. Our prankster is some sort of hacker using computer tricks to conceal his tracks, that's all. Yet even as he seized on this explanation, Browning found it unconvincing. Though no computer geek, he knew of no way that a posting to a news group could be visible to one user and invisible to everyone else.

He clung to the hope that he was mistaken; perhaps one of the newsroom's techies could offer an explanation.

The alternative, an idea so absurd that no sane person would even entertain it, made even less sense: that the message really was from Maria Callas, reaching out to him from beyond the grave. Browning was not a religious or superstitious man, and while he maintained a prudent neutrality on the possibility of an afterlife, he was inclined to doubt it. The notion that a spirit world might actually exist, and that one of its luminary residents had somehow tapped into the Internet to contact him, was well beyond his ability to comprehend or willingness to accept.

Browning found he couldn't sit still for more than a minute or so. His mind was racing and his pulse pounded heavily in his ears. Although it wasn't a warm evening, he was perspiring heavily. Maybe I am going crazy, he thought. He was having trouble catching his breath. His heart felt as if it might burst from his chest and dash down the hall.

Jumping Jesus, I'm having a heart attack!

This was one of Browning's deepest fears. Both of his parents had died of heart disease and Browning was convinced the family curse would claim him, too.

Christ, I'm only 47! Too young to die!

Browning staggered to the telephone and punched in 911. He gasped out his address. "What's the nature of the problem?" the 911 attendant asked with what seemed to Browning as preternatural calmness. "Heart attack!" he wheezed, then collapsed dizzily onto the hide-a-bed. He was still there ten minutes later when the paramedics broke down his door and carted him off to hospital.

~

THE YOUNG EMERGENCY-WARD doctor sat down beside Browning's hospital bed. He peered at his patient, who had been showing all the symptoms of a coronary when the medics brought him in three hours earlier. Though still white-faced and shaken, Browning's heart rate was back to normal, the pain in his chest had vanished and he was breathing easily.

"Well," the doctor began, "I have some good news for you. You haven't had a heart attack."

Browning stared at the physician. "If that wasn't a heart attack, what in hell was it?"

"Not absolutely sure, but likely a panic attack. We'll have to run a few more tests to be certain, but I'd wager a year's salary that's what it was. Have you ever felt anything like that before?"

"Christ, no. That was the most frightening feeling I've ever had. I was sure I was going to die. No, I've never felt anything like that. I'd remember," Browning said fervently.

The doctor smiled slightly. "I'm sure you would. Panic disorder causes symptoms that are every bit as real to the sufferer as a heart attack: pounding heart, cold sweat, trouble drawing a breath. The first time, most people are convinced they're on death's door. Yet physically, there's nothing wrong with them. The whole thing is a convincing mirage."

"You mean it's all in my head? I imagined all those symptoms?"

"Yes and no. The symptoms were real enough — your heart was pounding; you really did have troubling breathing. But they were triggered by your mind, not any physical problem. The mind is a powerful thing. It can make us well and it can make us ill. And it can fool the body into believing it is sick when it is not."

Browning pondered this for a moment. "You said people often think they're dying 'the first time.' Are you saying this is going to happen to me again?"

"Probably. Panic disorder is a result of failing to deal with stresses and fears we all are prey to. The longer we ignore the root causes, the more the pressures build inside us. Eventually we crack. That's probably what happened to you tonight. We can give you medication to control the severity of the attacks, but until you deal with the problems and fears that trigger them, you're likely to suffer more episodes."

Browning was torn between relief that his heart was apparently sound (for the time being, a small voice reminded him) and dismay at this new and unexpected affliction. Panic disorder? The very name was unmanly, suggesting weakness or cowardice. If I must be sick, why couldn't it be a virile disease, he thought. Brain cancer, perhaps. "Poor Bliss," he imagined co-workers whispering to one another. "Did you hear? Brain cancer. They don't give him much time." That would be a disease worth having, a disease people could respect. But panic disorder? Just another embarrassment for him to conceal from a sneering world.

The young doctor interrupted these maudlin meditations. "Have you been under unusual stress lately?"

Browning tried not to laugh. That certainly was one way to put it. The episode at the health club, the threat to dispatch him to Botswana, the piss-cutter from the publisher, the mysterious messages from "Callas" — yes, he thought, that qualifies as unusual stress, even by his lofty standards.

"I suppose," he acknowledged cautiously. "Work pressures, that sort of thing."

"Well then, that's likely the trigger. If my diagnosis is confirmed, I'd advise a complete break from all stressful situations for at least two weeks, preferably three. You need to give your mind a break while you figure out what's causing this problem."

Browning brightened. This was a silver lining indeed. With two or three weeks away from work, many of his immediate problems likely would evaporate. Renata Richter would forget her insane plan to dispatch him to Africa. *God willing.* And Reid Hartley's anger at him would blow over. In the time freed up from work, he might even be able to get to the bottom of the Callas mystery.

"Well, alright doctor," he said meekly. "If you say I must, then I must."

~

THE SUN WAS RISING when Browning finally made his way home from the hospital. His apartment door, ripped from its hinges by the paramedics, had been propped into the doorway to form a crude, if easily defeated, barrier. I'll have to get the superintendent to fix that right away, he thought dully. But for now, exhausted by his sleepless night at the hospital, Browning cared only for the downy comforts of his bed.

Shifting the door aside, he slipped into his apartment. Everything was as he left it: the racks of CDs, the stereo system, the hide-a-bed upon which he had collapsed in what, for all he knew then, were his final moments on Earth. Yet Browning sensed that appearances were deceiving. The feeling that something meaningful had changed was powerful, though Browning was too tired to do much more than note its presence. Propping the door back into its frame and pinning it in place with the hide-a-bed, he peeled off his sweat-stained clothes and fell into bed. He didn't even glance at his laptop. But had he looked closely, he might have seen, amid the screen-saver's soaring peaks, the faint outline of a woman's face.

CHAPTER 4

IT WAS BLINDINGLY BRIGHT. THE SUN SEEMED TO FILL THE CLOUDLESS sky, scouring the rocky ground below of any trace of cooling shade. Browning had forgotten his sunglasses, and had trouble seeing in the glare. He sensed, rather than saw, the others. They were staring at him, pointing, laughing. He realized with a start that he was naked, and that they were laughing at him, at his penis, which was grotesquely small, like the genitals of a Lilliputian welded to the groin of Atlas. Browning tried to cover his shame, but his arms were leaden and try as he might, he couldn't move them. Then one of his tormentors came into sharp focus. It was the red-faced man from the health club. His upper lip was curled in scorn, and he was recounting Browning's disgrace in the shower room.

Dimly at first, but growing louder, Browning heard a familiar electronic sound. With startling speed, the sun faded to black, the red-faced man and the others fell silent and the sound filled his head. He opened his eyes. The telephone was ringing insistently on the night-stand by his bed. Groggily, he reached for the receiver.

"H'llo?" he croaked.

"Blissy boy!" Browning groaned. Not him. "So you're home. Hope I didn't wake you, but I just wondered if you were planning to honour us with your presence today. That is, if it's not too much trouble." Few could manage derision as cuttingly as Ryan Young.

"Hi, Ryan," Browning said wearily. "Had a bit of a health problem last night. Didn't get to bed till after six. I should have called in, but I was just too exhausted. Let's make this a vacation day and call it even."

"Sorry, Blissy boy, no can do. Don't really care how hung over you are, you're gonna to have to drag your sorry ass into the office today. Richter's got her knickers in a knot over this stupid trip you're taking to Africa. Why the fuck she chose *you* has us all stumped, though. If she really wants to blow that kind of dough, we should send a real writer, Dylan Mosely or someone."

Mosely was the newsroom's acknowledged star, the only member of its staff to win a national writing award. Success had bloated his already sizable ego, though, and he was widely regarded as a prima donna, rejecting assignments he deemed beneath his eminent status. He was cordially loathed by most of the paper's editors and writers.

Sleep-sodden though he was, Browning was alert enough to recognize a useful idea when he heard one.

"Dammit, Ryan, I don't want to go to bloody Africa. But Mosely would be perfect; he'd do a terrific job. Do you think we can convince Richter to send him instead of me?"

"I don't know," Young said doubtfully. "She seems pretty hot on you, for whatever the fuck reason. But if you told her point-blank that Mosely would do a better job, she might listen. Christ, it's worth a try."

For the first time, Browning glimpsed a dim light at the end of his personal tunnel to hell. "I'll be right in," he said.

"JESUS, YOU LOOK LIKE SHIT." And indeed, the spectre that stood before Ryan Young was an alarming sight. Black half-moons of fatigue rimmed Browning's red eyes and a day's growth of stubble shadowed his jaw. A tuft of uncombed hair jutted from the side of his head at an angle that raised grave doubts about Newton's physical laws. An unnoticed stain of tomato sauce from the previous night's pizza bloodied the sleeve of his taupe dress shirt, whose tail had almost completely escaped the restraining hold of his grimy Dockers. Only Browning's shoes were presentable, gleaming with the sheen of a recent application of wax.

Browning looked levelly at his supervisor. "I told you I wasn't well, Ryan."

"You could have at least cleaned yourself up a bit, for fuck sake. I've seen better-dressed crackheads." Young looked at Browning with distaste. "Never mind, never mind. Might even help us convince Richter you're not fit to send half-way around the world."

"When do we see her?" Browning asked. He was anxious to get this over with.

"She's in one of her damn meetings. Should be free in half an hour, but you know her. Find something useful to do and I'll call you when she's ready."

Browning wandered over to his desk. His chair was missing. He sighed but made no effort to locate it. He looked for Harrison Howard, but the books editor was nowhere to be seen.

Browning leaned heavily on the side of his desk and surveyed the *Advocate* newsroom. At this time of day, late morning, it was fairly quiet. A few reporters pecked away at stories on their laptops, but most were out of the office, chasing down tips, meeting with sources or just poking the pooch, a time-honoured tradition among *Advocate* writers. The editors on the news desk were handling stories for inside pages in a desultory fashion; inspiring stuff such as advice columns, fashion news, stories about miracle cures for hemorrhoids and colossal tumors removed from the large intestines of Eastern European women.

Mick Mulligrew was on the phone as usual, consulting his broker. Mulligrew was a talented news desk editor with the personal charm of a rabid hedgehog. Embittered at being overlooked by his feckless bosses, he exacted retribution by doing as little as possible for his paycheque. When not discussing the markets with his broker, Mulligrew enjoyed trapping other *Advocate* staffers in endless, tedious conversations, in the apparent belief that his revenge was more complete if he could prevent others from being productive, as well.

In the sports department, Flynn Cahill, the *Advocate*'s crusty and beloved sports columnist, was declaiming loudly to a colleague about the previous night's hockey game. Cahill had been writing a sports column for the *Advocate* for more than two decades. He was an institution in the city, Mr. Ottawa Sports to his legion of readers. To his colleagues, though, he was less reverently known (though not to his face) as "Fuck" Cahill, for his propensity for employing the earthy anglo-saxonism with comical regularity. When writing his column, Cahill could somehow command his fingers to avoid his signature word. When he opened his mouth, though, it interjected itself in every imaginable spot of every sentence. Like someone afflicted with Tourette's Syndrome, Cahill seemed unable to control this bizarre verbal tick.

Yuri Alexandrov, the *Advocate*'s foreign editor, had his feet propped on the blizzard of papers that covered his desk, and was shouting into the phone in Russian. Alexandrov, a former Tass editor who emigrated to Canada around the time of the collapse of the Soviet Union, liked to keep in touch with events back home, usually by means of interminable and ruinously expensive telephone calls to places like Minsk. Bright but unscrupulous, Alexandrov was one of Richter's most prized recruits. Most *Advocate* staffers considered him a pompous windbag.

In an office across the newsroom, Browning could just make out Anita Wilson, the *Advocate*'s energetic young city editor, in conversation with Kimberley Taylor, the glamorous medical reporter. Wilson was another of Richter's proteges, but actually had the smarts to go far. According to the buzz around the office, she was being groomed as the paper's future editor. Already, her success had attracted the usual jealous sniping from less gifted rivals. As for Taylor, she was a whip-smart redhead in her late 20s and an object of lust for every sentient male in the newsroom, including Browning. Several had made a play for her, without apparent success. Except for a few mumbled hellos, Browning had never spoken to her. But it was terror, not indifference, that froze his tongue. Kimberley Taylor was a wonder of nature.

Chuck Bigras, the paper's chief copyperson (copyboy in an earlier, less gender-neutral age), was eating a hot meatball sandwich from Sassy's Bar and Grill at his seat on the copy desk. Inhaling might be a better word. Bigras seemed to be trying to gulp the sandwich whole, like a boa ingesting a small mammal. Bigras had been a copy person for nearly 30 years. He was the idiot relative of a former publisher and his living legacy at the newspaper. He couldn't type, couldn't spell anything but one-syllable words (and not even all of those) and had never figured out the mysteries of the office phone system – he was always cutting off callers or directing them to the wrong extension. Verbally abusing readers who called with questions or complaints gave him special lunatic pleasure.

As he surveyed this scene, Browning marvelled anew that this collection of misfits and oddballs was able to publish a newspaper every day. Truly the daily miracle, he thought dryly, as the familiar newsroom voices overlapped like characters in a bad Robert Altman film.

"...fuckin' Harris should get the fuck off the team if he isn't willing to fuckin' pay the price..."

"... nyet, Alexei, nyet, nyet, nyet..."

"...when it hits $25, sell 500 shares..."

"... what do you expect me to do about it? I just work here ..."

"... then buy again when it drops to 22..."

"... fuckin' asshole doesn't know shit from shinola..."

"... I don't give a shit if you cancel, lady ..."

"... fuck him ..."

"Blissy boy!" Young's braying voice broke through this discordant symphony. "She's ready to see us now. Shake your booty!"

Please God, thought Browning, let this work. Let Renata Richter see the wisdom of sending Dylan Mosely to Africa. Let her see the madness of sending me. Do this for me, and I'll never take your name or that of your dear son in vain again. That's a solemn promise.

"GODDAMN IT! JESUS FUCKING CHRIST!"

The meeting with Richter had not gone well, and Browning's agnostic inclinations were veering sharply towards atheism. At the very least, if there was a God, He harboured some unfathomable grudge against him.

From the moment he and Young had entered the editor's office, the atmosphere had been peculiar. Richter had smiled brightly at Browning, who looked like Death after a hard day at the mortuary and chirped: "Bliss! You look great!"

Browning, caught off guard by this non sequitur, had mumbled something about not feeling his best. But Richter had plowed ahead, oblivious to his words.

"Good, good," she said encouragingly. "So, when do you leave for Africa?"

"Well now, Renata," said Young, smoothly picking up his cue, "that's what we're here to talk to you about. See, Blissy bo ... that is, Browning, thinks we'd be better off sending someone else."

"Oh?" said Richter, arching her eyebrows and turning her laser gaze on Browning. "And who might that be?

"Dylan Mosely, Miss Richter," Browning said with deference that crossed a line into craven. "He's our best writer by far, and this really needs a writing job. Besides, to tell the truth, I'm not all that keen on the trip myself. Something of a nervous traveller," he added with a forced smile meant to be apologetic.

Richter frowned. "Nonsense!" she snapped. "I wouldn't dream of sending Mosely. He's a good writer, granted, but he's done nothing recently to earn this kind of perk. Besides," she beamed at Browning, "I really want you to go. It would do wonders to establish you as travel editor."

"But Renata," argued Young, "Browning here hasn't written a story in years. We don't even know if he *can* write. Travel's just a glorified advertorial section anyway. Why blow our travel budget to send a second-rate editor halfway around the world to write for a section nobody gives a slurpy shit about?" Young glanced at Browning. "No offence."

"None taken," Browning replied, with a tight smile.

"Ryan, Ryan, Ryan," Richter clucked, as if scolding a naughty schoolboy. "You just don't get it, do you? The reason our travel section doesn't get the respect it deserves is because we haven't promoted it enough. We haven't made an effort to showcase Bliss's talents. Your cause and effect are completely reversed."

Browning was getting desperate. "Look, Miss Richter, I appreciate your confidence in me, but the fact is I just don't think I'm up to this assignment. I've never been to Africa before. Hell, I've never been anywhere before."

"Well, well. This won't do at all," Richter said, wide-eyed. "A travel editor who has never travelled? It's unacceptable, totally unacceptable. The sooner you get a few frequent flyer points under your belt, the better off our readers will be."

Browning, who'd been saving his trump card for just such a crisis, decided this was the moment to play it.

"I'm afraid that just isn't possible right now. Last night I was rushed to hospital with what was later diagnosed as panic disorder." Browning saw Young's skeptical look and added quickly: "Awful. Felt certain I was going to die. Anyway, my doctor has ordered me to book off work immediately for at least four weeks" (what the hell, Browning thought, I could use the extra week) "and rest in a stress-free environment."

"But that's perfect!" Richter cried. "What could be more restful than a nice all-expenses-paid safari vacation in Africa? It will be a complete change from your usual routine, and you'll return a new man! And when you get back, you can write about your adventures for the travel section. It's a marvelous fit."

Richter picked up her phone. "Judy, call our travel agent and have her book a safari trip to Botswana for Bliss Browning. Yes, as soon as possible. He badly needs this vacation." Richter winked conspiratorially at Browning, who hissed at Young: "Do something, Ryan!"

But Young just sighed heavily and shrugged. He'd seen enough of Renata Richter to know when resistance was futile.

"There," said Richter. "It's settled. With any luck, you'll be on your way to Botswana by the end of the week." Richter gazed happily at Browning, as if she'd just granted his fondest wish. "I really envy you Bliss. You're going to have a great time." She had a sudden thought. "Nuts! It's the high-water season on the Zambezi. That means no white-water rafting below Victoria Falls. Pity — that's one of the most thrilling white-water trips in the world."

No white-water rafting below Victoria Falls. Damn, Browning thought. That eliminates drowning and being devoured by crocodiles from the list of hazards on this trip.

NORMAN PUGSLEY WAS ALONE, head tilted back, eyes closed, sitting at his spotless teak desk. An early season baseball game burbled quietly on a television set in a corner. Young knocked discreetly.

"Hi, Norm," he said. "I've got Browning here. She didn't go for it."

"Christ on a bicycle," the *Advocate*'s managing editor muttered, with a resigned sigh. He opened his eyes, slowly turning toward Young and Browning, who were standing uncertainly in the doorway. "Well, come in, come in, for Chrissake. Tell me about it."

Young briefed Pugsley on the events in Richter's office, punctuated by much eye-rolling, groaning and the occasional expletive from the managing editor. "Bloody hell," he fumed, when Young had finished, "have you ever heard such unmitigated crap in all your life? The woman is insane, gentlemen, in-fuckin'-sane."

Pugsley glanced at Browning, who had been silent to that point. "Well, Browning," he barked, "I guess you're going to Africa, whether we like it or not. Hope you've had your shots."

"Shots?" This was something Browning hadn't even considered. "Jesus, no, I haven't. What do I need?"

"Oh, the usual. Typhoid, cholera, yellow fever, that sort of thing."

Pugsley stifled a yawn. "And of course, anti-malaria pills. You'll need those. Africa's a cesspool of malaria."

"My God!" whispered Browning. "I really am going to die! Can't you do something, Mr. Pugsley?"

"Love to, Browning, love to, but when Richter makes up her mind, such as it is, it's pointless to argue. Besides, Hartley's a big fan of hers, for some bloody reason. No percentage in getting into a big dick contest with her. Assuming she had one," he added. Young snorted, but Browning flinched involuntarily at the turn of phrase.

"So, I'm doomed," Browning said dully.

" 'Fraid so," said Pugsley distractedly, pausing to watch a three-run homer land in the upper deck. "Christ, what a blast!" he cried. "Did you see that thing leave the park? Like it was running on rocket fuel!"

Pugsley watched raptly as the TV replayed the mighty shot. He seemed to have forgotten all about Browning. "I tell you, Ryan, this is the Jays' year," he enthused. "I can feel it."

"Don't know, Norm, their pitching's weak. Good hit, no fuckin' pitch. Not a recipe for a ring if you ask me."

"Shit, they're going to score so many runs this year, they won't need any pitching." Pugsley finally tore his eyes away from the television screen. He noticed Browning cowering miserably beside Young.

"Well, come on, Browning, hop to it. No sense standing there like a turd in a toilet bowl. You've got a lot to do if you're leaving for Africa in a few days."

Browning quickly reviewed his options. He could refuse to go, but he'd almost certainly be fired, and he couldn't afford to lose his job. Who else would hire a mediocrity like him? Suicide was out; he feared death too much to even consider it. A crippling injury might get him off the hook, but Browning didn't care much for pain, either. The alternatives, in short, were even more unpalatable than facing the terrors of Africa. And the doctors had told him he had to confront his fears if he wanted to overcome his panic attacks.

Browning ran his fingers through his thinning brown hair and nodded unhappily at Pugsley.

"OK," he said, resigned. "I'll start packing."

~

THE FOCUS on the Botswana trip had allowed Browning to briefly put the mysterious messages from "Callas" out of his mind. But as he turned the key in his apartment door (noting with approval that the superintendent had reinstalled it on its hinges), the anxiety came flooding back, tightening his chest and generating rivulets of sweat on his back and forehead.

He entered his bedroom and stared silently at his laptop, once so benevolent and now so malign. Perhaps it's a good thing I'm going to Africa, he thought: whoever's sending those messages might pick another target if I disappear for a while.

But even as he formed this thought, Browning rebelled against it. The Callas news group had become so pivotal that he could scarcely conceive of life without it. He treasured the feeling of belonging, of being valued and admired. He could not easily give that up. Yet he feared he'd lose credibility with the other Callas contributors if he did not get to the bottom of the mystery. Once again, it seemed that his only course was to confront his fears and accept the consequences, whatever they might be.

With a sense of foreboding, Browning called up the Callas group and began to read the latest postings. The first few were further responses to his appeal the previous night for information about the "Callas impostor." He was unsurprised to learn that, like the earlier posters, none could find any sign of the clandestine Callas. But he was hurt and alarmed by the increasingly mocking tone of the responses. "Our Canadian friend is having delusions of self-aggrandizement," sneered one; another graciously offered to take Browning and "Callas" on a tour of Bedlam, the notorious British asylum for the insane, the next time they were in England.

Grimly, Browning kept reading. Most of the other postings were typical of the group's discussions: debates about Callas's greatest role, enthusiasm for this or that of her recordings, invidious comparisons with present-day sopranos. But just as Browning was about to log off, he noticed a posting that hadn't been there only moments before. It began with the now-familiar salutation.

"My dear Browning. I'm glad to see that you're alive and apparently well. I was beginning to worry. I hope that your crisis of faith has passed, and that you are ready to accept me for who I am. I am anxious to get past this annoying skepticism and get on with the task at hand. However, I've read those moronic messages from other group subscribers, and I appreciate that our current method of communication is uncomfortably public for you.

"I have a suggestion: I understand this Internet has something called e-mail, where two people can communicate privately. I think you will agree that would be more satisfactory than the public conversation we have been conducting so far. If you use this e-mail to send messages, I will use it to respond. Since my access to this system is, shall we say, unconventional, you will have to trust that I will find your messages. At this point, I think I deserve a bit of your trust."

As Browning stared at the electrifying words on his computer screen, he thought, just for an instant, that he saw the outline of a familiar woman's face gazing back at him. Browning rubbed his eyes. Jesus, he thought, now I'm hallucinating! He had a sudden thought: what if this whole thing was just one big, ongoing hallucination? It was possible. Perhaps his mania for Callas had triggered a latent subconscious suggestion. Perhaps the stresses that had caused his panic attack were generating some sort of hysterical dementia. Maybe a nice vacation — in Botswana! — was what he needed after all.

Browning groaned. None of this made sense. On impulse, he opened his e-mail, typed a message and posted it to his own mailbox. "To Maria Callas, or whoever you are," it began. "OK, I admit it, you've got me at a disadvantage. You obviously know who I am, but I'll be damned if I know who you are. I'm supposed to believe that you're Maria Callas, who's dead, need I remind you. To have faith. Well, I'm sorry, but I don't even have faith in myself. How am I supposed to believe in some phantom speaking to me through my laptop? It's absurd. No sane person would swallow that. And in spite of everything,

I'm pretty sure I'm still sane, though there are days when I wonder about even that. The best I can do is talk to you and try to figure this out. Maybe you're just as desperate as I am. Maybe you're just crazy. But if you really can find my messages anywhere, respond to this now."

Browning waited a few minutes, then checked the Callas news group. There was no sign of an answer from his mysterious correspondent. He wasn't surprised: only someone who knew his personal password — BrowNose — could access his personal mailbox and read the message there, and he alone knew it. What did surprise him, though, was the stab of disappointment he felt at the absence of a reply from "Callas." Good God, he thought, could it be that I was actually starting to believe this crap?

On impulse, Browning checked his inbox. And froze. There, directly below his own message, was the reply he had both longed for and feared.

"My dear, baffled Browning. You really do lack faith. You should do something about that, you know — everyone needs someone or something to believe in. Life is horridly empty otherwise. Oh well. I suppose we'll just have to work around your skepticism, and hope that in time you can overcome it. At least you're willing to talk to me; that's a start. And believe me, my dear Browning, we have much to talk about."

CHAPTER 5

FOURTEEN YEARS EARLIER

FOR MORE THAN AN HOUR, he had watched as the most stunning woman he had ever seen had danced and flirted with a succession of eager men in the smoky bar. Her golden tresses hung to her waist, a long, flowing cascade that shimmered and swayed like wind-whipped prairie wheat. Her body, only nominally concealed by a clinging red mini-dress, had the trim lines of an athlete. When she laughed, which seemed to be constantly, her face crinkled in childish delight, and her green eyes widened, discharging sparks of light. She danced like a wild animal, lithe and feral, hips shimmying to the pounding rock 'n' roll beat, arms beating the air like a swimmer in the grip of an undertow. Men competed for her favour, imagining her compact body under theirs. Browning, rivetted by this vision but lacking the confidence to approach her, could only look on and fantasize as he nursed his beer at a corner table.

It was the first time that Browning had been in the bar, one of several nightspots in Ottawa's Byward Market that featured live entertainment. The area had long since transcended its roots as a farmer's market to become the city's nightlife hub. Though Browning wasn't normally attracted by the club scene, he was new to the city — he had just started his job as a copy editor on the night desk at the *Daily Advocate* — and craved human contact.

The club, The Albatross, was a narrow dim room that smelled strongly of beer and hard living. An elaborately carved wooden bar ran the length of one wall, and a sprinkling of round tables and chairs was arrayed around a sunken central dance floor. The entertainment, a '70s cover band whose repertoire drew heavily from the catalogue of Led Zeppelin and Kiss, was installed at one end of the room. When the band cranked up its amps and crashed through a set, anything approaching conversation ceased.

Since this was a Friday night, The Albatross was packed with people in their 20s and 30s determined to welcome the weekend. The club was not a classic singles bar — for one thing, the punishingly loud live music obliterated most pick-up lines — but it attracted its share of unattached young adults hoping to find love (or at least a night's cordial company) amid the sweating bodies and sloppy drunks. Browning's expectations were not so ambitious; he merely wanted to be where others were, to witness their frantic pleasures, to briefly ease his terrible aloneness.

At 33, Browning was still a virgin, though not out of religious conviction or abstract fidelity to a bride he had yet to meet. He'd had opportunities to shed his unwanted innocence, but had literally come up short, fearful that his puny privates would inspire ridicule rather than desire. Whenever a relationship reached the unzipping stage, Browning would recoil. His spurned partners seldom gave him a second chance.

Browning stared moodily at his draft beer, rapidly warming in the body-heated air. He had viewed the move to a new city, a new job, as a fresh start, a chance to reshape his own destiny. But he was settling into the same old patterns, sabotaging himself with his insecurities and self-doubts.

The band had finished its first set. Browning looked around for the captivating blonde and spotted her across the room. To his surprise, she was looking in his direction, and their eyes met. She waved, a quick, jaunty gesture that encouraged a response. Surprised, he replied with a tentative hand-waggle of his own. With a mixture of dread and delight, he realized that she was walking purposefully his way.

She marched up to his table and gestured in the direction of an empty chair. "Mind if I sit down?" she asked in a girlish voice.

"Um, no, fine, go ahead," Browning stammered.

"My name's Krystal Connors. Krystal with a K," she added, eyeing him quizzically. Rattled by her bold approach, it took Browning an awkward moment to realize that she was expecting a reciprocal introduction from him.

"Browning," he finally sputtered. "Bliss Browning."

"Bliss? Your name is Bliss?" She stifled a giggle. "Gawd, what kind of a name is *that*?"

Browning was nonplussed by her unselfconscious bluntness but charmed at the same time. "Well," he began, a bit calmer though his heart was pounding, "I suppose it is a bit unusual. But it's a perfectly fine name. Many people have had it before me."

Krystal pondered this for a moment. "Bliss. Y'know, it grows on you. I sorta like it. Pure Bliss." Her face crinkled into a dazzling grin. "That's what I'm going to call you. Pure Bliss. Are you?"

"Am I what?"

"You know, pure Bliss. Do all the women you make love to just die, like, of sheer pleasure?"

Browning felt a blush racing across his cheeks. "Well, to tell the truth, not many have had the opportunity."

"Oh sure. Next, you'll tell me you're, like, still a virgin or something."

Browning was caught up in Krystal's reckless candor. Impulsively, he blurted, "As a matter of fact, I am."

Krystal stared at him. "You're serious, aren't you? Oh my God, you're not, like, a priest or something, are you? You're not gay?"

Browning laughed tensely, a bit aghast at his own impetuosity. "No, not a priest and not gay. I just haven't met the right woman yet, I guess." Krystal's eyes widened. "Jeez, I've never met a guy your age who's never had sex. What are you, like 30?"

"Thirty-three, actually. I guess it's uncommon, but I think sex should be reserved for the person you love."

"And what about you, Pure Bliss. Haven't you ever loved anyone?"

"No, not really. I thought I did, once or twice, but I really didn't. They say you know love when you see it. I'm not so sure. I think love is a chameleon, a master of disguise. It likes to tantalize you, to make you think what you're feeling is real. But it's something else — lust, I suppose, or infatuation. Something less permanent, anyway. Love is somewhere else, hiding and watching, having a giggle at your expense." Browning stopped abruptly, embarrassed by his own volubility.

Krystal was gazing at him with interest. "I like listening to you. You're not like most men I know. All they care about is sex, sports and booze. You're different — deeper, like. What do you do for a living, Pure Bliss?"

"I'm an editor at the *Daily Advocate.*"

"See, I knew it! I knew it was something like that! You're smart, I can see that already. So, you're the editor!"

"No, not *the* editor; just one of many editors who handle pages in the paper. I'm pretty low on the totem pole, believe me. You read the *Advocate* then?"

"No, not really. Well, if I see a copy I'll check out, like, the comics and Dear Abby. And the horoscope. I always check my horoscope. I'm a Libra. What's your sign?"

"I don't know."

"You don't know your sign?" Krystal was flabbergasted. "How can you not know your astrological sign? That's like going through life with your eyes shut. My God, I'd be lost without my horoscope. When were you born?" she demanded.

"June 14th."

"Well, see, that makes you a Gemini. That's good. Geminis are creative, warm, caring people. Isn't that interesting?"

"Very interesting."

The band returned with a thrash of guitars, ending all hope of further conversation. Krystal leaned in Browning's direction. "Dance?" she screamed.

Browning wanted to say he wasn't much off a dancer (which was true: his moves were instinctive rather than learned) and beg off. But he realized he couldn't be heard over the band's din. Instead, he shrugged and nodded assent. Krystal grabbed his hand (how small her hand felt in his, he thought) and led him onto the crowded dance floor.

She immediately launched into an elaborate series of moves, while Browning shuffled his feet and jerked his arms spasmodically. He felt foolish and out of his depth, but his delight at being with the ravishing Krystal overwhelmed his fears. He began to relax, loosen up, let go of his inhibitions. Inspired by his partner's skillful steps, he began improvising a few moves of his own: a sudden pirouette, a waggle of the hips, a soft-shoe step borrowed from Gene Kelly. Krystal laughed delightedly whenever he tried one of these, sparks flying from her gorgeous green eyes. Browning was entranced.

When, at the end of the night, she invited him back to her apartment, Browning cast aside his usual caution and accepted. And when, in the low light of her living room, Krystal slipped off her red dress and led Browning to her bed, for once he followed willingly. Tenderly, Krystal undressed him, and if she was dismayed by the inadequacy of his endowment (then at its zenith) she gave no sign. She guided him expertly inside her and Browning, virgin no more, brought her rapidly to climax, seconds ahead of his own. Browning remembered his words about love's elusiveness earlier that evening and smiled ruefully. This time I've caught you, he thought. This time there is no trickery. This time it's really love.

~

THEY SPENT the rest of the weekend together, much of it in bed, emerging only to nourish their suddenly ravenous bodies and take long, languid walks in the glorious spring sunshine. They made love constantly, from every conceivable angle. Browning's shyness and innocence delighted Krystal, who initiated him, like an older woman, in the arts of Eros. He proved an able student, pleasing his instructor repeatedly with his newly acquired skills. When the weekend was over and they parted to resume their lives, Browning felt a void such as he had never experienced. At work, he was wholly unable to concentrate. He edited errors into stories, wrote headlines that made no sense. His supervisor spoke sharply to him twice about the quality of his work. He lived for evenings, when he and Krystal could be together.

Browning proposed the following weekend. After a moment's surprised hesitation, Krystal accepted. They were married a week later in a civil ceremony at City Hall, attended by a mob of Krystal's friends. Harrison Howard, the only person Browning knew well enough to invite, was best man.

Krystal said she'd never met anyone like Pure Bliss. He was educated, intelligent, kind and sensitive, not at all like the boorish men who usually pursued her with Only One Thing in Mind. She never dreamed that a professional man like Bliss — a journalist! practically the editor! — would be attracted to her, a mere sales clerk with a high school education. His sudden and consuming ardour made her feel good about herself in a way she hadn't felt before. And she was deeply impressed that Browning had chosen to surrender his jealously guarded virginity to her. "I'm the one, aren't I, Pure Bliss?" she had demanded. "The one you've been waiting for all these years?"

Browning was no less astonished by Krystal's attraction to him. In the universe that he was familiar with, stunning women like Krystal were snapped up by star quarterbacks, not the inept losers among whose ranks he had always numbered himself. Her interest in him had the force of an emotional tsunami, sweeping aside all reason and leaving only one desperate imperative: lock up this treasure while you can. His proposal of marriage had been borne of this desperation, but he hadn't allowed himself to believe she might accept. When she did, it was as if all the heaviness of life had miraculously evaporated, and for the first time, he felt profoundly at peace. It was, truly, Pure Bliss.

For their honeymoon, they went to Niagara Falls. Krystal told Browning she knew it was a cliché, but she'd dreamed of honeymooning in Niagara Falls since she was a girl, so he didn't object. Besides, it didn't involve foreign travel, which suited Browning.

They stayed at the Honeymoon Kort Motel, where every room was equipped with a heart-shaped whirlpool bath and a king-sized bed fitted out with Magic Fingers. Both amenities delighted the new bride. A complementary bottle of Canadian champagne and a vial of Passion Pulse massage oil came with the room. Out of empathy for exhausted honeymooners, breakfast was served daily until 1 p.m. in the Newlyweds' Cafe. The motel was a couple of blocks from the actual falls, but just down the street from the wax museum, which Krystal was keen to visit.

Since neither had been to Niagara Falls before, they took in the sights. The falls themselves were the first stop. Browning was impressed and more than a little daunted by the roaring cascade; he couldn't help imagining what it would be like to be sucked into the terrifying abyss. But after a few minutes of restless gazing, Krystal had had her fill. "It's okay, I guess, but let's face it, it's just a lot of water rushing over a cliff. Once you've seen it, you've seen it." She was much more enthusiastic about the wax museum and Ripley's Believe It Or Not, pleased enough with their trip to the top of the Skylon Tower (though she noted pointedly that Toronto's CN Tower was much taller) and manifestly uninterested when Browning took her to nearby Lundy's Lane, site of a famous battle between British and American forces in 1814.

They had their first real fight over the *Maid of the Mist*. Krystal was fascinated by the tiny boat braving the whirlpools at the bottom of the falls, but the very idea of boarding it made Browning weak in the knees. "Oh, for God's sake, don't be such a sissy boy!" she exclaimed. "I'm sure if it was, like, really dangerous, they wouldn't let tourists on it." Browning continued to resist, but after Krystal refused to speak to him, he relented. She was thrilled by the adventure; he was seasick. When it was over, Krystal looked at him thoughtfully. "I don't know you very well, do I?" she said. "No," said

Browning, miserably, wiping vomit from his chin. "I suppose you don't."

That night, as Browning undressed in their room at the Honeymoon Kort Motel, Krystal, propped on one elbow in the huge, vibrating bed, said something that chilled Browning's blood. "Like, I never really noticed before, but when you're not erect, your thing almost disappears, doesn't it?" Browning's hand instinctively dropped to his genitals. "Does that bother you?" he asked, fearing the answer.

"No, I guess not. I just hadn't noticed before. Never seen you without an erection. It doesn't look so small when you're, like, aroused." She got a faraway look on her face. "Jeez, you should have seen the willy on this guy I balled once. I swear it was, like, a foot long. And thick, too. Like a zucchini. It actually hurt when he screwed me." She glanced at Browning, who had a stricken look on his face. "Not that I really minded."

Browning, crushed, climbed into bed but found he couldn't perform. All he could think of were zucchinis. Krystal was not sympathetic. "It's, like, our honeymoon," she wailed. "If you can't get it up now, what's it going to be like 10 years from now?" Browning didn't answer. He could feel her slipping away.

The rest of the honeymoon was a disaster. Krystal went back on the *Maid of the Mist,* without Browning. She spent hours around the motel pool, reading Harlequin Romance novels (which moved her to tears) and ignoring Browning, who moped around miserably. She did the rounds of the town's souvenir shops, returning with armloads of gaudy trinkets whose tackiness appalled him. When he remarked mildly on their cheap appearance, Krystal flared. "You think you're so damn smart," she sneered. "Mr. Editor. Well, let me tell you something. You don't know everything. You're boring, Bliss Browning. I don't know what I ever saw in you."

She left two weeks after the honeymoon, and filed for divorce a year later, the earliest opportunity under law. And Browning, whose bruised and battered heart mourned his loss, vowed never again to link his fate with another. Love, the chameleon, had bested him. It would not get a second chance.

CHAPTER 6

THE E-MAIL MESSAGE FROM "CALLAS" SENT BROWNING BACK TO THE emergency ward in the grip of another panic attack, even more severe than the last. Along with dizziness, heart palpitations and shortness of breath, he was wracked by an intense nausea unlike anything he'd experienced, as if an army of Nazi bacteria had launched an assault on his duodenum. He knew he wasn't dying this time but given the severity of his symptoms, he wasn't sure if that was a good thing or a bad thing.

The emergency ward doctor — coincidentally the same one who treated him the last time — clucked sympathetically and renewed Browning's prescription to control future attacks. Browning clutched the precious prescription like a lifeline in his right hand and walked unsteadily to the hospital taxi stand. This second attack stiffened his resolve: he must take charge of his life, or he feared it soon wouldn't be worth preserving. He remembered a line from the Baz Luhrmann film, *Strictly Ballroom,* whose trite truth now struck him with the force of revelation: *A life lived in fear is a life half-lived.* He had lived in fear most of his own life. Unless he could banish his demons, his half-life would continue to ebb.

Browning hailed a cab and eased his lumpy frame into the back seat. The cabbie, a bristle-bearded Sikh with a tightly wound turban, gave him a questioning look. "Laurier and Bay," Browning grunted as the driver flicked on his meter and pulled into the late-evening traffic. He considered his situation. His first step, he told himself, was contact "Callas" and find out what she or he — it? — wanted from him. The e-mail message had shaken his conviction that his mysterious correspondent was an everyday fraud. But accepting her identity at face value had implications too enormous to consider. For now, he resolved to proceed with caution. Faith, he was convinced, was the domain of wishful thinkers.

As for his other problem, the dreaded expedition to Africa, Browning had passed through denial, anger and resignation and was sidling up to acceptance. He was starting to view the trip as a type of psychological enema: unpleasant to endure, but ultimately purging. While the prospect terrified him, his rational self knew many of his fears were probably overblown; by confronting them, he might finally banish them. Assuming he survived the trip, that is, which in his mind was not at all a forgone conclusion. Still, he understood he couldn't continue in the state of paralysis that had characterized his life to that point. It was time to seek the missing half of his existence.

~

IT WAS LATE when the taxi dropped Browning at his apartment, but he wasted no time logging on to the Internet. He opened his e-mail and typed these words in the subject line: To 'Maria Callas' from Bliss Browning. Barely pausing lest he lose his nerve, he quickly wrote: "I think it's time we had that little talk." Then as before, he posted the message to his e-mail address.

Almost immediately, his in-box pinged in response. "My dear Browning," the message began. "Delighted to hear from you. I was wondering when you'd take up my invitation."

Browning felt his heartbeat accelerate. He was clammy with perspiration. I will not allow this to happen again, he told himself sternly. I will not. He took several long, deep breaths and tried to purge the confusion from his mind. When he felt calmer, he began to type again.

"Sorry for the delay, but messages from you have a remarkable effect on me. I seem to become quite unhinged."

Again, the response was instantaneous. "My poor Browning. I keep forgetting that to you I am a ghost, an apparition, with all the superstitious human baggage that entails. Let me assure you that I'm not here to haunt you. I don't even think of myself as a spirit — I'm just Maria Callas in another dimension. Though I admit it's far different from your world."

Browning decided to play along. "Tell me about your world," he typed. "Does everyone go there when they die? Are there others there, too? People you knew in life?"

"Alas, my dear Browning, I cannot say much. Just as on Earth, there are rules and regulations here. Civilizations may rise and fall, but bureaucrats are immortal, you know. Under the rules of this place, anyone in contact with the Other Side can reveal only the most general information. You can understand why. If the human concept of life after death were stripped of its mystery, if the afterlife became just another exotic destination, it would lose its ability to inspire the living. All the world's religions gain their power and influence from the idea that our earthly lives are just a dress rehearsal for eternity. Too much knowledge would replace that energizing faith with prosaic certainty. The virtue of faith would be lost and, with it, humankind's ability to believe in anything it can't see, touch, taste or smell. What a sad, diminished world that would be!"

Browning pondered this for a moment. "That's fine for those who are able to believe," he replied. "But wouldn't knowledge of the afterlife help people like me, who find the whole concept implausibly far-fetched? Wouldn't a bit of certainty compensate for our lack of faith?"

Again, the answer was swift.

"My dear Browning, faith is as essential to life as oxygen. Without faith — in yourself, in others, in things that can't be proven by science — there's no hope. It was faith in my own ability, an unverifiable belief that I had a rare and precious talent, that sustained me through the endless hours of practice and rehearsal, that allowed me to rise above the envy of others to become the greatest soprano of my time, if I may be so bold as to say so. Could I have done that without faith? Absolutely not! I believed in myself and I was certain that, in time, others would share that belief.

"Even when faith is scorned, it has value. I had faith in Aristo. Though he hurt me more than I can tell you, my faith in him was never really shaken. I knew that he didn't really love the Kennedy woman, even if, for a time, he thought he did. He married her for status, which he craved above all else, foolish man. Me, for a time he truly loved, and my faith in that sustained me through many miseries. No, my dear Browning, there is no substitute for faith. Without faith, there is no light. Without faith, darkness descends."

Browning read this testament with a sinking heart, overlooking, for the moment, the ludicrous circumstances of the conversation. "I'm afraid that faith is one thing I lack," he confessed. "I have little in myself and even less in others. But why should I? What reason do I have to believe in myself? I'm just a hack journalist who has never accomplished anything lasting or important. And why should I believe in others? If they think of me at all, it's most often with contempt and scorn."

If this outpouring of self-pity dismayed "Callas," her response didn't show it. "My dear, befuddled Browning," she began. "Faith must begin with you. If you lack faith in yourself, you can hardly expect others to believe in you. Faith begets faith. You must trust me on this."

"Hell, I don't even believe in you," Browning replied, his skepticism reasserting itself. "But I'm trying to keep an open mind. There must be something you can tell me about your so-called world without breaking the rules. How are you able to communicate with me, for instance?"

This time there was a short pause before his in-basket filled with his mystery correspondent's reply.

"In the old days, people in the Zone — that's what it's called here — who wanted to communicate with the living had to use the tried-and-true methods: apparitions, rattling chains, whispering voices, that sort of nonsense. These were crude devices and, understandably, people usually responded in terror. Mediums and clairvoyants are a more effective channel, but you can't use them to initiate contact. You can only respond if someone is trying to reach you. And that doesn't happen often.

"When television arrived, it opened new channels of contact. Inhabitants of the Zone could tap into TV signals and appear as images on television sets. Later, when cable TV became widely available, we were able to gain access through coaxial cable links. But television still limited our contact with the living to largely non-verbal forms, which meant the message was often unclear. Because the Zone is a non-corporeal place, its inhabitants have only a limited ability to speak; it takes more energy than we have to make anything but the simplest sounds. That's why most 'ghosts' are usually either silent or manage little more than moans. "The Internet has given us a vastly more effective channel to reach the living. In theory, anyone in the Zone can communicate in writing with anyone whose computer is linked to a network. Once Zone authorities give their permission and clear a channel, we can tap into any computer exchange simply by choosing to do so. But that's the catch: we can only enter cyberspace with permission, which is not easily obtained. You must first endure a battery of tests and answer endless questions. Even then, if you don't score in the top two per cent of applicants for what the authorities here call the Paranormal Visitations Assessment, they'll turn you down flat. I was fortunate: my PVA score just made the cut."

Browning read all this with mounting disbelief. What a concoction, he thought. "You make the afterlife sound like some sort of bureaucratic wet-dream. Rules, regulations, PVA scores . . . it doesn't sound like any version of heaven that I recognize."

"My dear Browning, who ever said this was heaven? Heaven is just a fanciful concept dreamt up by religion to ensnare the faithful. It bears very little resemblance to the reality of the Zone. The problem is, people think of life after death as either a reward for good behaviour or punishment for misconduct. It is neither — it's simply another dimension of existence, where your essence, or soul as you call it, resides after your earthly body dies. Whether you've lived a life of virtue or sin is irrelevant: everyone ends up here. You come into the Zone with a fresh slate, just as you enter life on earth innocent and unsullied. How you behave determines your treatment here."

Browning shook his head at this but decided to play the straight man a little longer.

"Are you saying that crime and punishment exist in the afterlife as they do on Earth?" he asked.

"Not as they do on Earth, no. But the concept is similar. I have to be careful, because we're starting to get into the details, but I can tell you that we in Zone are held to account. There are some obvious differences from how things work on Earth. In a non-corporeal world, crimes against property and person are logically impossible — theft, assault and murder are alien concepts here. Crimes have much more to do with your thoughts. Enforcement is no problem; the authorities are aware of everything you are thinking."

In spite of himself, Browning gasped. "My God," he wrote, "it sounds like the ultimate totalitarian society."

"Not really. Once again, my dear Browning, you are applying your Earthbound standards to judge another reality. Here in the Zone, we call that Earthism. We encounter it a lot when dealing with your lot. You have to realize this is a different plane of existence, much more refined than the rather crude societies on Earth. Here the authorities are beyond reproach. There is none of the human fallibility, ill-will or caprice that makes the idea of Big Brother so threatening to people on Earth. The rules here are utterly rational and exquisitely moral, administered with scrupulous fairness. All utopian societies ever devised on Earth failed because of the frailties or corruption of the living. But in the Zone, utopia is possible. Indeed, utopia exists."

Browning's head was spinning as he struggled to absorb what "Callas" was telling him. "Just who are these wise and all-knowing authorities anyway? Are you saying they're God?"

"They are whatever you want to call them. They are omniscient, and in that sense, they resemble the earthly concept of God. But in other ways, they're like no God anyone on Earth ever imagined. All that really matters is that they are good, just, honest and reliable. More than that I cannot say. In any case, my dear Browning, I think I've given you enough to think about for today. I suggest we end this conversation now and talk again tomorrow. You know how to reach me."

Browning stared at the screen, uncertain what to think. He could not possibly have just communicated with the "essence" of Maria Callas. Could he? Yet this was no longer merely a prank. Was he deranged, mad, out of his mind? He ran his fingers through his hair. He needed time to think. But time was one luxury he didn't have.

BROWNING AWOKE the next morning to the jangling of his telephone and again, the grating voice of Ryan Young.

"Blissy boy! Hope I didn't wake you, but here's the dope on your trip to Botswana," Young said with a snicker that made it clear he knew just how unwelcome his news would be. "You're booked on British Air to London on Saturday, with a connection from there to Harare. That's in Zimbabwe, which isn't the nicest place in the world these days, but it's as close to Botswana as you can get without a lot of messy connections. From there, you're booked on a bus to Victoria Falls, where you'll pick up a Botswana safari run by an outfit called The Elephant's Trunk. Pack light — you're limited to 25 pounds of luggage on safari."

Browning rubbed his sleep-encrusted eyes. "Jesus, Ryan, Saturday's just three days from now. I can't possibly be ready that soon."

"Sorry, but that's the gig. You don't have any choice. All the arrangements are made."

Browning groaned. "Alright, alright. What do you want me to do?"

"First, get yourself organized. I assume you have a valid passport?"

"Are you kidding, Ryan? Why would I have a passport?"

"Well, get one. Today. And you need some shots and some anti-malaria pills. And Richter wants you to drop by at three for a planning meeting. You'll get your tickets and a cash advance. So you see, Blissy boy, you can't afford to lie in bed all day. You should thank me for waking you."

"Thanks a lot, Ryan," said Browning, making no effort to conceal his false gratitude. "You're a prince."

Young cackled. "Fuckin' A."

~

HIS RIGHT ARM throbbed from a gamma-globulin shot to ward off hepatitis. A vial of anti-malaria pills he really should have started taking two weeks earlier distended the right front pocket of his pants. He'd swallowed his first chloroquine tablet at the doctor's office, discovering their vile chalky taste. When he'd asked about getting shots for typhoid and cholera, the doctor had told him it was too late for them to be effective. But no matter, he'd assured Browning: travellers rarely contracted those diseases in southern Africa if they took sensible precautions. Browning wasn't comforted. His sense of impending doom deepened.

The stop at the passport office had been nearly as trying. Staffed by two harassed women, it was crammed with agitated people seeking their documents. Browning had endured a two-hour wait, only to be chastised by one of the clerks for not applying weeks earlier. The stress triggered another of the now alarmingly familiar attacks, which Browning managed to short-circuit by downing one of his precious pills. The clerk, suspecting that Browning was unstable and possibly dangerous, promised to expedite his application and instructed him to return in two days. Browning fled the passport office wondering how he was going to survive the stresses of travel preparation, let alone the Kalahari.

Head throbbing with such preoccupations, Browning stepped out of the elevator into a newsroom humming with activity. Editors were busily preparing early pages for the next day's editions (except for Mick Mulligrew, on the phone as usual), and reporters were working the phones or groping for the right turn of phrase for the stories they were writing. Browning headed across the newsroom toward Renata Richter's office.

"Hello, Bliss." The words had a soft, sensuous sound that was entirely alien to Browning's ears. It was Kimberley Taylor, her red mane dazzling his eye like an exotic flower.

"Uh, he-hello, Kimberley," he stammered, too rattled to meet the medical reporter's friendly gaze.

"I hear you're off to Africa," Taylor said with an encouraging smile. "Lucky you. I'd love an assignment like that."

"Well, yes, I suppose I am lucky," Browning replied cautiously, though lucky was the last thing he felt. "So, how'd you hear about it?"

"Are you kidding? It's all over the newsroom. I mean, the *Advocate* doesn't exactly make a habit of sending writers to distant locales. The most glamorous trip they've ever sent me on was to Moncton, New Brunswick."

This was by far the longest conversation that Browning had ever had with the divine Kimberley, and though he was late for his meeting with the editor, he didn't want it to end. He wracked his suddenly paralyzed brain for something non-idiotic to say.

"No, I guess not," he finally agreed, lamely. "I've never been anywhere, really. Well, once to Lake Placid, but I didn't particularly like it. Too commercial. I was in Niagara Falls once, too. Didn't like that either." He knew he was babbling, but to his grateful astonishment, Taylor didn't seem to notice.

"No, I didn't like Lake Placid or Niagara Falls either. But travel is my passion. I love Tuscany and just adore the Greek Islands. I think Crete is my favourite: so diverse, so beautiful." She blinked at Browning. "When you get back, you'll have to tell me all about your adventures. Africa fascinates me; I'd love to go there."

Browning smiled blandly. *Say something, idiot.* But he could think of nothing that didn't sound moronic. "Well. . ." he exhaled, trailing off stupidly.

Taylor glanced at her watch. "I'd better get back to work. Got a big feature due today. What a sweatshop, eh?" she laughed. Her laughter reminded Browning of the tinkling sound melting ice makes when rivers are swollen with spring runoff.

"Browning! Hey, Browning!" It was Dylan Mosely. The newsroom star rarely deigned to speak to Browning, deeming him unworthy of his august attentions. "I hear you got the Botswana trip. Who'd you fuck?" Mosely was smiling, but tightly.

"Sorry, Dylan, I recommended you but for some reason Richter was fixated on the idea that I should go," Browning shrugged.

The smile remained on Mosely's lips, but his eyes were cold. "Well, I just hope you don't disappoint her, Browning. Have you ever written anything before?"

"Not for a while, Dylan, not for a while," Browning replied. "I'm pretty rusty. Just have to do my best, I guess."

"I guess. It just seems odd that Richter would pluck someone like you from the ranks for a plum assignment like this, when they're basically squandering my talents on routine news and features. I guess they just don't believe in rewarding excellence around here. Makes me wonder if I shouldn't make myself available to an organization that would appreciate me more."

"I don't know, Dylan. I think they appreciate you here. This is just some crazy notion of Richter's. I wouldn't read too much into it."

Mosely glowered. "I'm just getting sick of the bullshit, you know? Christ, *The New York Times* doesn't jerk its stars around like this. Richter better wise up or she's going to lose good people like me."

Browning had suddenly had enough of Dylan Mosely's whining. In Browning's view, Mosely had it made. He was successful, insanely handsome and could write like an angel. Yet he was moaning like a four-year-old denied a second helping of chocolate fudge ice cream.

"Oh, for Christ's sake, Dylan. The world does not base every judgment on what's good or bad for you. Most of the time, it doesn't even know you exist. The editor thinks that I'm the right person for this assignment. That's the end of the story. Get over it."

Mosely stared at Browning, and a flicker of something that might have been wary respect crossed his chiseled features. Without a word, he turned on his heel and stomped off. Browning smiled sheepishly to himself. That had felt good. This fear-conquering stuff might not be so bad after all.

Renata Richter greeted Browning effusively. "Ah," she cried. "There he is, our world traveller! Like Stanley, set to journey into darkest Africa in search of his own private Livingstone! How are you Bliss? Ready to risk life and limb for the dear old *Advocate*?"

"As ready as I'll ever be, ma'am, though I wish you wouldn't make it sound quite so perilous."

"Oh, it's not, it's not at all," Richter assured him. "I'm just trying to whip up a little wind in your hair. You'll be perfectly safe, I'm sure. Anyway, I'm counting on you to share your adventures with our readers, so don't go getting trampled by an elephant or anything."

"I'll do my best," Browning promised, sincerely.

"Now Bliss," Richter continued, "I've been thinking about this assignment, and here's how I'd like you to tackle it. I think you should keep a daily journal in which you can record everyday events on safari as well as your reflections on the political, sociological and cultural environment of the country. I'd like you to go beyond mere travelogue writing and make this a profound meditation on a vanishing world. Nobody knows how long wild animals will be free to roam Africa, but they could have little more than a generation left. You have a unique chance to record this world before it disappears and offer your prescription to save it."

"I don't know, Miss Richter," Browning said doubtfully. "That sounds pretty ambitious for someone like me. I just want to survive the trip."

"Nonsense, Bliss. You have great ability. I know you can do this; I have faith in you. And for God's sake, call me Renata: 'Miss Richter' makes me sound like a schoolmarm."

Browning looked sharply at Richter, searching for signs of the hyperbole that too often sullied her praise. He decided that this time, she was sincere: she really did believe in him. Was she misguided? Or was it he who couldn't see clearly?

"Okay, Renata," he said at last. "Somebody told me recently that faith was essential to life. If you have faith in me, I guess the least I can do is have some faith in myself, too."

"Good, good, that's settled. Before you leave, be sure to pick up your tickets from Judy. Oh, and take a camera; you'll need some pictures and video to illustrate your series. And get them to issue you a laptop, too. You can get a jump on the writing that way."

Browning began to laugh. "Some vacation," he said ruefully.

"Yes, it is, isn't it," said Richter, seriously. "You are one lucky man, Bliss Browning."

And at that moment, for some unfathomable reason, Browning actually felt lucky. Damned if he could figure out why.

CHAPTER 7

THE NEXT TWO DAYS WERE A FRENZY OF SHOPPING, PACKING, RESEARCH and paperwork. Browning haunted the city's wilderness outfitters, rapidly acquiring three pairs of walking shorts with Velcro pockets; four T-shirts, all in no-bug beige; a pair of light-weight walking boots; some aviator-style sunglasses; a Swiss Army knife with all the doodads; a pair of compact, folding binoculars; three bottles of mosquito repellent; a small flashlight with a powerful, penetrating beam; a cotton hat in the shape of a pith helmet; a sleeping bag, comfortable to a temperature of -10 Celsius; a relief map of Botswana; and a length of light cotton cloth, useful as a wrap to ward off the intense Kalahari sun.

To supplement his woeful knowledge of Botswanian history, culture and contemporary concerns, he raided the city's main library branch. Its modest collection on these topics was fully available, reflecting the less-than-pressing interest they commanded amongst the city's literate population. Together with a burgeoning stack of travel books, they formed a not-inconsiderable body of more-or-less expert knowledge and opinion about his destination. And though he half hoped the clerks at the Passport Office would respond to his rush request with the usual bureaucratic lassitude, another part of him identified this for what it really was: a desperate desire to cling to the familiar. As it happened, the Passport Office rose to the challenge, issuing him a crisp new passport within two days of his application. Browning took it as another sign that he was fated to make the trip.

He spent his few remaining moments attempting to pack. At first, he simply piled as many of his belongings as possible into a cavernous cream-coloured suitcase purchased for his ill-fated honeymoon a decade earlier. But when he tried to lift the beige behemoth, he staggered under the load, like a weightlifter beyond his limit. A closer look at the safari company literature revealed that baggage was restricted to 25 pounds, roughly a third the weight of the suitcase. He needed a new piece of luggage and a new packing strategy.

Another trip to the outfitters store supplied the first — a canvas travel pack that he could strap to his back or tote by its handle — but the second proved more difficult. No matter how he packed his new, streamlined bag, something vital had to be omitted. Finally, after a painful cull that left several safari garments in a dresser drawer, he was able to fill his pack with a representative sampling from all the essential clothing groups. In what at the time seemed a stroke of genius, he reasoned that he could further expand his wardrobe by doubling up on clothing he wore: two pairs of socks, two jockey shorts, two T-shirts.

What was missing from this list of tasks, preparations and busywork, of course, was any contact with "Callas." Their last conversation, with its fantastical sketch of an unrecognizable afterlife, had assumed a dreamlike quality in Browning's memory; he wasn't entirely convinced that he hadn't hallucinated the whole exchange. Nor was he sure that he really wanted to know more. The trip to Botswana was a blessing in disguise, the ideal excuse to ignore the self-styled phantom knocking insistently at his cyberspace door. Browning found himself doing an unaccustomed thing — steering clear of the computer in his bedroom, as if it harboured a deadly virus that could, in a moment of incaution, possess his body. The world, always a menacing place to Browning, had acquired a new and unexpected peril.

HARRISON HOWARD SOPPED up a puddle of marinara sauce with a piece of bread and popped the soggy works into his mouth. Across the table, Browning downed his last bite of lasagna and washed it down with the remnants of a bottle of Italian red. He looked at Howard, feeling a bit drunk, the traces of a smile playing at the corners of his mouth.

"A satisfying little wine," he intoned solemnly. "I'm sure you'll be amused at its pretension."

Howard grimaced at the weak jest. Truth be told, he didn't want to be there. Howard was something of a gastronome, and the Impresario, though Browning's favourite restaurant, was hardly his idea of haute cuisine. But he had agreed to join Browning for what the travel editor only half-jokingly referred to as "the last supper" because his friend clearly needed his support.

So far, their conversation had been typical of their social get-togethers: desultory speculation about the sex lives of various colleagues, bitter complaints about the manifest ineptitude of their bosses and general teeth-gnashing about the parlous state of newspapering in the early 21st century. Browning's impending journey to Africa had barely come up, but now, as the waiter brought them two glasses of cognac, Browning cautiously broached the subject.

"Harry, I'm curious about something," he began. "What are people in the office saying about this trip I'm taking?"

"Well, they're jealous as hell, if that's what you mean."

"That's not what I'm getting at. What I'd like to know is, do people think Richter's crazy to send me?"

"Jesus, Bliss, people think Richter's crazy about everything. Why would this be any different?"

"Seriously, Harry, you're the only person I can trust to be straight with me. What are they saying?"

Howard looked levelly at his friend for a moment, then let out a long, slow sigh. "Alright," he said at last. "You asked, so I'll tell you. Just about everyone thinks Richter's really on drugs this time. They can't figure out why she picked you to handle an expensive foreign assignment that begs for a Hemingway. Who, by the way, they don't think you are."

Browning nodded. "I don't suppose that anyone has considered that, as travel editor, I might not be a totally illogical choice for a job like this."

"Bliss, you know the *Advocate* never sends editors on writing assignments. And let's be honest, you haven't exactly carved out a reputation as a wordsmith. I mean, you're a solid editor, and twice the little worker that Mick Mulligrew is" — Browning stuck out his tongue at this jibe — "but I haven't noticed any National Newspaper Awards cluttering up your desk."

Browning listened to his friend's comments with resignation. His encounter with Kimberley Taylor had raised his hopes that at least some of his colleagues saw nothing bizarre in his assignment. Howard's blunt assessment exploded that fantasy.

"On the other hand," Howard continued, "what the hell do they know? Richter may be an idiot savant, but her savant side is overdue for an appearance. You've never really been given a chance like this. Who's to say you won't knock their socks off? I, for one, expect you to ace this thing." Howard raised his glass. "A toast to Bliss Browning, Great White Hunter. May you do for travel writing what Henry Miller did for sex."

Browning smiled weakly. "I'd rather do for sex what Henry Miller did for sex, but under the circumstances, your proposition is a good second choice." He raised his glass, feeling the cognac burn into his belly and proceed directly, without passing Go, to his brain. "Whoa," he grinned woozily, "I'm getting a bit buzzed."

Howard nodded. "Me too, pal. And there's no one I'd rather get pissed with."

The two men fell silent as they sipped their cognac and basked in their easy comradeship. Shared sorrows had forged a powerful bond between them. After Browning's marriage ended, it was Howard who helped right him, listening patiently as the shattered man poured out his anguish and humiliation. And when Howard's son was killed in a freak bicycling accident four years ago, Browning had reciprocated, handling Howard's duties at the office, and acting as a sponge for his pain. Their closeness allowed Browning to reveal things he wouldn't dream of sharing with anyone else. Even so, it took a bottle of wine and several glasses of cognac before he was loose enough to tell Howard about his exchanges with the entity claiming to be Maria Callas.

"Really," his friend exclaimed, after Browning hesitantly broached the subject. "And what form do these close encounters take?" Howard grinned drunkenly. "Diaphanous arias from a translucent diva? Has she kept her weight off?"

"I don't know. I haven't actually seen her. We've just exchanged messages through my computer."

"Messages? What sort of messages?"

"Just conversation. You know, I ask her questions, she tells me about life after death."

"Ah. Those sorts of messages. Sounds harmless enough. What's the problem?"

"The problem, smartass, is that I really don't know what to think about it. Every bone in my body tells me it's a hoax, that the very notion of Maria Callas using the Internet to post messages from the Great Beyond is loony beyond belief. Yet I can't come up with an explanation that makes sense."

The liquor was making Browning's head swim. He forced himself to concentrate, enunciating his words with exaggerated clarity. "Harry, this person can do things with the Internet that haven't been invented yet. And there's something about the things she says, and the way she says them, that ... well dammit, they sound like I imagine Callas would sound."

"Waida minute," Howard interrupted. He noticed he was slurring his words. "Are you tellin' me you actually think that Maria fuckin' Callas is speaking to you through your laptop?"

"I don't know, Harry," Browning said morosely. "Maybe. No. Of course not. No. Absolutely."

Howard stared at his friend, who was just slightly out of focus. "As our esteemed managing editor Norman Pugsley would say, 'Christ on a bicycle'. You need this holiday worse than I thought."

"So, you don't think it could ... possibly be Callas?"

Howard snorted. "Let's just say it would surprise the fuck out of me. Look, Bliss, it's clear what's going on here. You're this big Callas expert, and somebody is obviously yankin' your chain, tryin' to bring you down a notch."

"You're right," said Browning dubiously, "I know you're right. It just seems so . . . real, I don't know."

"Real, shmeal. It's a con, Bliss." Howard flung a comradely arm around his friend's shoulders. "What you need to do is go to frickin' Botswana, forget about all this, and prove that Richter knows what she's talking about for once in her life. This is your chance, Bliss. Don't go wiggy on me now."

Browning smiled despite himself. "Okay, Harry. That's good advice. I can always count on you to set me straight, can't I?"

"Who else, eh?" Howard said with tipsy gruffness. "Who the fuck else?"

~

IT WAS NEARLY 11 p.m. when Browning, hand unsteady from drink, eased the key into the lock of his apartment door and lurched inside. His new travel bag, bulging with the winning items in his hotly contested packing lottery, sat on the living room floor near the door, next to his company-issue laptop and a carry-on bag containing his tickets, camera and various reference books. His plane left for London tomorrow afternoon, with a connection to Harare. Now that departure was imminent and there was nothing to do but wait, Browning's anxiety level was on the rise. Astonishingly, he had never flown before; the notion of sealing himself in a steel tube and racing somewhere at near-supersonic speeds thousands of feet in the air had always struck him as insane.

Sleep was out of the question, so Browning flipped on the TV and channel surfed, searching for something to distract his mind from his impending trip. He paused at the local news, but it was astoundingly tedious: the top story was an interminable item about a rare stamp causing a stir at a convention of philatelists. The sports channel featured a water polo match between Guyana and Mali, the Women's Network was debating whether men were rapists by nature or by choice, and the arts channel was presenting a troupe of dancers, supine and twitching spasmodically. Browning skipped quickly past a National Geographic film about hippos (a little too on the nose) and settled on an infomercial hawking tapes guaranteed to improve your sex life. But the infomercial was cunningly light on excerpts from the tapes, and Browning turned the set off in disgust.

Wandering over to his CD racks, he selected one of his favourite Callas discs, a 1961 recording of Bellini's *Norma* with the La Scala orchestra under the baton of Tulio Serafin. Cranking the volume only modestly in view of the late hour, he reclined on the couch and let the passionate voice of Callas wash over him. Soon enough, the moving strains of the opera's most famous aria, Casta Diva, filled his head with its familiar, soaring melody. Though he had listened to Callas's performance of *Norma* innumerable times, he found himself caught up anew in the power of her portrayal of the doomed Druid priestess. Mentally, he followed Norma into the flames with Pollione, the Roman pro-consul whose fickle nature was insufficient to shatter her epic love.

As the last Callas note faded away, Browning stayed on the couch, unmoving though not unmoved by the glorious sound. He thought of his impending journey into the heart of darkness as it seemed, melodramatically, to him, and realized how much he would miss that sound if it were denied him. Life, which he usually regarded as burdensome, suddenly struck him as infinitely precious, and he wondered why he didn't treasure it more. He was astonished to find himself weeping, not the dainty tears of sweet esthetic sorrow, but fully engaged, chest-wracking sobs.

Browning rose from the couch and plucked some tissue from a box on the coffee table. He wiped his coursing eyes and let out a long, shuddering sigh. He was vaguely embarrassed by his unstable emotions, yet in the aftermath of the purge he felt calmer than he had in days — calm enough, in fact, to consider sleep for the first time. Turning off the living room lights, he shuffled into his bedroom.

Immediately he sensed that something was wrong. Looking around the room, he saw at once what it was: his laptop was switched on though he hadn't used it in nearly three days.

Puzzled, he walked over to the machine and touched a key. The screen-saver vanished, revealing the following urgent message:

"My dear Browning. What has happened? I haven't heard from you in days. Time is running out. It is vital that we talk. Please contact me at once. Callas."

Browning stared at the message. I should ignore this. He remembered Harrison Howard's advice: forget Callas, focus on the trip. That's wise. That's what I should do. Instead, he sat down, opened his e-mail and with a few rapid keystrokes typed the following words: "Bliss Browning to 'Maria Callas': Piss off. Leave me alone. I'm not interested. Get it? Find another sucker." But before he could shut down his computer, his inbox pinged with a reply. Despite himself, Browning read the words.

"My dear Browning. Thank goodness you're there. I was afraid something had happened to you. But then, something has, hasn't it? Why are you so hostile? Why haven't you been in touch?"

In a fury, Browning bashed out his reply. "Because, whoever you are, I'm tired of being played for a fool. And even if I wasn't sick of your games, I have more pressing matters to worry about right now. Now please, if you have a merciful bone in your body, leave me alone."

"But my dear Browning," came the calm reply, "I don't have a bone, merciful or otherwise, in my body — in The Zone, bones simply are not part of the physiology. And I cannot leave you alone. You are my only hope. If you reject me, all is lost."

"What are you babbling on about?" Browning asked. "All I've heard from you is a lot of new-age blather about faith and a ludicrous story about some mystical place where bureaucrats can get inside your head. I'll tell you frankly: I don't know who you really are. I don't see what I can possibly do for you."

There was no immediate reply. Browning was about to shut down the computer when five short words appeared that caused the hair on the back of his neck to stand up as if zapped by electric current.

"You can find my son."

"Son?" Browning replied, recovering from his shock. "What son? Maria Callas had no children — everyone knows that."

"Oh, they do, do they? Have you never heard, my dear Browning, that when everyone knows something, it usually isn't true? It is a law of nature, I think. In any case, it applies in this instance. Shall I tell you the story?"

Browning knew he should end the conversation now. He hesitated, then slowly typed: "Go on."

"Good. I would have told you sooner, but I wanted to give you time to get used to me. Now there is no time. I must explain why I have contacted you and hope that you can find the faith to believe and help me."

"Spare me the commercial," Browning answered gruffly. "Just get on with it."

CHAPTER 8

"I'LL START WITH WHAT IS KNOWN, OR AT LEAST WHAT PEOPLE THINK they know. It is common knowledge that I had a lengthy affair with Aristotle Onassis, whom I met when I was 36 and at the height of my powers. He was a difficult man — temperamental, unfaithful, a bully even — but I loved him. Oh, how I loved him. I never met anyone so captivating, so charming ... when he wanted to be. He was a 20th-century buccaneer, and you know how attractive that sort is to women. And he was the only man I ever met who wasn't intimidated by Callas the legend, who treated me like a woman, not an icon.

"All the time we were together, right from the beginning, I longed to have children with this man. When his marriage to Christina ended — I suppose I have to accept some responsibility for that — I thought, My God, is it possible? Can we marry, have a family? Can I find some meaning in my life more enduring than an audience's bravos? But as the world knows, Aristo refused to marry me. He loved me, he needed me, but he wouldn't marry me. I think he was afraid that marriage would somehow limit his options. He was, after all, an unrepentant womanizer. As I grew older, I clung to the hope that he would change his mind. But time was against me. My child-bearing years were slipping away.

"Then, a miracle. In 1966, when I was 43, I became pregnant. I was overjoyed. I was sure that Aristo would marry me and accept the child. But he wouldn't. Quite the opposite — he told me if I had the child, our relationship would be over. It was a cruel ultimatum, and it left me in anguish. I had to choose between the two things I wanted most in the world: Aristo's love and my unborn child. The world believes that I chose Aristo and aborted the baby. That's the story I told Aristo and my friends, and I have no reason to doubt that they believed it. But the truth is quite different.

"You have to understand that I was a desperate woman. This was 1966; abortion was not the common thing it is today, and I was a devout Catholic. I could not kill my child, even if I wanted to. And I most assuredly did not want to. With all my success and fame and accomplishments, I had always felt as if something critical was missing. If I couldn't have a family of my own – and I was resigned to that – at least I was determined to save my child, to give him life.

"But it had to be done with the utmost discretion; if Aristo heard anything about it, our relationship would be over and my child would quite possibly be in danger. Aristo was a very powerful and ruthless man, after all. I needed to hide this child where no one would ever find it, and I needed a trustworthy intermediary to make the arrangements. But who could I rely on? The jet-set world that I was part of was not notable for its discretion; it was a world of gossip and envy. I could not look there for assistance. There was only one person: my godfather, Leonidas Lantzounis, the doctor who delivered me and a lifelong mentor and friend. He was by then very old, but still alive in New York City, where he moved a year before my parents in 1923. Leonidas did not let me down; he never let me down, come to think of it. He was originally from Meligalas in the Peloponnese, just like my parents, and it was his idea to place the baby with a trusted family in that town. He made the arrangements; I didn't want to know the details, only that my baby would have a good and loving home. Leonidas promised me that he would, and that was good enough for me.

"The hardest part was concealing my condition from Aristo. I told him I'd had an abortion, of course, but pregnancy is not an easy thing for a woman to hide. So when I could no longer conceal my swelling belly, I concocted a story. I told Aristo that I had always dreamed of travelling through China and intended to make a lengthy visit. I knew he wouldn't object; by this point he was already well along in his courtship of Jacqueline Kennedy and would welcome my absence. Of course, I didn't go to China. Leonidas set me up in a secluded spot in upstate New York, where I waited out my confinement.

"When the time came, Leonidas was there to deliver the baby. It was a difficult labor, what's called a breach birth. The child had turned sideways in my womb, and Leonidas had great trouble with the delivery. For me, the pain was excruciating, so severe that even the painkillers couldn't mask it. Finally — I think it was just as Leonidas succeeded in turning the child and grasping its head with his forceps — I could stand the pain no longer and passed out. By the time I regained consciousness, my son had been delivered and whisked away. I was dismayed, but Leonidas said it was better that way. It would make our separation easier for me to bear. But he assured me he was healthy, an eight-pound boy with dark hair.

"Many times over the next decade I longed to see my son. I imagined him as a boy, resourceful and robust, roaming the hills and valleys of the Peloponnese with his playmates. What is he like, I wondered. Can he sing? Does he have his father's cruel streak, or his mother's insecurities? Yes, insecurities. If you know me as well as you say, you cannot be surprised by that. Once, in a weak moment, I tied up my hair, put on simple clothes and went to Meligalas to see if I could spot him. I did not intend to approach him or try to speak to him. But my eyes hungered for the sight of him. I just wanted to see what he looked like, to ensure that he was well. I drove slowly around the town, scanning the faces of the young boys for one who looked familiar, one who bore the mark of Callas or Onassis. But no one I saw had the look I sought. I left, crushed by my failure, but half relieved as well. For I do not truly know what I would have done had I found him."

BROWNING, who had read this tale with mounting incredulity, sat silent for a full minute. Whoever this cyber-spectre is, he thought, her story is extraordinary. He realized, with a start, that he no longer felt any animosity toward his mystery correspondent. Her tale had changed something indefinable but significant.

He willed his fingers to type a response. "Even if everything you say is true — and I must tell you that it seems fantastical to me — I still don't understand what you think I can do about it."

"My dear Browning," came the now-familiar salutation, "I know it is a lot to ask, but I want you to help me do in death what I never did in life. I want you to go to Greece, find my son and tell him who his parents were. I want you to help him understand who he really is. And I want you to tell him that I did what I did out of love, not indifference. It is important to set the record straight."

Stunned, Browning responded with the first words that entered his head. "It's out of the question. My God, in a few hours I leave for Africa. If I somehow survive, you expect me to jet off to Greece to search for a mythical son who could be God knows where by now? I'm crazy, but not that crazy."

"My dear Browning, I know how you must feel—"

"No," Browning interrupted. "I don't think you do. I don't know how you picked me for this assignment, but you couldn't have made a worse choice. Travel terrifies me. Anything new and different terrifies me. And you, this conversation, everything about this situation, terrify me."

"Perhaps that is why you were chosen."

"What do you mean?"

"My dear Browning, the authorities here selected you, not me. They move in mysterious ways, but never without purpose. If they picked you as my earthly contact, they had a reason. Perhaps they saw your fears and believed that this would help you overcome them. Perhaps there is something in your destiny that impels you on this course."

"Bullshit. Fate and destiny are nothing more than excuses for not taking responsibility for your own life."

"As you have done?"

For a moment, Browning was silent, stung by the uncomfortable truth of the observation. "You're right," he replied at last, "I have not taken control of my life. But it is my own fears and weaknesses that have stopped me, not some fatalistic pre-determined design."

"Knowing that, my dear Browning, why do you flinch from dealing with them? You have the power to change your life's course if you truly want to. If you choose not to act, are you not willfully embracing your own unhappiness?"

"Give me a break. I'm going to Africa, aren't I? For me, that's huge."

"True, it is. Unfortunately, it's not an indulgence I can afford."

"Meaning what, precisely?"

"When the authorities in The Zone approved my request for earthly contact, they imposed strict conditions. One was that I must persuade you to undertake the assignment within 10 days. That time expires tomorrow. If you agree to help, I am permitted a further six weeks contact with you. That's all. After that, I will be unplugged, so to speak — unable to receive or respond to your messages."

"But that's absurd. You have all of eternity. What's the rush?"

"Admittedly, it seems a bit bureaucratic, but the authorities here have their reasons. They believe that if we can't persuade an earthly contact of our bona fides within 10 days, it's unlikely that we ever will. And the six-week rule is designed to clear space on the channel for others in The Zone waiting their turn."

"What do you mean, clear the channel?"

"The channel between The Zone and earth is strictly limited to 1,000 contacts at any one time, not because of technical limitations — the authorities are all-powerful, after all — but because of the need to preserve the mystery about this place. If contacts such as this were too numerous or common, that would be undermined."

"Let me get this straight. If I don't buy into your plan by tomorrow, you're off the air, right?"

"That's not how I would phrase it, but yes, essentially that's correct."

"And even if I do take your bait, I'll only be able to contact you for the next six weeks?"

"Correct again. That's what I meant when I said time was running out. And that's why you must depart for Greece at once if you are to locate my son before my time expires."

"Well, clearly that's not possible. I'm spending the next three weeks in Africa, God help me. So you see, I'm obviously the wrong man for this job."

"My dear Browning. I know that what I'm asking is difficult. But sometimes life demands a leap of faith. If you spurn me now, my son's best chance to learn his true heritage will be lost, and with it my hope of making amends for my errors in life. You may say, 'So what? It's not my problem.' But, my dear Browning, perhaps it is your problem, after all. You were chosen for this assignment for a reason. Whatever that reason may be, it too will be lost if you fail to act. You said yourself that we shape our lives through the choices we make. If you choose not to help me, your life will be different, perhaps much worse. Africa isn't going anywhere; you can go there another time. I am here so very briefly. If what I accomplished in my life means anything to you at all, I implore you not to reject me now. In the name of the human compassion that I know you possess, please help me."

Despite himself, Browning read this fervent appeal with emotion. If this was a hoax, it was a cunning one. Callas's tale was affecting and Browning, who also yearned for children he was resigned to never having, was touched by her story. Yet the situation was impossible. Even if he could somehow manage the leap of faith Callas wanted, he simply could not postpone the Africa trip now. He imagined explaining the situation to Renata Richter. "Sorry about that, Ren, but I really must pop off to Greece to search for Maria Callas's son. Yes, the opera singer. We're great friends, you know." He shuddered and ran his fingers quickly over the keyboard.

"I'm sorry, but the answer is no."

CHAPTER 9

BROWNING ARRIVED AT OTTAWA'S AIRPORT FOUR HOURS BEFORE HIS flight for London, so early that the check-in counter had not yet opened. He lined up anyway, determined to avoid any risk of misadventure. Half an hour later, an Air Canada clerk took pity on the forlorn figure and began check-in a few minutes early. "My, my" said the clerk, a tall young man with a permanent expression of faint amusement, "you must be eager. On vacation?"

"Mmmmm?" Browning murmured, distracted. The airport had activated his phobias, and his concentration was pinging off in several directions simultaneously. "Um, yeah. More or less. Sort of a working vacation, I suppose. Off to Africa, actually." He grinned miserably. "Can't wait."

He stuffed his ticket and boarding pass into his carry-on bag. With hours to kill before his flight, he undertook a full tour of the airport's services and amenities. By ambling like an arthritic octogenarian, he was able to consume nearly 20 minutes in this manner. A stale doughnut and vile cup of coffee from a fast-food outlet disposed of another 15.

Having exhausted the airport's diversions, Browning decided to proceed to the departure lounge and wait out the remaining time there. Provoked by his jangled nerves, flop sweat poured from his forehead and drizzled saline fluids into his eyes, leading staff at the security checkpoint to eye him with suspicion. But a thorough pat-down and search of his carry-on bag failed to turn up anything untoward, and they reluctantly waved him through.

Browning ambled slowly to the departure lounge, a sea of molded-plastic seats interrupting the broad sweep of the long hall near his gate. He picked a spot and settled in. After an hour or so of discomfort and tedium, it occurred to him that he hadn't tested his laptop to ensure that it was working. Cursing softly, he turned on the machine, used the airport's free WIFI to connect to the Internet and composed a message to Harrison Howard:

Hi Harry,

I'm writing this from the "departure lounge" of Ottawa airport. In less than an hour, I'll be strapped into my seat on an Air Canada jet, bound irrevocably for London and the great unknown. Short of a full-scale mental breakdown (which I'm not entirely ruling out), I don't suppose there's any escape now. Seriously, I'm nervous, but proud of myself for doing this. Of course, this is the easy part; I'll probably crumble like a feta cheese once I'm actually on foreign soil. Pray for me, Harry, and I'll see you in three weeks, God willing.

Ciao, Bliss

p.s. Took your advice on that Callas thing. Thanks.

Browning clicked the send button. At once, the screen filled with words.

"My dear Browning! Thank God I found you! I've been desperate with worry that my time would elapse before I could contact you again. You must listen to me. Lives depend on what I am about to tell you. My case officer at Central Office has given me information that casts my request in a more urgent light. Something is about to happen to my child; she wouldn't say what, but strongly hinted that people could die. She said, and I quote: 'Too bad your Browning lacks faith. He could make a difference.' I'm sorry this is so vague, but that's how they talk at Central Office. So you see, my dear Browning, it is imperative that you go to Greece. I am powerless to save my son, but you can. You can save him, and in the process, redeem both our lives. Three lives saved: how can you turn me down? You can't. You mustn't. Bon voyage, my dear Browning. Do not fail me."

Browning sat quite still, struggling to make sense of what had just happened. No mortal hacker could do this, he thought. *You can save my son and redeem both our lives.* That's what the message said. All he needed was a little faith. Okay, a lot of faith: a giant leap, in fact. But wasn't that what "Callas" had told him? Sometimes life demands a leap of faith? Perhaps this was one of those times. If he rejected her now, would he be missing his chance to affirm the sovereignty of his mind over the tyranny of his fears? He remembered his marriage, the last time he had recklessly pursued something, and the memory sent a shiver through his body. He'd be an idiot to take a risk like that again. And what about his job? What about Renata Richter's expectations? How could he jeopardize all that?

Through his brain-fever, Browning only dimly heard the announcement. It sounded something like "final call for Air Canada flight 463 to London," but that wasn't possible. Surely his plane wasn't due to depart for at least half an hour.

He glanced at his watch. It was fifteen minutes from departure time. Fighting off waves of panic, he stuffed his laptop into its carrying case and sprinted for the gate. Once there, he couldn't produce his boarding pass, and realized that it was in his carry-on bag, still sitting where he'd left it, by his chair in the departure lounge. Another cross-lobby sprint to retrieve the bag, a flash of his boarding pass and he was aboard, moments before the airplane crew locked down the door.

Buckling his seatbelt, Browning examined the plane's cabin. It was an alien place to him, its sleek plasticity as strange as a UFO and nearly as unsettling. He was surprised that the plane's staff looked normal — he'd half expected them to resemble beings from another planet, with oversized heads, perhaps, or lizard eyes. He watched closely as they ran mechanically through the standard pre-takeoff safety spiel and felt a stab of icy dread when they described procedures for ditching over water, an eventuality that ranked just behind a helpless plummet on his list of airplane horrors.

So intently was he following the safety instructions that Browning barely noticed the plane had reached the end of the runway and was awaiting clearance for takeoff. Suddenly the huge engines roared and the airliner began its transition from lumbering leviathan to airborne swan. The sheer noise and power startled Browning. He had never experienced anything like it. He clung fiercely to the seat's armrests as the plane hurtled ever faster down the runway. Just as he was convinced that the plane would crash ignominiously at the end of the tarmac, its wheels lifted and the jet climbed effortlessly over the city.

It made a long, looping arc as it ascended toward cruising altitude, and Browning found himself gazing in wonder at the receding city below. He looked for his own apartment block but couldn't pick it out from amongst the towers in the city core. Then the plane cut through a cloud bank and there was nothing outside his window but a vast expanse of blue, carpeted with white shag. It was a calm and peaceful place, with none of the sensation of speed or menace Browning had anticipated. He began to relax.

The couple on his left, piqued that his late arrival had robbed them of privacy and space, was ostentatiously ignoring him. But Browning was secretly glad. The last thing he wanted was five or six hours of captive conversation with strangers. He had much to think about. The last, urgent message had shaken him badly, and he needed to figure out how to respond.

The notion that lives depended on him was both novel and frightening. No one had ever depended on him for anything more vital than a page in the next day's newspaper. Yet the sense of responsibility he felt was oddly pleasing. A part of him wanted to embrace it, but how could he? If he took responsibility for Callas's son, he would renounce his obligation to his employer. Renata Richter had dispatched him on this mission in good faith, and he had accepted, however reluctantly. How could he abandon that commitment now?

A stewardess offering beverages interrupted these ruminations. He accepted a beer and a micro-package of nuts, which he devoured in a single gulp after a brief wrestle with the wrapping.

True, he reasoned as he munched, I agreed to go to Africa, but that was before I fully understood what was at stake with Callas. The situation has changed, for reasons nobody could have predicted. Browning took a swig of beer and swirled the malty liquid around in his mouth. Was this all just rationalization? Was he just looking for an excuse to bail out of a trip he'd really rather avoid?

The more he turned these thoughts over in his mind, the more confused and despairing he became. His brain hurt, and he decided to give it a rest. Perhaps a little soothing music would help, he thought. Plugging in the ear buds distributed shortly after takeoff, he found the channel dial on his armrest and turned up the volume.

He immediately recognized the moving strains of *Dei tuo figli*, a heartbreaking aria from the first act of Cherubini's *Medea*. The voice was unmistakably that of Maria Callas. Browning normally would have been delighted, but right now the coincidence was too much. He quickly switched to the next channel. Callas was singing the same aria there, as well. He swiftly ran through all 12 channels: only Callas was on offer.

Browning felt the panic rising. Surely this wasn't normal. Callas's popularity with airline passengers could not possibly be so universal that her music was offered to the exclusion of any other. He plucked the in-flight magazine from the mesh pouch on the seatback ahead and thumbed through it until he came to the section detailing in-flight services. Under audio, he found descriptions of the offerings on the various channels. They encompassed a wide range of styles, from alternative rock to Strauss waltzes. On the classical channel he discovered the Callas aria, but it was just one of nearly a dozen selections.

In mounting confusion, Browning summoned a steward. "Is there a problem with the audio program on today's flight?" he asked.

The steward frowned. "Not that I'm aware of, sir. Why? Isn't yours working?"

"Well, I seem to be getting the same song on every channel," Browning said, with an apologetic smile.

"Really?" said the steward. "That's odd. Let me have a listen."

Browning passed over his ear buds, drawing poisonous looks from the aggrieved couple next to him. The steward listened for a moment, twirled the channel dial a few times and, with a puzzled expression, handed them back to Browning. "Well, it seems to be working fine now, sir."

Browning mumbled embarrassed thanks and reinserted the ear buds. Callas was still singing. Somehow, he wasn't surprised. Nor was he surprised when a quick flip through the dial revealed that she was still on every channel, seemingly performing for his ears only.

It was impossible, even for Browning, to ignore the signs any longer. Whether or not it really was Callas, the moral arithmetic was clear: what was a newspaper assignment when weighed against a life? How could he pretend that writing a travel story was more important than doing what he could to prevent pain and loss and death? And how could he spurn an urgent appeal from a legend, albeit a dead and maddeningly unverifiable one, who also happened to be the source of his life's greatest pleasure?

By the time his plane landed at Heathrow airport, Browning had decided. He would go to Greece. And deal with the consequences later.

~

IT WAS BARELY 6 a.m. London time when Browning bolted gratefully from the Air Canada jet and entered the sleek precincts of Heathrow airport. Even at that early hour, the airport was bustling with transitory life, as travellers reclaimed their baggage or scurried to catch connecting flights. Browning was comforted to discover that Heathrow, while huge and confusing, was not unduly alien. The signs were in English, and many of the airport's inhabitants resembled Canadians, at least superficially. Still, his heartbeat was dangerously elevated, and he quickly popped a couple of pills to ward off an untimely attack. His decision to go to Greece had imposed an urgent agenda on him. He could not afford any weaknesses.

His first priority was to recover his bag. Fortunately, his luggage had not been checked all the way through to Africa. In Ottawa, he had seen that as a burdensome annoyance; now, with his change of plans, he thanked the fates for their prescience.

Unsure where to go, Browning allowed himself to be carried along by the torrent of passengers. He eventually arrived in a large hall filled with half a dozen baggage carousels, each spitting out the belongings of travellers arriving from all corners of the globe. Browning stood for 20 minutes beside one of the massive conveyer belts before realizing it was disgorging suitcases from a different flight.

Looking around, he recognized his hostile seat-mates collecting their bags at the next belt and deduced that he should be there instead. Almost immediately, he spotted his bulging canvas pack, disappearing around a bend in the conveyer belt. He set out in hot pursuit, but before he could navigate the crowds surrounding the carousel, his bag disappeared through an opening in the wall. Browning gazed helplessly at the departing luggage, convinced that his ineptitude had cost him his belongings, which even now, he feared, were being loaded for shipment to remote and distant lands. Then, to his immense relief, the bag reappeared through an opening in the wall on the other side of the conveyer belt. Backtracking, Browning zeroed in on his wayward luggage, nabbing the bag just as it began to loop back toward him. The relief he felt at this minor accomplishment was tempered by chagrin: if a simple thing like capturing his luggage was so challenging, how would he cope with the more severe tests certain to lie ahead?

Callas had said she needed his answer by the end of the day or she would be disconnected. Was that Ottawa time or London time? There was no way of knowing, and he couldn't afford to take a chance: he had to contact Callas at once.

Loading his luggage onto an airport cart, he set out toward a row of seats at one end of the hall. He unsheathed his laptop and connected to the airport's WIFI. With trembling fingers, he typed a brief message. "To Maria Callas: I am ready to help. Please reply. Browning." To his relief, though no longer to his surprise, another message appeared almost instantly.

"My dear Browning. Thank God. I had almost given up hope. Is it true? Will you really help me?"

"Yes, it's true. I've probably lost my mind, but I will go to Greece and search for your son, if that is what you really want."

"I've never wanted anything more. It is the answer to my prayers. I cannot begin to thank you."

"No, you probably can't. But it feels good to believe in something for a change. And incredible as it sounds, I do believe in you. Like you said, a leap of faith."

"My dear Browning . . ."

"Now, let's get down to business. Can you tell me anything that will help me find your son?"

"Not very much, I'm afraid. Only that he was born on Feb. 13, 1967. And that he was raised by a family in Meligalas, in the south-western Peloponnese."

"That's not much to go on. Is there nothing else? A name of someone in Meligalas who might know who adopted your son?"

"I don't know . . . As you know, I was born in New York and never lived in Meligalas. I was only in the town once, the time I went looking for my son. I did have cousins there, though; One I can remember was named Petros Demitros. I met him when I lived in Athens during the war. He was just a boy then. He must be into his 80s now, if he's even still alive. Look for him; perhaps he knows something. I'm sorry I can't be more helpful, but the whole idea was to make my son disappear, from me, from Aristo, from the whole hostile, dangerous world. Leon succeeded too well."

"What about Leon? Is he still alive?"

"Alas, no. He died two years before I did, in 1975."

Browning grimaced. "So, the bottom line is that you can't give me anything more definite than a birth date, a town and the name of someone who may or may not be alive and may or may not know anything about your son."

"I'm afraid so. It's not much, is it?"

"No, it's not. But I'm a journalist. I'm trained to track things down." Browning blushed as he typed this. It had been years since he'd worked on anything more difficult than an unruly headline. "Just so I'm clear on this: now that I've agreed to help you, you can stay on the air, so to speak, for another six weeks, right?"

"That's right."

"Then stay by your cyberphone. I've got things to do now if I'm going to Greece, but I'll be in touch soon."

"Alright, my dear Browning. Godspeed. And thank you."

PUSHING his baggage cart before him like the hull of an icebreaker, Browning cut through the airport's thronging crowds in search of a British Airways desk. His flight to Zimbabwe was scheduled to depart in less than two hours, and he needed to find a flight to Athens and change his ticket.

To his surprise, his travel inexperience wasn't as much of a handicap as he'd expected. Years of editing stories for the *Advocate*'s travel section had equipped him with more practical knowledge about the vagaries of travel than he had ever dreamed he possessed. It had seeped through his pores and now occupied a previously untapped but sizable space in his frontal lobes. Drawing on this unsuspected knowledge, he recalled that switching a ticket at the last minute was usually possible. He could not expect an immediate refund, but the *Advocate* would eventually be reimbursed for most of the cost of his unused ticket. As for getting to Greece, he had to hope that space was available on an early flight. Since he was travelling outside of the peak tourist season, though, his chances were good.

After a long hike through Heathrow's maze of corridors and lounges, Browning finally spied a British Airways transit desk. Though it was early morning, it was doing a brisk business. A couple newly arrived from Pakistan was trying to resolve a seemingly intractable problem with a BA official, and others awaiting their turn were growing restive, rolling eyes and sighing theatrically. At length, the problem was resolved, and the pace picked up. Still, the better part of 30 minutes had passed before Browning reached the head of the queue.

He briefly explained he was travelling on business and had had an unexpected change of plans. "Bit last minute, old chap," the airline official scolded, though not unkindly. "See what I can do for you, though." He flipped rapidly through schedules on his computer. "Right, here's one. We have space on a flight, leaving at 11:40 a.m., arriving Athens at 5:30 p.m. local time. Should I book it?"

Browning handed over his credit card. Given the implications of the act, his hand trembled surprisingly little as he did so.

~

WITH THE SUDDEN luxury of time, Browning parked his possessions and sat down on a padded bench. It was time to take stock of his situation. He unbuttoned his shirt and pulled a bulging billfold from the pouch slung around his neck. He had $5,000 in American currency (a healthy cash advance courtesy of the *Advocate*'s business office) and his trusty credit card to finance his trip to Greece. That should be enough, he calculated, though the margin for extravagance was thin. And of course, he'd have to repay his cash advance when he returned to Canada. The idea of walking back into the newspaper office sent a shiver down his spine. His only consolation, and it was a slim one, was that the humiliation would be short-lived, for he would surely be fired on the spot.

He really ought to advise Renata Richter of his change of plans, he told himself. She wouldn't be at the office at this hour; he'd have to e-mail her. That suited him. The idea of speaking directly to Richter was not at all appealing.

He fired up his laptop and quickly composed a terse message: "I know this will be hard to understand, but something has come up that prevents me from going to Africa. Must go to Greece instead. Will explain fully when back in Canada. Browning." He hit send, deriving austere amusement from the uproar he knew it would cause back home. He felt a surge of something unfamiliar — was it exhilaration? It struck him that confounding the drab expectations people had of him was oddly pleasurable. There would be time enough to regret his impetuosity; for now, he could enjoy the rare indulgence of acting the rebel.

His course set, Browning suddenly felt immensely weary. The stresses of the day had exacted a toll. If he was to get any rest, this was the time to do it, before hustling Heathrow geared up to its full daytime roar. He looked around for a cozy spot to relax. Everywhere, molded plastic seats sprouted with the pernicious profligacy of a virus in a kindergarten class. Whatever their virtues — and these seats were unquestionably cheap to produce and easy to clean — they were not designed for human comfort, and certainly not for slumber.

Just as he was about to abandon hope and stretch out on the marble floor, Browning spotted a relic from an earlier era that had somehow evaded detection by the airport's sentinels of efficiency: a black faux-leather lounge, upon which it was not only possible to sit in comfort but actually to recline. Browning swiftly asserted his claim, luxuriating in the lounge's soft padding. He shut his eyes and the din of the airport gradually faded to a comforting white noise. Within 10 minutes, he was asleep.

PART II

Faith is the substance of things hoped for, the evidence of things not seen.

- Hebrews ch 11, v. 1

CHAPTER 10

THE HOTEL ROOM WAS FIT FOR HUMAN HABITATION, BUT ONLY BARELY. A large brown water stain embellished the white ceiling. In one corner, a section of festering plaster sagged alarmingly. The wallpaper looked as old as Athens itself — a gloomy flecked red pattern that made the tiny room seem even smaller than it was, if that were possible. A metal-frame bed, a plywood veneer armoire and a threadbare rug that only partially concealed the linoleum floor completed the decor. The toilet was down the hall. It didn't seem like much for 105 euros, but the friendly cabbie who had driven Browning in from the airport had assured him the hotel was one of Athens' undiscovered gems. And surely the driver wouldn't deceive him — why, he had even given him a discount fare to the city centre, generously declining to turn on his meter in favour of what he called his "special tourist rate."

In any event, Browning had been desperate to get to a hotel and rest his weary body. He had slept fitfully on the lounge at Heathrow, twice disturbed by a wild-eyed zealot determined to enumerate the failings of Britain's Labour government. The flight into Athens had been unusually bumpy, and Browning had spent much of it firmly clutching his arm-rests while fighting off the waves of panic that washed over him whenever the plane hit an air pocket.

The airport itself was already a blur: long lines of travellers inching through customs in the noise and heat of the terminal; the immigration official with his brusque and puzzling questions in barely comprehensible English; Browning's confused replies, which even to him sounded evasive; the baggage retrieval area, where passengers waited so long that some wandered off to file missing-luggage reports for suitcases that eventually appeared; the money-change counter, where Browning received disappointingly fewer euros than he had somehow expected to get; and finally, the taxi stand, where insistent men vied for the privilege of carrying his bags to their waiting automobiles.

Fortunately, George the taxi driver had prevailed in the scrum around Browning's bags. Fortunately, because George (Browning knew him only as George) spoke English and was a font of information about this strange land in which Browning had so precipitously arrived. Since Greece was a last-minute change to his travel itinerary, Browning had, of course, done no research for the trip. It was as if he had been plunked down on another planet, innocent and bewildered.

Not only did George give him his special rate and direct him to one of the finest hostelries in the much-coveted Plaka district (by coincidence, owned by a cousin), he also recommended a taverna for dinner (run by his brother, so he could vouch for the food) and a travel agent (another cousin) for his rambles within Greece. "And don't miss the Parthenon, whatever you do," he added helpfully. With this sort of insider assistance, Browning reckoned he couldn't go far wrong.

Still, tired as he was, Browning had been dismayed by what he saw of Athens on the trip in from the airport. The fabled city was an unsightly, sprawling mess of decaying prefabricated concrete buildings, none of which remotely reminded him of the glory that was Greece. And for good reason: Except for a few ruins and a handful of older buildings, Athens was almost entirely a 20th-century creation. And for the most part, it was the 20th century at its least memorable: cheaply built structures devoid of architectural merit, many seemingly candidates for demolition a decade after they were built.

The streets were choked with vehicles of all description. Scooters and motorcycles, whose unmuffled engines gave off a cacophonous roar, filled any gaps too tight to accommodate an automobile. Buses and trucks belched sooty fumes into the dank air, clearly visible as a yellow haze in the broad Athenian valley. Only in its centre, at the sweeping expanse of Syntagma Square, did the city hint at its former grandeur. Even there, the stately houses of Parliament had to compete with the airline offices, tourist-trap restaurants and faded hotels that ring the other sides of the square.

But the urban blight of Athens was not foremost in Browning's mind as he arrived at his hotel. What he yearned for above all else was a bed, someplace he could safely go unconscious for several hours. This overwhelming need blinded him to the hotel's tacky lobby, its unlit staircase and the decorative deficiencies of his room. It had a bed, however lumpy. It had a door, however flimsy. It was his, however temporarily. He stripped off his clothes and collapsed like a dead man.

Before long he awoke, bathed in perspiration. The hotel was not air-conditioned, and though it was only late April, the oppressive heat and humidity for which Athens is notorious had already started to build.

Cursing softly, Browning rose wearily and tried to open his room's lone window. It wouldn't budge. He hammered at the frame with the palms of his hands, crouching low for maximum leverage until, with a shuddering screech, the window reluctantly capitulated. Immediately, the room was filled with the most incredible din: the full-throated roar of scooters, the shouts and cries of Plaka pitchmen and revelers, and somewhere nearby, the pneumatic hammering of a heavy drill.

Browning flopped on the bed and groaned. A spring, half-liberated from its mattress napping, poked him saucily between the shoulder blades. The roar of one of earth's noisiest cities washed over him like a cyclone of sound. As if to mock his effort, the faintest breeze stirred the fetid air through the open window.

Browning was thoroughly miserable. Then, borne by the same light breeze, so faint he wasn't sure if he was imagining it, he heard music. It was an aria from *Madame Butterfly*. The singer was Maria Callas.

"YOU'RE HIS BEST FRIEND," said Renata Richter, looking accusingly at Harrison Howard. "Can you shed any light on this extraordinary turn of events? Why in the name of God would Browning go to Greece instead of Africa?"

Howard had been summoned to an urgent meeting in Richter's office, convened in response to Browning's astonishing message from Heathrow. The missive had caused a sensation in the newsroom, where its extraordinary contents had rapidly circulated, and consternation in the executive suite. As well as Richter, managing editor Norman Pugsley, news editor Ryan Young and publisher Reid Hartley, whose presence signaled the gravity of the affair, had gathered to consider what to do.

Howard was as flabbergasted by Browning's aberrant behaviour as anyone, although he had a pretty good idea what had prompted his sudden change of course. His challenge now was to offer an explanation without making it sound as if his friend had completely taken leave of his senses (though that was pretty much what Howard believed had happened).

"Well," he began, "I can't be certain, but I may be able to shed some light on this. The night before he left, Bliss and I had dinner together. He told me he was on the trail of a really sensational story about Maria Callas."

"Saw a stripper once named Maria Callous," interjected Pugsley. "Talented girl. What she could do with ping-pong balls—"

"For chrissakes, Norm," snapped Hartley. "This is neither the time nor the place. Browning wasn't talking about some damn stripper. He meant the opera singer." Hartley looked at Howard, who nodded.

"Please continue," said the publisher. "What was the nature of this 'sensational story'?"

"Ah, well, that I'm afraid I don't know. He was pretty tightlipped about it. But I do know it was preoccupying him when he should have been concentrating on his Africa assignment. I even told him to forget about Callas. He said he would take my advice."

Hartley grunted. "Guess not."

"I don't understand," asked Ryan Young, clearly lost. "What does all this have to do with Browning going to Greece?"

"Maria Callas was Greek," Howard replied patiently, as if explaining to a simpleton how to boil water. "That is, she was born in New York, but her parents were straight off the boat from Greece. She spent most of her teen years in Athens, and, of course, had a famous affair with Aristotle Onassis."

"Sure, sure, I know that," Young said irritably, though clearly this was all news to him.

"So you think Browning went to Greece to track down this Callas story?" asked Richter.

"It's possible," nodded Howard.

"But why would he do that?" Pugsley cried. "What's so goddamn important about Maria fucking Callas" — Pugsley glanced guiltily at Richter, whose lips had pursed disapprovingly — "that Browning had to blow off an assignment that's costing us eight big ones?"

The assembled group pondered this question in gloomy silence. There was no answer. Browning's actions were simply incomprehensible. Nobody at the *Advocate* had ever done anything remotely similar, except for the time Yuri Alexandrov travelled to Kiev while on assignment in Moscow to close a deal with a Russian wholesaler for a cargo ship full of frozen turkeys from Texas. That had caused a ruckus that only subsided when Alexandrov presented Pugsley with a case of vodka, and a solemn, though insincere, promise never to do anything like that again.

But this . . . this was unprecedented. *Advocate* staffers were generally so thrilled to get one of the paper's rare foreign assignments that they worked themselves to the point of exhaustion in response. For someone to receive such a plum and then bail out, to take the money and run, as newsroom whispers put it, was beyond bizarre: it was prima facie evidence of madness.

"However good this Callas story might be, and it had better be a National Newspaper Award winner," said Hartley at last, breaking the silence, "the fact remains that Browning has misappropriated our money and our trust. We sent him to Africa, not Attica. To cover orangutans, not opera singers. We can't tolerate this sort of insubordination. Next thing you know, reporters will want to assign themselves. From there, it's a short, slippery slope to anarchy. No, we have to put a stop to Browning, and now."

"What do you suggest, Reid?" asked Richter. "I mean, we don't even know where he is in Greece."

"Then find him," barked Hartley. "Find him, and bring him back here, so I can have the pleasure of firing the son of a bitch myself."

"How are we supposed to do that?" asked Richter.

"Christ, woman," Hartley snapped, "do I have to tell you everything?" Richter coloured. "You're all journalists. You're supposed to have investigative skills. Send someone to Greece and track him down. How hard can it be?"

Howard spoke up. "I'll go," he said quietly. "Bliss trusts me; it will be easiest for me to find him."

"That's exactly why it shouldn't be you," Hartley shot back. "This is no job for a friend. It's time to send the sheriff, someone senior who has the authority to bring Browning back into line. I think Norman should go."

"Me?" spluttered Pugsley. "I can't go off on a wild goose chase to fucking Greece." His mind flashed to the home opener between Ottawa's triple A baseball team, the Lynx, and the Toledo Mud Hens, for which he had seats behind home plate, and next weekend's media golf tournament, invariably one of the best drunk-fests of the year. "I've got too much on my plate here."

"Nonsense, Norm," said Richter. "There's nothing so urgent that it can't wait a few weeks. I think you're right, Reid. Norm is the perfect choice." She turned to Pugsley. "I'll have Judy book you on the first available flight to Athens."

Pugsley looked mournfully at Richter and Hartley. "Christ on a bicycle," he muttered.

THE BROWNING SCANDAL had the newsroom rumor mill, fevered at the best of times, cranked up to new levels of delirium. Speculation hardened into irrefutable fact within nanoseconds: Richter was being fired for sending a screwup like Browning on such an important assignment. Interpol had been enlisted to track down Browning. Hartley himself was booked on the next flight to Athens.

So when Howard emerged from the war council in Richter's office, his newsroom colleagues descended like scavengers on carrion. Half a dozen of them accosted him before he'd taken 20 steps.

"So, what are they going to do?" demanded Dylan Mosely, who had been taking open pleasure in reminding people that he'd predicted disaster from the moment that Browning — rather than someone qualified, like himself— was picked for the assignment.

"Are they callin' in the cops?" mumbled Chuck Bigras, between huge, ripping chomps on a colossal submarine sandwich.

"Is Richter toast?" cried Mick Mulligrew, off the phone for once.

"Has anyone heard from Bliss?" asked Kimberly Taylor.

"What the fuck's happening?" summarized Flynn Cahill.

Howard held up a hand. "Calm down, for chrissakes, calm down. Jesus, I've never seen such indecent interest in someone else's misfortune."

"Harry, we know you're Browning's buddy," said Mosely, "but even you have to acknowledge that this is a pretty spectacular cluster-fuck. You can't expect us to be indifferent to something of this magnitude. We may never see ineptitude on such a colossal scale again."

Howard glared at Mosely. "You know, Dylan, I've never liked you. I just remembered why."

"Never mind fuckin' Mosely," said Cahill. "Just tell us what the fuck's going down."

"Alright, alright," said Howard. "I think Bliss went to Greece to track down a story about Maria Callas—"

"Fuckin' guy," muttered Cahill.

"—and they're sending Pugsley to find him and bring him home."

"Pugsley!?!" exclaimed Mosely. "Why Pugsley? The job clearly calls for an investigative reporter. Like me, for instance. I'd find the bastard quick enough."

"Shut the fuck up, Dylan," said Cahill. "Yes," agreed Kimberly Taylor, her divine features twisted with disgust, "we're heard enough from you, Dylan." Mosely said nothing, but stuck out his tongue.

"They think they need someone senior, with the authority to make Bliss come home," explained Howard.

"That's it?" asked Mulligrew, who was already reaching for the nearest telephone to spread the news. "Nobody's getting fired over this?"

"Well, only Bliss," said Howard.

"Poor fucker," muttered Cahill. "Fuckin' innocent abroad. Didn't know what the fuck he was doing."

"Oh, I think he knew, alright," said Howard. "He deliberately chose to blow off the Africa assignment and go to Greece. What I don't understand is what made him change his mind."

"What mind?" interjected Mosely, breaking his brief silence. "The guy's a cretin. He was in way over his head."

"What they needed was someone like you," Howard suggested.

"Damn right," said Mosely, oblivious to irony.

"Fuck you," said Cahill, genially.

"Mmmnpphhh grnnfff," added Chuck Bigras, struggling and failing to be understood with a mouth full of sandwich.

Howard suddenly felt sickened by his colleagues' lust for hurtful gossip. Sometimes, he reflected, people were only too eager to believe the worst of others, and to revel in their misfortunes. It was a sickness in the human soul.

He turned away and walked to his desk, determined to get on with his work. Slumping at his terminal, he checked his e-mail for book reviews he was expecting from freelancers. The message at the top of his in-basket leapt out at him immediately. "From Bliss Browning," it said.

He began to read.

"Hi, Harry,

You probably know by now that I didn't go to Africa. I'm in Athens instead. I can't tell you too much about my plans here — I'm still working them out myself — but I can say that I know I'm doing the right thing. I now believe that my Internet correspondent really is Maria Callas, and that I have been chosen, for reasons I can't begin to understand, to perform an important task for her. I know it sounds crazy, but you have to believe in something in this life, and I choose to believe in this. Please assure Richter that I'm okay and tell her I'm sorry about Africa; I'll make it up to her somehow. And don't worry about me. I've never felt as alive as I do right now.

Take care,

Bliss"

CHAPTER 11

BROWNING WAS RAVENOUS. HE HAD BEEN TOO EXHAUSTED TO EAT AFTER arriving in Athens the previous night; in fact, he'd eaten nothing since choking down a plate of polymerized airline chicken on the flight from London nearly 18 hours earlier. Fortunately, breakfast was included in the price of his room. Eagerly, he set out for the hotel dining room, visions of scrambled eggs, sausage, toast and cereal reviving his spirits.

Since it was still quite early, he was alone in the small, starkly furnished dining room. He settled into a wicker-bottomed chair (which he couldn't help noticing was intensely uncomfortable) at one of the half-dozen bare wooden tables in the room and waited for service. After several minutes, a woman appeared with a tray, whose contents she unloaded on Browning's table. There was a glass of watery yellow liquid of indeterminate origin, a cup of something that might have been coffee, several pieces of Melba toast wrapped in cellophane and two small packets of marmalade. With the certainty of a man facing a firing squad, Browning understood that this was breakfast.

Cautiously, he took a sip of the yellow fluid. It was almost flavourless. As far as he could tell, it was a glass of water minimally diluted by a powder derived from some citric source. The coffee was recognizable, though of a particularly vile instant variety that incited no desire for a refill (just as well, as none were offered in any case). The Melba toast was characteristically dry and bland, a condition only marginally improved by slathering on the packaged marmalade. Browning glumly wondered what sort of country couldn't even manage to serve a decent breakfast.

But even the dismal meal could not extinguish his excitement at the prospect of finally getting down to business. Armed with a map of Athens and the address of George the taxi driver's travel agent cousin, he plunged into the streets and alleyways of the Plaka, the old heart of 19th century Athens. Browning strolled down Adhrianou, a main pedestrian street, his eyes taking in souvenir shops selling ceramic reproductions of the Parthenon and pewter vases in Mycenean motifs, taverna touts enticing passersby to ranks of sidewalk tables, and jewelers, their shop windows glittering with gold. A large black dog sprawled limply in the middle of the road, whether dead or merely comatose Browning could not immediately discern. Scrawny cats with large ears and alert eyes loitered near outdoor tables, hoping for a scrap or two. And occasionally, at an intersection, the towering bulk of the Acropolis, crowned by its clutch of ancient temples, announced its unmistakable presence.

Turning onto Nikis Street, Browning quickly spotted Hellas Travel. George's cousin turned out to be a wiry, efficient man named Yiannis originally from Kalamata in the southern Peloponnese. His English, honed by years of dealing with tourists, was more than passable. And he was very familiar with Browning's objective, Meligalas, which was less than 30 kilometres northwest of Kalamata.

"You can't stay there," he told Browning. "There is no tourists, so there is no rooms. But there is village few kilometres to south, is called Mavromati. Is site of ruins of ancient Ithomi, and is rooms to rent there. With car, no problem."

"A car?" repeated Browning. "You want me to drive there? From Athens?"

"Of course," said Yiannis with a broad smile. "You see — no problem."

Browning shook his head slowly. "I don't think so, Yiannis. I've seen enough of your Athenian drivers to know when I'm in over my head. How else could I get there?"

Yiannis thought for a moment. "You could fly — there is airport just outside Kalamata — but very expensive." Browning grimaced. "Or you could take train or bus to Kalamata and pick up car there," Yiannis said. "Is not hard to drive in Kalamata, and once in countryside, you practically have road to yourself."

"Alright," said Browning dubiously. "That sounds like a plan. But let's make it the train. Buses make me nauseous. I'd like to leave tomorrow if possible. Is that OK?"

Yiannis flashed another beatific smile. "No problem."

HAVING ACCOMPLISHED what he could for the time being, Browning decided to spend the rest of the day fulfilling a modest fantasy he'd often entertained but never expected to experience. At 61 Patission Street in Athens — the address was as familiar as his own — Maria Callas had lived with her mother Evangelia and sister Jacquie from the late 1930s until she returned to America in 1947. Evangelia Kalogeropoulos had left her husband George and uprooted her daughter from their New York home in 1937 to further her ambitions for Maria, then barely into her teens.

Even then, Maria's voice was winning admirers. On the liner *Saturnia,* which had carried the two back to Greece, Maria had sung for the captain and passengers at dinner. She ended with the Habenera from *Carmen,* tossing the charmed captain a rose she snatched from a vase when the song ended. He rewarded her with the only doll she ever owned. Evangelia Kalogeropoulos was not given to frivolity when it came to her gifted daughter.

The top floor apartment at 61 Patission Street was an almost mystical site to Browning. So much had happened there that was part of the Callas legend. The apartment had been young Maria's home during the crucial years when she developed her talent and reputation under the tutelage of such teachers as Maria Trivella and Elvira de Hidalgo. It was there, during the brutal Axis occupation of Athens, when tens of thousands starved to death, that Evangelia and her daughters had hidden two British officers for six weeks. The day after they left, Italian soldiers raided the apartment after receiving a tip. Because she feared the soldiers might find incriminating evidence of the officers' presence — which would have meant swift execution — the 17-year-old Maria rushed to the piano and began singing arias from *Tosca*. Suckers for Puccini, the Italians fell under the young diva's spell and forgot to search. They were so enchanted that they returned the next day with bread, salami and macaroni, pleading for an encore.

Earlier that same year, the Germans had issued a proclamation against making noise in public. Maria responded by pushing a piano onto her balcony and defiantly singing arias at the top of her voice. On one memorable occasion, when she was singing the role of Tosca to the rooftops of Athens, an unseen "Mario" answered with stirring music of his own.

In October, 1944, after the Germans had finally been driven out of Athens, Maria, her sister and her mother had cowered in the apartment for 20 days with no heat or light and little food as thousands of Athenians died in battles between liberating British troops and the communist-led ELAS resistance. Once they narrowly averted death when ELAS gunmen strafed their bedroom from the street. They finally reached safety after being offered sanctuary at the British High Commission on Syntagma Square.

Browning had been mesmerized by the romance of these tales. In his imagination, 61 Patission St. was a place where miracles were an everyday occurrence. The chance to visit this shrine was too compelling to pass up. Consulting his map, he saw that Patission Street began just north of Omonia Square, not more than a 20-minute walk from the Plaka. His heart pounding in anticipation, he set out at a brisk walk through the narrow streets.

Before long, he was hopelessly lost. The Plaka's twisting alleys and lanes were like a maze; even his map was only of limited help in navigating them. After a few minutes he emerged into a broad platia. This was Monastiraki, the site of the central Athens flea market. Carried by the tide of a steadily building crowd, Browning was swept down a teeming pedestrian street into the heart of a Middle Eastern bazaar.

Hundreds of tiny shops offered an astonishing array of goods for sale: shirts, shoes and socks, high-topped leather boots, brightly patterned boxer shorts, jogging pants, costume jewelry and diamonds, intricately patterned backgammon and chess boards, fans, antique furniture, Victrolas with curling megaphone speakers, tools and workshop bric-a-brac of all descriptions, coins in collector sets, pieces of engines and machinery, hats, icons, faded pictures in weathered frames, wicker chairs, statues of Hermes, chintzy plates, earrings, bracelets and necklaces, camouflage pants, muskets, fake Trojan helmets, faucets, bouzoukis, Greek videos, packaged colognes sold from rolling carts, leather jackets, skewered grilled meats, mounds of pistachios and, here and there, items whose purpose was simply impossible to fathom. And as a soundtrack to all of this, the monotonous drone of itinerant lottery-ticket vendors, appeals for charity from legless beggars, boisterous sales pitches from braying shop owners and the ominous beep-beep-beep of travel alarm clocks, whose stellar qualities were evidently best demonstrated by allowing their alarms to sound ceaselessly.

Overwhelmed by the noise, humanity and merchandise, Browning ducked down a small alley and escaped to less congested streets. Consulting his map, he located Eolou Street, a wide pedestrian mall lined with workaday stores, which turned into Patission just past Omonia Square. After the claustrophobic crush of the Monastiraki market, Eolou's uncrowded sweep was both a relief and an anticlimax. For as much as the market's hubbub and clamour had unsettled Browning, so too had it exhilarated him. He'd never encountered anything quite like the tumult of the market, and now that he was free of it, he felt oddly deflated. Eolou, by contrast, seemed domesticated, even dull.

That impression evaporated, however, when Browning glanced

down the street behind him. He was staggered by what he saw. The Acropolis hovered over the city on its limestone plateau like a caller from a distant past, the Parthenon incongruously framed by the parallel sweep of Eolou's nondescript stores and offices. Browning could only gape in wonder at the man-made marvel before him. In that transcendent moment, he forgave Athens corrosive pollution, disastrous architecture and nightmarish traffic. Any city that can offer a spectacle such as this, he thought, can't be judged by the usual standards.

Omonia Square's rusting metal balconies and garish billboards advertising cigarettes and beer brought Browning abruptly back to earth after the sublime spectacle of the Acropolis. He hurried past this place of gritty commerce, anxious to reach 61 Patission and recapture the magic. Just north of the Archeological Museum, across a six-lane boulevard, he found it.

He recognized it at once, of course; he'd studied pictures of the building often enough. Still, there was something surreal about being there, as if it were a mirage or a practical joke directed at him for unknowable reasons. Seized by a need to touch the building physically, he stepped off the curb to cross the street and was nearly run down by a speeding taxi. More cautiously, he tried again, reaching the safety of the traffic island in the middle of the boulevard, then dashing across the remaining three lanes before reaching a broad stone-block sidewalk just outside the tall wood-and-glass doors of No. 61.

The building was five stories high, and except for a few painted signs in Greek that festooned the bottom level, plain at first glance. But closer examination revealed some flourishes that distinguished it from its more prosaic neighbours. A triptych of bay windows adorned the facade from the second floor to the fifth, the stonework decorated with elegant carvings. Just below the windows on the top level, a narrow concrete balcony encircled the building — the very balcony, Browning realized with a start, from which Callas had sung *Tosca* in wartime Athens.

On the front of the building, an unobtrusive plaque announced in Greek that Maria Callas had once lived there. But no crowd of gawking tourists, no throng of opera pilgrims, encircled the site. There was only Browning, summoning the nerve to step inside.

Slowly, he passed through the tall doors, ascended nine marble stairs (adorned with a series of potted plants fighting a losing battle for photosynthesis) and entered a small lobby. In the middle was an ancient wooden lift with bright stained-glass panels on the side, encircled by a black metal cage. To Browning's left, an open door led to an office where a middle-aged woman sat working at a desk. Browning caught her eye and nodded. Now or never, he thought.

Drawing a deep breath, he approached the woman and asked, in Pidgin English, if she knew that Callas had once lived there. Shrugging, she called out in Greek to a man in the next office. "Yes?" he said, studying Browning closely.

"Do you speak English?" Browning asked.

The man shook his head, then brightened. "Parlez-vous Francais?"

Browning, taken aback, struggled to recall his high-school French. "Oui," he responded cautiously. "Un peu."

Concentrating fiercely, as if his very life depended on his ability to comprehend the man's labored French, Browning learned that an institute of occupational education was now the building's prime tenant. Callas had lived on the top floor, but the man couldn't say who lived there now.

Exhausted by this second-language interrogation, Browning thanked his informant and walked toward the lift. With pounding heart, he entered the small cage and pressed the worn call button, imagining Callas's finger on the same button more than half a century earlier. The elevator began a slow, shuddering ascent, stopping with a lurch when it reached the fifth floor. Browning opened the door and stepped into a small, pale green hallway, unadorned except for a radiator painted the same utilitarian shade of green, and two heavy brown doors, standing at right angles to one another. One bore a small brass plaque upon which was engraved a single word in Greek. The other was unmarked.

This, then, was the inner sanctum, the place that Callas lived while developing her gift. Browning, knees trembling, imagined Maria, an overweight teenager redeemed by a voice that angels would envy, waiting here for the lift, treading these very floors, entering her wartime home through these same doors. Shutting his eyes, he tried to hear the music she made, the arias that flew from these rooms to gladden the hearts of Athenians in their darkest hours. But all he could hear was the relentless sound of Vespas, trucks and automobiles roaring past on the street below.

He yearned to go through those doors. But something stopped him from knocking: respect for the privacy of the current occupant, perhaps, or fear of finally confronting a holy place, with all the attendant risk of shattered expectations. Abruptly, he turned and descended the stairs to the main floor, oblivious to the meaning of the Greek word on the door, whose meaning, had he known it, would have unlocked the mysteries within. For the word on the door was "push."

IT WAS dark before Browning was able to break free of the spell cast by 61 Patission. After his enchanted ascent to the very gates of Callas paradise, he had been delighted to discover a small tree-lined pedestrian mall immediately south of the building. One side of the street was lined with tables and chairs sheltered by umbrellas proclaiming, in English, "Coors — America's premier beer." Directly opposite, a thumping disco beat issued from the Cafe Appthon. Gratefully, Browning had taken a seat at one of the tables and ordered a beer. Lost in thought and well-supplied with Amstel by the Appthon's attentive staff, he had passed contented hours gazing at his secular shrine. It was only when he noticed the fading light that he reluctantly paid his bill and with one last lingering look behind him, started none too steadily back down Patission toward his hotel.

Moderately drunk, he took a wrong turn at Omonia Square and found himself on Socratous, a gritty, narrow street that reflected scant glory on the famous philosopher after whom it was named. Even in Browning's condition, the street's grotty, down-at-the-heels ambiance made him a bit apprehensive. However, he was reassured to see several young women taking the night air, perched on white molded plastic chairs at intervals on the sidewalk ahead.

There was something odd about those young women, though. They all wore tight skirts, which struggled and mostly failed to reach mid-thigh, and form-fitting sweaters that cast their bosoms in sharp relief. Many had long, straight ash-blond hair. And their faces, without exception, were garishly painted: vivid lips the colour of Lobo apples, eyes ringed with mascara, rouged cheeks blushing like maidens caught with their knickers down. Nor, on closer inspection, were the women all as young as they first appeared. Some were middle-aged and bore the scars of a life lived raw. With a mixture of horror and fascination, it dawned on Browning that these were hookers, brazenly plying their trade on the sidewalks of Socratous.

Careful to avoid eye contact, Browning passed the procession of prostitutes, ignoring their low calls and hissed invitations. The whores would assume that he, a single man walking alone, was in the market for their services, and he was anxious to do nothing to reinforce that impression. At Sofokleous Street, Browning turned left, hoping to leave the Athenian tenderloin behind. But Sofokleous, like Socratous, was teeming with women desperate to sell themselves to strangers, and Browning wondered how those venerable ancient Greeks would react if they could see the streets that bore their names.

A ravaged woman with a grotesquely painted face sidled out of the shadows toward him. "Meester," she rasped. "You want fuck?" She leered sickeningly, running her tongue over her lips in what she evidently thought was a suggestive manner. Browning, trying to hide his revulsion, smiled politely and shook his head.

But the aging whore was not so easily deterred. Sliding a hand slowly up her right thigh, she lifted the hem of her short skirt until the fur of her sex was plainly visible. "For you, a bargain. Just 20 euros," she purred. "Come . . . I have room nearby."

Tearing his eyes away from the woman's crotch, Browning stuttered a reply. "N-no, really, thanks very much. I'm really not interested."

The crone's demeanor changed abruptly. "You no like?" she demanded, insulted. "You sissy?" She minced, fluttering her hands with limp wrists. Glaring, she unleashed a torrent of what could only have been Greek curses, punctuated by a series of emphatic gestures. Then she stalked off, leaving Browning speechless on the sidewalk.

"I VISITED your old apartment on Patission Street today."

"Patission Street . . ." replied Maria Callas, her words scrolling across Browning's computer screen. "I remember that place very well. Those were dark times, my dear Browning. Dark times."

Shaken by his encounter with the whore, Browning had returned to his hotel, the crone's words still ringing in his ears. Twenty euros, he thought. Less than $30. For perhaps the first time in his life, he had wondered what sort of self-loathing could lead someone to value herself so lightly — and others to accept that valuation so readily. He was not entirely blind to the irony of the thought.

Feeling terribly alone, Browning suddenly had wanted more than anything to talk to Callas. Needless to say, there was no Internet in his dismal room. But during his morning rambles through the Plaka, he had spotted a cybercafe near his hotel. Walking there briskly now, he dispatched an urgent appeal to her attention. She had replied almost instantaneously.

"Thank God," he had typed. "It's been an unsettling day; I needed someone to talk to. I hope you don't mind."

"Not at all. I have nothing but time now. And you are doing me a great favour. I'm not one to abandon my true friends."

"I'm honoured. And I'm determined not to let you down."

"I know that you won't, my dear Browning."

"When I knew you only through books, videos and your music," wrote Browning, "I believed that I knew everything about you. How arrogant I was! Standing outside your old apartment today, I understood how little I really know of your life. How could I truly conceive of the hardships you endured? Yet somehow, in the midst of all that horror, you found beauty within yourself and shared it with the world around you."

"My dear Browning, that's a lovely thought. But what a hopeless romantic you are! I did no such thing. I didn't discover the beauty within me, as you put it. First of all, beauty is not what I'd call it. It was an impulse, something irresistible. Whatever it was, it was struggling to get out and be seen. Nor is it correct to say I shared it with others, as if it were an act of generosity on my part. I sang because I had to sing — nothing more, nothing less. It was an act of compulsion, not volition."

"Call it what you will," Browning replied. "The fact remains that not many young women would have paid the price that you did to cultivate it."

"Not many young women are driven by forces beyond their control or comprehension," Callas shot back. "Do you really think I practised day after day until my throat was raw and my body limp with fatigue, because I wanted to? Do you really imagine that I didn't care about missing out on a normal adolescence, that I preferred to spend my time in the company of people two or three times my age? That I didn't yearn for the love of a boy, the friendship of people my own age? Look at me then: fat, pimple-faced, unattractive. Was that the body of a person who perceived beauty within herself? No, I worked like a slave because some unfathomable impulse forced me to do so. I could no more have resisted than I could have willed myself to stop breathing. That is not beauty. That is a type of tyranny, of totalitarianism."

"And yet," replied Browning, "this tyranny produced some of the most magnificent art of the last century."

"My dear Browning, you are making a common error — confusing the song with the singer. I thought that you, of all people, would appreciate the difference. True, my artistry was of a high order. But it was achieved at a cost no person should have to pay. Even a cursory examination of my private life makes this clear: my absurd marriage to a man more than twice my age, my estrangement from my mother and sister, my compulsive attraction to Aristo, my fearsome public image, my death . . . My God, I was just 53! But I was too sad to live. Sorrow killed me, my dear Browning, a life of sorrow and pain."

"But that sorrow and pain fuelled your art, gave it a universal dimension that connected with millions around the world. Without it, your art might never have soared so high."

"Why not? Must art wallow in despair to have power? Can't it move by filling hearts with joy and hope, rather than anguish and woe?"

Browning considered this. "Of course. Great art can be uplifting, too. But sorrow is the great conjoint of human experience. Every life contains sadness and grief. Art that expresses that, that can speak to people's sorrows and fears, serves a great and noble purpose. That is why I love opera so much, and your music in particular; its focus on the tragic speaks to my own disappointments and pain."

"But the artists are martyred in the process," Callas reminded him. "Their lives are a misery of suffering and loss. Take a close look at my life. I was loved for my art, perhaps, but who loved Callas the woman? Certainly not Battista; he married me for status. I was a trophy wife, to use the vernacular of your day. Aristo loved me, I think, but even for him I was a possession, a bauble. If I had not been a famous opera singer, there is little chance he would have given me a second glance.

"Even my art was a fragile thing, driven to premature decay by my obsessive approach to singing. Do you know that even at the height of my triumphs, in the 1950s, my voice was dying? It's true. By the '60s, it was gone. Finished. A decade of artistry — that's what I was granted. The rest was a desperate effort to beat back the forces of decline. Even the solace of a family was denied me. No children, no husband worthy of the name, not even a mother's love to comfort me. Think of it, my dear Browning. No one would willingly choose such a life, and no one has the right to demand it of another."

"Are you telling me that you regret your life? That if you had to live over again, you would choose contented mediocrity over tortured genius?"

"If I had been given that choice, perhaps. Wouldn't you?"

"No. I mean, I'm not sure. Think about the loss to the world had you not been driven to perfect your art. There would have been no Callas."

"No, there would have been no artist named Callas. But Callas would still exist. She would have been a different person, perhaps loved for who she was rather than for what she did. She would have been a human being, not an icon. Isn't that what we all want — to be loved for who we are, to be accepted and cherished with all our faults?"

Browning started to respond but couldn't continue. The truth of Callas's words was irrefutable. Yet the love and acceptance she yearned for seemed, for him, hopelessly out of reach. He felt his eyes fill with tears. Tears for Maria Callas, cursed with a genius that brought her fame at a terrible price. Tears for her lost son, who might have changed her fate. Most of all, tears for himself.

CHAPTER 12

STATHMOS PELOPONNISSOU, THE ATHENS TERMINUS FOR THE RAIL LINE that circles Greece's Peloponnese peninsula, crouches in a charmless district of ramshackle concrete office buildings and tawdry hotels. Parked cars block the narrow sidewalks, forcing pedestrians to chance the choked streets for passage, and huge cranes and the shells of partly constructed buildings mar the skyline.

The station itself is a decaying turn-of-the-twentieth-century edifice more suited to a sleepy backwater than the heart of a vibrant, modern city of four million. Unlike Stathmos Larissis just up the street, a bustling terminus for sleek trains travelling to the north of Greece, Stathmos Peloponissou is nearly deserted. Fewer than a dozen trains a day pass through the station, most heading to Patra, a major ferry port on the north coast of the Peloponnese. The poor condition of the ancient narrow-gauge tracks on the southern route to Kalamata precludes speedy service, which keeps both passenger demand and prices low.

The station was eerily empty when Browning arrived an hour before his 9:30 a.m. departure for Kalamata. There was no queue at the lone open ticket window, and barely half a dozen people occupied the wooden benches in the station's small main hall. The station's stillness struck Browning as ominous, the calm before some unseen storm gathering just out of sight.

Forcing such thoughts from his mind, Browning focused on the mission before him. Assuming all went well, he would arrive in Kalamata by mid-afternoon. Yiannis had booked a rental car from an agency near the city's beach strip. With luck, he could pick up the car, drive to Mavromati and be settled in his room by nightfall. From that base, he would make the short drive to Meligalas to search for Callas's cousin Petros, or anyone else who might be able to help him with his quest. He knew the language barrier would be a problem, but was counting on his rusty journalistic skills to help him meet the challenge.

Plotting strategy seemed to take the edge off Browning's anxiety. He felt himself becoming calmer, and realized with surprise that it was the very imminence of action that was reassuring. In prospect, the assignment had seemed overwhelming, but now that it was about to start, he could break it down into manageable pieces: the train, the car, the hotel, the town. The search for Callas's son remained a daunting task, but at least he knew how to begin.

The sound of an air horn interrupted these thoughts, followed by the thunderous arrival of the train to Kalamata. Despite the noise, it was surprisingly modest — just three cars, including one split between the engine compartment and the first-class cabin — and looked to be of 1960s vintage. Browning grabbed his pack and climbed into the small first-class cabin. Decorated in low-maintenance tones of beige metal, it was anything but luxurious. The narrow gauge of the Peloponnese track meant there was only room for a dozen passengers in the undersized coach, which had a double row of seats down the right-hand side and just a single row down the left. But the seats were comfortable enough and, with persistence, could be induced to recline. Browning stowed his pack in an overhead rack, settled into his assigned seat and waited for the train to begin its circuitous crawl through the mountains and valleys of the Peloponnese.

With a blast of its horn, the train jolted into motion at 9:30 a.m., precisely on time. An auspicious sign, Browning thought. He was amazed at his composure; even a week ago, the prospect of travelling on a rickety train through the unfamiliar Greek landscape would have horrified him. But now he was doing it, and feeling not fear but a strange exhilaration he could not explain.

The train moved slowly through inner-city Athens, gradually gathering speed. The engineer leaned often on the horn, announcing the train's arrival at a series of level crossings. It passed within metres of buildings that showed little of the decay usually associated with proximity to urban rail lines, low-rise apartment blocks, neat if nondescript, with balconies brightened by bougainvillea and cyclamens. The life of the city seemed close enough to touch — a woman glimpsed through a window washing dishes, a man watering his plants, children waving.

Captivated by the intimacy of the scene, Browning lowered his window and cautiously poked his head outside. The train was rounding a gentle curve, and he had a clear view of the track ahead. The train began to accelerate as it approached a small park filled with fir trees. Except for a lone figure standing near the tracks a couple of hundred metres ahead, the park was deserted. Browning drew a deep breath. The breeze in his face, perfumed by the clean, fresh fragrance of the fir trees, was intoxicating. It had been a long time since he had felt so grateful to be alive.

As the train drew nearer, Browning saw that the figure in the park was a middle-aged man. And he was not alone after all; he had a toddler in his arms. Browning raised his right arm to wave. But something in the man's expression made him freeze in mid-gesture. The man was staring straight ahead, ignoring the child, whose face was twisted with sobs. Browning realized with a sudden shiver of apprehension that they were dangerously close to the tracks. He shouted a warning, but his cry was swallowed up in the clatter of the speeding engine.

What happened next had the quality of a nightmare. The man, still holding the howling child, took three quick steps and stood on the tracks, back to the onrushing train. With a grating scream of metal on metal, the train's engineer braked violently, tossing Browning into the aisle. As he struggled to regain his footing, one image filled his head. Just before stepping in front of the train, just before the awful collision between metal and flesh and sinew and bone, just before taking the steps that snuffed out two lives in an instant, the man, inexplicably, had smiled.

~

EVEN BEFORE THE train had fully stopped, Browning had bolted out the cabin door in the mad belief that he could do something to help. The first thing he found was the body of a child. After that, he remembered little. Police later told him he was sobbing when they arrived on the scene, but he had no memory of that.

Browning was the only eyewitness to what police called "the tragedy." None of the other passengers had been leaning out their windows (it was, after all, officially discouraged). And the engineer had been momentarily distracted, fiddling with a knob on the engine console just before the man stepped onto the track. Browning alone had seen him take the fateful steps. He alone could testify that the man appeared to have followed his suicidal path freely, that he had not been pushed or fallen onto the tracks, that he had deliberately chosen to end his own life and that of the child in his arms.

Once Browning was able to convey what he had seen, he quickly became the object of intense interest to Athens police. They were facing a particularly horrible and public murder-suicide, and needed answers.

Browning was whisked to a large police station near Omonia Square, where he was politely but thoroughly interrogated no fewer than four times by detectives with varying proficiency in English. To each he numbly repeated what he had seen: the man, child in arms, standing near the tracks as the train approached, the smile, the fatal steps. Each answer provoked a torrent of rapid conversation in Greek as the interrogator translated Browning's words for other officers in the room and they debated whatever police debate in such grim circumstances.

Browning sat silently through these incomprehensible exchanges. In truth, he was too shocked to do otherwise. He'd never seen anyone die before, much less seen something so gruesome. It still seemed unbelievable; he half expected the man to walk through the door, child in arms, and announce that it had all been a macabre joke. He could feel himself slipping in and out of shock.

It was the smile that haunted Browning. What could possibly explain such a response in someone about to end two lives? He turned to his English-speaking interrogator. "Who were they?" he asked softly.

The cop scrutinized him for a moment. "A father and daughter," he said finally, running his hands through his hair. "His name was Andreas Mourtzinos. His daughter was Vasilio. She was only two."

"Why?" It was more cri de coeur than question.

"Who knows why madmen do anything?" the cop shrugged, not unkindly. "There was trouble in the marriage, apparently. Maybe he did it to punish his wife."

Browning tried to digest this information. Somehow, knowing their names and a possible motive made these people more real; these strangers, barely glimpsed in life, who now loomed so large in death. All this perhaps because the love that once bound two people had come unravelled. Madness indeed. Yet even as these thoughts jostled for space in a mind suddenly too small to contain them, he felt anew the pain of his own disastrous marriage. When love disintegrates, it leaves wounds that are slower to heal than any other. It is not the body that is marked, but the soul. Whatever scarred Andreas Mourtzinos must have been agonizing indeed to provoke such deadly rage.

From deep within the fog of these thoughts, Browning gradually became aware that the police officer was speaking to him. "I'm sorry," he said, "could you repeat that?"

The officer regarded him with something close to pity. "I was just asking where we can reach you in case we need to talk again."

"Actually, I'm on my way to the Peloponnese."

A look of consternation flickered across the cop's phlegmatic features. "May I ask if you are here on vacation?"

"No, business. That is, I'm on an assignment of sorts. Quite urgent, actually."

"I'm sorry, Mr. Browning, but I'm going to ask you to stay in Athens for a few more days, until the investigation is complete. It's vital that you are here to answer any questions that may come up."

Browning fought a rising wave of panic. This was intolerable. Lives were at risk, Callas had said. He simply couldn't afford to lose time.

"Listen, I've told you everything I know — four times. I really must get back to the business that brought me here."

"And what, if I may ask, is that business?"

"Er, research. I'm working to a very tight deadline."

The cop looked apologetic but unyielding. "I'm very sorry, Mr. Browning, but you are the only witness to a very serious crime. Lives were lost. Whatever brought you to Greece can't be more important than that. I must insist that you remain in Athens until further notice. Of course, the department will pay for your hotel room."

Browning stared at the cop miserably. It appeared that he had no choice but to comply. He had no stomach for action in any event. "Okay," he said finally. "I'll stay. But please try to finish with me as soon as possible. For me, time is of the essence."

HE SAW her first at police headquarters. He had collected his pack from the desk sergeant and was about to leave the building when she emerged from an office, accompanied by a sharp-eyed detective.

He knew her at once. She was younger than him, probably no more than 40. Her pale face, streaked with the tears of the newly bereaved and roughly framed by dark strands of uncombed hair, looked prematurely aged, as if grief had dissolved the thin veneer of her fading youth. She shuffled down the corridor, leaning on the detective's arm for support, with the slumped gait of one who has suffered an irreversible blow. There was something about her that Browning found impossible to ignore, though he couldn't put his finger on just what it was.

As if in a dream, he moved toward her. "Mrs. Mourtzinos?" he said softly, regretting his inability to speak even a few words of Greek.

She looked at him distractedly. Though rimmed red from weeping, her dark, liquid eyes were striking behind the thick, tortoise-rimmed glasses that kept slipping down her nose. "I'm sorry, do I know you?" she asked in clear, lightly accented English.

"I was on the train," Browning said softly. He was astonished at himself for undertaking this difficult conversation, but he seemed in the grip of a force beyond his control.

Her eyes widened in sudden understanding. "You're the witness. You saw it."

He nodded gravely. To his consternation, her face crumpled. "Vasilio," she cried. "My poor Vasilio. Why you? If he hated me so much, why not kill me instead?"

The officer glared at Browning, and put his arms around the distraught woman. My God, Bliss thought, they've already told her it was deliberate, not an accident. The cop made comforting sounds in Greek, and slowly her sobs began to subside. Browning stood rooted to the spot, paralyzed by the woman's sorrow. He felt an irrational sense of guilt and shame, as if witnessing Andreas Mourtzinos's fateful act made him complicit in his murderous design. But most of all, he felt intense compassion for the stranger before him, this woman whose life had been so brutally and abruptly transformed.

"I'm terribly, terribly sorry," he whispered when the woman's sobs finally stopped. "I can't begin to imagine how you must feel."

The cop waved at him irritably. "Leave her alone," he said roughly. Browning nodded slowly and turned away.

"No, wait!" The woman's voice stopped him in his tracks. "Please, don't go," she said, dabbing her eyes with a tissue. Browning turned and faced her. How forlorn she looks, he thought.

"Forgive me," she said. "Please. Tell me what you saw."

Browning glanced at the cop, who nodded reluctantly. He had to force himself to speak, because the words seemed to catch in his throat. "I was leaning out the window when I saw your husband standing near the tracks. At first, I didn't see your daughter, but when we got closer I could see that she was in his arms. I thought they were just there to wave at the train. But when I saw his face, I knew something was wrong."

"What did he look like?" she asked, eyes wide, though she looked as if she were fearful of the answer.

"It's hard to describe. Determined, I suppose. He had a look of concentration, as if he were thinking very hard. He was staring straight ahead, not even looking at the train. I remember thinking that was very odd."

"Yes . . . odd. My daughter. How was she?"

"She was crying."

The woman bowed her head. "My poor, poor Vasilio," she murmured, and the sadness in her voice made Browning's heart ache. He turned to go.

"Wait," she called. "I should ask ... you were the last person to see my husband and child alive. I don't even know your name."

"Browning," he said, haltingly extending a hand. "Bliss Browning."

She took his hand gravely in both of hers. He felt her eyes searching his face. "Thank you, Mr. Browning," she said quietly.

"And you?" he stammered, wondering exactly what he was asking, since he knew she was now a widow named Mourtzinos.

"Matina Mourtzinos," she replied, a bare whisper. "You may call me Matina."

CHAPTER 13

NORMAN PUGSLEY WAS WOOZY WITH FATIGUE AND OVERINDULGENCE. After travelling for nearly 15 hours, he'd finally arrived in Athens, charged with the task of tracking down and retrieving the *Advocate*'s delinquent correspondent, Bliss Browning. To make the numbing hours of travel more bearable, Pugsley had soaked up all the airline booze his body could tolerate, which was considerable. Now, sprawled in the back of a cab speeding towards his luxury hotel on Syntagma Square, it was all he could do to keep his eyes from closing.

Yet Pugsley knew he had to keep his wits about him. For he was in alien territory here, surrounded by people whose very alphabet was incomprehensible. Norman Pugsley was not a well-travelled man. His idea of an adventurous vacation was a few days at the slot machines and casino tables of Las Vegas. He had been to Europe only once, on a whirlwind bus tour that passed through six countries in 13 days. He hadn't much liked it then, and didn't expect to like it this time, either.

Pugsley's xenophobia was fuelled by his conviction that foreigners viewed North Americans as walking billfolds ripe for plunder. Already, he'd had to get stern with his taxi driver, someone named George, who'd fed him some cock-and-bull story about a special tourist fare in lieu of the metered rate. But Pugsley had belligerently insisted that the driver turn on his meter. "I don't know what sort of suckers you're used to dealing with, pal, but you'll turn that thing on or you'll be sorry," he'd shouted at the driver. He'd watched with grim satisfaction as the driver sullenly complied. He'd failed to notice, however, that the meter was set for the night rate, twice the regular fare, though the sun was still only part way through its daily transit of the blue Greek sky.

As Pugsley struggled to retain consciousness, he considered the task before him. Finding Browning, he knew, would take sheer bloody luck. Pugsley had been a pretty decent reporter in his youth, but he was far removed from those days. And the fact that people here spoke a foreign goddamn language was inconvenient, to say the least. His plan, to the extent that he had one, was to position himself in a strategic location — a popular bar, perhaps — and wait for his quarry to come to him. It made as much sense as anything else, and he could enjoy a few libations while he waited for Browning to appear. If he had to be here on this damn-fool mission, Norman Pugsley was determined to be as comfortable as possible.

Pugsley's taxi pulled up outside the Hotel Grande Bretagne on Syntagma Square. The Grande Bretagne was the dowager of Athenian hotels, imposing and venerable. It was the pinnacle of old-world elegance, at least by the standards of Athens, a city not overly endowed with either the old world or the elegant. Still, Pugsley was displeased. He had been expecting a gleaming temple to modernity, with fitness clubs, chic shops and acres of chrome. The Grande Bretagne's faded elegance promised subtler pleasures, and Pugsley was not a subtle man.

Leaving his two heavy suitcases for a bellboy to carry, Pugsley marched through the hotel lobby to the front desk. "Pugsley from Ottawa, checking in," he barked at the clerk, leaning wearily on the counter. The clerk, accustomed to boorish foreign guests, barely blinked. "You have a reservation, Mr. Pugsley?" he asked neutrally. Pugsley nodded briskly. "Damn straight," he growled. The clerk did some rapid typing on his computer keyboard. "Could you spell your name for me, sir?" he said.

"P-u-g-s-l-e-y," the *Advocate*'s managing editor replied irritably, muttering under his breath: "How else would you spell it?" These people were already getting on his nerves, as he knew they would.

There was another flurry of keystrokes. "I'm sorry, Mr. Pugsley," said the poker-faced clerk, "but we don't have any record of your reservation."

"What?!" Pugsley exploded. "My office just made the damn reservation two days ago. What kind of operation are you people running here? Christ on a bicycle!" Pugsley glared at the clerk. "Lookit, I've been travelling forever. Just give me a room and I'll forget all about this screwup."

"I'm afraid I can't, sir," said the clerk smoothly. "We're fully booked."

"Don't give me that crap!" Pugsley cried. "You people always have something in reserve. You mean to tell me if the president of the United States walked in here right now, you'd turn him away?"

"With regret, sir, yes," replied the clerk. "Besides," he added with just the faintest hint of malice, "you're not the president of the United States, are you, sir?"

"Fuck you!" screamed Pugsley, his thick neck red with rage. "You can take your shit-pile of a hotel and stuff it up your ass!"

With that, Norman Pugsley spun on his heel, collected his two overstuffed suitcases and, staggering slightly under the load, stormed off into the Athenian afternoon.

"THERE'S BEEN A DELAY," Bliss Browning told Maria Callas. After a tumultuous day, he was at last ensconced in a comfortable hotel not far from Syntagma Square, recommended by the Athens police department. He'd been relieved to discover that his room in the hotel, which catered to visiting businessmen, came equipped with WIFI, simplifying his communications with Callas. But he was still too shaken to fully grasp just how commodious the room was, though with its feather-soft bed, sleek contemporary furnishings and en suite bathroom, it was a world apart from the glorified slum he'd occupied in the Plaka.

"I knew it," Callas replied. "I've been uneasy all day, but I couldn't say why. What happened?"

Browning told Callas about the collision and what had provoked it. "It really shook me up. The man, Mourtzinos — I'll never forget his face. So cold, so resolved. And that horrible smile! Bad enough to end your own life like that. But to kill an innocent child, and smile while you do it . . . it's monstrous."

"Yes," replied Callas. "It's just like Medea."

"What do you mean?" asked Browning, not immediately grasping her point.

"The smile gives it away. Killing the child was his ultimate revenge, just as Medea murdered her own children to avenge herself on their father after he spurned her for Glauce. Believe me, I performed the role often enough; I should know what motivates someone when the furies of the heart are unleashed."

Browning digested this theory. "But why did Mourtzinos kill himself as well as the child? Medea's rage was directed at her betrayers, Jason and Glauce. She did not end her own life."

"My dear Browning, life imitates art, but never precisely. Medea was a sorceress with great and terrible powers. Your Mourtzinos was a mortal man. For his revenge to be complete, his wife needed to know that he had killed their child. That left him with two choices: spend the rest of his life in prison for a heinous, unforgivable crime, or take his own life. It's obvious which he preferred."

"Even if you're right, why choose such an extravagant and public means of revenge? Why not use poison, or even a gun? I mean, stepping in front of a train, for God's sake . . . it's almost operatic."

"Precisely. And that's just what he wanted. Revenge on a grand scale. Remember how Medea killed Glauce; the poisoned jewels, placed on her forehead at her wedding, before all of Corinth? And the children; killed in the temple as Jason and the crowd converged, howling for her blood? These were very public acts. Medea wanted the world to know of her vengeance. So, I fear, did your Mourtzinos."

"Why didn't he kill his wife, too?"

"My dear Browning, that should be obvious. Killing her ends her torment. Forcing her to live, to endure her loss, that is truly cruel."

Callas's words triggered something in Browning. "You sound as if you speak from experience. Was that how it was for you after Onassis died?"

There was no response for a moment. Then the words again started to scroll across the computer screen.

"My dear Browning, you are more perceptive than you seem. Yes, in spite of his brutishness, his cruelty, his arrogance, when he died, the only light in my life was extinguished. My voice was only a memory — my gruesome concert tour with Giuseppe De Stefano in the 1970s proved that beyond a shadow of doubt. I was barely into my 50s, and I faced the appalling prospect of decades of life devoid of purpose or meaningful companionship. Is it any wonder that I chose death instead?"

"Chose death? Maria, what are you saying? Are you telling me that you committed suicide?" Browning typed the words fearfully, almost afraid of the answer.

"Committed suicide. An oddly sterile phrase, don't you think? It hardly conveys the momentousness of the act. Choosing to end your own life, to deliberately stop your beating heart forever, deserves a description filled with drama and portent. More operatic, as you might put it."

"Maria . . ."

"Yes, yes, I know. I haven't answered your question. Well, you've learned a great deal about me. What do you think?"

"I think . . ." Browning faltered, searching for the right words. ". . . that you were capable of taking your own life."

"That, my dear Browning," replied Callas, "is an evasion. Did I do it, or didn't I?"

Browning closed his eyes. There had been speculation, of course. Callas had been relatively young, and despite a depressive reclusiveness, had not been seriously ill before her death in Paris in 1977 of what was officially described as a heart attack. There had been no autopsy, though, and her body had been cremated with a speed that some found unseemly.

Yet Browning had always rejected the suicide rumours out of hand. Indeed, whenever they had surfaced in the Callas discussion group, he had rebutted them with withering force. It was simply alien to his conception of Callas as a heroic figure that she could author such an ignoble end. The very possibility, he thought, diminished her legend.

Yet as he turned over these ideas in his head, Browning realized that he had been guilty of a kind of myopia. Because Callas had achieved perfection as an artist, he had invested her with perfection as a person. He had excused her erratic behaviour and questionable judgment as the understandable eccentricities of genius.

But the Maria Callas he had met on the Internet, disembodied though she was, was nevertheless more truly human than the woman he had worshipped through her music and videos. The latter was a wraith, a reinvention without substance and depth. The real Callas, he was learning, was deeply flawed and riven with contradiction. The real Callas was easy prey to the forces that push people to end a life that has become, for them, intolerable.

"Yes," wrote Browning, "I think you did it."

"Bravo," Callas replied sardonically. "You are beginning to understand me. And now, I suppose, you are disillusioned with your heroine?"

"No," Browning answered, and what surprised him was that he meant it. “I am only sad that your life was so empty that death seemed more attractive to you than life. It changes nothing about my feelings toward you."

"My dear Browning," said Callas, "you do surprise me. Could it be that we are both becoming a bit more fully human, each in our own way?"

"Perhaps. This has been an extraordinary day; I wouldn't rule anything out."

There was no response for a moment. Then Browning read these words from Maria Callas: "I wish I could embrace you, my friend."

Blinking back tears — whether of joy, sorrow, exhaustion, shock or some odd blend of them all was unclear — he responded: "And I you, dearest Maria."

And though it was not literally possible, at that moment the connection between them was as real and tangible as any touch. To Browning, wracked with the trauma of the day's events, it felt like serenity. And, blessedly, like love.

A LIGHT KNOCK awoke Browning from a sound sleep. He groped for his watch and focused on the hands: 10 a.m. My God, he groaned, I've been sleeping for nearly 12 hours. He pulled on a robe supplied by the hotel and approached the door.

"Who is it?" he called uncertainly.

"It's Matina Mourtzinos." The voice was small and tentative, like that of a shy child.

For a moment, Browning, mind still befogged by sleep, struggled to place the name. Then with a rush of dread, he remembered. The train. The smile. Matina, the bereaved wife and mother, here, outside his door. "Just a moment," he said, buying time as he struggled to think what to do.

Finally, there seemed no alternative but to open the door. Which he did, with a sense of apprehension that was palpable.

"Forgive me," she said, looking frightened and miserable, "but I asked the police where you were. I had to talk to you."

Browning didn't know what to say. Then some latent politeness reflex kicked in. "Of course," he said, struggling to recover his poise. "Please come in."

She was carelessly dressed, as if she had thrown on her clothes in the dark. One black button on her white cotton blouse was in the wrong buttonhole, and her socks were distinctly different shades of blue. Her face was puffy, as if she'd had little sleep, her hair disheveled, her glasses visibly stained with what Browning could only assume was the residue of tears.

"You must think I'm insane, barging in on you like this," she said, wringing her hands. She noticed, apparently for the first time, that Browning wasn't yet dressed. "Were you still in bed? I'm so sorry." She looked confused, and tears welled up.

Alarmed, Browning moved toward her. "Are you okay?" he asked anxiously. "Can I get you a drink or something?"

"No, no thanks," she said, removing her glasses and wiping her eyes on her sleeve. "I'll take a tissue, if you have one." She stared vacantly at her tear-stained glasses.

Even in her current bedraggled condition, Browning couldn't help noticing that Matina was attractive. He grabbed some clothes from his pack and disappeared into the bathroom, quickly pulling on a shirt and pants.

Matina, slumped on the edge of his unmade bed, barely looked up when he handed her a fistful of Kleenex. She blew her nose softly, and, after dabbing her eyes with more of the tissue, slipped her glasses back on. "Thank you," she said quietly.

"Forget it," said Browning.

Matina looked at him. "You're wondering why I'm here, of course," she said dully. He looked at her closely. She was obviously still in shock.

"Actually, yes," said Browning. He was also surprised that she appeared to be by herself.

"I know it sounds stupid, but when I got up this morning, I had an overwhelming urge to see you. I was alone, and I'm not used to that. Before, there was always Andreas or Vasilio." Her voice trembled and she seemed again on the verge of tears.

"Don't you have any friends or relatives in Athens?" asked Browning, disconcerted.

"No, we only moved to Athens six months ago, and I really don't know anyone here. Andreas wasn't very sociable," she added.

"Where are your relatives?"

"My mother is in Areopoli, in the Mani. My father died years ago."

"What about brothers and sisters? Or your husband's family?"

"I have no brothers or sisters. My parents had given up hope of having children when I came along, at the last moment. Mother was 42. There were no others after me. As for Andreas's family, his father is alive but very old and not at all well. His mother is dead. And his brothers have had nothing to do with us for years. Andreas, you see, he wasn't ..." Her voice trailed off, as if she had suddenly reconsidered whatever she was about to say.

Browning finally broke the lengthening silence. "Does your mother know about your husband and child?" he asked cautiously.

"Yes. I think she does. I spoke to her by phone last night. But she's becoming quite addled. You never know what she's retaining."

Browning looked at Matina thoughtfully. The woman did seem to be truly alone. And she obviously was still in a stupor after her husband's mad act. It struck him as bizarre that she would turn to him, a stranger, for comfort. Surely there were better candidates.

"Matina, I don't want to sound cruel, but I'm not sure what I can do. I'm a stranger in this country, we've barely met and I'm here on urgent business. As soon as the police give me permission, I must leave. I'm not exactly in a position to help you."

Matina jumped to her feet. "You're right, you're right," she said, a flush of embarrassment colouring her expression of numb misery. "It was wrong of me to bother you." She tried to smile, but what emerged was more of a grimace. "Don't worry," she said, averting her eyes, "I'll go now."

"Wait a minute," said Browning. He had been too brusque. What harm was there in letting the woman talk for a while? "I have nothing planned right now. Let's have coffee somewhere. You can tell me anything you like."

Matina searched his face with her eyes. "Really? You don't have to if you don't want to."

"I want to," said Browning firmly. And if that wasn't the truth, it wasn't entirely a fabrication either.

He found them a free table at a sidewalk cafe just off Omonia Square. On Matina's recommendation, they ordered frappés, tall glasses of iced coffee with a creamy head sipped through bendable plastic straws. Somewhat to his surprise, Browning found the drink's chilled caffeine flavour invigorating.

Matina gazed at him gravely: "Why were you on that train?"

The question made Browning squirm. He could hardly tell this stranger the real reason for his visit, yet he had neither the nature nor the talent for outright deceit. He opted instead for mild dissembling.

"Well, I'm a journalist," he began. "I work for a newspaper in Canada; I'm sure you've never heard of it — the Ottawa *Daily Advocate*. I'm the travel editor."

"You're right," said Matina, "I've never heard of your newspaper. But I do know Ottawa. It's the capital city, isn't it?"

"Yes, it is," said Browning, surprised. "How did you know that?"

"My parents. Before I was born, they lived for many years in Montreal. But they couldn't take the winters. Once they made some money in Canada, they returned to Greece. They taught me English. They thought I should learn because it is the language of the world, and who speaks Greek except Greeks?"

Browning smiled. "Well, they taught you well. Your English is very fluent."

"Thank you," she murmured. "You're very kind to say so."

There was an awkward pause. "I'm sorry," said Matina, "You were starting to tell me why you were on that train."

"Yes, well, I'm here researching a story for my newspaper about Maria Callas, the famous opera singer. As I'm sure you know, she was of Greek heritage. Anyway, her music is enjoying renewed popularity in North America, and my editor felt we should do a feature story about her life. Callas's family was originally from Meligalas in the Peloponnese, and I was heading there to find out more about their life there."

"Oh," said Matina, almost somnambulantly.

“It's kind of a travel story, too," said Browning, rushing on. "I'm writing about the places associated with Callas — Athens, Milan,

Verona, Paris, New York — so people can retrace her life if they want to." This was well beyond mere dissembling, and Browning quickly moved the conversation back onto firmer, and more truthful, ground. "I'm a devoted Callas fan."

"I don't think I've ever heard her sing," said Matina, "but then I don't listen to opera very much. It's too tragic."

"But that's much of the attraction," said Browning, dismayed at the woman's cavalier dismissal of an artist, and an art form, that meant so much to him. For a moment he forgot that sorrow overwhelmed the creature in front of him and launched into a lecture on the art form's attractions. "Opera appeals to the tragic sense in us all. At its best, it creates a terrible beauty out of suffering. When Callas sings a tragic aria, it's like standing in front of an emotional blast furnace that purifies everything it touches. Opera opens the heart and lets us feel. By sharing another's pain, we become more compassionate, more fully human."

Browning abruptly stopped and looked at Matina. To his consternation, her eyes were filling with tears.

"I'm sorry," he said, alarmed. "I get carried away sometimes, especially when I'm talking about Callas. Please forgive me."

Matina shook her head. "Don't apologize," she said. "You've done nothing wrong. Your words moved me deeply."

She let out a long, shuddering sigh. "I've always borne my sorrows alone, because it never occurred to me that anyone else would care. Why should they? They have their own problems to worry about. But if sharing another's pain purifies the soul and opens the heart, then I am wrong to hoard my sorrow. By hiding it away, I am diminishing the storehouse of compassion in the world. Do you see?"

"Yes," said Browning slowly, "that's very insightful." In fact, it had never occurred to him that what was true of his emotional response to opera might be equally true of his response to life. Yet instinctively he knew Matina was right. When Harrison Howard's son was killed, Browning had mourned his friend's loss as if it were his own. The two had shared the despair and heartbreak, and had emerged with an unshakable connection. Howard's compassion for Browning after the collapse of his short-lived marriage had been just as indispensable.

But as he mulled this over, Browning realized that these episodes were exceptions in a life that had made a virtue of withdrawal and disconnection. His deepest emotional responses were reserved for the manufactured tragedies of art. From life's misfortunes, most often, he recoiled. He was at a loss to explain the double standard. He knew only that it had to end.

"Mrs. Mourtzinos," he said, looking her square in the face, "there's something I must tell you about your husband."

"My husband? What?"

Browning took a deep breath. "I saw his face just before he stepped in front of the train. I don't know why, but he was smiling."

Matina's face was utterly without expression. "Yes. I know," she said tonelessly. "The police told me."

"You knew?"

"Yes."

"But why? Why would he smile at such a time?"

"You'd understand if you had known Andreas." She looked wearily at Browning. "He was a brutal man. Marrying him was the mistake of my life. Finally, I had had enough. I told him I was leaving. He went berserk, started screaming that I couldn't just walk out on him, that I'd be sorry if I tried."

Her lower lip trembled. "He knew Vasilio was the only person who mattered in my life. I suppose he thought that taking her from me was his ultimate punishment — the bastard!" She spat the last word. Her composure entirely deserting her now, she slumped heavily onto the table. Her body convulsed with wracking sobs that brought conversation in the sidewalk cafe to a halt and drew alarmed looks from passers-by.

Momentarily aghast at her display of bitter sorrow, Browning at first just stared helplessly. Then he did something that surprised even him. He rose from his chair, walked around to where Matina lay crumpled on the table and gathered her tenderly in his arms. And held her as the tears poured out.

CHAPTER 14

BROWNING FELT A CURIOUS SENSE OF LOSS AS MATINA'S BLACK-AND-yellow taxi merged into heavy traffic along Stadiou, one of the Athens arteries that radiates from Omonia Square. He watched as it travelled slowly up the busy street until other vehicles obliterated it from view. It was very odd. He barely knew the woman, hadn't even wanted to talk to her, and certainly didn't want to share her sorrow so intimately. Yet now that she was gone, he missed her. For a loner like Browning, it was an unfamiliar feeling.

To fill the surprising emptiness, he took a walk. Already the noise and confusion of Athens was less threatening to him. This, too, came as a revelation. All his life, he had harboured an unshakable conviction that the world was a forbidding place. That belief had governed his every action, tethering him to his small known universe as firmly as a safety harness secures a window-washer to a high-rise. The train tragedy should have cemented that life view. Instead, he was finding that while the world held its share of terrors, he could navigate them well enough. The discovery gave him a feeling of competence that he'd scarcely believed possible.

Ambling through the streets of central Athens, Browning saw the city around him with fresh eyes. True, Athens was all the things its critics asserted: noisy, astonishingly ugly in places and unforgivably polluted. But it was also, he was beginning to perceive, a place of endless fascination. He had been struck earlier by the contrast between the Acropolis and the 20th-century city surrounding it. Now, he began to find unexpected delights in the people and places of modern Athens itself.

The bazaar along Athinas and Eolou and the streets in between, were to everyday commerce what the Louvre is to art — a huge and varied repository that engaged and overwhelmed the senses even as it satisfied every imaginable need. Each block was devoted to one specialty or another: tools here, clothing there, paint and brasswork to the east, glass products to the west. The most astonishing section was the meat and seafood market in the middle, where shoppers browsed stalls laden with great slabs of meat, body parts like hocks, hearts and snouts, and all manner of creatures scaly and squirming from the seas off Greece. A walk through the market was intoxicating and nauseating at the same time. But amid the carcasses and teeming crowds, Browning felt the pulse of life more forcefully than he ever had in his carefully modulated existence.

The Greeks themselves were one reason for that. Boisterous, passionate and social to a fault, their messy embrace of life repelled and attracted him at the same time. He found himself studying squat matrons haggling with ruddy-faced merchants over the price of red mullet and kalamarakia. He watched as boisterous, swarthy men quaffed ouzo and strong coffee in kafenios, debating the important and trivial issues of their lives with force, conviction, often anger. The contrast with the distant people of his own city, who lowered their defences only under the influence of strong drink, could hardly have been more striking. Browning, too, was part of that legion of the dour and distant; he had believed it necessary for survival. But the Greeks on the streets of Athens were proof that there were other ways to live, ways that didn't require you to shut your heart to the neighbours and strangers who shared your city.

These thoughts were ripening when Browning spotted something that made him stop short and stare. In the window of a shop selling used records and tapes was a display devoted to the music of Maria Callas. That in itself was enough to gladden Browning's heart, but what made it pump faster was the sight of a small cardboard rectangle near the centre of the display. It was, Browning realized immediately, a rare 1953 LP recording of *Norma,* featuring Maria Callas and the La Scala chorus and orchestra under the baton of Tullio Serafin. Browning's own CD collection included reissued excerpts from the same recording session, but copies of the original vinyl record were all but impossible to find. Even inquiries posted to the Callas news group had failed to turn up a copy. Now, he was looking at this much-desired prize lying casually in plain view in a shop window. It was as if Heinrich Schliemann, the German archeologist who unearthed the legendary city of Mycenae in 1874, had spotted the death mask of Agamemnon in a curio shop on the Kurfurstendamm.

There was never any doubt that Browning would have to buy the album. He didn't even hesitate when the shopkeeper told him the price: 45 euros. Browning willingly peeled the bills from the wad of currency in his wallet. His hand trembled slightly as he handed the money over and received the precious three-album set in return. Athens, he thought. What a bloody great town.

~

"YES, I'm here, no thanks to you people," Norman Pugsley bellowed into the phone line that linked him to the *Advocate* office in Ottawa.

"What do you mean?" asked Ryan Young.

"The fucking hotel had no record of my reservation, that's what. I had to tramp all over goddamn Athens before I found a place that looked halfway decent. And even this place is only marginally better than the Black Hole of Calcutta. I swear, Young, this city is the asshole of the world. People are up all night racing their motorcycles outside your window — it's a miracle I got any sleep at all."

"Jeez, Norm, it sounds awful," said Young, quietly enjoying his boss's discomfiture. "Should be able to file for hardship pay, though."

"Are you mocking me, Young?" snarled Pugsley. "Cause if you are, you're in more shit than you can possibly imagine."

"Christ, no, Norm," said Young, scrubbing the tell-tale note of amusement from his voice. "Jesus, we all feel for you, travelling halfway around the world to retrieve a putrid piece of shit like Browning."

"Yeah, well, Browning better hope I don't find him. Cause if I do, I'm going to rip his lungs out, do you hear me Young? I'll carve him a new sphincter." Pugsley was warming to his subject. "Hell, I'll carve him a dozen new sphincters. When I'm through, he'll walk with a permanent limp."

"Uhhh, Norm," said Young, interrupting this tirade, "Renata's here and she'd like a word."

"No, Young, Christ, tell her I've just hung up. I don't want to ta—"

"Norman?"

Pugsley stifled a groan. "Hello, Renata."

"Wonderful to hear your voice, Norman. How's Athens? Marvellous city, isn't it? Absolutely replete with the most astonishing antiquities. Have you been to the archeological museum yet? No, of course you haven't — you're working, you don't have time for such pleasures, do you? Any luck finding our AWOL reporter?"

"Christ, Renata, I only got here yesterday. Give me a break."

"Of course, of course. Look, Norman, try to have a little fun while you're there. Learn a little Greek, soak up some of the history. Oh, be sure to try the mezedes at that superb little place in the Plaka. They make the most amazing octopus. Now what's it called again . . ."

"Octopus? You gotta be kidding. And what the hell, pardon my French, is mezedes?"

"Are mezedes, Norman, are mezedes. It's a collective noun, so it takes a plural verb. Look, I'd love to talk, but the publisher just walked into the newsroom. Must go." With a hollow click, the line went dead.

"Christ on a bicycle," muttered Pugsley, staring at the receiver in his hand. "I'm working for a fuckin' fruitcake."

"YOU'LL NEVER GUESS what I found today," said Bliss Browning to Maria Callas. He paused for a few moments until Callas rose to the bait.

"Well?" she prompted.

"A vinyl copy of your 1953 recording of *Norma*!"

"Wherever did you find that relic?"

"A used music store in the Athens bazaar. It was sitting in the store window, calling to me. Do you think your old pal fate had anything to do with it?"

"Perhaps, though the interventions of fate are usually reserved for more momentous matters than the purchase of an album of music. More likely it was just dumb luck. You know, that exists too, my dear Browning. Not everything is ordained by higher powers."

"Now you tell me," Browning replied wryly. "I was starting to believe that I was just a pawn in someone's master plan."

"I don't know where you got that idea," said Callas, taking the riposte seriously. "Certainly not from me. You have a destiny, to be sure, but there's no guarantee that you will fulfill it. To do so you must act, and to act you must have the courage and faith to do what's necessary, even if it may seem undesirable or even impossible. It was my destiny to be a great diva, but it didn't happen by chance. It happened because I devoted decades of my life to that objective. Fulfilling a destiny is hard work, my dear Browning."

"Yet in your case," interjected Browning, "you were driven by powers beyond your control. Almost against your will, you say. And in the end, you were miserable, so miserable that you preferred death to the pain of life. So how much choice do we really have over the way our lives unfold?"

"True, I was compelled by forces I didn't understand to fulfill my destiny. Yet at some fundamental level, I was a willing participant. Why? Because I knew that I could accomplish something extraordinary. That sort of temptation is hard to resist. Of course, had I known the cost . . . but I only learned that much later. But it is a grave error to suppose my life can teach you much about the nature of destiny. I was a freak, a mutation. There was nothing typical about my life, so you should not read any lessons into it. Your life, now, that's another matter entirely. You, my dear Browning, are burdened with none of my extraordinariness. You are the quintessential everyman."

"Thanks, I think."

"Please don't take offence. All I meant was that you have been spared the unwholesome mania that governed my own life. The very plainness of your life means that you have the freedom to choose how it unfolds. If you doubt me, consider your life before we met. Had you not deliberately withdrawn from the life around you? And have you not now made an equally considered decision to abandon that caution in order to help me?"

"Yes," replied Browning, "but were those really choices? My life until now has been governed by fear — I certainly wouldn't have chosen to live that way."

"But you did, my dear Browning, you did. Nothing says our choices will be wise, or will make us happy. But they are choices, nonetheless. True, your fears have ruled your life. But you let them. Fears are intangible things that can be conquered with enough resolution and courage. But most people avoid the battle because it's easier than resisting."

Just as Browning was about to reply to this provocative volley, the telephone on the bedside table jangled urgently. Uncertainly, he answered it. It was Matina.

"I just wanted to thank you for your kindness today," she said. Her voice on the telephone was steadier and had a warmth he hadn't noticed when they were together. Browning was surprised how pleased he was to hear from her again.

"It was the least I could do," he said. "I'm glad I could help."

"You did. I'm much calmer now. My neighbours just left. They fed me lunch. Amazing what some mezedes and companionship can do." There was a tiny bleak laugh, which died quickly in her throat. "What have you been up to since I left?"

"Oh, just walking. I bought an old LP of Callas singing Norma. It's incredibly rare — I can hardly wait to get back to Ottawa so I can play it." Immediately he regretted the statement. What could his own frivolity mean to a woman who had just lost a beloved child?

There was a silence on the other end of the line, and for a moment, Browning feared his insensitivity had caused offense. "Matina?" he asked. "Are you okay?"

"No, I'm fine," she replied, distractedly. "I was just thinking ... I have an old record player in my apartment. If you'd like to listen to your Callas record, you could do it here."

"Are you sure?" Browning doubted that a visit was appropriate under the circumstances. "I mean, this is such a difficult time for you."

"I could use the company. Why not come around 8 tomorrow? I'll make a proper Greek dinner."

"That sounds like too much trouble."

"No, really. I have people to phone. To explain," her voice trailed off, "what happened." Then, more urgently: "But I am alone. Please come."

Browning hung up the phone and turned back to his portable computer. "Sorry," he apologized, "but I had a phone call."

"Oh?" said Callas.

"It was Matina. We're becoming friends, of a sort. She came to see me earlier today, and we had quite a talk. Now she's invited me to come to her place for dinner, to play your record."

"How generous of her."

"Generous doesn't cover it. The poor woman has just suffered a terrible blow. Her child is dead, for God's sake. In her shoes, I would want nothing more than to be left alone. I certainly wouldn't be inviting strangers for dinner. It's remarkable. She's remarkable."

"It sounds to me, my dear Browning, as if you are attracted to her."

"Maria! How can you say such a thing? It's monstrous," Browning scolded. "This is hardly a time for romance."

"My dear, dear Browning. There is no such thing as an inappropriate time for love. You must seize love whenever it appears, for it may not pass your way again."

Callas's relentless omniscience was beginning to get on his nerves.

In exasperation, he typed a snippy response: "Is there anything you don't know, Maria?"

The reply came after a short pause. "Just one thing," said Maria Callas. "I can't tell you how to make someone love you."

MATINA'S APARTMENT was a walkup on the second floor of a nondescript low-rise in Athens' northern suburbs. The neighbourhood bore the scars of the city's too-rapid post-war development. Concrete buildings hastily erected in the late '50s and early '60s were already deteriorating, some little more than shells. Matina's building was indistinguishable from dozens of others on her street — three to four stories of insipid greyness interrupted only by an occasional burst of colour from a balcony bougainvillea.

Just before 8 p.m., Browning stepped out of the cab that delivered him to this forgettable place. He was clutching his Maria Callas album in one hand; in the other, a bouquet of flowers. He had agonized over the flowers. Would bringing them be inappropriately personal? Would Matina interpret the blossoms as an expression of unwanted affection, or cheerfulness at the worst moment? In the end, he decided to bring them and hope for the best.

He climbed the steep staircase to the second floor and, placing the Callas album securely under his right arm, knocked briskly on the door of apartment 201. There was the sound of light footsteps from within, then Matina was there. He was astonished at the transformation in her appearance. She was wearing a simple black dress and matching leather pumps. Her hair fell in graceful waves to her shoulders. Even the heavy glasses seemed less severe than he remembered.

"You look ... better," he said, suppressing the word "wonderful".

"Thank you," she said with a quick, tight smile. "I've been so miserable."

Browning presented the bouquet. "I hope this is okay," he said.

"They're beautiful," Matina murmured appreciatively. "You didn't need to do that, Bliss." Browning beamed and dropped his head shyly.

"Make yourself at home while I put these in water," Matina ordered, disappearing into the kitchen with the flowers. While he waited, Browning took in the living room in a glance. The tiny room was sparsely furnished: two elderly upholstered chairs, a small utility table, a couple of lamps and a small braided rug. The room was dominated by a monstrous old television set, a relic from the early 1970s, on top of which sat a record player of even older vintage. A hallway near the door led to the kitchen and what appeared to be the apartment's lone bedroom.

"It's not much, is it?" said Matina, catching the look on his face as she emerged from the kitchen with the flowers, now neatly contained in a green ceramic vase. "When we moved here from the Mani, we could only take what we could carry. We didn't have a car and couldn't afford to pay a mover. Since we've been here, I've been haunting the flea markets. That's where just about everything you see came from."

A look of such sadness suddenly flashed over her features, that Browning felt compelled to say something lest she burst into tears.

"Under the circumstances, you've done wonders. It's very homey," he said, hoping the words didn't sound as trite to her as they did to him. Apparently they did not. She brightened and gestured at the ancient record player. "Do you think you can play your album on that?" she asked.

Browning surveyed the apparatus. "I suppose so," he said doubtfully.

"Then put it on," said Matina.

Gingerly, Browning extracted the first disc from its sleeve. A careful inspection had satisfied him that the albums were in decent condition, with only minor scratches visible. Still, until the records were played, he couldn't be certain that all was well. So it was with considerable anxiety that Browning placed the record on the well-worn turntable and lowered the stylus onto the outside groove.

For a moment, all they could hear was the pop and crackle of the needle on the record's surface. Then the first luminous strains of the overture filled the small apartment. Browning glanced at Matina, but she was sitting with her eyes closed, absorbed in the music, he presumed.

She sat immobile until Callas made her first entry. On hearing her fluid, soaring voice, arresting even through the tinny speakers of the battered phonograph, Matina opened her eyes and looked at Browning in surprise. But now he was in another dimension, transported by the lyric beauty and intensity of the performance. This was Callas at the height of her powers, one of a handful of sopranos in the history of music with the imagination, technique and dramatic sense to bring Bellini's great opera fully to life.

There was a moment of silence when the record ended. Then Browning, not daring to look at Matina, let alone speak to her, got up and turned the disc over, repeating this procedure for each of the remaining records in the set. All the while, Matina said nothing, sitting with her head bowed as if in prayer. Lost in their private thoughts, they listened to Callas's aching invocation to the 'chaste god' in the famous aria Casta Diva; the lovely soprano duet in Act II between Norma and her unwilling rival for Pollione's affections, Adalgisa; the two great duets between Norma and Pollione; and the stirring trio that ends the opera on a note of high drama.

When it was over at last, Browning's eyes were damp with emotion and for several moments, he could not speak. Struggling to regain his composure, he was embarrassed to find Matina gazing at him with a look of pure empathy, as if he were the one who now needed comforting. She, too, had been crying.

"You really love this, don't you?" she said softly. He nodded, not confident of his ability to speak. "I understand why," she said. "It's lovely. I had no idea the music would be so moving. Thank you for sharing it with me."

Brushing his eyes, Browning took a deep breath. "I'm sorry," he said, with a rueful smile. "You must think me feeble-minded for getting all weepy over music."

"No," protested Matina quietly. "I admire a man who isn't afraid to let his emotions show. Much of the problem with men is that they bottle up their feelings, as if they're afraid to let anyone know that they're vulnerable, as if by being human they're somehow less than men.

"That's such bullshit," she added, with a sudden vehemence that caught Browning by surprise.

"Men acknowledge only one emotion," she continued fiercely, staring past him as if she'd forgotten he was there. "Anger — they're good at anger. Apart from that, most are emotional cripples. To them, kindness and compassion are weaknesses, sorrow is something you never acknowledge, and love is a flag of convenience unfurled only to legitimize lust."

The pain that fuelled Matina's words tore at Browning's heart. He wanted to reach out to her, assure her that she was mistaken, that men were not all as she described. But something, perhaps an apprehension of hypocrisy, made him hesitate. For was he not himself guilty of many of the offences she had enumerated? Had he not pulled a draw-string over his feelings, burying his sorrows and hoarding his compassion? Did he not limit his own displays of emotion to the safe, second-hand sanctuary of the tragic arts?

He had long consoled himself with the thought that his passion for Callas was purer, and hence more virtuous, than the necessarily flawed and messy relationships between real, breathing human beings. But he saw now that this was an elaborate fantasy, carefully nurtured to justify his withdrawal from life. By constructing a parallel universe with Callas at its core, Browning had sheltered himself from the whims and vagaries of the world around him. By responding with such feeling to Callas's music, he'd found a way to express his emotional turmoil without risk.

But risk is the essence of true emotion. Love is a leap into the unknowable, with no sure landing in sight. Compassion begets involvement, with unpredictable consequences. Outrage risks confrontation and conflict. Sorrow flows from loss. Risk is inherent in every honest human emotion. Not since the humiliation of his marriage had Browning dared to risk anything substantial, preferring the safe emotion that flowed from his CD player to the real thing. But now, sitting in Matina's apartment, against a backdrop of death and ruin and anger, he felt ready, even eager, to risk again.

"What you say is true, Matina," he said, jumping restlessly to his feet. Her head jerked at the sound of his voice, as if reminded of his presence. "Many men act as if their feelings are enemies, to be suppressed at all cost. I should know; I am one of them. Sure, a Callas aria can make me weep, but that's art. Life is another matter entirely."

Matina said nothing, so Browning continued. "I was married about 10 years ago — it was over before it began — and since then, I have given life a wide berth. I was determined never to be hurt again, and there are only two ways to be sure of that — withdraw or die." Browning's lips puckered into a small, pained smile. "I didn't have the guts to die, so I withdrew."

Matina was watching him carefully now, her eyes focused tightly on his face. "But I've been kidding myself. Withdrawal is just another form of death, only slower. It's safe, yes, but it is the safety of the grave. I'm sick of safety. I want to live."

"You may have had enough safety," Matina said quietly, "but I crave it. You've lived too little, but I've lived too much. My daughter is dead, Bliss," she said, pronouncing the words with an emphasis that made it clear she found them unbelievable. "She was only two years old. The police won't even let me bury her until they're finished their investigation. That's real. That's life. Is that what you want?"

Browning returned her gaze but said nothing. There was nothing he could say. He could hardly tell her that he, with her, felt more alive than he ever had. She wouldn't understand. He wasn't sure that he did.

"I want to know you," he said at last. "I want to know everything about you. Will you tell me?"

She hesitated, perhaps weighing whether she had the strength to undertake such a journey into memory. "Okay, Bliss Browning," she said after several seconds. She straightened in her chair, as if shaking off a weight, and furrowed her brow. "Now, where to begin."

"At the beginning, of course," offered Browning.

"Alright, then," she said softly. "At the beginning."

CHAPTER 15

"I WAS BORN IN ONE OF THE MOST DESOLATE PLACES ON EARTH. IF you've never seen the Mani, it's difficult to understand just how barren it is. The Mani peninsula is like a long, bony finger that separates the Ionian Sea from the Aegean. It's as far removed from an earthly paradise as you can imagine.

"The whole peninsula is dominated by the Taygetus Massif, which runs down its spine like a fortress — a fortress so impenetrable that the outside world barely left a mark on the place until this century. Mount Taygetus itself is enormous, second only to Mount Olympus among Greek mountains. Further south, the pine trees that soften the mountains in the north give way to stark, sun-blasted rock, where no living thing survives. For the final 40 or 50 kilometres to the sea, the mountains are a huge grey mass, scorched and ravaged by heat in summer and icy winds in winter. They are close to what I imagine Hell to be. In fact, the mythical entrance to Hades is at Cape Tenaro, at the Mani's southern tip.

"Those who live in the Mani cling to the coast, along the narrow dry plain that separates the mountains from the sea on the west, or around the few bays that offer sanctuary along the east coast. But it is a harsh life, offering little more than survival to even the most intrepid. The ground is stony and infertile, mostly useless for growing crops. In a few places, people have somehow persuaded olive trees to take root, or nurtured a few stalks of corn or wheat, but only nettles, thistles and prickly pears thrive. And rocks are everywhere — you can't walk two paces without stepping around them or on them. They are the only thing the Mani has in abundance.

"In summer, the sun broils this poor land like meat on a grill. People's skin turns as black and leathery as the hide of an ox. In the middle of the day, the heat is so intense that it's sometimes hard to breathe; work is impossible. The best option is to try to sleep until the sun drops and conditions are bearable again, but even that is often hopeless in the baking heat.

"Weeks pass between rainfalls. What little rain does fall is hoarded like gold. It is a paradox: all around the rocky coastline is the sea, with its bountiful supply of water useless for human consumption, yet the land is as dusty and dry as a desert. It is as if God is mocking us.

"As if all this were not enough, the people who live in this harsh land, the Maniots, made life even more difficult by warring among themselves. Blood feuds fuelled by rivalries between powerful clans were common until early this century. These feuds even shaped the architecture of the area. The tower houses that you find in every village — tall stone buildings built to repel attack — are the legacy of those murderous times. Most are empty and crumbling now, though some are being restored for tourists, who have started to come now.

"But when I was born, visitors were rare and the poverty was unrelenting. My father and mother moved from Montreal to Areopoli, the Mani's principal town, not long before I was born. I've never understood why. My father was always vague when I asked what possessed him to move to such a god-forsaken place. He'd only say that the winters in Canada were unbearable and that he missed his homeland. But Greece is full of beautiful places where life is so much easier than in the Mani, I'd say; why come here? And he'd always answer: 'I feel safe here.' Ironic, in light of what happened later.

"My birth gave their lives new purpose. And they were good, loving parents. I do not recall my father, during the years that God granted him, ever lifting his hand against me; the discipline, such as it was, fell to my mother, who was scarcely more severe. Like most children, I could behave badly — once, I remember, I sat down in the town square and screamed and kicked my feet until my mother bought me a sweet I wanted — but my parents were too delighted by my existence to be truly stern.

"I don't remember much about my earliest years; just a general impression of being loved and happy. Even though my father had no steady job, we were comparatively well off because of the money he'd saved from working in Canada. We owned a modest house on the edge of town, and kept a few goats and chickens in our yard. These provided a steady supply of eggs, milk, feta cheese and, from time to time, a special dinner. Mother planted a small garden and grew tomatoes, chickpeas, onions and garlic for the larder.

"Father picked up odd jobs around town, everything from construction work to harvesting the few crops that grew in the area. That brought in a few drachmas. But the thing he enjoyed most was crewing with one of the fishing boats that sailed out of Limeni, Areopoli's port, just north of town. When he returned, he'd always have a box of fresh fish in his arms. And let me tell you, there are few things more delicious than freshly caught fish, drenched in olive oil and lemon juice and grilled.

"It was a simple life, I suppose, but not an unpleasant one. I had playmates — not a lot, because even then most young people left for greener pastures as soon as they were of age — but enough to keep loneliness at bay. When my friends were unavailable, I could always read a book — my parents brought boxes of books in English back from Canada with them — or listen to a record. We had a fairly modern record player, though primitive by today's standards, and my parents loved a wide range of music, from big-band jazz and balladeers to traditional Greek songs and classical music.

"And, of course, I had the Mani itself, a fantastic playground for a child. One of my earliest memories — I must have been about four — is of my father taking my mother and I out on a fishing boat with him. He had borrowed the boat for a few hours, and was anxious to show us what our home looked like from the water. I can vividly recall images from that trip: holding my mother's hand tightly so I would not fall overboard; the luminous turquoise of the water near shore; the looming presence of the mountains, with their tops shrouded in cloud. I suppose it was the first time I understood that there was a world beyond Areopoli.

"But for most of my childhood, the outside world might just as well have been on Mars, for all I knew of it. Once they settled in the Mani, my parents had little desire to leave, even briefly. Only rarely would my father get on a bus — we had no car, since there was little need of one in Areopoli — and strike off for Kalamata, a metropolis that seemed to me as distant and awesome as Athens itself. Usually, these trips were prompted by the need to purchase something not available in our little town.

"One day, father returned from one of these exotic outings carrying a large box; it was heavy, too, judging from how he staggered under its weight. He carried it into our living room and set in on the floor with a sigh of gratitude. I was beside myself with excitement. What could it be? As mother and I watched, he sliced open the flaps with a knife and pulled out . . . a television set! It was the first TV we had ever owned, and one of just a handful in the town. It became my window on the world, introducing me to things — beautiful, horrible and banal — that I had never imagined before: figure skating, ballet, Western movies, traffic jams, haute couture, skiing, war, famine, death.

"But amazing as that television world was, it had stiff competition from the stories told of the Mani itself. For this was a land of myth and legend as magical and fearsome as anything the outside world could offer. Old men sipping coffee in the town square were delighted to dandle youngsters on their knees and fill their heads with tales of Gorgons and Centaurs, of the magnificent Beys who ruled with an iron fist, of the dolphins who rescued men from the sea and the nereids who enchanted sailors.

"Of all the stories, it was those about nereids that captivated me most as a child, perhaps because of their grace and benevolence. For unlike most creatures from mythology, they rarely mean to harm anyone, though their fickle passions could cause much inadvertent misery. Nereids live in water, mostly freshwater streams, springs and fountains. But in the Mani, the sea is their domain, as well. Their forms are feminine and of unearthly beauty, a beauty that never fades during their thousand-year lifespan. They dress in white and gold, and are skilled at cooking and at spinning flimsy fabrics. I remember a neighbour tasting a dish prepared by my mother and offering her highest praise: 'Cooked by a nereid!' It's an expression that once was common, but is heard less often now that the Mani is more a part of the modern world.

"Nereids are sexually voracious, and any man who crosses their path — especially if he is young and brave — risks being carried off to a secret grotto for carnal pleasures. But their wanton nature makes them incapable of fidelity. Before long, their ardour cools and they're off in search of another, leaving their jilted lovers melancholy and prone to illness. If a mortal falls in love with a nereid, the only way to keep her from running off is to seize and hide her kerchief. She'll turn into frightening shapes in her efforts to recover the kerchief, but if the mortal is resolute, she'll eventually return to her natural form and submit to his wishes.

"Nereids are drawn to pretty children, and this, too, can lead to harm. They are known to abduct youngsters from their cradles and substitute their own sickly offspring, who usually die of sorrow at being abandoned. Sometimes children run away with them and dance for days, an experience from which they rarely recover. Even goats and sheep can fall under their spell, deserting the flock and wasting away.

"As a child, I yearned more than anything to meet a nereid. I was a plain, awkward child and their mixture of beauty and freedom was hopelessly attractive to me. I used to stand in front of my bedroom window, gazing out to sea, hoping that a nereid would come for me. But needless to say, I was always disappointed.

"Then one day, when I was 12 years old, I was walking along the cliffs overlooking the sea just outside of town. Dolphins had been spotted off the coast, and I was searching the waters in hope of seeing one. All at once, I became aware of a form rising from the water below, just off shore. But it wasn't a dolphin; it was unlike anything I had ever seen before. It was dressed in a diaphanous white gown, and long golden tresses flowed like honey from its head to the top of its legs. As I watched, unable to move or say anything, the creature raised its head from the water and looked directly at me. Its face was astonishingly lovely — it took my breath away to see it — and though it said nothing to me, I distinctly heard these words: 'I have taken him. He is safe.' Then, as quickly as it appeared, the creature was gone.

"That night, some people from the town came to our door and spoke to my mother. I was in the next room, but even from there, her cry of anguish chilled my blood. I rushed to the door and saw mother crumpled on the floor, sobbing. Two women were bent over her, comforting her and trying to help her to her feet. Several men were there as well, looking grim. One of them noticed me and took me aside. I'll never forget his words. "There's been an accident," he said. "A squall came out of nowhere and capsized your father's fishing boat. Most of those on board were rescued. But your father has disappeared. We're searching for him — there's still hope."

"But I knew they'd never find him, because the nereids had taken him. And I was right — they never found his body. Though I was devastated at his disappearance from my life, I was comforted by the knowledge that he was not really dead, just in some other world in the company of the nereids. For years, I expected him to show up one day at the door when the nereids finally tired of him and allowed him to return to his old life. But he never did; I presumed that they loved him too much to let him go.

"Of course, I could never share any of this with my mother. It would only have upset her, and she wouldn't have believed me anyway. After my father disappeared, she seemed to age a decade overnight. She discarded every colourful piece of clothing she owned — and she had been a stylish dresser by Mani standards — and wore only the traditional black of the widow. To this day, that's all she will wear. For her, it is a sign of respect for my father, but you don't see

Greek men shrouding their bodies in black and withdrawing from life when their wives die. In fact, most are anxious to remarry as soon as they decently can. But not Greek women, and certainly not my mother.

"Our lives became harder after that. Though we still had some savings, father had no life insurance and we had no income. I was too young to work and mother was getting older. Besides, what few jobs there were, almost without exception, went to men. The Mani was a very traditional society.

"We struggled by for a few years, sinking deeper into poverty as our savings shrank. We became experts at the art of making a little go a long way. Sometimes, the chickpeas and onions in our garden were all we had to eat. We went years without buying new clothes; everything we wore we made ourselves, or picked up second-hand. Yet difficult though our lives were, we were not miserable, not really. The saving grace was that we had each other. Mother had always been loving and attentive, but after father disappeared, I became her reason for living — no daughter ever had a more devoted mother.

"As for me, losing father made me treasure mother all the more. After all, she was my sole living relative. I soaked up all the love she had to give and returned it in equal measure. I suppose I was looking for security, something solid to hang onto in what suddenly seemed a frighteningly changeable universe.

"Still, by the time I was 18, our financial situation was desperate. The last of our savings was gone, and we were surviving, though just barely, on the charity of our neighbours. I needed a job so badly I could think of little else. Even when I was asleep, my dreams were filled with images of me shuffling despondently from place to place, begging for work. Of course, there was little available in Areopoli, and I began to think about leaving for Kalamata, or even Athens, anywhere I might be able to find a job. But I hated the idea of leaving mother alone; she was nearly 60, and already showing signs of the memory loss and disorientation that would later afflict her.

"To that point in my life, I hadn't had much contact with boys. Like most teenage girls, I had daydreamed about finding the perfect man, falling in love and marrying, and raising a family. But the old-fashioned values of the Mani itself, where such modern-day practices as dating were mostly unknown, conspired against romance.

"Besides, in my early teen years, I was no prize. I was gangly and awkward, and that made me very self-conscious and shy. All that began to change around the time I turned 17, though. My torso started to catch up with my arms and legs. I became almost graceful. Of course, my mother had always told me I was attractive, but I discounted that as a mother's blindness. But other people started to remark on my transformation from ugly duckling to swan, and I became aware of appreciative looks from the young men in town.

"One of the young men who suddenly seemed interested in me was Andreas Mourtzinos, the only son of one of the most prosperous families in Areopoli. It was well-known that the Mourtzinos family was related to the billionaire shipping tycoon, Aristotle Onassis — they were distant cousins, I think. When Onassis died, his will stipulated that every relation should receive a portion of his enormous fortune. For the Mourtzinos family, this amounted to about a million drachmas, an insignificant amount to someone like Onassis, but a huge sum in a place like Areopoli.

"The Mourtzinos family invested the money wisely, and by the time Andreas was a young man, it had grown to three or four times its original size. Andreas himself, however, was less of a success. Perhaps because of the money, or some inbred character flaw, he had little ambition. He seemed content to spend his days lounging in one of the cafes on the main square, drinking ouzo and coffee and arguing with other men who haunted the ouzeri.

"But while his laziness dismayed his parents, Andreas was considered the most eligible bachelor in town by all the girls I knew. His family's wealth was part of the attraction, of course, but there was much more to him than money. He was slim and athletic, with dark, feverish eyes and a wide, sensual mouth that always seemed fixed part way between a smile and a sneer. He was brimming with bravado; he didn't walk, he swaggered. And he was wild — wild in the way that young girls find fatally attractive.

"His stunts were legendary. Once someone stole the bell from the church tower in town — no mean feat, considering that the thief had to scale a 30-metre tower and somehow detach and lower a 200-kilogram bell. There was a huge uproar until Andreas finally admitted that he, and several other idle young men, had abducted the bell and dropped it into the sea near town. The bell was never recovered, and the church replaced it with electronic chimes, paid for in part by the Mourtzinos family.

"Then there was the Great Car Epidemic. One day, not a single car in town would start; it was as if a mysterious illness had afflicted everything automotive. The next morning, people awoke to find a pile of engine parts in the central square. Andreas and his cronies had removed them from every car under cover of darkness.

"Adults strongly disapproved of such exploits, of course, but they only made Andreas even more attractive to my girlfriends and I. There was something a bit dangerous about him, a bit crazed, that was very appealing to impressionable girls living dull lives in an isolated small town.

"Andreas could have had pretty well any young woman he wanted, and as it turned out, he wanted many of them. He flirted outrageously, which secretly delighted the young women. But Areopoli's respectable citizens were scandalized. This was still a very traditional society, remember. Even the idea of sex outside of marriage was unthinkable, let alone the act itself. Yet unconfirmed rumours circulated that he had impregnated one or two young women, and at least one girl I knew did suddenly leave town, never to return.

"So as you can imagine, when he finally turned his attentions to me, I responded with a mixture of pleasure and alarm. He was 25, a full seven years older than me, and if the rumours were true, all too experienced. I was as innocent and naive as a nun. I was flattered by his interest in me — more than flattered, to be honest, because he was one of the young men I had fantasized about. But at the same time, his reputation made me wary. I was quite prepared to love him, but I did not want to be just another one of his conquests.

"So when he first came calling, I was cool to him and rebuffed his advances, though it tore at my heart to do so. He was unaccustomed to resistance from women, and my refusal only seemed to inflame his passion for me. He redoubled his efforts to woo me, inundating me with flowers, sweets and other gifts. For a girl unused to luxury of any sort, it was a heady experience. Yet still I resisted him, not out of coyness, but because I was not yet convinced that his intentions were honourable. I even told him as much. 'Andreas,' I said, 'I am not like the other girls you use and throw away. When I fall in love, it will be with a man who wants to share his life with me, who will provide for me and be a good father to our children. Nothing you have done in your life so far makes me think that you are that man. You have no job, you bounce from woman to woman, you spend your days drinking in the square. You are a bad risk.'

"He said nothing, but looked at me thoughtfully. The next day, he appeared on my doorstep to announce that he had found a job as a clerk at the town hall. 'It is my first step to convince you that I am worthy of your love,' he said. I have to admit that I was touched, and at last I dared to believe that love between us might be possible. That day I kissed him for the first time, and I was surprised by the ardour between us. I guess I hadn't admitted, even to myself, how desperately I wanted him.

"Even so, I was still cautious. A leopard doesn't change its spots, after all, and I wanted more evidence that his new behaviour would last. Over the next couple of years, Andreas worked diligently at his job and shunned the cafes that used to be his second home. Everyone in town noticed the change, and there was much talk that I had inspired it.

"Andreas and I were spending more and more time together, and always he was on his best behaviour. He would spend whole evenings in the parlour, talking to my mother and me, and charming us both. And his generosity knew no bounds. He knew we had little to eat, and would deliver bags of fresh fruit and vegetables, cheese, even meat and fish, and insist that we accept them. We tried to say no, but our grumbling bellies made it difficult not to accept his gifts. And as my suspicions about him faded, the love that I had suppressed flowered and grew by leaps and bounds.

"On my twenty-first birthday, Andreas took me down by the cliffs at the edge of the sea, where I had seen the nereid the day my father disappeared. We stopped and gazed out across the bay to the hills of the Messinian peninsula, which were barely visible as ghostly outlines on the horizon. Then Andreas took my hands and looked at me with his great dark eyes. 'Matina,' he said, 'you once told me that you could only love a man who wanted to spend his life with you, care for you and raise your children. Perhaps when we first met, I was not that man. But I hope you can believe that I am now. My parents are delighted by the change in me and have promised us a wedding gift of a million drachmas if we marry. With that, your mother can live in comfort for the rest of her life. I love you dearly, and I want more than anything to be your husband. Please, Matina, marry me.'

"How could I resist? This man had mended his dissolute ways to prove his love for me. Now he was offering me not only his love, but salvation for my mother, to whom I owed everything good in my life. And I truly did love him, more than I had ever believed possible. I couldn't have been happier. I felt I was the luckiest person alive.

"We were married six months later, a big church wedding that most of the town attended. Andreas moved in with mother and I, and for a while, everything was as wonderful as I had imagined. Andreas's job provided a modest but steady income, and the generous cash gift from his parents allowed us to refurbish and re-equip the house. For the first time in years, mother and I didn't have to wonder where our next meal would come from.

"And Andreas was a marvelous lover, introducing me with gentle skill to the pleasures of my body. Within months I was pregnant. I was pleased, of course, but Andreas greeted my pregnancy with something close to ecstasy. He talked ceaselessly about his plans for his son (he was convinced the baby would be a boy). When I in fact delivered him a son, you can imagine his joy. It seemed he didn't stop smiling for weeks. We called him Petro, after Petrobey Mavromichalis, the

Maniot leader who helped to free Greece from Turkish rule in the 19th century.

"The baby was beautiful, as Andreas knew he would be. So beautiful, in fact, that I remember feeling uneasy, worried that the nereids might find him irresistible. I know it sounds absurd, but remember, as a child I believed that nereids had taken my father. What was to stop them from doing the same to my son?

"As it turned out, my fears were justified. Not of the nereids, who so far as I know stayed away, but of something even more dangerous and unpredictable: pneumonia. It started as a quiet little cough and slight fever. I was worried, but it seemed minor. Within a couple of days, the cough had turned into a harsh bark so awful it hurt every time I heard it. Then, with appalling speed, his tiny lungs filled with fluid and his breathing became laboured. The town doctor took one look at him and said he should be hospitalized at once. The nearest hospital was in Kalamata, 80 kilometres away. Andreas drove over the mountain roads like a madman, but Petro died in my arms just before we reached the city. He was just seven months old.

"Everything changed after that. The baby's death was a blow from which Andreas never recovered. He lost interest in everything — his job, his family, me — and withdrew into his own private world. Within weeks, he had quit his job and returned to the cafes, spending his time and a growing piece of his inheritance on drink and his layabout friends. When I'd question him about it, he'd wave me away and say, 'what difference does it make?'

"Even worse, his attitude toward me changed dramatically. He blamed me for the baby's death, saying I should have done something sooner. I didn't need that — I was already tortured with guilt — and we'd have terrible quarrels, literally screaming at each other. He never hit me then, but I could tell he wanted to. The hatred was plain on his face. At a time when I needed his comfort and love, he offered only blame and rejection. I was devastated.

"It was as if whatever was hopeful and optimistic in Andreas died with Petro. Somehow, my love had lifted him for a time out of his life of idleness, but Petro's death plunged him back into that world with a vengeance. The loss of our son reaffirmed his cynicism about life, its pointlessness and random unfairness.

"His money, which had once seemed such a blessing, became a curse. Stripped of both the will and the need to earn his own way in the world, Andreas could indulge his worst instincts. And that's just what he did. He spent more and more time drinking and carousing with his friends. Often, I wouldn't see him from morning until he fell into our bed late at night. Sometimes, in his drunkenness, he would paw me and demand sex. But I always refused. I would have welcomed his love, but this drunken lust repelled me.

"One night, he came home stinking of ouzo and made his standard demands. As usual, I said no. But this time, there was a crazed look in his eyes when I refused. 'Who are you to refuse me?' he roared. 'I'm your husband. You belong to me!'

"'Then act like a husband, instead of a drunken lout!' I said, and something inside him seemed to snap. He let out an unearthly moan of rage and anguish, and leapt on top of me, pinning me to the bed. Then he struck me, hard, on the face. It was the first time he ever hit me, but it was not to be the last. I was stunned by the blow, but he wasn't through yet. He seized my nightgown in his hands, tore the fabric from my body and raped me.

"He left me alone for a long time after that. I think even he knew that he had gone too far, though he did not apologize or change his behaviour. It was after this that I first started hearing whispers that he was seeing other women. I'd confront him with the rumours, and he wouldn't even bother to deny them. 'What I do is my own affair,' he'd tell me.

"Why did I put up with it? It's a fair question — obviously, I should have left him years ago. But you have to understand that divorce in Greece is rare, and for someone from the Mani, it was unthinkable. You made your match, for good or ill, and lived with the consequences.

"And there was another consideration: my mother. She was growing more and more confused as her dementia worsened, and she needed me there to care for her. Even though Andreas wasn't working, his inheritance gave us enough income to live in reasonable comfort. That would be lost if I left him. How would I look after mother then? If it had just been me, perhaps I could have summoned the courage to leave earlier. But I couldn't when I knew that by doing so, I would be condemning mother to poverty.

"And so we continued, with Andreas slipping deeper into the abyss and mother and I coping as best we could. Andreas came and went as he pleased, and when he couldn't get satisfaction elsewhere, he'd get it forcibly from me. This happened more and more as time passed, always accompanied by a beating or threats of violence. Eventually, I stopped resisting. It was easier just to submit passively and let him have his way. Sometimes he'd hit me anyway and call me a whore. In a sense, I suppose he was right.

"This continued for years. I was almost reconciled to it. This was my life. Then, about three years ago, I became pregnant again after one of these marital rapes. For a few months, while I was big, Andreas softened towards me. At times, particularly when we were talking about the baby I was carrying, he was almost tender. He'd get a wistful look on his face and say we should treat this child as a fresh start, a chance to reclaim what was lost after Petro died. He'd insist that he was going to clean up his act, get a job. Sometimes I almost believed him.

"But after Vasilio was born, he quickly lost interest again. I think it might have been different if the baby had been a boy. But girls in the Mani are considered more of a burden than a blessing, useful only for breeding more boys. It's an attitude that goes back to the days when blood feuds were a way of life, and no family could have too many fighters.

"In any case, Andreas fell back into his old patterns and paid little attention to his new daughter. But she was the consolation of my life, a reason for enduring the pain of this world. As I held her small body next to mine, I imagined her future. I was determined to make it as good as possible for her.

"Andreas saw how much I loved her, and it seemed to irritate him. 'If you paid even half as much attention to me as you do to that child,' he'd say, 'you'd be a proper wife.' Of course, he didn't really want my attention. What he wanted was for me to share his misery. He could no longer abide any sign of happiness on my part, and Vasilio made me very, very happy.

"I was prepared to go on indefinitely like this. I figured I could endure Andreas's cruelty now that my purpose in life was clear at last. But what I didn't know was that the one dependable thing in our lives — the thing that made this whole dysfunctional arrangement possible — was about to change. Without telling me, Andreas had been eating away at the principal of his inheritance for years to finance his drinking and partying. Now, he finally admitted, the money was almost gone.

"As usual, he blamed me. 'If I didn't have to support you and that demented mother of yours,' he'd say, 'I'd still have plenty of money. And now there's another useless mouth to feed.'

"For a while, we survived on the largesse of Andreas's parents. They were as disgusted by his behaviour as anyone, but they couldn't allow their son's family to starve; the shame would have been too great. Andreas's reputation in town was so bad that nobody would give him work, so Mr. Mourtzinos pulled a few strings and got him a government job in Athens. It paid quite well and would let him support his family properly. But his father told Andreas this was his last chance; he could count on no further help from his parents.

"The thought of leaving the Mani, where I'd spent my whole life, for a huge city like Athens was terrifying. But we had little choice. We could stay in Areopoli and starve or go to Athens and hope for a better future. I wanted mother to come, of course, but Andreas wouldn't hear of it, and mother, in her lucid moments, was against the idea as well. She said she was too old to start over again someplace else. Andreas' parents offered to let her live rent-free in a small house they owned just around the corner from their home. I didn't like to leave her, but I knew they'd make sure that she was cared for. And it meant she could sell her own house and live off the proceeds in reasonable comfort.

"We arrived in Athens just over six months ago. It was as overwhelming as I had imagined — full of people and noise and the most astonishing pollution. But I was surprised at how quickly I overcame my fears and embraced my new home. There was a current of energy and excitement running through the place that was entirely absent in the Mani, and I found it invigorating.

"Andreas reported for work at his new job, and things went well — for a few weeks. Then he started coming home later and later each night. He said he was just socializing with his work mates, but it wasn't long before he was out till dawn, and sometimes he didn't come home at all. When he was home, he was surly and demanding. And violent — he scared me all the time now. There was something new about his violence in Athens, a frenzy that wasn't there before. He would hit me for no reason, no reason at all, and when he wanted sex there was a cruelty to his methods that I hadn't seen before. He'd want me to do things to him, dreadful, degrading things that I'd never known people did to one another. It was then I realized: he was seeing prostitutes. That's who was teaching him his foul tricks.

"Even during the worst of this, Andreas still got up and went to work. Don't ask me how he did it. I used to wonder, but I was too frightened to ask him. But last month, after one of his all-night binges, he didn't get out of bed at the usual hour. I tried to wake him, but he just rolled over and buried his head deeper in the covers. 'Andreas,' I said, 'you've got to get up and go to work. It's late.' 'Doesn't matter,' he said, irritably. 'I'm quitting.' I don't know why I was surprised, but I was. I really didn't think that Andreas would walk away from this job, if only because there was nothing left for him to fall back on.

"I backed quietly out of the room and tiptoed to the telephone in the kitchen. My mind was racing . . . I was confused. I thought if I called Andreas's office and made an excuse for him, said he was sick and wouldn't be in, that I could buy some time and somehow salvage the situation. But when I phoned, his boss came on the line and said Andreas had been fired. He said he had been showing up to work hours late or not at all, and in grim shape. 'There's a limit to what we can tolerate,' he said. 'I don't care how many friends he has in high places.'

"I remember putting the phone down and thinking: 'It's over.' I had stuck with Andreas for nearly 20 years, hoping against reason that he would right himself. I had lost my own self-respect in the process, but now I finally had to acknowledge that it was never going to happen. Andreas was doomed. If my child and I were going to make it through this life, we were going to have to do it without him.

"Somewhat to my surprise, I felt enormous relief at this decision, as if by taking it I had shed a burden. I was unsure of myself, of course, and more than a little afraid of what the future might hold, but it was liberating to act after years of passive suffering.

"I didn't immediately tell Andreas of my decision. I was frightened of how he might react, and besides, I needed to make some plans before breaking with him. I started to look around for work, and within a few weeks I found a part-time job at a bakery. It wasn't much of a job, but I was thrilled. It was my ticket to a better life. I found a small apartment that I thought I could afford, and prepared to tell Andreas of my decision.

"I'll never forget the night I told him. He was broke, so instead of going drinking or whoring, he stayed around the apartment, tormenting me. He wanted sex, of course. I tried to ignore him, but he was persistent, grabbing at me every chance he could. Suddenly I had a vision that chilled my blood, a vision of this violent, twisted man and my daughter, Vasilio. I knew that he was capable of anything, and I knew that for my daughter's safety, if nothing else, I had to get away from him as soon as possible.

"Suddenly I felt calm and sure of myself. I turned and looked him in the eye. 'Andreas,' I said, 'I'm leaving you. Our marriage is over.' He laughed a little uncertainly, and sneered, 'Where would you go? I'm all you have in the world.'

"'You're wrong,' I said. 'I have Vasilio, and she means more to me than anyone.' I told him I'd found a job and an apartment and would be moving out as soon as possible.

"The colour drained from his face. 'You can't do this to me,' he whispered. 'You're all I have.' He sounded so pathetic, I almost felt sorry for him. But then I remembered all that he'd done to me, the threat he posed to my daughter, and I hardened my heart. 'I'm sorry,' I said, 'but I'm already gone.'

"That seemed to jar him out of his stupor, and his face flushed with anger. For a minute, I thought he might attack me, even kill me. He was shaking with fury. But instead, he stormed out of the apartment without another word. It was the last time I saw him alive.

"The next day, I left Vasilio with a neighbour while I made arrangements to move to our new apartment. While I was out, Andreas appeared, broke down the neighbour's door and took Vasilio. You know the rest of the story.

"He killed Vasilio because he knew that was the thing, the one thing, he could do to hurt me. He killed himself because he was in a trap of his own making and saw no way out. And he left me alive to suffer the consequences, because he knew nothing could be crueler."

CHAPTER 16

NORMAN PUGSLEY'S FEET HURT. HE'D SPENT MUCH OF THE DAY tramping through central Athens, fruitlessly showing a snapshot of Bliss Browning to a succession of hotel desk clerks. None could remember a guest who looked anything like the morose man in the picture. Not surprising, thought Pugsley, resentfully flexing his toes. Browning is such a nonentity it would be surprising if anyone could remember him.

Pugsley groaned as a spasm shot up his right leg. He had to get off his dogs before they really started to howl. Spotting a kafenio across the street, he hobbled to the door and stepped inside. Though it was mid-afternoon, the place was nearly full of boisterous Greek men, all apparently with nothing better to do than laze about swilling tiny cups of strong dark coffee, half-litre bottles of beer and a milky liquid that Pugsley could not identify. Their tumultuous presence irritated Pugsley, who badly wanted a quiet drink in peaceful surroundings. Grumpily, he found an empty chair at a small round wooden table and waited to be served.

After several long minutes, during which Pugsley's thirst and annoyance grew exponentially, a lanky young waiter ambled over and nodded expectantly. "About time," Pugsley muttered under his breath. "I'll have Scotch, straight up," he said, scowling at the waiter.

"No Scotch," the waiter replied, matter-of-factly.

"No Scotch?" repeated Pugsley, fixing the waiter with an incredulous stare. "What kind of bar is this? Can you make me a martini, then?"

"No martini."

"Mother of suffering Christ!" Pugsley cried. "What in hell do you have?"

"Beer. Ouzo. Metaxa." The waiter recited the brief list in a bored, let's-get-on-with-it tone of voice that grated on Pugsley's nerves. These people, he thought.

"Hell of a selection, pal," he said, with what he hoped was sarcasm obvious enough to cross cultural barriers. Then, with a theatrical sigh designed to convey long-suffering exasperation, he fixed the waiter with his best managing-editor glare and said gruffly: "Better bring me a beer, then." The waiter nodded curtly and was turning to leave when Pugsley had second thoughts. "Wait," he called. "What the hell, bring me one of each. I'm not sure beer will be enough."

The waiter shrugged and, with a sideways comment that provoked snickers from a group of men at the next table, sauntered off to get the drinks. Pugsley slipped off his shoes and flexed his throbbing arches. "Jesus, they never used to ache like this. Was a time when I could have walked the legs off any man around. Must be gettin' old, Norm, gettin' old. Or maybe it's just this effn country . . ."

The waiter returned with four glasses and a bottle of beer. One glass was empty and another was filled with water. The other two each contained a small amount of liquid, one amber in colour and the second clear. The waiter smoothly set the four glasses and the beer on Pugsley's table and turned to leave.

"Not so fast, buddy," Pugsley called. The waiter spun and looked at him quizzically. "The beer and the water I can handle, but you'll have to help me out with these," Pugsley said, gesturing at the two unidentified fluids. The waiter gave him the sort of look Pugsley usually reserved for simpleton reporters. He pointed to the amber liquid.

"Metaxa brandy," he said gravely. "Drink straight up." Then he picked up the glass containing the clear liquid. "Ouzo," he intoned. "Put in water."

"I should put the, uh, orzo in the water?" Pugsley asked, confused.

"No, no, no. Put water in ouzo," the waiter instructed. "Like this." He picked up the glass of water and poured it into the glass of clear liquid until it was nearly half full. Immediately, white clouds began to form. Within seconds the liquid had turned completely white. It looked exactly like skimmed milk.

"Holy shit!" cried Pugsley, fascinated. "Lookit that, willya?"

The waiter smiled. "You try," he encouraged, handing Pugsley the glass containing the opaque liquid.

Pugsley accepted it doubtfully. Lifting the glass to his nose, he took a cautious sniff. At once, a powerful odour of anisette assaulted his nostrils. "Licorice!" he exclaimed. "Smells just like licorice." The waiter nodded expectantly, and Pugsley realized that the four men at the next table were following the proceedings with keen interest.

"What the hell," Pugsley said, lifting the glass to his audience, "down the old hatcheroo."

Eager to impress his audience, Pugsley took a large swallow of the ouzo — rather too large, in fact. The liquor's strong flavour burned in his throat, and he started to choke.

"Christ!" sputtered Pugsley, wiping his mouth with his sleeve and eyeing the ouzo with new respect. "Stuff packs a wallop." The Greeks nudged one another and smirked. "It's not bad, though. Yeah, I kinda like it. Let me try the other stuff, whatsit, mariah?"

"Metaxa," corrected the waiter.

"Whatever," said Pugsley, lifting the glass to his lips. The Greeks at the next table leaned forward expectantly. More cautiously this time, Pugsley took a sip of the brandy. It was as rough as the waterfront district in a harbour town.

"Interesting," Pugsley said, suppressing a grimace. "Kinda prefer the orzo, though."

"Ouzo," corrected the waiter. The Greeks snorted.

"You from America?" one of the olive-skinned drinkers at the next table asked Pugsley.

"Christ, no," he replied, offended. "I'm from Ottawa."

"What's an Ottawa?"

"Ottawa, man, Ottawa," barked Pugsley, simultaneously amused and annoyed at the same time. "It's only the fuckin' capital of Canada. You have heard of Canada, haven't you?"

"Yes, Canada," smiled the man with the olive complexion. "Montreal, Toronto, Vancouver."

"That's right, that's right," encouraged Pugsley. "And Ottawa. Ottawa's the capital."

The man looked at his companions and shrugged. "Sorry, I don't know this Ottawa."

Pugsley shook his head sorrowfully and took another gulp of ouzo. "Christ on a bicycle," he muttered.

"What you do in this Ottawa?" asked the man, whose skin, Pugsley now saw, was actually closer to brown than olive.

"I run the newspaper in town," he boasted. Hell, it's true. That dipstick Richter couldn't run a hundred-metre dash.

The brown-skinned man seemed impressed. There was something odd about his face, and Pugsley realized with a start that he had a glass eye. He quickly took another swig of ouzo, relishing the warm glow radiating from his midsection.

"What you doing here?" asked the one-eyed man.

"Here on assignment," said Pugsley, draining the ouzo. "Waiter," he cried, "better bring me another of those." He passed over his empty ouzo glass and took a long, cleansing draught of beer.

"On assignment?" prompted his interrogator, whose mouth, Pugsley noticed, tended to twist to the left when he spoke.

"Yeah, publisher sent me to find one of our employees. Bastard was supposed to go to Africa. Instead he comes here, not so much as a by-your-leave. Now I've got to track him down and haul him back to Ottawa."

Pugsley accepted a new glass of ouzo from the waiter and deftly poured in some water as if he'd been doing it all his life. He took a long satisfying swig of the beverage, holding the glass up for appreciative inspection when he was done. "Stuff's damn good," he enthused.

"How you gonna find the guy?" asked the crooked-faced man.

"Won't be easy," said Pugsley, "but if he can be found, I'm the guy who'll do it. Used to be a crackerjack investigative reporter before I got kicked upstairs. Ripped the lid off more stories than anyone in the business, I did. 'Page One Pugsley' — that's what they used to call me. Can you imagine? I mean, can you fuckin' imagine?" He emptied the glass of ouzo. "Waiter!" he bawled. "I need a goddamn refill here!"

The waiter grabbed a small bottle of ouzo and a pitcher of water and set them on Pugsley's table. "Help yourself," he said with a broad smile.

"Don't mind if I do," Pugsley replied amiably, pouring several ounces of the licorice liquor into his glass and filling it to the brim with water. "Bottoms up!"

"Any luck?" asked the man with the crooked face.

"Luck with what?" said Pugsley.

"Finding your man."

"Naaahhh. Been flashin' his picture all over town, but ain't nobody's seen him."

"Let's see," said the man, rising awkwardly from his chair. Pugsley saw at once that his left leg had been amputated just below the knee.

"Yow!" he cried, pointing to the missing limb. "How'd you lose that sucker?"

"What?" said the one-legged man, startled. "Oh, that. Fishing accident." He smiled. "A very long time ago." He hobbled over to Pugsley's table and sat down. "Let's see picture."

Pugsley fished out the shot of Browning, taken at work for his security pass. He had a typically vacant, moronic look on his face, Pugsley thought.

The brown-skinned, one-eyed, crooked-faced amputee studied the picture. "No, I'm sure I haven't seen him." He passed the picture to his friends and said something in rapid Greek. Pugsley poured another glass of ouzo.

There was an excited exclamation at the next table. Pugsley

glanced at his new friends to see what all the fuss was about, but for some reason, he was having trouble bringing their faces into focus.

"Whatzit?" he asked his horribly disabled companion. "Whaddar they sayin'?"

"Constantine thinks he saw your man. He took someone to train station the other day who looked just like him. They argued over fare."

Pugsley was suddenly alert — or as alert as a man who has consumed a quarter-litre of ouzo can be. "Does he know where he was goin'?" he managed to ask.

"Kalamata," said the blind cripple. "He said he was going to Kalamata."

"Where's that?" Pugsley demanded.

"In Peloponnese. Only short flight from Athens."

"Hah!" whooped Pugsley. "I knew I'd find you, Browning. You can run, but you can't fuckin' hide, buddy." Pugsley reached under the table and started fumbling for his shoes.

"Going somewhere?" asked the gimp.

"Airport," mumbled Pugsley, as if in a trance. "Gotta go to the airport. Fly to Kalamazoo."

"Plenty time for that tomorrow," his sightless friend said soothingly. "Tonight, we fix you up with sexy woman who make your dream come true. Hokay?"

Pugsley pondered this offer for a moment. Come to think of it, he didn't feel much like travelling just now. And a sexy woman sounded a whole lot better than an airport.

"Okay," he agreed. "Sexy woman it is."

"THE POLICE HAVE RELEASED THE BODIES." Matina's voice on the telephone was little more than a whisper.

"I know. They've been in touch with me, too. They say the investigation is closed. I'm free to go."

There was a long, shuddering sigh on the other end of the line. "Oh, Bliss." Matina sounded as if she were choking back a sob. "I'm sorry. All I can think about is Vasilio and the train and the collision . . ."

"Matina, stop," said Browning gently. "It's pointless to torture yourself like this."

"I know, I know. But what am I supposed to do? She was my whole world. What have I got to live for now?"

"Matina, for God's sake. Most of your life is still ahead of you. You've suffered a terrible blow, but time heals all wounds." *God,* thought Browning, *master of the trite cliché.*

"What would you know about it?" snapped Matina, unaccountably furious. "You've never lost someone you love." Matina's words cut into Browning with the bite of a bullwhip. "Love is risky, Bliss, and now I'm paying the price. But at least I was willing to take the risk. At least I didn't run away from the rest of the world."

Browning, stunned by her unprovoked attack, said nothing. There was really nothing to say. In the silence that followed, Matina's fury passed as quickly as it had flared. "I'm sorry, I'm sorry," she whispered, suddenly remorseful. "I don't know what got into me. I'm just so upset."

"Forget it," Browning replied, more roughly than he had intended, for Matina's attack had stung him. He thought of telling her more about his brief marriage. I have loved and lost, too, Matina, he thought. I have earned my own badge of honour on the battlefields of the heart. But there was enough truth in her accusations that he reigned in his turbulent emotions and changed the subject instead. "What will you do now?" he asked.

The muffled sobs and sniffles on the line testified to Matina's struggle to regain control. "I'm taking the bodies back to Areopoli for burial," she finally managed to gasp. "Athens is not their city — they're like aliens here. They should not have to spend eternity in a strange place. Not even Andreas deserves that."

"How will you get them there?" asked Browning, his hurt swept away by a wave of compassion for Matina.

"I've arranged space on the 11 a.m. train to Kalamata tomorrow.

Andreas's father and the priest will meet me there for the last part of the trip back to Areopoli."

"He's not joining you here?" Browning's mind rebelled at the idea of Matina being left to handle this grim but necessary task alone.

"He wanted to send someone — they all did — but I told him not to," she said in a small, wistful voice. "He's old and tires easily. It's a long, slow, bumpy trip from Athens to Kalamata — it would exhaust him, and I'd just end up taking care of him, too."

"Maybe," said Browning, jumping to his feet as an inspired idea began to take shape, "but I hate the idea of you making that trip alone. Look, Matina, I have to go to Kalamata too. Let me travel with you. I don't have any experience at this sort of thing, but at least I can offer some support."

"You don't have to do that, Bliss," protested Matina.

"Matina, I want to. Really."

There was a short pause. "If you really don't mind," she said, in a small but relieved voice. "I don't know why you're being so kind when I've just been so cruel to you."

"Let's just say I could use some support, too."

HARRISON HOWARD WAS PROOFING the main books page for the coming Sunday's *Advocate* when the phone rang. "Howard, books," he answered automatically.

"Hi Harry."

"Bliss! Jesus, is it really you?"

"You know it is."

"Holy shit, Bliss, where are you?" Howard turned his head and cupped the receiver covertly in his hand, as if others in the newsroom might be able to tell that he was in conversation with a fugitive from journalism. "Half the goddamn *Advocate* is out searching for you."

"I'm in Athens, Harry," said Browning impatiently. "Remember that story I told you about Maria Callas?"

"How could I forget?" said Howard, knowing what was coming next.

"Well, guess what — I think it really was Maria Callas, after all. There's just no other explanation for what's been happening."

"Exactly what has been happening, Bliss?" asked Howard carefully.

"It's amazing, Harry, absolutely amazing." Browning's voice had the same bright, insistent inflection that Howard had heard from readers who called to rave about their latest literary "discovery". "Callas wants me to track down her long-lost son."

"Son? What son?" said Howard, straining to recall snippets of knowledge about the famous diva. "Callas didn't have children, did she?"

"So you think, Harry — you and the rest of the world," said Browning, the words tumbling out breathlessly. "But that's the whole point. She had the kid secretly, gave him up at birth, and now she wants him to know who his parents really were."

"And she's telling you all this through your computer?" Howard could not keep the incredulity from his voice, but Browning was oblivious to it in any case.

"Right," he chirped. "I know it sounds fantastic—"

"Fantastic?" interrupted Howard. "It sounds fucking loony, Bliss, fu-cking loony."

There was a sullen silence on the line.

"Bliss?" Howard said anxiously, pulling the receiver closer to his lips. "You still there?"

Browning gave a short but heartfelt sigh. "Yeah, Harry, I'm here. Just a little disappointed in your attitude, is all. I thought you, of all people, would believe me."

"Christ, Bliss, I'd like to believe you," said Howard, peering around him to ensure he wasn't being overheard, "but who in their right mind could swallow a crock like that? Why couldn't you be tracking Martians or searching for Atlantis or something? It would be easier for people to accept."

"Laugh if you like, Harry, but I'm telling you, this is for real.

There's no way a hacker could do what she's doing. And I know I'm not hallucinating."

Howard ran his fingers through his short-cropped hair. "Alright, Bliss, for the sake of argument, let's say you're right. Let's say Maria Callas really is talking to you from the Great Beyond. What's in this for you? Near as I can see, best case scenario is you lose your job. If old man Hartley doesn't calm down, you could be facing fraud charges, too. So why are you doing this?"

"I've decided it's time to change my life," Browning said cryptically.

"So change it," snapped Howard. "That doesn't mean you have to take orders from computerized phantoms."

"But what if it's true?" Browning's voice pulsed with an uncharacteristic urgency that made Howard more than a little uneasy. "Just think about it, Harry. It's the goddamn story of the century — locating the lost son of Maria Callas and, by the way, confirming the existence of an afterlife in the bargain. How could I resist?"

"No one will ever believe you," said Howard flatly. "You know that."

"Maybe not. But I'm doing this for me for once, not for others. This is the most purely selfish thing I've ever done, Harry, and it's long overdue."

"So you're determined to proceed, then?" Howard suddenly felt very tired.

"Never been more determined in my life."

"Nothing I say will change your mind?"

"Nothing."

"Then I'll just say 'take care' and stop there," said Howard, resigned. He remembered something. "By the way, they've sent Pugsley to Greece to bring you home. You'd better keep an eye open for him."

"Pugsley's here?" said Browning, surprised. "In Athens?"

"At last report."

"Jesus," said Browning. " Thanks for the heads-up. I'm leaving for the Peloponnese tomorrow morning, so I'll lay low until then. And Harry . . ."

"Yes?"

"This is just between us, okay?"

"Bliss! I'm insulted. You know you can rely on me."

"Just making sure. I'll be in touch when there's something to report."

"Bliss?"

"Yes?"

"Give Maria my regards."

"Fuck you."

NORMAN PUGSLEY'S head felt like a sack of wet cement, into which someone was driving a pointed steel pike with the relentless regularity of a metronome. Ka-thwang! Ka-thwang! He opened his eyes, but quickly closed them as blinding light seared his retinas. Goddamn, he thought, it even hurts to blink.

More cautiously, he opened his eyes again, squinting crinkle-eyed at the dingy, unfamiliar room. Ka-thwang! Willing his aching brain to function, he tried to recall how he had come to be there. Dimly, through the hangover's fog, he began to remember.

He had come here with a woman, that much he could recollect. His new friends in the bar had introduced them. She was blonde and sexy as all hell and wore too much makeup, and he'd liked her straight off. She seemed to like him too, setting herself plunk on his lap and sticking her tongue in his ear even before they were properly introduced. She definitely wanted him — still got the old dame appeal, eh Norm? — and within minutes they were off to some hotel. This one, apparently.

They'd gone up to a room and . . . something about 200 euros. Pugsley tried to focus. Damn ouzo . . . hard to think.

He remembered her unbuttoning her blouse and stepping out of her mini-skirt and . . . Shit! She wasn't wearing any panties! She was standing there, bare-ass naked, and . . . Two hundred euros! She wanted 200 euros! Christ on a bicycle! A whore! She was a whore!!

Pugsley had done his share of whoring in his day, but it had been years. But then he thought, what the fuck, the *Advocate* owes me one, and he'd peeled the bills from a large wad of cash in his wallet and tossed it down in front of the trollop. She'd tucked them safely away in her clothing and, with a quick look of . . . boredom? Was that possible? . . . she'd reclined on the bed and spread her legs.

Yes, it was all coming back now. Tugging off his clothes in a frenzy of desire, climbing on top of the supine woman and . . . something wrong . . . can't understand . . . never happened before . . . damn ouzo. Then she was soothing him, saying don't worry, everything will be fine, just rest a while and we can try again. After that, nothing. Until now.

Despite the wet cement clogging his brain, and the sadist with the iron pike, Pugsley couldn't resist a rueful smile. Damn fool, that's what he was. Tanked up on liquor and acting like a man half his age. Well, no harm done. Only his pride hurt . . .

With a groan, Pugsley sat up and reached for his watch. Every fibre ached, and for some reason, he couldn't make a fist. The watch was nowhere to be seen. Annoyed, Pugsley struggled to his feet and conducted an unsteady search of the small, bare room. Still nothing. Goddamn it, thought Pugsley, hope I haven't lost it. After all it is a Rolex and—

Pugsley froze in mid-thought as another, far more ominous idea creased his tortured frontal lobes. Wallet! Where the fuck is my wallet?

Frantically this time, Pugsley lunged around the room, opening drawers, turning out his pockets and shifting furniture. It was no good. The wallet — and the 2,000 euros and credit cards it contained — was gone.

Pugsley slumped on the yellowed floor as the full horror of his predicament began to penetrate the haze that still clouded his faculties. An Athenian cockroach scuttled past his left foot, but Pugsley was too dispirited to squash it.

Then some primordial instinct kicked in, and Norman Pugsley's brain was flooded with the cleansing balm of righteous anger. Not at the whore, who had, after all, only done what any whore in the same situation would do. Not at himself. His only sin was to be too trusting of strangers. Not even at Athens, though Pugsley's low opinion of the ancient capital had hardly been improved by this turn of events.

Instead, Norman Pugsley's anger was directed with venomous force at one target, and one target alone — Bliss Browning. "Browning, you bastard," he bawled, "you'll pay for this! Goddamn it, you'll pay big time!"

He was still shouting imprecations when hotel staff unlocked the door, helped him dress and hustled him, penniless, into the sullen morning streets.

CHAPTER 17

THE TINY WHITE COFFIN ON THE RAILWAY PLATFORM AT STATHMOS Peloponnissou looked incongruous next to the much larger pine box beside it. It was inconceivable that it contained the body of a child. It was much too small and fragile for such precious cargo. Browning and Matina stood, unspeaking, next to the coffins, he craning his neck to watch for the approaching train and she head down, lost in private thoughts. It was unseasonably warm, and Browning fretted silently about the effect of the heat on the deteriorating husks inside the wooden shells. An involuntary shudder ran through his body as a horrifying memory of the accident scene flashed through his brain. He forced himself to think about something else.

He turned toward Matina, still and silent beside him. "Are you okay?" he asked. She nodded but said nothing. He looked at her closely. Her chin was quivering and she was biting fiercely on her lower lip. From beneath her glasses, thin rivulets streaked both cheeks with a sorrow no self-control could suppress. Browning reached for one of Matina's hands, found it clenched into a fist, opened and smoothed it, and took it gently in his. They stood like that, her hand folded inside his, until the train arrived and railway workers loaded the coffins gingerly into a baggage car.

They said little as the train left the station and headed out of Athens, though Matina sat rigidly and stared out the window when the train passed the park where the lives of her husband and daughter had ended so violently. A morbid fascination that he could neither explain nor ignore drew Browning's gaze as well. What struck him most was how innocuous it looked. Nothing hinted at the horrors that had taken place there. He wasn't quite sure what he'd expected to see, but whatever it was, it was not this . . . negation. He marveled at how quickly the present scours away the past.

With surprising speed, the train cleared the central area and moved into more open country, chugging past expansive orchards and tracts of suburban housing that stretched to the bottom of the scorched hills ringing Athens. The countryside was a monochrome of yellows, beiges and pale browns broken only rarely by a market-garden splash of green, startlingly vivid in such an arid landscape. Farther out still, the vista was scarred by a series of factories, open pit mines and refineries, each competing to exceed the others in ugliness.

Browning fidgeted in his seat. He had insisted on buying Matina a first-class ticket, calculating that the added comfort would make the journey more bearable. But the lever that allowed his own seat-back to recline had malfunctioned, and he realized that he was obliged to make the entire seven-hour journey sitting bolt upright. The plush blue seat-back in front of him bore the dusty imprint of a running shoe left by a previous, presumably disgruntled, occupant of the defective chair.

At least Matina is comfortable, he thought. He peeked covertly at her reclining form in the chair beside him. Her eyes were closed, though she did not appear to be sleeping. He felt a rush of warmth at the sight of this slight, bruised woman — a feeling out of proportion to the brief time they had known one another. Why this should be was something of a mystery, but Browning was content for the moment to simply bask in the unaccustomed comfort of human connection.

The train, which had been moving at a sedate pace to that point, gained speed as it left Athens behind. As it did, the carriage began to jostle and buck like a horse in a canter. Matina sat up and pulled her seat-back forward. She looked at Browning with sorrowing eyes.

"Do you think they're alright?" she asked.

"I'm sure they are," Browning said, though he nursed private concerns of his own.

Silence.

"Maybe I should check on them."

"Matina, relax," Browning ordered. "They're in good hands. There's nothing to worry about."

More silence.

Out his window, Browning caught his first glimpse of the blue waters of the Saronic Gulf, confined by the hills of Salamina Island, off whose shores an ancient outmanned Greek fleet trounced the Persians in 480 B.C. The train hugged the coastline, giving Browning a ringside seat as a flotilla of tankers jostled for position in the bay between the island and the mainland.

"It's strange." Matina's mournful voice drew him back into the swaying train carriage. "It was just six months ago that I made this trip in the other direction." She spoke in the dreamlike cadences of one recalling distant events with difficulty. "It seems much longer than that. So much has happened."

Browning touched her hand lightly, but said nothing.

"It was the first time I'd ever been out of the Mani." She looked at Browning with the alert, astonished expression of a deer catching a scent of danger. "Imagine that — almost 40 and I'd never been anywhere." Another shake of the head. "I was so naive. I really thought going to Athens would change our lives." A bitter laugh. "I guess it did."

"Matina-" Browning began.

"I was excited, Bliss," she said, brushing aside his intervention. "Leaving home, going to Athens, a fresh start — I thought, 'maybe this is really it. This is the beginning of my real life. Now, at last, we can try to be happy.'" She lowered her head. "So naive."

Browning started to say something, then stopped. Matina, he sensed, needed to talk more than to listen right now.

"I had such dreams for Vasilio . . . such dreams." She seemed to be talking as much to herself as to Browning. She smiled at some private memory. "She was going to be an Athens girl, smart and worldly and contemporary — all the things I wasn't. She would grow up understanding the world in ways that I never could. She would not be bound by old prejudices and traditions — she was going to embrace the present." She paused, and Browning sensed rather than saw her struggle to maintain her composure. "That's what I wanted for her," she finally whispered. "That's all."

Matina slumped back in her chair and shut her eyes. A feeling of helplessness swept over Browning. He cursed the mental blankness that denied him the words that might ease her grief. But any words that came to mind seemed laughably inadequate. So he settled for simple sympathy.

"Matina, I'm so sorry."

She opened her eyes and touched his right hand. "I know," she said.

~

AN HOUR OUT OF ATHENS, past the bustling port town of Megara, the train hugged the coast, hemmed in by sheer cliffs rising hundreds of feet above the Saronic Gulf's sparkling waters. At times, the rock face, pocked-marked with caves, was so close that Browning felt he could reach out the train window and touch it. Through the heat haze that hung over the gulf like muslin, he could just make out the mountains of the Eastern Peloponnese. Browning gazed at the jagged horizon. Somewhere out there was the mystery he had undertaken to solve. A frisson of something between excitement and apprehension rippled through his body.

The train slowed as it neared the Corinth Canal, the six-kilometre-long scar that divides Attica from the Peloponnese. It stopped briefly at Isthmus station before edging onto the bridge that spans the century-old canal. Browning caught a glimpse of a strip of blue at the bottom of a deep trench of blasted rock, and a tinker-toy oil tanker far below.

Awed by this bravura feat of 19th century engineering, he shot a quick glance at Matina. She, too, had marked the train's passage over the canal, and seemed as transfixed as he was.

"Impressive, isn't it?" he murmured.

"Yes. It's amazing what humans can do when they set their minds to it." A shadow darkened her features for a moment. "And how much harm they can do without even trying," she added.

The train was skirting Corinth, a monument to history's fickle temperament. In classical times, Corinth was a wealthy and powerful city of 750,000, an astonishing population for its era. Now, the ancient city is little more than a widely scattered series of ruins, while the modern port that carries its name, ravaged by earthquakes, is an ugly agglomeration of characterless concrete. Glory is such a fleeting thing, and sorrow so enduring.

"I know what you mean," said Browning. "The woman I married really meant me no harm. In fact, I couldn't have been less important to her." Matina looked at him in surprise. "But I'm still recovering from the damage she did to me."

She shot him a quick look. "I'd forgotten that you were married. What was her name?"

"Krystal." Browning's jaw tightened at the unfamiliar sound of her name from his lips. "With a K," he added inanely.

"So what happened?"

"Nothing. That was the problem."

"Meaning?"

"Meaning that we never should have gotten married. We had nothing in common — less than nothing, actually."

Matina studied him. "Why did you marry her, then?"

Browning gave a short, mirthless laugh. "Because she bewitched me." He saw her impatient expression. "No, really," he said, "that's just what she did. She picked me out in a bar and took me home to her bed. She was blond and beautiful and full of life, and she wanted me. That had never happened to me before, to be selected by someone so desirable. I didn't know how to handle it. Next thing I knew, we were married." He shrugged helplessly. "Bewitched."

Matina frowned. "Sounds like you didn't exactly fight her off. Why did it end?"

"It never really started," said Browning with a rueful smile. Except for Harrison Howard, he had never talked to anyone about his fleeting marriage. He was surprised how easy it was to talk about it with Matina. "The marriage didn't survive the honeymoon."

Matina's eyes widened. "Seriously?"

"God's truth."

A low murmur of astonishment. "Must have been quite a fight."

"No, that wasn't it." There was something liberating about this discussion, as if by raising a subject long taboo he was finally clearing a mental attic cluttered with recrimination and regret. "It was more like we drifted apart, but at high speed. We compressed 20 years of marital disillusionment into a single week."

Matina laughed, then covered her mouth apologetically. "No," said Browning, "it is rather funny, I suppose. Though it wasn't at the time. I thought it was the end of the world. I figured I'd wind up one of those pathetic gibbering men you sometimes see in shopping malls, cackling insanely to themselves through toothless gums, driven mad by their own company." He glanced at Matina; she was smiling faintly, but attentive.

"You don't still feel that way, do you?" she finally asked, to break the lengthening silence.

"Most of the time." He shifted his gaze to the Peloponnese landscape rushing past as the train neared Mycenae. Ranks of mountains retreated into the mist like talismans of ancient civilizations, and the valley and hillsides were verdant with vineyards and olive groves.

"Why?"

"Why not?" he asked. "I'm no prize. Who'd want me?"

Matina clucked her tongue. "You came to my rescue. Most people would have turned away, found some excuse not to get involved. But you didn't. You listened when I needed a sympathetic ear, offered your shoulder when I needed a good cry, held my hand when I was alone and afraid. And you did all this for someone you didn't even know a week ago. I call that extraordinary."

Browning felt a flush creeping across his cheeks. Matina's words pleased him, but he was uncomfortable with her praise. Still, she was right; his response to her plight had been unusual, especially for him. Could it be that one leap of faith begets another? Or was there something about Matina that gave him the courage to show himself to another for once?

"I'm not normally so bold," he confessed. "For most of my life, I would have found some excuse not to get involved. But something has happened here. Maybe it's Greece, maybe it's you—" a helpless shrug — "I really don't know. All I know," he turned to her shyly, almost afraid to meet her gaze, "is I'm glad I can help."

Matina stared at him for a long moment. "Me too," she said fiercely.

"YOU DON'T MEAN to say you lost everything?" Even from a distance of 4,000 miles, the disbelief in Renata Richter's voice was apparent.

"Afraid so, Renata," said Norman Pugsley. He was torn between chagrin at having to report this humiliation, and resentment of Richter, Browning and the world in general for putting him in this position. "They got it all — the euros, the credit cards, the works."

There was a long-suffering sigh, clearly audible at the other end of the long-distance phone line. "Well, what happened, exactly?" asked Richter, her note of impatience further chafing the raw wound of Pugsley's irritation.

"There was a whole gang of them, I dunno, maybe 10 or 12." No sense telling Richter the truth, Pugsley thought; she'd never understand the urges of a healthy, heterosexual male like himself. "I'd been out all day, tracking down fuckin' Browning, pardon my Bulgarian, and I was heading back to my hotel when they caught me alone on a dark street. 'Course they're all dark in this sinkhole of a city." Pugsley was warming to the tale; no harm in gilding the lily a bit, especially since the lily was actually a dandelion. "They forced me into an alley and started to shove me around. I got in a few good licks — put several of 'em on the deck — but there were just too many of 'em." Pugsley's chest puffed out at the memory of his heroic stand. "They put a knife to my neck and threatened to cut my throat if I didn't hand over all my money. There was nothing I could do. It was submit or die!" he concluded, with a flourish.

There was a momentary silence at the other end of the line. Pugsley wondered uneasily if he'd overplayed his hand. "Sounds like you did the right thing," Richter finally said, dubiously.

"Damn straight!" exclaimed Pugsley, indignant at her plain skepticism. "You don't know what this place is like, Renata. It's a cesspool of crime and corruption! And it's all aimed at ripping off visitors like me! We're like fresh meat to them! Christ on a bicycle, I'm lucky to be alive!!"

"Yes, I'm sure," Richter said icily. "Tell me again why you were carrying so much cash?"

"Well, Jesus, Renata," yelped Pugsley, "what else could I do?" Her lack of empathy was infuriating. "I couldn't leave it at the hotel — the place is a dive. Christ, I've been in better bordellos . . . er, on assignment, of course."

"Of course," said Richter, her tone as dry as the Kalahari. "But you must have been carrying some traveller's cheques when you were robbed. You can get them replaced, at least."

"Traveller's cheques?" repeated Pugsley, stupidly. "No, I cashed them all in at the airport."

"Norman, for God's sake!" Richter's exasperation was the verbal equivalent of a hand-slap to the temple. "The whole reason people carry traveller's cheques in the first place is for security. What possessed you to convert all of them to cash the moment you left the plane?"

There was a sullen silence at Pugsley's end of the line. When he spoke, his voice shook with barely suppressed fury. "Look, Renata, I didn't ask to come here. To be honest, I'd much rather be in my living room, suckin' on a beer and watchin' the Jays, instead of risking my life looking for Asshole Number One!" He was nearly shouting now. "Maybe I'm not doing things exactly the way you would! Maybe you'd do better!!" The veins on his forehead were bulging, like dangerously over-inflated balloons. "Fine! Pull me outa here!!" he screamed into the malevolent black receiver. "Replace me!! You won't hurt my feelings, I promise!!"

Pugsley's hands were shaking, his breath coming in short bursts. He caught his red-faced reflection in the hotel-room mirror. Gotta calm down. A sudden, startling pain gripped his chest like a clenched fist. He sat up in surprise and opened his mouth, but no sound came out. Christ on a bi—

The receiver slipped from his hand and fell heavily to the floor, followed seconds later by the unconscious form of Norman Pugsley.

~

A LITTLE MORE THAN three hours out of Athens, past the ancient city of Argos, the train carrying Bliss Browning, Matina and their grim cargo turned inland, travelling through low mountains and narrow rock-cuts. The landscape, formerly expansive and larger than life, became crimped and constricted, almost claustrophobic. Browning was aware of a tightness in his chest and a dankness in his nether regions. It was as if the very smallness of his surroundings was confining him like a ligature to an uncertain fate. Finally, the train broke into a broad valley ringed by the soaring peaks of Arcadia and Lakonia, and he could breathe more easily again.

He glanced at Matina in the seat next to him. She had drifted into a fitful sleep, interrupted only by the relentless conductors, who needed regular reassurance that passengers were properly ticketed. Browning too tried to sleep, but his racing brain and ramrod-straight seat-back made that impossible. Now that he was truly launched on the unlikely mission that had brought him to this unfamiliar land, all his old doubts were resurfacing. What if the messages on his computer weren't from Callas at all, but a resourceful impostor toying with him for unfathomable reasons? And how could he hope to pick up a trail nearly four decades old in an alien land whose language he didn't speak?

Finally, what of Matina? The bond between them, though born of trauma, had rapidly strengthened into something real and comforting. Yet in a few hours she would leave to bury her dead and pick up the shards of her own shattered life. Would he ever see her again? How could he cope without her, alone in a lightly travelled region of rural Greece? The thought struck him that he needed her, desperately. Absurd. How could he tell her that? It would be unfair, unreasonable, unthinkable.

Browning wrestled with these thoughts as the pokey Peloponnese express jostled across the sweeping valley, through soaring highlands into the lush and fertile lands of Messenia, where lank cypress trees punctuated the landscape, and the bleached-white city of Kalamata lay shimmering beneath the ominous peaks of the Taygetus.

~

MATINA AWOKE JUST as the train was passing through the urban detritus that surrounds Kalamata. "Where are we?" she asked groggily, rubbing her eyes.

"Nearly there, I think," answered Browning, grateful for her return to consciousness. He checked his watch; it had been nearly seven hours since the train had left Athens. He stretched stiffly in his seat.

"What if your father-in-law isn't at the station to greet you?"

"He'll be there, maybe with some other family or friends," Matina said grimly.

"Still," said Browning, "I'll stay with you until I'm sure everything is okay."

"No, you won't," said Matina, alarmed. She looked at him severely, then her expression softened when she saw the hurt on his face. "It's not that I don't want you to," she said more gently, "it's just that Mr. Mourtzinos is a traditional man from a very old-fashioned part of Greece. He would think it was highly improper if I stepped off the train with any man, let alone a divorced man from Canada. Women in the Mani just don't do that sort of thing."

Browning was only slightly mollified. "What are you saying?" he demanded. "That we have to pretend we don't know one another?"

Matina nodded apologetically. "I'm afraid so."

"But that's intolerable! Matina, I know I've only known you a short time, but we've shared so much. I regard you as a very dear friend, and I'll be damned if I'll abandon you just to please some chauvinistic old goat."

Matina shook her head emphatically. "You don't understand, Bliss. It has nothing to do with pleasing him; we're talking about my life. This is where I come from. This is where my roots are. And where I come from, widows in mourning do not arrive for the funeral on the arm of another man."

Browning gave her a stricken look. "Will I see you again?"

Matina turned away and gazed out the window for a long, silent moment. "I don't know," she said at last. "Maybe. Probably not."

The train was slowing now as it neared Kalamata's modest station. Browning felt a rising desperation tinged with despair. The idea that these might be his final minutes of contact with Matina was appalling to him. Surely there was something he could say or do to alter such an unthinkable fate. But instead, he turned to her and said gruffly, "Then I suppose we'd better say good-bye now."

Matina nodded mutely. She took his hand and looked searchingly into his eyes. "You're a true friend, Bliss Browning," she said gravely. "I won't forget you." With that, she half rose from her chair, leaned toward him and brushed her lips lightly against his. It was the briefest of kisses, but it conveyed more depth of feeling than the most unbridled embrace. Browning felt dizzy.

"I'll miss you," he whispered.

"I know."

The train entered the station and slowed to a near stop. Matina rose from her seat, collected her suitcase and walked to the end of the first-class car. Then without a backward glance, she stepped onto the platform before the train was fully at rest.

Browning watched her from his seat, immobilized and numb. He watched as she approached a stooped man with a weather-lined face and magnificent white mustache who was waiting on the platform with a group of other men. He saw her embrace the man, who closed his arms around her with the awkward grace of someone unaccustomed to public displays of emotion. He saw her shoulders shake, and knew that she was sobbing. Whether for her daughter Vasilio, her husband Andreas or for him, the stranger on the train whose affection she dared not acknowledge, he could not say.

PART III

God helps the sailor, but he must row.
—German saying

CHAPTER 18

BROWNING STAYED ON THE TRAIN UNTIL MATINA AND HER FATHER-IN-law were gone. Then, rising stiffly from his seat, he collected his baggage and stepped onto the nearly deserted platform. The late-afternoon air, stirred by a hint of sea-breeze, embraced him gently. But Browning barely noticed. Feeling lost and alone, he stood motionless on the platform, unable to muster the will to move.

A shabby man with an olive-oil complexion edged furtively in his direction. Browning noticed him at the last moment and instinctively placed a hand on his wallet.

The man grinned uncertainly. "You want taxi?" he asked. The question seemed to shake Browning out of his lethargy. "Yes. Yes, as a matter of fact, I do. Do you speak English?"

The man nodded vigorously. "Speak English. Very good," he insisted. Browning looked at him dubiously, but continued. "I need a hotel for the night," he said, enunciating carefully. "Can you recommend one?"

The man smiled and nodded, but said nothing. "Can you take me to a hotel?" Browning asked again, more loudly, as if volume alone might penetrate the veil of incomprehension that separated them. "Do you understand?"

The man grinned again. "Speak English. Very good," he said, with less conviction. "Oh, this is hopeless," said Browning, exasperated. He grabbed his bags and walked into the small railway station, his would-be benefactor trailing expectantly behind. Spotting a ticket-seller behind the station's lone wicket, he strode to the counter and leaned in.

"Excuse me," he said. "I've just arrived and I need a place to stay."

"How much you want to pay?" the man responded.

"You speak English," said Browning, relieved.

"Of course," said the ticket-seller, mildly indignant. "I went to school in New Jersey for five years. So how much you want to pay?"

"As little as possible. I'm on a tight budget."

"Then I have just the place for you. The Arizona. It's a little pension near the waterfront. Run by my aunt, so I can vouch for the place." Browning winced involuntarily, memories still fresh of the overpriced flophouse the airport cabby had steered him to in Athens. "Just 50 euros a night," the ticket-seller continued, easing his fears of another rip-off. "And all the earthquake damage has been repaired."

"Earthquake?" repeated Browning, alarmed. "What earthquake?"

"You didn't read about in Canada? In 1986, earthquake levelled half the city. Killed 20 people. Another 12,000 lost homes. Even today, we are still recovering."

A shiver of apprehension rippled through Browning, and he wiped his palms on his pants. This was a dangerous place he'd come to, where the very earth beneath your feet could not be trusted. "Have there been any more, ah, earthquakes since then?" he asked.

The ticket-seller shrugged. "Odd tremor. Nothing serious," he added, but Browning wasn't reassured. "Your aunt's pension," he asked tentatively, "was it badly damaged in the last earthquake?"

"Not too badly. Roof caved in a bit, and walls and floors cracked, that sort of thing." The ticket-seller spat noisily into a tobacco tin. "But it's solidly built. Not like a lot of newer hotels in this town." He looked meaningfully at Browning. “A strong wind could knock them over."

Browning stared at the ticket-seller in horror. "Alright," he said faintly. "I suppose it's your aunt's place, then. Can you tell my friend here," Browning gestured at the taxi driver, still bobbing and weaving by his side, "to take me there?"

"Of course," the ticket seller nodded. He turned to the taxi driver and the two had a rapid-fire conversation in Greek that seemed, to Browning, to take far longer than necessary. Finally, the ticket-seller gestured to Browning. "Okay, he'll take you. And don't let him charge more than eight euros. That's all it should cost."

Browning looked at the man in surprise and gratitude. "Thank you, sir," he said. "You are an honest man." The ticket-seller waved him away. "There are enough crooks already," he said, turning back to his work. "They don't need my help."

~

THE ARIZONA WAS a bland three-storey structure that offered comfortable, if spartan, rooms with large canopied porches affording fine views into the living rooms of apartments across the street. Browning's quarters were unremarkable save for the presence of a large, load-bearing pillar in the middle of the room, next to the bed, that he had to take care to avoid when rising to his feet.

A matronly woman in her late 50s, presumably the ticket-seller's aunt, presided over the pension. She spoke little English, but with liberal use of mime, was able to perform the rudiments of check-in. To her delight, Browning offered payment in advance. Beaming broadly, she stuck a beefy hand into her blouse and extracted a handkerchief containing a bulging roll of bills, to which she added Browning's 50 euros. Then, as Browning watched in wonderment, the whole apparatus — a minor fortune from all appearances — vanished into the enveloping folds of her bosom.

By chance, Hellas On Wheels, the rental agency through which ever-efficient travel agent Yiannis had booked Browning's car, was just around the corner from the pension. Restless after his long, confining journey, Browning decided to stroll to the agency to confirm that all was in readiness for the car pick-up at 10 the next morning. He found the office easily, but though a sign promised office hours until 8 p.m. and it was not yet 7, the tiny office was dark and the door bolted. It was not, Browning noted, an auspicious sign.

Unwilling to return so soon to his bare room, Browning turned down the broad avenue running along Kalamata's waterfront. It was an attractive enough street, lined with hotels, banks and restaurants on one side and ranks of tables for al fresco drinking and dining on the seaward side. Browning selected one of the tables at random and ordered an Amstel, offering silent thanks for Greece's limited range of beer brands.

From his vantage point near the water's edge, he could see the menacing Taygetus range, just a few kilometres to the east. His eyes followed the scabrous peaks south along a peninsula that jutted into the sea and vanished into the settling dusk. It was the Mani. Somewhere down that jagged coastline was Matina with her cargo of sorrow, back in the harsh and strange land of her birth. He could not think of her without a dull ache of loss. He peered at the receding finger of coastline, trying to conjure up her face. But no matter how hard he tried, he could not see her there. He drained his beer, paid the bill and walked slowly back to his room.

THERE WAS no sign of life at Hellas on Wheels when Browning arrived at the agency's darkened offices the next morning. Fighting off unease, he installed himself at a sidewalk table outside a kafenio across the street, ordered a tiny cup of bitter Greek coffee and waited. Precisely at 10 a.m., a small fluorescent-blue hatchback screeched to a halt in front of the rental office. An unshaven man with a face redolent of hangover climbed from behind the wheel and unlocked the office door. With palpable relief, Browning paid his bill and hurried across the street.

"Hello," he called. The rental agent looked at him through bleary eyes. "Meester Browning?" he croaked. Browning nodded. "Thank God," said the agent. "I'm very sick, not well at all." He massaged his temples with his fingers. "I wouldn't have come to work at all except for you," he said in a vaguely accusatory tone, as if Browning were to blame for the overindulgence that was obviously responsible for his distress.

"Very sorry to inconvenience you," Browning said, but his sardonic inflection was lost on its target. "No problem. Let's get this over with so I can go back to bed," said the agent, beginning to scrawl on a rental contract. But evidently his synapses were misfiring, for after a few minutes he stopped and stared balefully at his handiwork. Then he ripped up the contract and started over, muttering Greek imprecations under his breath.

The formalities completed at last, the agent handed over the keys to the hatchback, a stubby German-made Opel, and gruffly informed Browning that the gas tank was empty. "You can get gas up street," he said, pointing vaguely to the north. Then he locked up the office and disappeared in the general direction of the waterfront bars, still rubbing his forehead.

Browning slipped gingerly behind the wheel of the unfamiliar car. Though tiny, it was nearly new and appeared to be in good condition. He ran the stick through all five forward gears and checked out the location of the turn signals, washers and headlights. Satisfied, he turned the key. The engine roared obediently to life. He did a sharp U-turn and headed north on Faron Street in search of the promised gas station.

He found it within a few blocks and pulled up to a pump. "Fill up," he said moronically, though the attendant seemed to understand his pidgin English. Browning was alarmed to discover it cost more than double the price of a fill-up for his own, larger car in Ottawa. This was an expense he hadn't reckoned on. Fortunately, the gas station accepted his credit card, allowing him to preserve his supply of euros.

After extracting directions from the attendant through a series of grunts and hand gestures, Browning pulled tentatively onto Faron Street. Traffic was light and key intersections well-marked in English. Within minutes, Browning had broken free of Kalamata and was travelling through rolling countryside toward his destination, the town of Meligalas.

Along with the vivid red soil and ubiquitous stands of olive trees, Browning noticed something new: thickets of prickly pear cactus lining the roadside, in places so numerous that they formed a continuous hedgerow. The huge cacti were laden with reddish-orange fruit, which a straggley succession of informal pickers were harvesting. Browning was seized with curiosity about this strange and exotic fruit. Beneath its spiky exterior, he imagined, must surely lurk a nectar that would make Zeus himself swoon. The thought of sinking his teeth into the velvety sweetness made his stomach rumble. Impulsively, he pulled over next to an imposing stand of cacti loaded with the barbed pears. He approached warily, a bit intimidated by the lethal-looking thorns protruding from the thick green cactus leaves. But the fruit itself looked relatively benign, its surface an acne of prickly pimples that posed little obvious threat.

Reassured, Browning gingerly picked one of the pears with his right hand. Almost instantly, a hundred pinpricks of pain flashed from his fingers to his brain, as if scores of microscopic needles had been swiftly imbedded in the fleshy parts of each digit. With a loud curse, he dropped the malign fruit and examined his afflicted paw. Dozens of minute yellow slivers, too tiny to be readily visible on the surface of the pears, protruded from the pin-cushion of each finger. Instinctively, he swiped his right hand with his left, trying to brush off the Lilliputian invaders. To his mounting horror, he succeeded only in transferring a batch of the insidious slivers from one hand to the other, effectively incapacitating both.

Browning staggered back to his car and slumped into the driver's seat. His first thought was to seek help in town. But the moment he tried to grip the steering wheel the searing pain in his fingers forced him to let go. His mind flashed to images of Hollywood villains who used toothpicks and fingernails in painful combinations to extract cooperation. If confession would end his torment, Browning would have complied gladly. But there were no torturers to appease, just the infernal slivers in his flaming fingers.

He slid his right forefinger into his mouth, taking care not to imbed the hellish spikes in his tongue. Gripping a few of the slivers with his front teeth and sucking gently, he managed to extract enough of the intruders to allow pressure on the finger without excruciating pain. He repeated the procedure with his right thumb, thus regaining limited use of his hand. Then he rummaged through his luggage with his two good fingers until he found a pair of tweezers that he'd packed in a moment of prescience. Gripping them with his newly opposable thumb and forefinger, he methodically removed a small forest of slivers sprouting from his fingers.

When at last he was done, he was bathed in a thin veneer of sweat and thoroughly rattled. For a moment, he was tempted to drive back to Kalamata and catch the first plane to Canada, a place mercifully devoid of such unforeseeable perils. But then he thought of Callas, who was counting on him, and Matina, who had become so important so quickly, and stiffened his resolve. He gripped the steering wheel gingerly, with only moderate discomfort from a few rogue slivers that had evaded eviction, and pulled onto the highway. Within minutes he was in Meligalas.

~

IT WAS early afternoon when Bliss Browning, sore of finger and empty of belly, cruised slowly down Meligalas's empty main street, looking for a place to eat. After his tussle with the demon prickly pear, he was badly in need of a satisfying meal to revive his spirits. But most businesses had closed for the afternoon. Houses were shuttered against the light rain that had started to fall, and the streets were uninhabited. Only a small cafe with a dozen or so tables arrayed under a green plastic awning was still open, though the place was empty save for a weathered man in the corner drinking Amstel. In the absence of an alternative, Browning parked and went inside.

After a couple of minutes, a beetle-browed man in his mid-40s, evidently the proprietor, emerged from a back room. He spoke no English, but Browning quickly communicated his desire for food. The owner led him into the darkened kitchen, switched on the lights and peered into a series of pots, searching for anything edible. He finally located a single forlorn piece of stewed chicken in a thin tomato sauce, and offered that, along with a salad of tomatoes, onions and olives, and a basket of thickly sliced bread. It was a humble meal, but the chicken, as stewed as a Bowery bum, was tasty and tender, falling off the bone at the slightest pressure from a fork.

The meal, washed down by a half-litre bottle of beer, did the trick. With a new spring in his step, Browning set out to explore the town. There wasn't much to see. Aside from a handful of young layabouts lolling on turquoise plastic chairs outside a bar across the street, and a scruffy man in yellow pants and an ill-fitting mauve jacket who was shuffling aimlessly up and down the road, the main street was deserted. In fact, the whole town had an air of abandonment, though the occasional crackle of a radio or television set from behind a shuttered facade offered hints of hidden life. The business hours posted outside a pharmacy gave some inkling of the town's rhythms: *Open from 10 a.m. to 12:30 p.m. and 6 p.m. to 8 p.m.*

Browning found the municipal offices. They were closed. He entered an imposing yellow church that dominated the centre of town. It was empty. He climbed to a smaller chapel and bell tower at the top of town, swatting at a plague of flies that swarmed around him. Still nobody to be seen. When a young woman emerged from a doorway and strode briskly past him, he was so startled that he was struck dumb; she receded before he realized that he should have tried to speak to her.

He returned to the bar and approached the young louts lounging there. They responded to his questions with shrugs and sniggers and remarks in Greek that Browning sensed were derisive. Footsore and frustrated, he decided that a strategic retreat was in order. He would secure his lodgings in nearby Mavromati and return later, when the town should be open for business.

Striding briskly to his rented Opel, he settled in behind the wheel and turned the key. To his mild irritation, another driver had parked inches from his front bumper, forcing him to back up. He slipped the car into neutral and, lifting up on the stick, slipped it down and to the right, where reverse gears of his acquaintance were customarily found. But though he struggled with the stick for a few moments, it refused to slide into gear.

Frowning, he peered at the knob on top of the gear-shift stick, seeking guidance about the location of reverse. No roadmap to the gears was imprinted there. Nor was there a manual of any sort that might unlock the mysteries of reverse. He jammed the stick in every direction that Opel designers, at their most fiendish, might hypothesize. Reverse remained stubbornly disengaged.

Browning slumped onto the steering wheel, panting from his fruitless exertions. He was discouraged by the day's reversals, yet like his balky vehicle, he felt impelled to go forward. Slipping the car into neutral, he put his shoulder to the frame and began to push. It didn't take much effort to move the tiny car back a few feet and allow him to escape. Such crude techniques would have to suffice, he thought, until he could return to Hellas on Wheels and exchange his defective vehicle for one capable of two-way locomotion.

ROOMS TO RENT ZEUS, a clump of modern, neatly furnished rental units with a shared kitchen area, sits above a jewelry store in the hillside village of Mavromati. Parking is in the rear, on a steep, narrow road that runs behind the property. Cleverly using the topography to his advantage, Browning backed neatly into his spot by rolling downhill in neutral. Getting out would be another matter — the road was too narrow for a U-turn — but Browning put that problem aside for the time being.

In his comfortable room, he was delighted to find a telephone. He called Hellas on Wheels to report the problem with reverse, and was unsurprised when no one answered. He had been unable to contact Callas since leaving Athens, but rather surprisingly, his small hotel was equipped with dial-up Internet. He quickly plugged in and dashed off an e-mail. As usual, she responded immediately.

"What do you do, sit by the phone all day, waiting for me to call?" he joked.

"My dear Browning, that's hardly necessary in The Zone," Callas replied seriously. "We know the instant someone tries to contact us. It's as plain as if you were here, talking to me."

"Maria, I was joking. You don't rely on earthly technology, God knows."

"I see. Sometimes your sense of humor puzzles me. It's nothing like Aristo's. There was never any doubt when he made a joke. He always laughed louder than anyone else."

Browning brought Callas up to date on what had transpired since their last contact, including his early impressions of Meligalas. But somewhat to his embarrassment, he found himself saying much more about Matina than he had intended. "It was hard to sit there on that train and let her walk away," he told her, "particularly when I know how much she still needs me."

"Forgive me, my dear Browning," Callas replied, "but it sounds very much to me as if it is you who need her."

Browning flushed at Callas's words, but he could not deny their accuracy. The truth was that he did need Matina, more than he'd been willing to admit. It frightened him, this need, because it exposed feelings that had been sealed behind impermeable barriers for nearly a decade. Now, without even trying or intending it, Matina had conjured the alchemy of hope, ardour and longing that he thought he had disavowed forever. It was unnerving.

"It's true," he admitted, "I am drawn to her. There is a dignity about her, an inner strength, that I deeply admire. This is a woman who had just endured the worst trauma imaginable — the murder of her daughter at the hands of her husband — yet somehow she has been able to carry on without sinking into despair. She's had a difficult life, yet her spirit is unbroken. That she would open her heart to me, a stranger, during her greatest sorrow — all of this is remarkable to me. *She* is remarkable to me."

"What are you going to do about it?" said Callas.

"What can I do about it? We're from different worlds. She's a grieving widow from rural Greece and I'm a journalist on the lam from Canada. I don't think a relationship like that has much of a future, do you?"

"That's entirely up to you, my dear Browning," said Callas. "Not to be trite, but love has a way of overcoming all obstacles. My love for Aristo even survived his marriage to that Kennedy woman."

"Yes, but it never brought you true happiness."

"You're wrong, Bliss." Browning was startled by Callas's use of his first name. "My love for Aristo gave me my greatest moments of happiness, my profoundest pleasures — as great as anything the concert stage or the adulation of an audience ever did. There is nothing more satisfying than a deep connection between two people. And that's what we had. If it fell short of my fondest hopes, well, perfection is always elusive. In every life there are perfect moments and perfect times. The fact that they don't last makes them no less perfect. Wise people embrace these moments of perfection, and don't waste time lamenting the imperfections."

"So what you are saying," interrupted Browning, unaccountably irritated by this line of reasoning, "is that I should abandon my country, my career and, oh yes, my search for the son of Maria Callas, and cast my destiny with a woman I barely know who lives on a barren peninsula in the Peloponnese?"

"I'm not telling you to do anything," Callas replied calmly, "That is for you to decide. But since you raised them, let's examine your list of concerns for a moment. Your career, if you can dignify what you do with such a word, has probably suffered a fatal reversal thanks to your presence here. Your country is no doubt admirable and very, very clean, but really, what's there for you? You have no family, very few friends — if ever a life was easy to leave behind, it's yours. As for your quest on my behalf, obviously I don't want you to abandon that. But it will be over soon, one way or another. And when it is, you will still be in Greece. And so will she."

"I think you've made your point," said Browning tersely. He was feeling quite grumpy and didn't want to continue this conversation.

He suspected his mood had something to do with Callas's relentless logic, which he found both compelling and infuriating.

"I hope so," said Callas. "Honestly, my dear Browning, for a clever man sometimes you can be quite obtuse."

Browning was strangely reassured by Callas's reversion to her more accustomed form of addressing him. For a moment, things had been a bit too intimate for comfort.

MELIGALAS AT NIGHT was a town transformed. The streets were filled with families taking the night air, shops were open for business, and sidewalk kiosks did a brisk business in cigarettes and lottery tickets. A steady stream of cars, mostly older models, cruised the main street, and in a club next to the headquarters of the New Democracy Party, boisterous men played poker, read newspapers and argued about the issues of the day.

Browning gravitated to the nameless bar with the turquoise chairs where he'd encountered the shiftless youths earlier. The plain, square, characterless room was much busier now, filled with men watching a soccer match on a television hung from the ceiling. He found an unoccupied table, ordered ouzo from an unshaven but efficient man, and was rewarded with a small complimentary plate of mezedes — a handful of olives, a piece of feta cheese, a few slices of tomato and cucumber, a piece of roasted meat secured with a toothpick to a square of bread. He sipped the ouzo gingerly, not sure he really enjoyed its strong anisette flavour. Before long, though, the liquor's warm glow had radiated from the pit of his stomach to the nethermost reaches of his body. The time had come to begin his quest in earnest.

Skirting a salesman vainly trying to interest bar patrons in his line of garish, brocaded curtains, Browning approached his bartender with ouzo-fuelled confidence. "Excuse me," he said, more loudly than he intended, "does anyone here speak English?" The waiter shot him a look that was appraising but not unfriendly. "I do," he said. "What do you need to know?"

Browning couldn't believe his good fortune. He explained that he was a Canadian journalist on assignment in Greece and needed to track down a resident of the town, Petros Demitros, who might have some information that could help him with his story.

"You want to speak to Petros Demitros," said the bartender, eyes narrowing perceptibly.

"Yes," confirmed Browning, impatiently. "Do you know where I can find him?"

"Sure. Try the cemetery. He died more than 10 years ago."

This was a setback. But a man with ouzo coursing through his veins is not so easily deterred. "What about relatives?" Browning demanded. "Did he have a family, or any close friends?"

The bartender chuckled softly. "My friend, you obviously know nothing of Petros Demitros. Old Crazy Petros, we called him. Oh, was normal enough once, I guess, but that was long ago. During war, bloody Germans kill everyone in his family for collaborating with resistance. He only survived by hiding under floorboards. But he heard his mother and father die, his sisters, brothers. He was never same. After the war, he become hermit, living in old house on edge of town." He paused to wipe up a wet spot on the bar, then squinted at Browning. "You ever hear of Maria Callas, she was famous opera singer?"

Browning felt as if he'd stuck a finger in one of the bar's ancient electrical fixtures. The ouzo buzz was gone, his mind suddenly clear and alert. "Of course," he said, with feigned casualness. "Why do you ask?"

"That's where Old Crazy Petros used to live, in old Callas family house. You probably don't know, but Callas's parents lived in Meligalas until they moved to America, just before Maria was born." He grinned ruefully. "As close as this town's ever come to fame. Anyway, when they moved, they sold house to Petros' parents. He inherit it when they die, but since he crazy, he let it fall apart. Is empty now, not much more than ruin. Damn pity, too; people say was fine house once."

Browning stared at the bartender. "What's your name?"

"George. George Kalagerakis."

"George," said Browning, looking intently at the bartender, "would you take me to this house and help me ask the neighbours a few questions?" He saw the dubious look on the bartender's face and hastily added: "I'll pay for your time, of course."

"No, no, not necessary," said the bartender. "I be happy to help you — hospitality is part of our culture." He frowned. "But I must work tonight, and tomorrow must take early bus to Athens. If you around for few days, I can take when I return Monday."

Browning tried to conceal his dismay. Monday was five days from now. He'd already lost nearly a week in Athens. Could he really afford to tread water for another five days? After all, he barely had a month left to complete his mission before his connection with Callas was permanently severed. "George," he said urgently to his new friend, "time is an issue for me. Could someone else help me?"

George shook his head. "This not tourist town. Not many here speak much English. I'm really man for job."

Browning thought quickly. This was his only real lead. Though he ached to race to the house and begin his search for clues at once, it was clear that he would need George's help. In the meantime, he could see what other information he might turn up. It wasn't ideal, but it was his only real choice.

"In that case, George," he said, "Monday it is."

CHAPTER 19

NORMAN PUGSLEY WAS HAVING A NIGHTMARE. HE WAS STRETCHED OUT on a hospital bed, tubes and monitors attached to various orifices and body parts, and when he opened his eyes, she was there: Renata Richter, the idiot-savant editor a capricious fate had bequeathed as his boss and personal millstone. It was impossible, of course — he was in Greece, tracking down the moron, Bliss Browning, and she was an ocean away, in Ottawa. He must be delirious.

But then the vision spoke, in a voice that dripped with the inane cultivation that grated like sandpaper. "Norman? Norman, are you awake? Oh, good Lord, Norman, are you alright?"

Pugsley groaned and clamped his eyes shut. Please God, not her. But when he cautiously opened his eyes again, there she was, staring at him wide-eyed, face twisted with concern. "Renata?" he croaked. It was hard to talk, almost painful. "Christ on a bicycle! What are you doing here?"

If Renata Richter was fazed by Pugsley's vulgarity, she didn't show it. "Norman, I came right away," she whinnied, "hopped on the first available flight. Harrison came too; he's off searching for Bliss. I'm going to stay here with you until you're well enough to go home. Oh Norman, we've been so worried about you."

As usual, the silly bitch was making no sense whatever. "For God's sake, why?" Pugsley grumped. "I'm fine, goddammit." But even as the words left his mouth, he had to concede that he didn't feel fine. In fact, he felt terribly weak, as if even sitting up would demand too much effort. And there was a dull ache on the left side of his chest.

"Don't be silly, Norman," said Richter, firmly but not unkindly. "You've had a heart attack. The doctors say you're lucky to be alive. If the hotel staff hadn't responded quickly, we wouldn't be having this conversation."

Pugsley tried to digest this startling news. "What are you talking about?"

"We were talking on the phone, remember? I heard a loud crash, and then you weren't there anymore. I was afraid something terrible had happened, so I called the hotel staff and told them to check on you right away. They found you sprawled on the floor, unconscious."

A thought began to form, unbidden, in the deep recesses of Pugsley's brain, an idea so astonishing that at first he refused to countenance it. "Are you trying to tell me," he asked Richter, already guessing the answer, "that you saved my life?"

"Not at all, not at all," she replied, with a dismissive flutter of her left hand. "If anyone saved your life, it was the hotel staff."

"But they wouldn't have known I was in trouble," Pugsley said slowly, "if you hadn't called them." The full implications were now sinking it. Pugsley looked at Richter as if seeing her for the first time. "I owe you my life," he said thickly, his choked voice full of astonished emotion.

"Don't get maudlin on me, Norman," Richter said, embarrassed by her crusty managing editor's uncharacteristic display. "Anyone would have done the same thing."

"Yes, but it was you, Renata," cried Pugsley, emotions suddenly surging. "It was you." His throat thickened and a sob escaped. "I've been so unfair to you, Renata," he blubbered, rubbing his welling eyes with his fists. "I've said so many terrible things, had such unkind thoughts." Richter wordlessly handed him a tissue and he blew his nose lustily. "No more," he vowed. "That's over. From now on, we're best friends. That is, if you'll forgive me," he added.

"For heaven's sake, Norman," said Richter, "there's nothing to forgive." But she was secretly pleased, for she'd often sensed Pugsley's scorn for her. They looked at one another for a long moment. "You just get better, okay?" she said with mock sternness. "That's an order."

Norman Pugsley smiled submissively. "You're the boss," he said, without irony for once.

~

BROWNING SPENT the days until George's return from Athens in a fitful and fruitless search of Meligalas for information about Callas's son. As George had warned him, most of the town's residents spoke only a few words of English. The few he found who were more fluent knew little about the hermit, Petros Demitros, and nothing about an adopted child who might have been Callas's son.

He wandered Meligalas's streets, peering narrowly at males who seemed to be in the right age bracket, wondering if they could be the one he was seeking. He even approached several to ask if they were adopted, but gave that up after one threatened him with a beating if he didn't leave him alone. The sensation that he was marking time he didn't have was overwhelming. By the time he went to bed Sunday night — the eve of George's return — he was so anxious he barely slept.

He arose at dawn to an otherworldly scene. The countryside was sheathed in an ocean of cloud that had slipped silently below the peaks of the low mountains to fill the narrow valley with a gossamer layer. Long after the rising sun had baked away all trace of the mist, he sat quietly in his hotel room, listening to the sounds of the waking village, a place so intimate that every conversation and quarrel, every debate and altercation, every giggle, belch, hoot and halfway decent fart was shared with the whole hillside.

A vendor hawking fruit and vegetables from the back of a pickup truck was blocking the road ahead when Browning climbed into the blue Opel for the return trip to Meligalas. With reverse gear still inoperative, he had no choice but to make the twisting descent to the village's tiny main square in neutral, backwards.

George was nowhere to be seen when Browning pulled up in front of the nameless bar in Meligalas, but he soon appeared, spouting apologies for his tardiness. In the daylight, George looked more careworn than he had in the bar's forgiving glow at night. Perhaps it was the permanent stubble that transformed his cheeks and chin into coarse sandpaper. But he was lucid and willing enough, and the two set off almost immediately for the short drive to the house formerly occupied by Petros Demitros.

Browning was surprised to find himself back on the road toward Mavromati. "It's out here?" he asked. George grunted and gave an affirmative nod. "Slow down," he warned as the car approached a crossroads hamlet, "you don't want to miss turn." George craned forward in his seat for a better view. "There!" he cried, so loudly he startled Browning. "There it is! Turn left there!"

Browning jerked the car sharply to the left, onto a narrow blacktopped roadway. Out of the corner of an eye he spotted a blue street sign bolted to the side of a white building. The white lettering on top was in Greek, indecipherable to his eye. But the gold-lettered transcription below leapt out as if written in neon: Marias Kalogeropoulou, it read, and underneath, in parenthesis, the single, electric word, (Kallas).

George directed Browning a short distance down this auspiciously named road, ordering him to pull over in front of a crumbling but largely intact building of grey and brown stone. "Well," said George, gesturing at the decaying house, "what do you think?"

Browning studied the ancient Kalogeropoulou homestead with barely suppressed excitement. Within these still-sturdy walls, the century's greatest opera singer was conceived by a young married couple who soon would be unable to stand the sight of one another. Part of the terra-cotta roof was missing and sections of stone above the two small boarded-up windows at the front of the house had long since fallen away. On the upper level, a doorway opened abruptly into thin air, its staircase or balcony lost to time and neglect. Yet the solid stone construction, and a few surviving decorative touches around the doors and corners, hinted at the fine house it once must have been. Gazing upon it, Browning was swept with an unaccountable sense of loss, as if his own past were somehow disintegrating with the house.

"Come on," he said roughly to George, "let's get on with it."

The two approached the house of the building's nearest neighbour and knocked on the door. A man of perhaps 50 emerged from the gloom within and stood blinking quizzically in the morning light.

Browning turned to George. "Explain that I'm a Canadian journalist looking for information about Petros Demitros," he instructed. "Ask him if he ever heard anything about Petros adopting a baby, or arranging an adoption for someone else in town."

George looked at Browning sharply, but did as instructed. The neighbour gave the two an incredulous look, then launched into a tirade in Greek that concluded with a contemptuous spitting sound. "He didn't like Petros very much," George translated for Browning, who had sensed as much. "He says he was a crazy man, always scaring the children and making trouble. He was glad to see the last of him."

"What about adoption?" Browning persisted. "What did he say about that?"

George shook his head. "He said Petros Demitros would no more be a father to a child than a wolf would suckle a lamb."

"That's it?" asked Browning, disappointed. "He never heard anything about Demitros being involved in an adoption? This would have been in the late '60s."

George nodded and spoke again to the neighbour. The response was swift and vehement. "He says Petros Demitros never cared about anyone except himself. He was a man at war with the world."

Other neighbours who had known Demitros said much the same. All scoffed at the idea the surly curmudgeon could have been involved in anything as life-affirming as adoption. He was so friendless, one confided, that when he died only two people showed up for his funeral.

"Only two?" asked Browning, perking up when George translated the man's remark for him. "Does he know who they were?"

"Only one," answered George, after a moment's consultation, "Theo Leventis, a very old man who lives a bit further out of town along this road. I know him slightly; he must be nearly 90 by now. The other," George shrugged, "was a stranger, someone from out of town."

"That's odd," mused Browning. "Why would someone make a special trip here just to attend the funeral of an anti-social old hermit?" He glanced at George, who shrugged again. "Who knows?" the bartender said, impatience in his voice. "What difference does it make?"

"Only this," said Browning, thinking out loud. "Perhaps the stranger came because he owed Petros Demitros a debt of gratitude. Perhaps Petros once did him an enormous favour — like arranging an adoption, for instance."

"Why are you so interested in this adoption?" asked George, a bit exasperated. "Who was this child?" It was time to trust George, at least a little bit. Browning motioned for him to come closer. "I'm on a mission of the greatest sensitivity," he confided in a low voice. "I'm looking for — can you keep a secret?"

"Of course!" cried George, indignant. "Trustworthiness is matter of greatest honour to Greeks!"

"Good," said Browning, patting George light lightly on the arm. "I have reason to believe," he began, glancing around as if to ensure that he wasn't being overheard, "that Petros Demitros assisted in the adoption of the child of the daughter of one of this town's most illustrious families."

George's eyes widened. "You don't mean Maria Cal—"

"Shhhh," hissed Browning urgently. "For God's sake, George, not so loud."

George nodded and, still staring at Browning, silently mouthed the name. With a barely perceptible nod of his own, Browning signaled silent confirmation.

"Mother of God!" George exclaimed.

"You won't breathe a word of this to anyone," Browning insisted.

"Not a word. On my most solemn oath."

"Good. Now, let's pay a call on Mr. Leventis and see what light he can shed on this mystery."

THEO LEVENTIS LIVED in what looked like a renovated chicken coop a couple of kilometres farther along Marias Kalogeropoulou Road. In fact, judging from the clutch of roosters and hens rooting in the dusty soil, it appeared he might actually be sharing his quarters with his feathered companions.

Leventis himself was a gnomish man, barely five feet tall, gnarled and wizened with age. Despite his years, a thick shock of snow-white hair still covered his head and a bushy white moustache drooped over his upper lip and spilled past the corners of his mouth. Wearing an ancient overcoat several sizes too large for his diminutive frame, he was painstakingly raking a barren plot of land next to his hovel-house when Browning and George arrived.

George introduced Browning and explained the reason for their call. Leventis said nothing, but watched Browning through watery eyes as George spoke. When he finished, Leventis was silent for what seemed like minutes, and Browning was sure that he hadn't absorbed a word. But then, in a raspy croak that made each word sound like a supreme physical effort, Leventis spoke.

George listened intently, his expression of concentration gradually giving way to one of distaste. "What?" Browning asked George anxiously. "What is it? Does he remember the stranger at the funeral?"

"Oh, he remembers, alright," he said disgustedly. "But he says this information must be very valuable if you have come all the way from Canada just to ask him these questions."

"What does that mean?" demanded Browning, enlightenment dawning even as he spoke. "You mean he wants money?"

George sighed. "I apologize for my countryman, Mr. Browning.

Most Greeks aren't like this." He spat contemptuously. "He is greedy old fool."

Browning was silent for a moment. "How much does he want?" he finally asked.

George turned to the old man and spoke to him gruffly. Leventis croaked a response, and George, face flushed with indignation, unleashed a torrent of high-volume Greek in return. The old man shrugged and turned away, resuming his methodical and evidently futile raking.

"What did he say, George?" asked Browning. "How much?"

"Is ridiculous," sputtered George. "Is embarrassing. He should be ashamed to think it, let alone ask."

"George," interrupted Browning wearily. "Just tell me how much."

"Two hundred euros." George shook his head sorrowfully. "Absurd."

Browning did a quick mental calculation. "Tell him," he instructed, "that we'll pay him 100. Not a euro more."

"But Mr. Browning," George protested. Browning held up a hand. "Just tell him, George. Please."

Unhappily, George did as instructed. Leventis stopped his raking and held out his right hand, palm upward. Browning pulled out his wallet, peeled two 50-euro notes from his billfold and handed them to the avaricious old fossil. Leventis examined both with gleaming eyes, folded them neatly and placed them in a pocket of his capacious coat.

"Now," said Browning, his excitement undimmed by the old man's greed, "ask him what he knows." He watched as George questioned Leventis, nodding as he spoke and interrupting him with sharply worded questions. The conversation seemed to go on forever, and Browning longed to break in for an update. But he was afraid to say a word, lest the canny old eccentric realize how anxious he was and demand even more money.

At last, George turned toward Browning. "Well, here's what you bought for 100 euros, though I doubt you'll think you got money's worth."

"Tell me," ordered Browning, impatient.

"He first met Petros Demitros nearly 70 years ago," George began, "when Demitros was just child. He was friend of boy's father. When the rest of family was wiped out by bastard Germans, he helped Demitros get back on feet. They stay in touch even when Demitros become hermit." George glanced at Leventis, who had resumed his raking. "He say he was his only friend. That's why he went to funeral."

"What about the stranger? Does he know who he was?"

"No. He say he never see him before in life."

A wave of disappointment swept over Browning. "Well, does he remember what he looked like?"

George paused, an odd look on his face. "Well, that strange thing. He say man —it was a man in mid-50s — this man seem to appear out of nowhere as they laying old Demitros in grave. He not see him coming, and he not see him leave. He just there, then suddenly, he not."

"Did they speak?" asked Browning.

"Only short time," replied George. "Stranger not very friendly. When burial complete, Leventis introduce himself and ask stranger where he from. From Mani, he tell him. And how you know Demitros? he ask. Once, long ago, he did me great favour, stranger replied. Oh? say Leventis, and what was?" George paused, a visible shudder rippling through his body. "Well?" prompted Browning.

"I sorry, Mr. Browning, but something old man tell me has me bit scare. When he ask stranger what Demitros do for him, man look at him with tender, sad eyes. Eyes, Leventis say, like deep wells, somehow not quite real, not quite alive . . ." George shuddered again. "Anyway, stranger say, 'He gave me a life.' Leventis say he feel eyes make him feel like he drawn into a frightening void. Finally, he have to look away. When he look back, stranger gone."

Both men digested this odd tale for a few moments. Browning spoke first. "He gave me a life. That's what he told Leventis?"

"That's what he tell him," confirmed George. "Whatever it means."

Browning's eyes shone with excitement. "Don't you see George? I was right — Demitros helped the stranger adopt Callas's child! What else could it mean?"

"Could be," said George, though he was far from convinced by this theory. "But who was stranger? Why he seem so odd to Leventis? How he appear and disappear so fast?"

"I don't know, George," said Browning, his mind racing, "but that's what I have to find out. And it looks as if I'll have to go to the Mani to do it."

The Mani. Strange land of blood feuds and nereids. And Matina. The thought of seeing her again, and perhaps even enlisting her help in his search, filled his heart with sudden longing.

They bade farewell to old Leventis, who'd resumed his raking and was paying them no heed. When they reached the car, Browning asked George to help him push it out of the laneway and back onto the road.

"Mr. Browning," said George politely, "why you no just back up?"

"Because George, the car won't go into reverse."

"No?" said George. "That strange. Can I try? I have gift with mechanical things."

"Be my guest," said Browning, with exaggerated courtesy. George slipped into the driver's seat and accepted the key from Browning. Sliding two fingers under a knob halfway down the stick that Browning had somehow failed to notice before, he lifted and pulled back in one smooth motion. Reverse gear engaged with a gentle thwunk and George had the car backed out onto the road and turned around before Browning could close his gaping mouth.

~

AFTER CHECKING out of his room in Mavromati, Browning returned to the bar in Meligalas to say farewell to George. It was in his mind to slip the bartender a few euros for his help. But before he could say a thing, a flushed and clearly excited George was clapping him heartily in the back and babbling something in Greek. "Whoa, George, whoa," said Browning. "Calm down, man. I can't understand you."

"Sorry, sorry," said the bartender, "but I have news that might make your search easier."

Browning caught his breath. "For God's sake, what?"

"I am telling a few of boys in the bar about you searching for Maria Callas's child ..."

"George!" Browning interjected sharply. "You promised you wouldn't say a word about that!"

"I know, Mr. Browning," said George, a sheepish grin bisecting his rough-hewn features. "But this is such big news. How could I not share it?" Browning glared, and George added hastily: "Besides, when you hear what I find out, you forgive me."

"I doubt that, George," replied Browning icily. "But try me. What did you find out?"

"The name of stranger!" he declared, triumphant.

"Really?" gasped Browning. "You know his name? How?"

"One of bar old-timers remember family from next village who move away in late 60s, after adopting child. They leave suddenly, without telling people where they going." Browning, mind racing, considered this startling news. The timing was about right — it had to be the family he was looking for. "What was the name?" he said, pulling out his notebook.

"Marinatos. The family name was Marinatos."

"WELL?" said Renata Richter, sipping on a glass of Boutari white wine. "What have you found out?"

"Bliss went to Kalamata by train three days ago and rented a car from an agency called Hellas On Wheels." Harrison Howard suppressed a smirk. "Helluva name, eh? Only the Greeks. Anyway, he told the rental agent he was going to spend a few days poking around in the ruins of ancient Messene, which is just a short distance north-west of Kalamata."

"Good work," grunted Richter, impressed. "Is there anything else?"

"Nothing solid," Howard admitted. "But I've been studying a map of the area. There are only three or four places of any size near the Messene site — a place called Androussa, another called Valira, a village called Mavromati and Meligalas, which looks to be the main centre for the region. My guess is that Bliss went to one or more of those places to track down his Maria Callas story."

Richter took another sip of wine. "Then I suppose you'd better go there, too."

"My thought precisely," agreed Howard. "I've already booked myself on the 6 p.m. flight to Kalamata." He gestured at the hospital across the street from the sidewalk cafe. "What about Norman?"

"Oh, he's out of danger, thank God. Trouble is, now he's like a born-again Christian, except that I'm his saviour," smiled Richter, shuddering slightly. "It's unnerving. I think I liked it better when he hated me."

Howard chuckled. "You're staying here, then?"

"For now. I'll stay with Norman until he's up and about, then I'll join you — if you haven't found Bliss by then."

Howard shot Richter a look. "I guess Bliss is in a lot of trouble, eh?"

Richter scowled. "He ignored instructions, absconded with a pile of his employer's money, and made me look like an idiot for giving him a chance. But you know," she continued, her voice softening, "part of me can't help admiring him for what he's doing. It takes a lot of spunk."

"Bliss has more spunk than most people think," nodded Howard. "More, even, than he himself realizes. I've always thought there was much more to him than met the eye."

Richter studied Howard shrewdly. "You're fond of him, aren't you," she said. A statement, not a question.

"Yes, I am. He's screwed up, sure, but who isn't? I just think he's one of the most decent people I know." Howard gazed levelly at Richter. "I just hope you can find a way to go easy on him."

Richter drained the last of the wine from her glass. "Let's find him first," she said. "Then we'll figure out what to do with him."

CHAPTER 20

NOT FAR FROM KALAMATA, THE COASTAL ROAD TO AREOPOLI BEGINS A vertiginous ascent up the rugged flank of Mount Taygetus. The drive along the two-lane highway, with its bounty of switchbacks and vistas of the twisting Maniot coastline, is one of the loveliest in Greece. But Browning, hands gripping the wheel in a mortal embrace, was too unnerved to notice anything but the sheer drop to his right and the roadside shrines erected where earlier travellers had met untimely ends. If Greek drivers fell off this road with such regularity, Browning reflected, what were the odds of him surviving the drive? But retreat was impossible — there was no place to turn around in any case — so he motored on, body tensed and tilted forward as if anticipating imminent attack.

At last, in a flurry of zigzags, the road descended to a narrow plain between the mountains and the sea. But almost before Browning's pulse had returned to normal, the route veered wildly back into the mountains, climbing to even more dizzying heights. The shrines were almost continual now, tiny white-stone chapels from within whose glassed-in chambers smiled photographs of the deceased, blissfully unaware of their dreadful fates.

Resisting a powerful urge to shut his eyes, Browning leaned

forward and tried to ignore the seductive blue expanse of the Messinian Gulf hundreds of feet below. He concentrated instead on the road, which took him past sprouting olive groves and rough stone fences, past blink-tiny villages with streets barely wide enough for a single vehicle, past ancient frescoed churches and hobbled grazing goats, past used-up Maniot women in wide-brimmed straw hats toting bundles of branches, past empty cliff-top settlements bristling with crumbling tower houses until, at last, Areopoli, named for the God of War, slouched sullenly into view from behind a bend in the road.

The town hunkered on a narrow plateau high above the sea, in the lee of the bare, cloud-capped Taygetus Massif,. Browning drove slowly through its quiet streets, past austere grey stone buildings and around its narcoleptic central square, peopled only by a few dozing townsfolk and a young backpacking couple hunched over a map. The square's focal point was a heroic statute of Petrobey Mavromichalis, the 19th century leader who united the Mani's warring clans and helped win Greece's War of Independence. It was ringed by tavernas, all but deserted at mid-afternoon, a hotel, a bakery and a few shops.

Somewhere in this town was Matina, whom Browning yearned to see again. But he couldn't seek her out, not in this place. That would only cause trouble. He would have to bide his time and find a discreet way to make contact. In the meantime, he would make Areopoli his base while he searched for the Marinatos family and the lost son of Maria Callas.

The hotel on the main square was full, booked by a German tour group drawn to town by the nearby and justly famous Diros caves. So Browning set off on foot through the narrow streets in search of a place to stay. Several of the tower homes had been converted into small, luxury hotels to cater to the region's modest but growing tourist trade. The rates were excessive at all but one, the Tsimova Museum Rooms, which billed itself as a combination hotel and military museum. The tariff was markedly cheaper than elsewhere, but the accommodations seemed comfortable, and the hosts jovial if incomprehensible. He gratefully booked a room and walked back to the square to retrieve his car.

When he returned, his hostess was waiting to direct him to an appropriate parking spot. A broad, beaming woman of about 50, she jabbered at him ceaselessly in Greek, seemingly confident that he understood every word. Fortunately, she punctuated her words with gestures for emphasis, and from these Browning was able to decipher her intent.

Collecting his belongings, he followed the babbling woman into the small hotel, a well-kept three-storey building of white stone and red mortar next to an attractive Greek Orthodox church with a multi-storied bell tower. Without a pause in her baffling commentary, the woman walked over to a darkened showcase and flicked a switch. At once the showcase was illuminated, revealing a jam-packed arsenal of muskets, broadswords, breech-loaders, daggers, pikes, antique revolvers, scabbards, even a miniature cannon. His hostess, briefly silent, beamed expectantly, and Browning understood he was viewing a museum of the Mani's bloody history. He made appropriate noises of appreciation and the woman, satisfied, snapped off the light and motioned for him to follow her.

To reach his room on the top floor, Browning had to climb a winding stone staircase cut roughly into one corner of the building. Where it turned a corner, the staircase narrowed until it almost disappeared, making its ascent only slightly less hazardous than rock-climbing. His hostess scampered up with an agility that belied her years and heft. Browning, burdened with his luggage, staggered and wobbled like a toddler taking his first steps.

He caught his breath while his hostess, cackling at her own incomprehensible wit, unlocked the door to his chambers. The room, an attractive rectangle of thick whitewashed walls, smooth stone floors and slotted wood ceilings, was arranged around its dominant icon: a huge and ancient colour television set, circa 1965, bristling with pushbuttons and knobs. It was clearly meant to inspire awe, for the woman immediately launched into an animated demonstration of its features. Browning nodded mechanically as she fired up the antique cathode ray tubes and produced, with a flourish of twirling buttons, grainy images on three different channels. She appeared unconcerned that they were unanimously in black and white, smiling triumphantly as each shadowy image materialized.

With obvious reluctance, the woman turned off the TV and, plumping the pillows and smoothing non-existent wrinkles from the bedspread, at last took her leave, still chattering obscurely. As her voice receded, Browning fell heavily on the bed, suddenly exhausted beyond reason. Within minutes, his robust snores filled the room.

About 45 minutes later, the bell tower of the church next door erupted in a cataclysm of sound. Gripped by the mental miasma unique to those ripped untimely from sleep, Browning at first couldn't fathom the source of the astonishing din. The sound came in waves, the pattern endlessly repeated, borne directly to his inner ear by highly amplified electronic bells: TA-dum, TA-dum, TA-dum! TA-dum, TA-dum, TA-dum!! TA-dum, TA-dum, TA-dum, TA-dum, TA-dum, TA-dum, TA-DUM!!!

At length, the cacophony ceased, followed by the timeless cadences of a priest singing the Orthodox liturgy. Wide awake now, Browning stretched out on his bed and let the chant-song's rhythms wash over him. The effect was profoundly calming. When the service ended, he watched from his window as three white-bearded priests, looking like refugees from a distant past in flowing black robes and high-brimmed hats, climbed into a late-model car and drove off to rejoin the 21st Century.

Inspired by this second-hand exposure to the spiritual world, Browning resolved to begin his search at once. Descending carefully from his aerie, he made a fruitless attempt to learn if his hosts knew a family named Marinatos. But the language barrier proved insuperable; the garrulous woman thought he was trying to introduce himself and repeatedly shook his hand, while her equally unilingual husband simply smiled and nodded. Defeated, Browning smiled and nodded back, and eased out the door.

Outside, the town was stirring from its afternoon somnolence. Stores were reopening, and the streets, if not exactly thronged with people, at least testified to their existence. Browning wandered down the narrow main street toward the square. To track down the Marinatos family, he would need to find an English speaker. But in the isolated Mani, few residents knew the language. His best hope was to concentrate on hotels, bars and restaurants, places where the ability to speak a variety of languages was advantageous.

His first stop was the central hotel, the one booked by the German tourists. As Browning had calculated, the desk clerk spoke decent English. But though he was a lifelong resident of the town, he knew of no family named Marinatos. "Are you sure that's the name?" the man asked, face twisted in puzzlement. "It isn't very Maniot."

"The family was originally from Messinia," Browning answered. "They would have moved to the Mani 25 or 30 years ago — a married couple with a young son."

The clerk shook his head. "No, I'm certain they're not here." He smiled ruefully. "You understand, not many outsiders move to the Mani. I'm sure I'd remember."

Browning made similar inquiries at the tavernas ringing the square. But the answer was the same: nobody had heard of a family named Marinatos. Browning's optimism was fading fast. Assuming they were still alive, they must be living in a more remote part of the Mani. To locate them, he would need help. Matina's help, he thought. Yet how could he ask her? Under the circumstances, it would be scandalous for her to be seen with him.

As he pondered his dilemma, an idea began to form. Retracing his steps to the hotel on the square, he approached the clerk, leaning conspiratorially over the counter. "It's me again," he began apologetically. "Sorry to be a nuisance, but I wonder if you could help me with something else." The clerk gestured expansively. "It would be my pleasure."

"Years ago, my parents met a Greek couple in Montreal," Browning said. "They became great friends. But the couple moved back to Greece, to this town, as a matter of fact. I would like to look them up, but I have forgotten their names. I remember only that they had a daughter named Matina."

The clerk gave him a sharp look. "You must mean Matina Mourtzinos." He shook his head. "Terrible, terrible," he muttered.

"Why? What's the matter?" asked Browning, feigning innocence.

"It's like the family is cursed," said the clerk, face darkening. "Years ago, Matina's father Nicholas was drowned during a storm that came out of nowhere. Then, just two weeks ago, Matina's husband Andreas killed himself and their daughter in Athens."

"How awful," Browning exclaimed.

The clerk spat disgustedly into a spittoon on the floor. "He was a bum, her husband, a no-good bastard. He had everything, but it wasn't enough."

"Where is Matina now?" Browning asked cautiously.

"With her mother, Eleni. They live in a small house on the edge of town. The old woman's missing a few marbles; half the time she doesn't even know who she is."

Browning fell silent for a moment, appearing deep in thought. "I would like to give my regards to Matina's mother," he said finally, "but I don't want to impose." He squinted at the clerk. "Would you be willing to call Matina and find out if she and her mother are up to a visit? I would be very grateful."

"Of course," said the clerk at once. "What should I tell her?"

"Just say," replied Browning, "that an old family friend, Bliss Browning, is in town and to call me at the Tsimova Museum Rooms if she'd like to arrange a meeting."

The clerk scribbled something on a piece of paper. "No problem."

"By the way," asked Browning absently, "what is Eleni's last name?"

"Karalis."

"Ah, yes, Karalis. That's the name, alright."

Congratulating himself on his cleverness, Browning thanked the clerk and strolled into the gathering twilight. His disappointment at failing to find the Marinatos family had evaporated at the prospect of seeing Matina again, for he had little doubt that she would respond to his message. Lost in thought, he barely noticed that the narrow road he was walking along led out of town. Within minutes, he found himself at sheer cliffs overlooking the sea. To the west, the sun was half-submerged in the Ionian Sea, colouring the water and sky cerise. To the east, the awful blankness of the Taygetus loomed oppressively, crowned by sunlit clouds that glowed first white, then pink. As the sun fell below the horizon, the fire dimmed from the clouds over the mountains, and the cerulean sky faded to grey and black. Between the mountains and the sea sat the God of War, its ancient towers silent and still and displaced in time.

Mesmerized, Browning gazed at the sea hundreds of feet below. He recalled Matina's vision of the nereid on the day her father died. This must be where it happened, he thought, peering into the dark water. But he saw nothing unusual. After a few minutes, he turned and walked back toward town, just as the milk-white figure of a woman of unearthly beauty slowly rose from the water near the cliff-bound shore.

~

MATINA WAS WAITING across the small courtyard when he stepped out the door of the Tsimova Museum Rooms early the next morning. Her black clothes, the traditional mourning garb of Greek widows, accentuated the darkness of her eyes and hair. Browning started to call out, but the words died in his throat when she abruptly turned and walked away. He stood stock still for a moment, uncertain, until she gave him a backward glance that clearly said: Follow me.

He trailed after her at a respectful distance, trying not to make it obvious that he was following. She never looked back, but kept walking at a brisk pace through the ancient, winding streets. Finally, near the point where the town melted away into the barren plateau, she opened the door of a modest single-storey stone house and stepped inside. Browning slowed, unsure what to do next. Then Matina appeared in a window of the house. With a quick look around that felt furtive even to him, Browning scampered up to the door and stepped inside.

Almost at once, Matina was at his side. He was startled by the rush of emotion he felt at being with her again, as if a long-stuck valve to his heart had re-opened. Without a word, he wrapped her in his arms, hunching slightly to match her shorter frame. She clung to him in response.

Then, Matina looked at him levelly, a slight frown on her serious face. Browning could only stare back, captivated by the curve of her neck and the quiet intelligence in her eyes. "I thought I'd never see you again," she said quietly, her eyes probing his. "I thought that when we parted in Kalamata, you were out of my life forever." Browning nodded, not trusting himself to speak.

"Then I got that phone call last night, saying you were here, in Areopoli, that you wanted to see my mother." She shook her head slightly. "At first, I didn't believe it. But then, somehow, I knew it was true." A tentative smile, then she again fell silent.

A fierce tenderness swept over Browning, and he understood that this brave and battered woman meant more to him than anyone he had ever known. It no longer surprised him that this was so. It struck him that his life — his real life, not the ersatz existence he had mistaken for a life — had begun only recently, midwifed by a long-dead opera legend, his own shaky convictions and the courage of the woman standing before him. But how could he say any of this to Matina? She had buried a child and a husband barely a week earlier.

"How was the funeral?" he asked cautiously, unsure whether he should raise the painful subject. But Matina smiled, though her eyes were brimming as she answered. "Very sad, but very beautiful," she said softly. "It seemed like the whole town turned out." She wiped her eyes unselfconsciously. "Everyone has been so kind." She frowned. "It was very hard on mama. At times I wasn't sure she would make it through the service."

Browning was at a loss for words, so said nothing. Again, it was Matina who broke the lengthening silence. "Why, Bliss?" she said, looking searchingly into his eyes. "Why have you come here?"

If he was to enlist Matina's help, Browning would have to be more forthright about his purpose. But not too forthright; he didn't want to scare her off with tales of ghosts. He took a deep breath. "Remember when I told you I came to Greece to research a story about Maria

Callas?" She nodded, her eyes never leaving his face. "Well, there's more to the story than I've told you. A lot more."

"Go on."

"I have reliable information that Callas had a son out of wedlock by Aristotle Onassis." Matina's eyes widened, but she said nothing, so Browning plunged on. "She kept the pregnancy hidden from him, because he would have disowned her had he known, and gave the child up for adoption to a family in the Peloponnese, not far from Kalamata.

"Since we parted, I have learned that sometime after adopting the child, the family moved to the Mani. Who knows why; maybe they feared that Onassis's agents would find the child and do him harm. He was a powerful and ruthless man, after all. I've also learned the family's name: Marinatos. I was hoping you might help me find them."

Matina's face sagged imperceptibly as Browning finished his explanation. "That's why you're here?" she asked dully. "To chase your story?"

"Yes," he said, adding quickly, "and to see you again, of course." Especially, he thought, but did not say, to see you again. "Of course," she repeated. Browning ached to say more, but the words would not come.

With a physical effort of will, Matina straightened up and gave Browning a wan smile. "Well then," she said, "I guess we'd better get to work. What did you say the family's name was?"

"Marinatos."

Matina frowned. "Can't say I know anyone by that name around here. Perhaps they live deeper in the Mani. That's where I'd go if I was trying to hide from the outside world."

"Can you help me search for them?" Browning asked.

"Of course." There was a note of impatience in Matina's voice that she couldn't quite disguise.

"What about your mother and your father-in-law? What will we tell them?"

"You've already concocted a pretty good cover story," Matina responded, and Browning coloured slightly at the memory of his deceit of the hotel clerk. "Let's stick with that. We'll just say you're the son of friends of my parents, here on vacation, and everyone thought it would be good for me if I was to show you around. Since you're like family, it's not improper."

"Will your mother believe that?"

"Mama's often . . . confused," Matina said quietly. "She won't recall your parents, of course, but . . ." She shrugged. "Don't worry. It will work."

Browning looked directly into her eyes. "It's good to see you again, Matina." She dropped her gaze. "It's good to see you too, Bliss," she murmured. Words he dared not speak hung in the sea-stung air like whispers from a half-remembered dream.

CHAPTER 21

"It's been three days since I've heard from you," scolded Maria Callas. "Where have you been?"

"I've been busy tracking down your son," Browning replied crisply, suppressing a prickle of irritation. "Besides," he added, in a flurry of keystrokes, "it's often impossible for me to connect with you."

"No need to get huffy," sniffed Callas. "I was only asking. When I don't hear from you, I get worried."

"Well, there's no cause for alarm," Browning shot back, but his annoyance was already waning. "I've been making good progress. In fact, I now believe I know the name of the family who adopted your son."

"Really? Tell me," Callas said, her urgency palpable even on his computer screen. Browning quickly filled her in on his research in Meligalas, including his conversation with Theo Leventis and his discovery of the Marinatos family name. There was no immediate response when he finished, and he feared the connection had been broken. Then this bald assertion, for that's the only way to describe it, appeared on his screen: "The stranger at Demitros's funeral, the one who spooked Leventis, that was Marinatos."

"How do you know that?" asked Browning, though he had already reached the same conclusion. "I just know," replied Callas. "The Zone is like that. Sometimes, for no apparent reason, you know with absolute confidence that something is true. While you were telling me your story, I suddenly knew who the stranger was. It was Marinatos."

"What else do you know about him?" probed Browning, his excitement growing.

"Only one thing. He was not alive at the time of Demitros's funeral."

"What do you mean, he wasn't alive?" said Browning, thoroughly confused. "I thought you just said he was at the funeral."

"I did," Callas replied calmly.

"Well, then, how could he have been—" Browning stopped typing in mid-sentence, aghast. "You're not saying. . ." he began,". . . that he was a spirit?" finished Callas. "That's precisely what I'm saying. The way he appeared and disappeared without warning was a clue. But as soon as I heard you describe his eyes, I knew. How did Leventis put it? 'Like two deep mysterious wells, like looking into a vast frightening void.' That's precisely how the eyes of the dead appear to the living. Of course," she added matter-of-factly, "in The Zone it's perfectly normal. Nobody gives it a second thought."

Even for Browning, who was accepting instructions from a dead legend, this was a bit much. "If it's that easy to pop down to earth and pay a visit," he asked, "why don't you do it? Why do you need my help?"

"My dear Browning, I never said it was easy. In fact, permission to materialize is rarely granted, and even then, only for brief periods. Our friend Nicholas Marinatos must have wanted to attend that funeral very badly indeed."

"Why would it matter so much to him?" asked Browning, still absorbing Callas's revelations.

"Obviously, he wanted to thank Demitros directly."

"You've lost me again," said Browning.

"I'm sorry, " Callas apologized, "I keep forgetting that you know nothing of The Zone. Look. Think of a funeral as an elevator that transports the souls of the departed from a waiting room on earth to the next plane of existence. By going to Demitros's funeral, Marinatos could ride that elevator with him. Once it reaches its destination, further contact becomes difficult, if not impossible. But I have said too much already."

But Browning's mind was already racing ahead. "Are you saying," he began, typing so quickly that his fingers had trouble keeping pace with his thoughts, "that I should be looking for a widow named Marinatos with a son?"

"Probably. Though I have no way of knowing if this Mrs. Marinatos is still alive, either."

"What," he teased, "can't The Zone's truth channel give you that information?"

"There's no need to be sarcastic, my dear Browning," Callas replied stiffly. "I told you it was a mysterious process. I know what I know. Nothing more."

"Sorry."

"Apology accepted. So how are you going to find Mrs. Marinatos and, more importantly, my son? Need I remind you that the clock, so to speak, is ticking?"

"No, you needn't," he replied, with an audible sigh. "I've enlisted the help of Matina Mourtzinos. Together, we're going to search through the Mani for Mrs. Marinatos."

"Matina?" Callas exclaimed. "Isn't she the woman you're besotted with?"

Browning's face reddened. "First of all," he wrote, "I'm not 'besotted' with her. I'm very fond of her, admittedly, but 'besotted' is not the word I would use."

"You can use whatever word you like," interjected Callas, "but it's clear to me that you are in love with her. Do you deny that?"

Browning considered Callas's question. Was it true? Did he love Matina — he, who had sworn never again to fall under passion's dominion? Had he not concluded that love was a chameleon, irresolute and traitorous, not to be entrusted with anything as fragile as his heart? He had even convinced himself that what people called love was usually something more impermanent and ignoble: lust's craving dressed up in respectable clothing, perhaps, or raw, naked need masquerading as caring. Love, he had concluded, was for the credulous and quixotic. It was not for people like him.

Yet Matina had thrown these smug rationalizations into question. For if love were a chimera, how could he explain his feelings whenever he thought of her? This was not the gonad-driven brain fever he remembered from his fleeting liaison with Krystal. It wasn't even the tongue-tied infatuation he suffered in the presence of Kimberly Taylor. Matina aroused feelings of tenderness, esteem, devotion. He was awed by her calm intelligence, her resilience in the face of adversity. Yet he was also alarmed by her precarious mortality, and yearned to keep her safe from the world's unbounded storehouse of perils. Most of all, he hungered to be with her, to wrap his body around hers, to lightly kiss her neck or lay a gentle hand on the swell of her belly. She was the miraculous embodiment of all that he held precious and had thought forever lost. How could he not love her?

"Well?" prompted Callas, determined to have his response.

With a shudder of resignation, Browning capitulated. "It's true. I love her. Are you satisfied?"

"No. Not until you tell me what you're going to do about it."

"Maria! Please, think of the circumstances. What can I do?"

"Damn the circumstances! Tell her how you feel."

"No!"

"Why not? Are you afraid to find out if she feels the same way about you?"

Browning started to remind Callas how improper it would be to woo a woman who had recently suffered so great a loss. But he broke off in mid-sentence, again considering Callas's words. What if what was holding him back wasn't Matina's situation at all, but the unspoken fears that had sabotaged him throughout his life? What if his concern about the appropriateness of a romance with Matina was merely a cover for his own private demons? Was that possible?

With a sinking feeling, he realized it was. Just thinking about declaring his love to Matina triggered a tightness in his chest and a queasy feeling in the pit of his stomach. Yet he believed that when her grief had faded and the time was right, Matina would welcome his love. So, what was he afraid of?

Could it be his old nemesis, his fears about the adequacy of his attributes, which had so often subverted past relationships? He considered this possibility for a moment, then somewhat to his surprise, rejected it out of hand. It struck him that his penis phobia had always been a flesh-and-blood metaphor for something more fundamental that was missing from his life: a sense of capability, of belief in himself. O ye of little faith, he thought with a wry smile. What silent damage you do!

But the last few weeks had swept away those subverting demons, or so he thought. His exchanges with Callas, his bold decision to accept her challenge, his ability to function well in a strange and alien land — all of these had exposed the Big Lie that life was a challenge beyond his abilities. Even his panic attacks had subsided.

But Matina. She was an entirely different matter. Declaring his love for her took more than self-confidence. It was the ultimate leap of faith. To bare our soul to another, to let someone see who we really are, without the barriers we erect to conceal our darkest secrets, takes true courage. Despite all the progress he had made since arriving in Greece, Browning wasn't sure he was ready to risk that yet.

"My dear Browning." Callas's familiar words scrolled across his computer screen. "You've been silent for a long time. What are you thinking?"

Browning smiled wearily. "Just trying to puzzle out an answer to your question," he said. "I'm not sure I've got one yet, but I think perhaps I am afraid. I feel like I've emerged from some sort of chrysalis and I'm finally ready to spread my wings and fly under my own power. It's exhilarating. But the stakes are so high, Maria. I am so new at this. If I declare my love to Matina and it's a mistake, I could crash and burn."

"That's true," replied Callas. "But risk is part of love. You must embrace it like a friend, or you will miss much of what is joyful. Think of what you risked to take on this assignment, and how much you have gained as a result. Do you have any regrets now?"

“No,” Browning admitted. “But how much risk can I bear?”

“That’s for you to decide, my dear Browning. For love, though, I would bear a lot.”

~

"MOTHER, I'd like you to meet Bliss Browning." Matina, radiant in spite of her widow's black, addressed a wizened, white-haired woman dressed even more somberly, if that is possible. "He's the son of some old friends of yours from Montreal, and they asked him to stop by on his vacation and look you up."

The old woman squinted at Browning suspiciously. "Friends of mine?" she asked querulously. "He's no friend of mine. Never seen him before in my life."

"No, mother," said Matina patiently. "He's not your friend. His parents are your friends." She shot Browning an amused look. "What are their names, Bliss?"

"Barton and Marjorie Browning, Mrs. Karalis," said Browning, with a slight deferential bow in the direction of Matina's mother. "They met you when you lived in Montreal, and when I told them I was coming to Greece, they insisted that I look you up."

The old woman looked confused, and passed a fluttery hand over her forehead. "Browning? Barton and Marjorie? No, I don't remember." She gave her daughter a look of frustration. "Matina, I can't remember them."

"It's okay, mother. You're just having one of your spells. It will come back to you later. You'll see."

Matina's mother nodded unhappily. "I hope so. It‘s such a pain, growing old." A look both wistful and plaintive crossed her lined features. "You forget all the things you want to remember, and remember only the things you'd rather forget." She was silent for a moment, then smiled politely at Browning. "How very nice of you to stop by," she said with grave formality. "You must thank your parents for thinking of me."

"I will," promised Browning. "They will be delighted to know you are well, and that God has blessed you with such a lovely daughter." At least that is true, he thought. The old woman beamed, while Matina lowered her head in embarrassment. "Yes, she is my greatest blessing," she said. She looked shrewdly at Browning. "Have you heard her sing?" she demanded. Browning, startled by the question, allowed that he hadn't.

"Come, come," said Mrs. Karalis, rising laboriously from her chair. "She has such a lovely singing voice."

"Mother, no!" protested Matina, alarmed by the sudden turn the visit had taken. "I'm sure Mr. Browning has no interest in hearing me sing."

"Oh, but I do," said Browning, with a gravitas betrayed by the mischievous twinkle in his eye. Sobered by Matina's look of genuine distress, he quickly added: "Of course, I would understand if Matina doesn't feel up to it right now."

"Nonsense," snapped the old woman. "Best thing for her. She needs to get her mind off ... " she paused, as if suddenly recalling things too terrible to mention, "... things she shouldn't dwell on. Come along, Matina," she instructed, shuffling painstakingly in the direction of an adjoining room. Matina followed reluctantly.

They entered a small oblong room crowded with furnishings. Crammed into the room, which was scarcely larger than a spacious bathroom, were two chairs upholstered in red velvet, and a loveseat in an unmatching green-and-yellow print. These were arrayed around the room's centrepiece, a well-travelled portable record player with two detachable speakers. To either side were racks filled with dozens of record albums.

Matina's mother beamed at Browning. "This is my music room," she said, gesturing grandly at the tiny chamber. "Music was always important to us. When we came back to Greece from Canada, this record player was one of the few possessions we didn't leave behind." She fell silent, a faraway look on her face, until finally Matina touched her shoulder. "Mother?" she said gently. The old woman started, then seemed to remember where she was. "I was drifting. That happens when you're old, you know," she said almost belligerently, as if daring someone to challenge her.

"It's okay, mother," said Matina softly. "What do you want me to sing?"

The old woman turned to the record collection and furrowed her brow. "Let me see, let me see," she muttered. "I know it's here somewhere." She traced a bony finger along the outer edge of the row of albums. "Aha! Here it is!" She slipped a hand between two albums and extracted a recording. "Please, Matina, sing the aria from 'Samson and Delilah' for us. You know the one. I love it so much, and you always do it beautifully."

Browning looked quizzically at Matina. "I didn't know you sang opera."

"I don't," she replied. "Only a few of the easiest arias. And not even them very well, I'm afraid. As you're about to learn."

Matina's mother was struggling to align the spindle on the turntable with the hole in the record's centre, but kept missing. "That's odd," she said, puzzled. "I never used to have trouble with this." She held the record up to the window's light and scrutinized it closely. "Matina, I think the record's warped."

"Let me try, Mrs. Karalis," offered Browning. The old woman looked at him in alarm, as if noticing him for the first time. "Who are you?" she snapped.

"Mother," said Matina, unruffled, "this is Bliss, the son of your Canadian friends Barton and Marjorie Browning. Let him help you with the record."

Reluctantly, Matina's mother surrendered the album to Browning, eyeing him distrustfully. Browning slid the vinyl disc onto the turntable and engaged the mechanism. "Track two!" the old woman ordered. "The aria is on track two!"

Browning obediently set the stylus down at the start of the second track. Almost immediately the opening violin notes of the Saint-Saens aria filled the room, followed seconds later by the unmistakable voice of Maria Callas singing the opening line: "Mon coeur ouvre a ta voix."

Then something happened that set Browning's heart racing with shock and amazement. Another sound filled the room, dwarfing Callas's recorded voice, a sound, he realized with a start, coming from Matina. Her voice slid effortlessly over the lyric's fervent affirmation of love. The declaration of Dalila's ardour flew from her lips with an urgency that belied her own tragic history.

As this unlikely duet continued, the two singers merged and became one. The distinction between Matina and Callas melted away; it was as if the great diva had rematerialized before Browning's disbelieving eyes. Barely daring to breathe, he concentrated on Matina's face as the two voices soared to the aria's climactic crescendo. In its expressiveness, its emotional vulnerability, its ineffable longing and desire, it was Callas's face he was looking at. It took his breath away.

The aria ended abruptly and the room was briefly silent except for the scratchy sound of the needle in the groove between tracks. Matina, trembling visibly from the emotion of the song — and perhaps her own turbulent memories — stood with head bowed; her mother sat in her chair, eyes closed, a radiant smile stripping years of care from her face. Browning stared at them both, the lump in his throat making speech impossible. Then the needle reached the next track, and the spell was broken. Jarred by the music's re-entry, Browning lurched for the turntable and lifted the stylus with a sandpapery scratch that earned him a reproachful frown from Matina's mother. But he was far beyond noticing such things.

"My God, Matina," he whispered, when at last he felt able to speak again, "where did you learn to sing like that?"

Matina raised her eyes. She had the look of a startled fawn. "I'm not sure," she slowly answered. "I've been singing that aria since I was in my teens, but believe me Bliss, I've never sung it like that before." She shrugged helplessly. "I can't explain it."

Browning nodded, eyes locked on Matina's face. "I was never able to see Callas sing," he said quietly. "I was born too late for that. But just now, in this room, listening to you, I understood what it must have been like." Matina started to protest, but Browning silenced her with an upraised palm. "I know what I'm saying. I've been listening to Callas for more years than I care to remember, and I'm telling you

Matina, what you just did was remarkable." He snatched a bouquet of fresh-cut orchids from a vase on the windowsill and, bowing slightly, presented them to Matina. "For the great diva," he said gravely, "in heartfelt appreciation for her brilliant performance."

Matina suppressed a smile with her right hand and with her left, gravely accepted her reward from Browning. Both became aware of a low sound, gradually building strength, emanating from the direction of Matina's mother.

"Bravo. Bravo! Bravo!! BRAVO!!!!" Mrs. Karalis had risen from her chair and was grinning at her daughter like a woman possessed. "O glorious music," she cried, in the grip of some transcendent ecstasy. "Thank you for this gift! Thank you for this daughter! Thank you for this life!!"

"Amen," whooped Browning, swept up in the old woman's fevered hosannas. She whirled and fixed him with a confused stare. "And who, exactly, are you?" she demanded anew.

CHAPTER 22

EXCEPT FOR A FEW STRAY CLOUDS HOOKED BY THE TAYGETUS, THE Mediterranean sky was a brilliant blue as Browning and Matina set off the next morning in search of Maria Callas's son. There had been a few frowns when Matina informed her mother that she would be guiding Browning on a motoring tour of the peninsula, but Browning's parents were dear friends, after all, and the hospitality impulse proved stronger than Mrs. Karalis's old-world sense of propriety. She gave the outing her reluctant blessing, but insisted that Matina, swathed from head to toe in black, sit in the back seat for decency's sake.

They headed south along the main highway toward Yerolimin, through a narrow, comparatively fertile plain between the sun-scorched mountains and the sea. Once they were clear of Areopoli, Matina asked Browning to pull over and sank into the passenger seat beside him.

"Are you sure?" he asked. "Your mother wouldn't approve."

"Don't worry," she answered, casting off her black headscarf and raking her dark hair with her fingers. "I'm a big girl now," she said with a sardonic laugh. It was the most carefree sound that Browning had yet heard from her. "Okay," he said, and put the car back into gear.

The highway snaked past an astonishing number of villages. Filled with ruined tower houses, most had an air of abandonment, ghostly monuments to a disappearing age. Matina directed Browning into the frail and failing hearts of these settlements. At first, they appeared deserted but invariably yielded a few old men marking time in the dying villages of their youth.

The men (for women were virtually absent) were friendly enough, perhaps even grateful that strangers had disturbed the changeless routine of their lives. They chatted amiably about the weather, the harsh landscape they shared, the last time a stranger had passed through the village. If they wondered what the young widow in black was doing with the visitor from Canada, they were too polite to ask. Or perhaps they were simply content not to inquire into matters that were none of their affair. Yet as soon as Matina asked if they knew a widow or a young man named Marinatos, she received only a blank stare, a curt head-shake or a gruff "no" in response. Then the old men would look away, suddenly recall urgent business that needed attending to or otherwise make it clear that, as far as they were concerned, the conversation was over.

"It's very odd," mused Matina, after several encounters of this sort. "I'm sure they know something, but it's as if my questions make them uneasy."

"Perhaps they are still protecting the Marinatos," Browning suggested. "After all, the family may have moved here to escape detection by Onassis. Maybe these villagers know that, and are protecting them against prying outsiders like us."

Matina frowned and shook her head. "That doesn't make any sense. First of all, Onassis has been dead for more than 30 years. If he was ever a threat to Callas's son, surely the danger has passed. And if the Marinatos family wanted to disappear in the Mani, they'd hardly share their secret with the entire countryside."

"I suppose you're right," conceded Browning. "But then why are they holding back? Why won't they tell us what they know? What are they afraid of?"

"I don't know," said Matina, "but I suspect that's the key to unlocking this whole mystery."

They stopped for lunch on the awning-shaded terrace of a taverna in Yerolimin, a small fishing port on a lovely natural harbor near the Mani's southern extremity. Except for seven cats and three dogs, which competed for scraps from their table, they had the place to themselves.

Tell her, thought Browning. This is your chance. But though he steeled himself to declare his love to Matina, somehow the moment was never quite right. Instead, he listened as she chattered about inconsequential things: her mother's cooking, the smell of the land after one of its infrequent but violent rainstorms, the time she caught a red mullet in this very bay. At one point, she stopped and discreetly touched his hand. "Thank you for coming here, Bliss," she said, seriously. "Just being able to get away with you like this does wonders for my morale." She smiled wanly. "I think you are good for me, Bliss Browning."

Now, surely. "Matina," he began, "there's something I've been wanting to tell . . ." But his pending declaration was cut short by ferocious snarling and hissing at their feet, a whirlwind of fur and flashing claws beneath their table. Browning and Matina scrambled as the taverna owner and two of his employees, brandishing brooms and bellowing their displeasure, scurried to break up the melee of domestic animals. When order was finally restored, the moment had passed.

After lunch, they continued south past Vathia, bristling with tower homes and perched imperiously on a mass of rock with a commanding view of the Mani coastline. Like most villages in the area, Vathia was part ghost town. But unlike the others, it was being restored as a tourist attraction. Someday, wealthy Europeans would pay handsomely to sleep in these medieval towers. But for now, the town held only construction workers and a handful of residents, unable or perhaps unwilling to shed any light on the mystery of the Marinatos family.

After Vathia, it was only a few kilometres to Cape Tenaro at the Mani's tip, continental Europe's southernmost point. Cape Tenaro was reputed to be the entrance to the underworld of ancient myth, a haunted and haunting place. "I haven't been there since I was a child," said Matina, a wistful look betraying her recollection of happier times. "Let me show it to you," she suggested impulsively. And though Browning questioned whether he could really afford the time, the look of urgency on Matina's face made it impossible to decline. If she could think of doing something so frivolous so soon after the tragedy, he would not refuse.

After a couple of false starts, they found the road leading to the Cape, though "road" is too generous a term for the rutted track that wound around the tapering spine of the Taygetus. In places, a chunk of the narrow lane was simply missing, perhaps washed away by the storms that periodically lash the Cape. Browning had to slow the car almost to a halt and gingerly steer around the gaping holes as best he could. Eventually, the road improved slightly, and they were able to move at the pace of a brisk jog. Minutes later, they arrived at a small clearing next to a couple of deserted buildings. Browning parked the car. They would walk from here.

A path of sorts led from the car park toward the Cape, visible in the middle distance. The landscape now was almost lunar, strewn with rocks large and small, and upholstered with blue-green thorns and thistles the consistency of steel wool. Every so often, a delicate purple wildflower found purchase amidst the rocks, as if thumbing its nose at its harsh surroundings. Though it was a warm late-spring day, Browning felt a shudder ripple through his body, accompanied by a curious feeling of foreboding he could neither comprehend nor define. Perhaps it was this place, with its malignant associations, that unsettled him. Or perhaps it was being here, alone with Matina, knowing that he must soon find a way to declare his feelings for her, yet dreading her response.

Though Matina moved easily along the rough path, Browning had to pick his way carefully to avoid turning an ankle or brushing up against the barbed foliage, which awakened still-painful memories of his tangle with the prickly pear outside Meligalas. After 30 minutes of vigorous hiking, they finally reached the barren, sun-blasted finger of rock known as Cape Tenaro. At its tip sat a lonely lighthouse, and just beyond, the Ionian and Aegean seas commingled in a maelstrom of eddies and clashing currents. A stiff westerly wind, unopposed since Italy, tore across the cape like a Japanese salaryman running for a plane. Browning could just make out the island of Kithira and the easternmost finger of the Peloponnese to the east, but nothing but open water was visible to the west. From Browning's perch, the vast expanse of blue made the huge cargo ships plying these ancient shipping lanes appear puny and insignificant.

"Well?" said Matina, gesturing expansively. "What do you think?"

"It's magnificent," gasped Browning, bracing himself against a particularly fierce gust of wind. "Wild and windswept and utterly untamed." He turned to her with a slightly crazed smile. "It makes me want to shout."

"Be my guest," Matina said gravely.

Now or never. Browning paused a moment, then cupped his mouth with both hands. "Hear ye, hear ye," he bawled into the gale. "I, Bliss Browning, love Matina Mourtzinos!" He dared not look at her. "I say again, I love Matina!!" A few curious seagulls, attracted by the bellowing man below, drifted in his direction. "I want to spend the rest of my life with her!!!"

He finally lowered his hands from his mouth and sneaked a quick look at Matina. She was staring at him, arms limp by her sides, mouth clamped shut. He turned to face her. "I couldn't seem to spit it out any other way," he said apologetically.

Still Matina stared, saying nothing. At last, with an effort that was almost physical, she averted her gaze. From far below a passing ship's horn sounded, faint and forlorn. Browning held his breath, afraid to break the lengthening silence between them.

Matina turned to face him again. Her eyes were moist, her face a mask of tenderness and sorrow. "Bliss," she began, speaking his name with a gentleness that briefly raised his hopes, "this is not our time." Her eyes seemed to be pleading for understanding. "Whatever I feel for you now, however much you mean to me, I cannot think yet of loving again."

Browning felt his heart sink, but held her gaze. "It has been just over a week since I buried my child," Matina said tonelessly. "She was killed by a man I once thought I loved." Her voice thickened. "I'm still trying to understand what happened. I can think of little else." The tears welling in her eyes traced salty tracks on her cheeks. "I miss her every minute of every day." She drew her sleeve across her face and shuddered. "Most of the time, I feel like I'm going crazy, or I'm stuck in a horrible nightmare. But I know I won't wake up. Not ever. This is my life now. I must make the best of it." She managed a sad smile. "So let's have no talk of love. Not yet. Not now."

Browning wanted to tell Matina that he understood. That he too had been damaged by love gone wrong. That he had run from love, as if from a pestilence. And had paid a terrible price for doing so. But his suffering paled in comparison to hers. He could not really claim to understand what she'd been through.

He had spoken too much, too soon. Yet he did not regret his impetuosity. If Matina's words were not the ones he had hoped to hear, he took solace from his impression that she was deferring his love rather than rejecting it. Most of all, he was exhilarated that he'd found the strength to declare his feelings. Whatever happened next, at least he had broken through the barrier of dread that had so thoroughly thwarted him in the past.

"Matina," he said, picking his words with care, "I don't need your answer now, or next week, or even next year. It is enough, for now, that you know how I feel. When you are stronger, when the time is right, you can consider what I have said. There is no rush." He smiled at her. "I'm not going anywhere."

Matina nodded slowly, gratitude and relief on her face. "Thank you, Bliss," she whispered. "You are quite remarkable."

"I know," he acknowledged gravely. "Women are always telling me that."

She studied him narrowly for a moment, trying to judge whether he was serious. It wasn't until Browning's facade of mock earnestness crumbled into a broad grin that she relaxed and both succumbed to giddy laughter. Beneath the limpid Greek sky, in view of the gods and curious sea-birds, near the place the ancients knew as the entrance to Hell, Bliss Browning and Matina Mourtzinos laughed until tears like cleansing balm flowed from their eyes.

THE SUN, hell-bent on immersion in the Ionian Sea, had fallen below the western ridge by the time they reached their car. A mile or two along the rough track leading to the highway, they were startled to encounter another vehicle, heading for the Cape. At least it had been heading there before becoming hopelessly lodged in a gaping pothole. The driver, a patrician gentleman in his early 60s, was leaning languidly on the right front fender of his car, having abandoned any pretense of trying to free his vehicle. He waved cheerily as Browning and Matina drove up.

"Jolly glad to see you two," he said in a broad British accent undiluted by years of expatriate life. He waved at his useless automobile. "Bloody nuisance, that. Stupid of me."

He introduced himself as Denzil Delacourt, a British travel writer based in the Mani for the past dozen years or so. "Fell in love with the wild beauty of the place, I suppose," he said vaguely, by way of explanation. He'd been on his way to observe the sunset from Cape Tenaro — a special pleasure of his — when the left front wheel of his Fiat had slipped into a monster pothole, and he'd been unable to extricate it. He'd been waiting for someone to come by and help. Browning and Matina would do splendidly, he said, with a disarming smile.

Bemused, Browning joined Delacourt alongside the trapped wheel while Matina slid into the Fiat's driver's seat. Delacourt counted to three, then he and Browning, grunting and straining, hoisted the car out of the hole as Matina slipped it into reverse and tromped on the accelerator. The Fiat shot backwards to liberation.

Delacourt took his rescue in stride. "There," he declared, rubbing his hands briskly, "that's done." He pulled an unfiltered cigarette out of a pack stuffed in his breast pocket and examined his rescuers, as if noticing them for the first time. "What brings you two out here?"

Without going into detail, Browning briefly explained that they were looking for a family named Marinatos. Delacourt observed him shrewdly. "I suppose that when you ask, people look uncomfortable or change the subject or some such," he said.

"Yes," said Browning, surprised. "How did you know that?"

Delacourt stuck the unlit cigarette in his mouth and grunted. "Just an educated guess. This is still a very backward part of the world, my friend. People here believe in sprites and nymphs and goblins. One of them goes by the name of Marinatos, or so the story goes. He's supposed to haunt grottos and springs and other watery places, and it's very bad luck to talk about him." Delacourt snorted, lighting his cigarette. "Superstitious rubbish, of course, but the villagers here believe every word."

Browning turned to Matina. "Have you ever heard of this?" he asked. She shook her head. Delacourt nodded at Matina and asked, in an exhalation of smoke, "Where do you live, darling?"

Matina blushed at his familiarity. "Areopoli," she replied.

"Ah, that explains it, then."

"Explains what?" asked Browning.

"The story about Marinatos is from the Deep Mani," said Delacourt. "Areopoli is right on the line between the Mesa Mani and the Exo Mani. It's too firmly in the modern world to take such claptrap seriously. That's why your friend," he raised his eyebrows expressively, "hasn't heard of him."

Despite Delacourt's scorn for those credulous enough to believe in spirits, Browning was fascinated by the story. It fit neatly with Callas's revelation that Marinatos was mouldering in the grave at the time he attended Petros Demitos's funeral.

"How do people know his name?" he pressed Delacourt. "I mean, how do they know he calls himself Marinatos?"

"They know," said Delacourt, mysteriously.

"But how?" Browning persisted. "Does he actually introduce himself or something?"

"Something like that." Delacourt was losing patience with Browning's questioning. "Look, people don't talk about this very much. A lot of the details are murky. Besides," he added, clearly wanting to bring the conversation to a close, "it's all a load of hogwash anyway, so what does it matter? And now, if you'll excuse me, I have a sunset to catch."

"Of course," said Browning dryly, "sorry to detain you."

"Not at all, not at all," said Delacourt, distractedly. "Actually," he added, as if suddenly recalling their role in his deliverance, "you've been most helpful."

"So have you, Mr. Delacourt," muttered Bliss Browning.

"WELL," said Matina, as they turned back onto the coastal highway, "That explains the odd reaction we got whenever we asked about the Marinatos family. No wonder — to these people, we were asking about a ghost."

He tore his eyes from the winding road just long enough to steal a glance at her. A look approaching contentment had taken up residence on her face, which was quite the loveliest face he'd ever beheld. He felt a rush of emotion so overwhelming that he nearly drove off the road, pulling back from the shoulder at the last instant with a sharp jerk on the steering wheel.

They drove in silence for a few minutes. It was fine; words were unnecessary. At length, Browning broke the silence. "Matina," he said, considering what Delacourt had told them, "do you believe in spirits?"

Though he did not look at her, Browning could sense her frown. "I'm not sure," she said finally. "When I was a child, I believed in ghosts and nereids and nymphs, all the inhabitants of a parallel universe hidden from us. And the nereid who visited me about my father — I don't know what I believe about that." She paused. "Since Vasilio's death, I suppose I've lost my faith."

"I understand," said Browning, "yet my experience is precisely the opposite. As a child, as a young man — until quite recently, in fact — I never believed in anything I couldn't see, touch or feel. And sometimes, even that wasn't enough. But now," he chuckled softly, "I'm awash in faith, like a big, thirsty sponge."

Matina gave him a searching look. "Why? What has happened to you, Bliss?"

He laughed. "You, for one thing. In a world that contains someone as remarkable as you, I figure anything is possible."

"Be serious," Matina protested.

"I am." She said nothing, waiting for him to continue. "Okay, it's not just you," he admitted. "I met someone exceptional recently, someone who helped open my eyes to possibilities I'd never dared to imagine."

"Who?"

This was not the moment to tell her about Callas. "I'll tell you the whole story," he parried, "but not now." Dusk was giving way to night, and he was eager to return his passenger to her mother before the old woman became anxious. He tromped on the accelerator, coaxing a bit more speed from the small engine.

Matina suddenly sat bolt upright in her seat and turned to him, eyes alight. "Bliss," she exclaimed, "take the next left. There's something I want to show you."

"I don't know," he said dubiously. The sense of unease he had felt at Cape Tenaro returned, only more strongly now. "Shouldn't we be getting you home before your mother sends out a search party?"

"No, it will be alright," she insisted. "It's still early." She pointed to an intersection in the heart of the small town they had just entered. "Please, Bliss, there's your turn."

"Okay," he said reluctantly, twisting the wheel. "Where are we going?"

"You'll soon see," she teased, milking the mystery. "Just drive."

The road wound down along the coastline, rapidly descending to sea level from the high coastal plain. Within minutes they arrived at an entrance gate. Browning stopped the car. "What is this place?" he asked.

"The Diros caves," Matina answered, pronouncing the words as if they were something fantastic and exotic.

The name rang a faint bell in the back of Browning's brain. "Wait a minute," he said as a mental tumbler clicked into place, "I've heard of those before. They're a big tourist attraction, aren't they?" There were advantages to being travel editor, after all.

"You're right," cried Matina, delighted. "They're also one of my favourite places on Earth. I've been coming here since I was a young child, and the caves leave me breathless every time."

Browning peered at the entrance gate, which was firmly shut. "Looks like they're closed for the day."

"Doesn't matter," said Matina. "They'll let us in. They know me here." She hopped out of the car and walked over to the ticket hut next to the gate. A moment later, a smiling young man emerged, opened the gate and waved Browning through.

"Come on," urged Matina, once they'd parked the car. "You have to see this." She greeted a swarthy, handsome youth, who handed her a key, with a suspicious glance at Browning. "They've just finished their shift, but we can go through the caves as long as we lock up and drop the key with security," Matina explained. "Follow me."

She led him down a staircase through a set of double doors to an underground wharf where half a dozen flat-bottomed boats were docked in a flooded cave. Picking up a long pole, she stepped nimbly into one of the boats. "Okay, climb in," she instructed, "but be careful."

Browning did as he was told, and Matina deftly used the pole to push the boat deeper into the cave. Though not a trace of natural light penetrated the gloom, strategically placed electric beacons cast a ghostly illumination over the scene. And what a wondrous, fantastical scene it was! As Browning stared with rapt attention, Matina poled the boat through crystalline water past ceilings dripping with stalactites, like melting candles in a topsy-turvy world. Elsewhere, the ceiling, rarely more than three or four feet above their heads, bristled like a giant pincushion with hundreds of lethal-looking spikes. Here and there, a stalactite and stalagmite had merged into a huge misshapen pillar of stone. The cathedral-like hush was broken only by the sound of Matina's pole on the cave walls and their own breathing. And throughout, the transparent waters, glassy as a newborn's eye, reflected the contorted ceiling shapes with absolute fidelity. It was as if they had been transported to a phenomenal new world.

"It's amazing," whispered Browning, though his voice seemed shatteringly loud in the silence of the cave. Matina nodded, and kept poling through the twisting subterranean channel, past more Brueghelian grotesqueries. "Fantastic," Browning breathed, goggle-eyed.

Before Matina could respond, the cave's lights blinked off, and the two were plunged into a blackness more profound than the grave, a dismal, inky negation of all that is welcoming and alive. Browning cried out instinctively, the guttural, primal noise of a child startled by something sinister in the night. Matina cursed. "Damn it! If they've turned off the lights, we're stuck here . . ."

Her voice trailed away, and though the lights remained off, Browning could just perceive the outline of her face, faintly illuminated by something behind him. For a moment, he thought it was the flashlight of another boat, dispatched to lead them back to safety. But then he noticed Matina's eyes, wide with surprise and something that might have been fear, and her mouth, soundlessly opening and shutting.

He swivelled in his seat and looked around. Not more than a dozen feet away was an achingly gorgeous woman, her golden tresses framing a porcelain face. She was partly submerged and was wearing a flowing white dress that glowed with a faint luminescence. Browning struggled to understand what he was seeing. With a shock of recognition, it came to him that she must be a nereid. But a greater shock was yet to come.

For beside the nereid, rising slowly from the still waters, was the unmistakable figure of a man in his early 50s. He was gazing directly at Matina, a look of great tenderness in his eyes — eyes that were like two mysterious wells. As the apparition rose from the transparent waters, the nereid seemed to speak, though her lips did not move. But Browning clearly heard her voice, heard her say the words, words that filled his heart with excitement and dread. "May I introduce" — her words floated in the air like the gossamer wings of a butterfly — "Nicholas Marinatos."

Then another sound filled the low, watery cave, a sound that overwhelmed the nereid's delicate voice and drove both spectral figures back to their shadowy world in an instant. The sound was coming from Matina.

She was staring at the man, at Marinatos, wild-eyed, screaming a single word over and over again.

Papa. The word was papa.

CHAPTER 23

WHEN THE LIGHTS CAME BACK ON, MATINA WAS SLUMPED IN THE bottom of the boat, limp with shock and moaning softly. Given the extraordinary encounter in the caves, it was hardly surprising that she was overcome. What was wholly unexpected, though, was Bliss Browning's response. He was composed, protective and, for once, clear of purpose. As Matina slipped into shock, he seized the guide pole and rapidly retraced their route into the cave, heedless of the jagged stone walls and low ceilings that tore at his shoulders and menaced his head. Within minutes, they were at the dock. Sweeping Matina into his arms, he carried her to the car and gently stretched her out on the back seat. Once satisfied that she was settled, he jumped behind the wheel and sped the few kilometres to Areopoli.

Matina's mother, watching as the car pulled up, saw Browning again gather her daughter in his arms. Before he had reached the door, she was rushing to meet him. "What happened?" she cried in a voice quavering with fear.

"She's had a terrible shock but she's fine," said Browning, with more assurance than he actually felt. "She — that is, we — saw her father in the Diros caves."

The colour drained from the old woman's face, and a hand flew involuntarily to her mouth. Browning feared she too might faint, but then she seemed to rally. "Come," she ordered. "Follow me." She led him, still carrying his precious cargo, to an airy room at the rear of the house. She gestured to a single bed topped by a thin comforter. "Put her there." Browning followed instructions as the old woman scurried out of the room, returning moments later clutching a damp cloth, which she laid on Matina's forehead. Her daughter's eyes fluttered. "Mama," she groaned.

"Hush," her mother soothed. "Don't try to talk. Just rest." She glanced at Browning. "She's in shock," she said, handing him a pillow from the head of the bed. "Remove her shoes and put this under her feet." As Browning did this, the old woman pulled a light blanket from a chest near the bed and laid it over her daughter's prostrate frame. "We should let her rest now," she whispered. Browning nodded, and together they withdrew, lightly closing the door behind them.

"Now," said Matina's mother, once they were back in the living room, "tell me exactly what happened." She listened closely as Browning recounted the events in the cave. She started when he mentioned the name Nicholas Marinatos but said nothing, nodding briskly to indicate that he should continue. Browning was struck by her alert, capable manner — quite unlike the confused, doddering woman he had met the previous night.

When he had finished, the old woman studied him intently. "Exactly who are you, Mr. Browning?" she asked slowly. "You're not really the son of an old friend, are you." It was more statement than question.

"I might ask you the same thing, Mrs. Karalis," he said, then parried: "Or is it Mrs. Marinatos?"

The old woman stared at him without speaking for a very long time, then sighed and lowered her gaze. "I've always feared this day would come," she said quietly. "Who sent you? Is it the Onassis family?" She gave him a pleading look. "Matina has no idea who her real parents are. She's no threat to you."

With a shock, Browning realized that she was afraid of him. "My God, no," he protested, "you've got it all wrong, Mrs. Marinatos — it is

Mrs. Marinatos, isn't it?" She nodded mutely, waiting for him to continue. "It's true that you've never met my parents, and somebody did ask me to find your daughter, but I mean neither of you any harm. On the contrary," he added recklessly, "I'm in love with Matina."

It was the old woman's turn to be shocked. "In love with Matina!" she exclaimed. "How is that possible?"

"I find it hard to believe myself," Browning conceded with a slight smile. "But let me assure you, Mrs. Marinatos, it is true." As Matina's mother listened with growing astonishment, he filled her in on the tragic circumstances of their meeting in Athens and their subsequent meetings and trip together to Kalamata.

"Does my daughter know how you feel?" she demanded when he had finished.

"I told her today."

"And what did she say?"

"It is far too early for her to say anything. She has suffered terribly."

The old woman slumped in her chair, clearly overwhelmed. "Why didn't you tell me this from the start?" she cried. "Why did you deceive me?"

"Matina thought you would not approve of me," said Browning, chagrined.

"Well, she was right," the old lady snapped, eyes flashing. "I do not approve." After a moment of awkward silence, Mrs. Marinatos continued with less heat but equal directness. "You said somebody asked you to find Matina. Who?"

Browning hesitated. But he had nothing to lose at this point. "It was her real mother," he said levelly.

"Her mother!" she exclaimed, unable to hide her consternation. "How could it be her mother? Even I don't know who her mother is."

"You don't?" blurted Browning, caught off guard by the admission.

"No." She frowned, as if concentrating intently. "When Petros Demitros brought Matina to us, he warned that she had enemies, powerful enemies. He told us to be wary of Aristotle Onassis, so we guessed that she might be his illegitimate daughter. But Petros never hinted at who her mother was." She glanced at Browning apprehensively. "Who is it?"

Browning took a deep breath. "I believe it was Maria Callas, Mrs. Marinatos."

The old woman gasped. "Maria Callas? The diva?"

"The same. She and Onassis were lovers, you know."

Mrs. Marinatos nodded slowly, ashen-faced. "Yes, it makes sense," she said, as if to herself. "The secrecy. The danger. And Matina's beautiful voice . . ." She stopped abruptly and gave Browning a searching look. "But you said her mother asked you to find Matina. And Callas has been dead for . . ."

"More than 25 years," supplied Browning. "That's correct."

"But how?"

"Mrs. Marinatos," Browning began, "do you believe in spirits?" The old woman hesitated. "I, I don't know," she stammered. "I suppose so."

"I do too," said Browning firmly. "I saw your husband in that cave tonight. And I have also been in contact with the spirit of Maria Callas. It was she who sent me on this mission, to tell her daughter who she really is. Except," he stopped, then added with a frown, "she told me I should look for a son, not a daughter."

"A son? If this fantastical story is true, how could she not know the sex of her own child?"

"I'm not sure," Browning confessed, "though it was a difficult birth, and the baby was whisked away before she saw it." He frowned again. "Why did her uncle tell her she'd had a son if it wasn't true?" He shook his head. "I'll have to pursue this with her."

Matina's mother was watching him closely. "Pursue this with her?" she repeated. "Don't tell me you're still in contact with her?"

"Of course," replied Browning absently, still pondering the confusion over the sex of Callas's child. "We talk on the Internet."

"Po-po-po!" cried Mrs. Marinatos, lapsing into Greek. "This is too much!!"

"I know it's hard to accept," agreed Browning. "But Mrs. Marinatos, there is much in this situation that is not as it seems, isn't there?"

"What do you mean?" she replied, flustered.

"Your name, for instance. I'm guessing that you changed it when you moved here to make it harder for Onassis's men to track you." She nodded, but said nothing. "But what about your Alzheimer's?" he continued. "Your behaviour just now has not been that of a person on the verge of senility. Is all that an act, too?"

The old woman looked away. "Not entirely," she said. "I do get a bit addled from time to time. But I have . . . exaggerated my condition somewhat." She shot him a conspiratorial look. "People are less likely to bother you when you're a bit, well, unbalanced."

Browning smiled briefly at the deception. "We'll have to tell her, you know," he said softly. "She deserves to know."

"I know," she said. "I always intended to tell her what I knew someday. The lies and deception just became such a habit." She smiled wanly. "It's a relief, in a way. That it's finally over."

"How do you think Matina will respond?" Browning asked. Mrs. Marinatos shuddered. "She won't believe it at first. That's understandable — it's hard to accept, that the people you've thought of all your life as your mother and father really aren't." A pause. "But Matina is a sensible girl. She'll be fine once she gets used to the idea."

"Do you want to tell her," Browning asked, "or should I? And is this even the right time?"

"No, I'll do it. Regardless of whose womb she emerged from, I'm still her mother. Always have been, always will be. She deserves to hear it from me." She looked directly at Browning. "And since you are on the scene, it might as well be now."

Browning nodded at the frail but resolute woman across from him. People always surprise you, he thought. Just when you think you've taken their measure, they surprise you. They are often stronger than you think, more resilient than you suppose, more capable of decency than you ever imagined. Perhaps that was what Callas meant with her talk about leaps of faith. Not in God, or fate or the alignment of the stars, but in ordinary men and women. People like Matina, her mother, Harrison Howard, or even, God forbid, himself.

"A DAUGHTER!" exclaimed Maria Callas. "No, you must be mistaken."

"I don't think so," replied Bliss Browning, tapping out the letters on his keyboard. "Everything fits. Petros Demitros arranged the adoption. He warned the Marinatos to watch for Onassis and his men. Plus, Matina is nearly 40 years old — exactly the right age. And she sings like an angel. She must be the one."

"Then why doesn't it feel right?" Callas demanded.

"I don't know. Maybe it's hard to adjust after believing you had a son for so many years. Perhaps you just need to get used to the idea."

"That's possible, I suppose," Callas mused. "And Leonidas knew me well. He might have misled me about the sex of my child because he knew that, sooner or later, I'd search for him. Or her. Still . . ." Even from the evanescence of The Zone, Browning could sense her frown.

"What about your truth channel?" he prompted. "Can't that confirm this for you, like it did the identity of Nicholas Marinatos?"

"In theory, yes. But it either happens or it doesn't. And right now, it's not happening."

"So what does that mean?" asked Browning. "That Matina isn't your daughter after all?"

"Not necessarily. As I told you before, it's an unpredictable process. Sometimes you know something is true, beyond a shadow of doubt. But more often you can't pick up anything at all. It's like listening to a short-wave radio. Just because you can't pull in a signal doesn't mean the stations aren't there."

"What a ludicrous system," Browning erupted. "What kind of supreme being would concoct something so random and unreliable?"

"You're right," agreed Callas dryly. "It's just like life."

"What do you mean?"

"Well, think about it. Consider all the things that can alter the course of your life: where you are born; whether your parents are wealthy or poor; whether you take a job at company A, which prospers, or Company B, which goes bankrupt; whether you go to a party and meet your true love, or turn down the invitation and miss your best chance at happiness. Even the most trivial things can change our lives. I once knew a man who had a heart attack and died while running for the bus to work. If he had been willing to miss that bus, he might have lived for many years."

"What you say is true to a point," Browning replied, "but surely life is more than just a series of random events tossing us about at their whim. Life is also about making choices, about knowing what you want, then working to make it happen."

"Really? For example?" taunted Callas.

Browning could feel his face reddening with annoyance. "For example, my love for your daughter," he replied. "I know that I love her, and I chose to act on that knowledge."

"Have you forgotten already?" chided Callas. "If you hadn't gone to Greece at my request, and if her husband hadn't chosen your train as a vehicle for his murderous design, you would never have met. Your example just proves my point. Life is a series of random connections punctuated by fleeting moments of certainty and knowledge — just like consciousness in The Zone. In my case, I knew that it was Marinatos at the funeral, but there is much more that I don't know, can never know. For you, love for Matina may be a certainty, but for most of the rest, you must rely on fate, chance and above all, faith."

Browning digested this for a moment. "Suppose you're right," he began at last. "Suppose that fate, chance and faith guide our lives, and knowledge and certainty play a minor role. Why, then, can't you accept on faith that Matina is your daughter?"

Callas's answer flashed across his computer screen almost before he'd finished typing. "Because the stakes are too high for that. This is my only chance to set this right, to ensure that my child knows the truth. I don't have the luxury of faith. I need to know."

"No leap of faith this time?"

"Please, my dear Browning, don't mock me."

"I'm sorry, but even you must see the irony," said Browning. "Since our first contact, you have been preaching the virtues of faith to me, how I needed to believe in you, in others, in myself. Now you refuse to make even the tiniest hop of faith yourself to accept something that is also supported by all the evidence: that Matina is your daughter. Suddenly faith is a luxury you can't afford, and you insist on a proof that no one, living or dead, can supply."

"No, you are wrong," said Callas, ignoring the scolding tone of Browning's words. "There is a way to know for sure."

"For God's sake, Maria," cried Browning. "What's is it?"

"It's right here, in Chapter 45, section 12 of The Zone Regulations," Callas replied calmly. "Zone residents require written permission from the Ministry of Revenant Relations before they are able to materialize to those on Earth. Any attempt to materialize without proper authority is futile, except when blood relatives are involved, in which case materializations are at the discretion of Zone inhabitants to a maximum of three per quantum.'"

"What the hell does that mean?"

"Why, my dear Browning, it's perfectly obvious. It means that if I am able to materialize for your Matina, she must be my daughter. Since I have neither sought nor obtained permission to materialize, if I am unable to do so, then it will be clear that Matina is not related to me by blood."

"Why didn't you tell me about this before?" Browning exploded.

"It was never relevant before," Callas replied mildly.

"Can I be present when you do it?"

"Certainly. You just won't be able to see me."

"I don't understand," said Browning. "I saw Matina's father when he materialized. Why can't I see you, too?"

"He must have Zone permission to materialize. Unless," she added, Browning sensing her frown from cyberspace, "the nereid division has different rules."

"Couldn't you get this permission, too?" he asked. "I'd love to see you with my own eyes, just once."

"My dear Browning," Callas said briskly, "that would defeat the whole purpose, wouldn't it? My materialization would prove nothing. No, I must proceed without permission. If Matina sees me, I'll have my answer. And so will she, if she doubts your story."

"Why," said Browning, surprised, "you don't think she'll believe me?"

"Quite likely. Let me remind you that I had to use every trick in the Zone handbook to convince you that I wasn't a fraud. You can't expect her simply to accept your story without question. Though from what you tell me, she has more capacity for faith than most people."

Browning thought for a moment. "You really think this will work?"

"It should. My only worry is that my contacts with you have drained my energy reserves. Materialization takes a huge amount of energy, and frankly I'm running on empty right now. But give me a good night's rest, and I should be fine. I hope so, anyway."

"Me too," Browning added fervently, "because if Matina isn't your daughter, I'm out of candidates. Of either gender."

NATURE HERSELF SEEMED restive when Browning awoke the next morning. A thick fog shrouded the Mani, turning its inhabitants into apparitions whose footfalls announced their presence long before the eye supplied confirmation. A misting rain filled the air, dampening everything without truly soaking anything. Periodically, a low rumble rolled down from the Taygetus, either sputtering thunder or the grumbling of the gods.

Browning dressed quickly, packed his laptop and walked through the haze to Matina's house. By now, he calculated, her mother would have told her the story of her adoption — and who Browning believed her true parents to be. How would she respond? And how would she feel about him? Would she feel deceived, used, tricked in some way? Did she have the strength left for such revelations? It was with much apprehension that he knocked on her door.

Matina's mother greeted him with a terse nod and gestured for him to enter. "Wait here," she instructed, then disappeared into the back of the house, leaving Browning, portable computer in hand, standing in the foyer. After a few moments, Matina emerged. She looked wan, a perception heightened by the black dress that covered her from neck to ankles. She greeted him warily, not smiling, avoiding physical contact.

"I suppose you're here to view your prize," she said abruptly.

"Beg your pardon?" Browning blurted.

"Well, that's why you've been hanging around, isn't it?" she continued. "Because you think your precious Callas is my mother?" She looked away. "It wasn't because of me."

"Matina!" Browning cried, taken aback, "How can you say that?"

"It's perfectly obvious," Matina snapped. "You're obsessed with this woman, this dead woman. She's all you truly care about. I'm just a vehicle for you to live out your fantasies."

Browning slumped into a chair, stunned. In his worst nightmare, he had not anticipated this reaction. He struggled to collect his thoughts. He knew his next words might be the most important of his life.

"First of all," he began, "I never imagined that you might be Maria Callas's daughter until we saw your father yesterday. Until then, I thought we were searching for a son. You know that," he admonished. Matina stared impassively at him, so he continued. "From the time we first met until that moment in the cave, the woman I knew was Matina Mourtzinos, not Matina Callas. When you burst into my room that night in Athens, I thought you were deranged by grief, and to be honest, I wanted nothing to do with you." Matina narrowed her eyes, but said nothing.

"I stayed with you because you needed a shoulder, and I seemed to have the only one available. But something happened that I didn't anticipate. You broke through the defences I had erected to keep feelings, unsafe feelings like love and involvement and caring, at bay. You made a connection. And though I didn't acknowledge it then, I was already falling in love with you."

Matina was listening now with greater attentiveness. "Over the next few days, the bond between us deepened. I didn't know what was happening — I certainly didn't want it to happen — but you were too powerful. By the time we parted in Kalamata, I knew I was in trouble. When you left me sitting on that train, you took my heart with you.

The ache you left in its place I haven't felt in a very long time — and never want to feel again. I thought you were out of my life forever. And that thought was almost impossible to bear.

"When we were reunited," he continued, smiling at the memory, "I could scarcely contain my joy and excitement. I felt sure it was a sign that we were meant to be together, that some higher power had decreed it. I tried to tell you how I felt a dozen times, but it seemed too soon. The time wasn't right. Until Cape Tenaro. Until we were alone, with only the wind and birds as witnesses. I felt for the first time that the world was a just and miraculous place."

Browning paused to wipe his eyes and clear his throat, both of which were suddenly brimming. He looked directly at Matina; she returned his gaze without blinking. "Perhaps I was drawn to you because I saw the qualities that I admire so much in Callas. Perhaps the gods thought it would be amusing to bring us together. Or perhaps it is nothing but chance that we met.

"None of that really matters. All that matters is that I loved you when you were Matina Mourtzinos, and I love you still. Whether or not you are Maria Callas's daughter makes no difference to me. It's you I care about. It's you who gives me strength. Matina, it's you."

Matina had listened to these fervent declarations without expression. Now, though, her face softened imperceptibly, suggesting that Browning's words had had an effect. Still, her voice was controlled when at last she spoke.

"You have given me too much to think about, Bliss, far too much." He nodded. "I need time to absorb all of this. Right now, I mostly feel confused." She paused. "If your feelings for me are genuine, you will have no trouble granting me as much time as necessary."

Browning started to speak, but Matina cut him off. "As for your claim that I am the daughter of Maria Callas, I must tell you that I find that even harder to accept than your declarations of love for me." She shook her head. "It's as if you were living a perfectly ordinary life, and right in the middle of it, someone announced that you were the only living descendent of the Czar. It doesn't fit with my concept of who I am."

Browning nodded. "I understand. Even I'm not certain that you're Maria Callas's daughter, though the evidence strongly suggests that you are. Frankly, if it were up to me, I'd say 'who cares, let's get on with the rest of our life.' But Matina," he said, gripping her by the hands, "I made a promise to someone that I feel obliged to keep. And it turns out there is a way to know once and for all."

"There is?" asked Matina. "How?"

Browning smiled uncertainly. "Let me tell you about it," he began.

~

BLISS BROWNING SAT in Matina's living room, hunched over his laptop computer. Matina stood behind him, watching dubiously as he typed a sentence. The sentence read: "Maria, it's time for your entrance." Within seconds, a response flashed across the computer screen. "I was always good at entrances. Let's hope I haven't lost my touch."

Matina jumped. "Is that supposed to be Callas?" she whispered. Browning nodded affirmation and tapped out another sentence on his computer. "Would you like to hear from Matina?" The response was immediate. "Please."

Browning gestured to Matina to sit down at the keyboard. "What would you like to say?" he asked her. She furrowed her brow. "I don't know. My God, this is so surreal. Let me think." She pecked laboriously at the keyboard, and slowly a message took shape.

"Hello," it began, "Bliss tells me that I am your daughter. I must tell you that I am having a lot of trouble with that idea. I already have a mother whom I dearly love, and to be honest, it would be very confusing to acquire another, even one as famous as you. To say nothing of the notion that you are communicating with me from beyond the grave. These are hard ideas for me to accept — almost impossible, really. So you will forgive me if I remain unconvinced.

"But life is full of surprises, and perhaps this is one of them. So let's pretend for a moment that you really are my mother. If that were true, what would I say to you? First, I suppose I would thank you for giving me this life. I would tell you that I understand how hard it must have been to give me up, but that I bear you no ill will. I'm sure you did what you thought was necessary. And my parents couldn't have been better to me. My life has had its hardships, but also much happiness."

Matina stopped typing for a moment and gazed at the screen. "That's what I would say if you really were my mother," she concluded. Browning put his hand on her shoulder. They waited.

"Hello, Matina." The words appeared on the screen like the tracks of a ghost. "I have heard much about you, but only last night did I learn that you might be the one I've been seeking. I, too, am having trouble getting used to the idea. Countless times I have imagined my son, growing to manhood, precocious and brave. But never, before last night, have I imagined a daughter.

"Please do not think that I am disappointed. My only disappointment is that I gave you up. You are kind to forgive me for that, but I was wrong to do it. After Aristo died, I had nothing to live for anymore. If I'd had you, my story and yours would have been so different. But it's pointless to wallow in regret. What's done is done. The absolute finality of life is both its greatest gift and its most terrible truth. We are defined by the choices we make, and there's no user's manual to guide us. That offers tremendous freedom, but it can exact an awful cost. I made my choice. It was a foolish one, but that's the risk that life imposes. I've had to live with it. So have you.

"I'll have to end this soon. I need all my energy if I hope to materialize and find out, once and for all, if you are truly my daughter. Whatever we learn, you will not be able to contact me again. Regulations in The Zone are quite clear about this. In any case, my energy level will be so low that I couldn't contact you even if I were permitted to do so.

"So this will be our only conversation. I hope that you are my daughter, but even if you are not, I take solace from that knowledge that you and Bliss have met. He is a fine man, though he too often fails to appreciate his own virtues. In time, I'm sure, you will be with him. Take good care of him, and thank him for all he has done for me. Perhaps, if the fates allow, we will all meet again."

Abruptly, the screen went blank. Browning reached over Matina's shoulder and typed a quick question: "What do we do now?"

"Nothing," came the reply. "Just watch. Let me perform; it's what I do."

Browning glanced at Matina. She was staring at the screen, as if transfixed. "Matina," he said gently, "I think she's said everything she had to say." Matina lifted her head and met Browning's gaze. "What if she really is my mother?" she said slowly. Then, more urgently, "Bliss, what if she's my mother, and that's all the contact I get?"

"We'll know soon enough. And if she is your mother, well, at least her life has been well-documented. You'll be able to learn a great deal—"

Matina suddenly sat up straight and shushed him urgently. "What is it?" he demanded. "I'm not sure," she answered, peering around the room as if searching for an intruder, "but I think something is about to happen."

Matina's agitation put Browning on high alert, though he neither sensed nor saw anything unusual. He scrutinized the room for evidence of Callas's presence, but except for him and Matina, the room appeared to be empty. "Callas warned that I wouldn't be able to see her," he told Matina, "so it's up to you."

All at once, Matina stood up and walked toward the door. "What is it?" asked Browning. "Do you see something?"

She didn't answer, but instead turned slowly until her back was to the door. Her gaze seemed fixed on a spot near the opposite wall. She was squinting, brow furrowed, as if straining to see through a heavy mist. Then her eyes suddenly widened and a hand flew involuntarily to her mouth.

"My God," she whispered slowly. Matina stood stock still, staring. Browning barely dared to breathe, lest he break the spell. The silence felt endless to him, though in truth it probably lasted no more than 10 or 15 seconds.

The sound of raised voices in the hallway broke the spell, though Browning was concentrating so hard on Matina, he was at first barely aware of the commotion.

Then someone flung the door open and a familiar voice called out, "Bliss! Bliss Browning!" He was startled to see Harrison Howard, a wide grin creasing his sun-bleached features. Right behind him, not smiling at all, was Renata Richter. Matina's mother brought up the rear, looking apologetic. "I'm sorry," she said. "I tried to stop them, but they wouldn't listen."

Browning blinked, too stunned to register the scene. It simply didn't compute that these people, who now seemed to him to be from another life, had suddenly materialized here, in Matina's mother's house, at so critical a moment. Their appearance was as jarring and incongruous as a streaker in a nunnery.

At first, still focused on Matina, he tried to ignore them, half hoping their appearance was some sort of bizarre hallucination. He was annoyed at their unseemly interruption at the climax of his quest. But gradually their insistent proximity drew him out of the magical realm into which he had withdrawn, and back to the banal world where jobs, bosses, actions and consequences hold sway.

He cleared his throat. "Hello, Harry," he said, adding uncertainly: "Um, you too, Renata."

Howard looked triumphant. "Told you we'd find him, didn't I?" he exulted to Richter. "Yes," she said coolly, "you did." She looked around appraisingly. "Will someone please tell me what's going on here?"

Browning opened his mouth, but no words came out. His brain seemed encased in cement. Then he remembered Matina. He whirled and turned in her direction. She was standing stock-still, arms limp, a stunned expression on her face. She had barely noticed the intruders.

"Matina," Browning cried, rushing to her side, "did you see her? Did you see Callas?"

"See Callas?" repeated Richter. "What's going on?"

"I'm not sure," Matina said dully. "That is, I saw something — someone — but I'm not sure who. It was a woman — I think. The image was very faint." She looked reproachfully at Howard and Richter. "It disappeared when these two people came barging into the room." Her face darkened. "Who are you, anyway? Who gave you the right to enter my home?"

"Matina," said Browning quickly, "I'd like you to meet my good friend, Harrison Howard, and our boss, the editor of the Ottawa *Daily Advocate*, Renata Richter. Somehow, they have managed to track me down."

"It was easy," said Howard happily. "Once I found out that you'd gone to Meligalas, it didn't take much to discover where you'd gone next. Chap who runs a bar in town was particularly helpful."

He rubbed his hands gleefully. "Good to know I still have the old reportorial royal jelly." So absorbed was Howard in his triumph, he seemed not to notice the grim look on Richter's face. But Browning saw it immediately.

"Guess I'm in trouble, eh?" he said to her. "You tell me," she answered with deceptive calm. "How would you feel about a reporter who took money for a foreign assignment, then disappeared without a trace, provoked a heart attack in the managing editor ..."

"Norman's had a heart attack?" Browning exclaimed.

"... and forced the editor herself," Richter continued, ignoring the interruption, "to spend several days in a foreign land trying to track him down? Would you say that reporter was in trouble?"

"Yes, I suppose I would," replied Browning quietly.

"You're bloody right!" Richter shouted, her face flushed. "I took a chance on you, Browning, and you made me look like a fool! I expect you to repay every cent of your advance, then I expect your resignation. Unless you'd prefer to be fired!"

"Just a minute!" Matina's voice cut through the hubbub like a high C in an opera house. She raised herself to her full height and faced Richter, eyes flashing. "I don't care who you are," she said, anger clipping her words. "I may very well be the daughter of Maria Callas, and nobody comes into my home and speaks like that to this man."

"Ho-ho!" cried Howard, clapping his hands delightedly.

"Shut up, Harry," snapped Browning. He looked levelly at Richter. "Renata, I know I let you down. For that, I apologize. And don't worry, you'll get your money back, and my resignation too, if that's what you want. But sometimes, there are things you must do that are more important than travel journalism. This was one of those times. I didn't plan it that way, but I'm comfortable with what I did, and I'd do it again in the same situation."

Richter seemed slightly abashed by her outburst. "You could at least have called," she grumbled. "You're right," said Browning. "I should have. But I didn't think you'd understand, and I've learned so much since then." He glanced at Matina, still glowering at Richter, and smiled.

Richter, further mollified by Browning's words, was almost conciliatory. "Well, if you repay the advance, I may be able to save your job." She gave him a conspiratorial wink. "Especially if you've got a world exclusive for the *Advocate*. We could both come out of this looking good yet. You've got to tell me the whole story, from start to finish. And don't leave anything out. I insist."

"Thanks, Renata," began Browning, walking over to Matina and tentatively draping an arm over her shoulders, "but I think I'll stick around here for a while. As for my story, let's just say you wouldn't believe it if I told you." His face dissolved into a slow smile, as if he were amused by a private joke. "You see, you'd need a great deal of faith."

Richter's eyes narrowed. "What, you mean you're not going to tell me? You're not going to f-f-fuckin' explain yourself?" Her tongue stumbled over the unfamiliar expletive, which in nearly half a century of refined living had rarely passed her lips, and never before in public. "Ooohhh, Browning, you are so fired!"

But Bliss Browning was no longer listening. He was looking at Matina, trying to fathom what she had seen, lost in the black pools of her eyes. Odd, he'd never realized just how beautiful she was. A bit like Callas, but different. Like Matina. Gently, he kissed her. On her lips, he could taste the future.

CHAPTER 24

NORMAN PUGSLEY WAS BEGINNING TO BOUNCE BACK. HE STILL SPENT most of his time supine in his hospital bed, innumerable tubes and monitors wired into his body. And the friendly but hopelessly foreign staff expected him to subsist on unrecognizable globs of hideous Greek fare. But the ache in his chest had subsided and with the help of the hospital physiotherapist, he could feel strength slowly returning to his limbs.

Even so, Pugsley wasn't prepared when Bliss Browning, bold as brass, strolled into his hospital room. "Christ on a bicycle!" he cried, his ticker racing alarmingly. "Is it really you, Browning?"

"It's really me, Norman. How are you?"

Pugsley studied Browning through narrowed eyes. Something different about the bastard. Seems more substantial, somehow. More present. "Well, I've been one fuck of a lot better, no thanks to you," he growled, a bit of the old, pre-coronary Pugsley resurfacing.

"Yes. I know," said Browning with quiet sympathy. "I heard. I'm sorry."

"You bloody well should be," glowered Pugsley. "If you hadn't gone fuckin' AWOL, I'd be home, cheering on my Jays."

The raucous sound of revving motorcycle engines roared in

through an open window, obliterating the brief silence. "How'd you find me, anyway?" Pugsley demanded.

"Harrison told me where you were. He and Renata tracked me down in the Mani." A small, rueful smile. "Renata isn't very happy with me right now. She feels I let her down."

"Well, hell's bells man, you certainly did. She believed in you, God knows why, and you betrayed her. She didn't deserve that."

"You're right, she didn't. I handled things badly."

"Fuckin' A." Pugsley fell silent, and it seemed for a moment that he had forgotten about his visitor. Then, in a low voice: "I wanted to kill you, you know."

"I know."

"No, I mean I really wanted to kill you. To rip your heart out, leave you for the vultures." He glanced up. "I was feeling really hostile."

"And now?"

"Now?" A quick, barking laugh. "Ah, shit. Life's too short. Y'know? Life's too goddamn short, Browning. I mean, you were an asshole to do it, but what the hell, I've been an asshole at times, too. We all get so wrapped up in our little ego trips. And where does it get us? You wind up alone, with a heart full of bile and regret." He shook his head. "Life's too short for that kind of crap."

"I'm glad to hear that, Norman," Browning said softly, "because you and I are going to be spending quite a bit of time together."

Pugsley's head jerked up. "What the fuck are you talking about?"

"I'm going to look after you until you're discharged from hospital. Then I'm going to take you back to Ottawa. After all, as you said, I'm responsible for this."

Pugsley stared at the unfamiliar man who used to be Bliss Browning. "Ah, shit, Browning, you don't have to do that. One of the others can take care of me."

"I'm afraid that's not possible, Norman. I've sent them home."

Pugsley sat bolt upright. "Sent them home!"

"They have work to do. Whereas I have all the time in the world." He smiled sweetly at his former boss. "Besides, I have to return to

Ottawa to clean up my affairs. I'm relocating. So you see, Norman, you're stuck with me."

Pugsley fell back onto his pillow and closed his eyes. He said nothing, but an image of Our Saviour, pedaling furiously, materialized behind his eyelids.

BROWNING HAD FORGOTTEN how yellowed and worn the newsroom of the *Daily Advocate* was. Curious to have forgotten that. He hadn't been gone all that long, really. Still, it felt like a lifetime. If not a lifetime, then at least a different life. There was no going back now. Not that he wanted to. His former life now seemed like an ill-fitting suit that he'd worn because he lacked the enterprise to acquire a better one. It would always be part of his story, but he could leave it behind without regret.

Since his own life was so different now, it struck him as odd that little appeared to have changed in the newsroom. Mick Mulligrew was still on the phone. Yuri Alexandrov was bellowing something in Russian. Flynn Cahill was wearing out his favourite adjective/verb/noun. Chuck Bigras was swallowing something enormous. Dylan Mosely was preening. Ryan Young was seated at his desk but, though Browning was pretty sure he had seen him, Young was paying him no attention. As a matter of fact, everyone in the newsroom was studiously ignoring him.

Browning suddenly understood that he had become the Typhoid Mary of the newsroom. Nobody wanted to risk infection by fraternizing with him. Nobody, that is, but Kimberley Taylor. The *Advocate*'s medical reporter had written too often about deadly diseases to be cowed by a mere career virus. "Welcome back, Bliss," she smiled expansively. "Sounds like you've had quite an adventure."

Confronted by the lovely Kimberley, the old Bliss would have stared at his shoe-tops, mumbled something nonsensical and edged away at the first opportunity, his heart pounding with unexpressed longing. This new Bliss, though still dazzled, was able to carry on a conversation that, if not quite suave, was at least sentient. "Kimberley," he said, "you wouldn't believe most of it if I told you."

"Even so," she replied, with a subtle but noticeable glance of reappraisal, "I'd love to hear about it sometime."

Browning smiled. "Sometime, perhaps. But not now, I'm afraid. I've got to talk to Harrison. Do you know where he is?"

Her eyes widened. "Haven't you heard? No, I suppose you wouldn't have, would you. There's been a bit of a shuffle around here. Norman Pugsley has taken early retirement. For health reasons, he says, but no one believes that. And Harrison is our new managing editor."

"No kidding!" Browning was delighted. The appointment was the first sensible move the *Advocate* had made in years. Maybe there was hope for the place yet.

"Just announced yesterday," said Kimberley. "You could have knocked us over with a feather. We're all terribly pleased, of course, but nobody dreamed this could happen. Guess Harrison and Renata bonded while they were over in Greece."

"Guess so. Where can I find him?"

"Try the M.E.'s office. He's just moving in."

"Thanks, Kimberley. For everything," he added impulsively.

~

HARRISON HOWARD WAS UNPACKING books when Browning tapped lightly on his office door. "An office of your own," he said approvingly. "Guess this means you've finally hit the big time, Harry."

Howard smiled broadly. "Good to see you, Bliss. Thanks for babysitting Norman. Can't have been the most pleasant chore."

"Wasn't so bad," grunted Browning. "Old Norm's not so disagreeable when you get to know him. Besides, his brush with death appears to have made a new man of him. Odd, because my brush with life has done the same thing for me. We've both been improved by our follies."

Howard snorted. "Not so much improved, Bliss, as liberated. There's always been more to you than met the eye. I knew that. Problem was, you didn't."

To his surprise, Browning felt unbidden tears welling in his eyes. He stepped forward and gripped the *Advocate*'s new managing editor in a bearhug embrace, which Howard returned with equal fervour.

"Congratulations, old friend," Browning said thickly. "Nobody deserves it more than you."

"Thanks, Bliss. That means a lot."

The two parted, Browning unselfconsciously wiping his streaming eyes. "Whew," he exhaled as he fought to contain his surging emotions. He fished into a pocket and pulled out a slip of paper. "Here," he said, handing it to Howard, "I guess this is for you."

Howard peered at the scrap of paper. It was a cheque, made out to the *Advocate*, in the amount of $5,652. "Full recompense for airfare and expenses," said Browning. "As promised."

Howard slowly shook his head. "You don't have to do this, Bliss. I'm the goddamn managing editor now, and I'm telling you, you don't have to do this."

"Yes, I do, Harry," said Browning firmly. "That money was given to me for another purpose. It was my decision to change the rules. It's my responsibility to make things right."

Howard thought for a moment. "You were supposed to use this money to write a series about being on safari in Africa, right?" Browning nodded. "Unless I'm missing something," Howard continued, "you still haven't completed your assignment. So here's my proposition: use this money to write the series you were assigned to do, and we'll call it even. Otherwise," he added, affecting an air of mock gravity, "I'm afraid you will have failed to live up to your obligations. We may be forced to consult our lawyers."

Browning stared at his friend for a long moment. Then he burst into laughter so raucous that heads turned in the newsroom. "Alright, you bastard," he said, snatching the cheque from Howard's outstretched hand. "Agreed." He smiled. "And thanks."

Howard waved off his gratitude. "Just doing my duty as M.E., however unpleasant," he parried. "Seriously, Bliss, is there any way I can convince you to stay on at the paper? It needs you. Hell, I need you. And don't worry about Renata. She thinks I can walk on water these days. I can make things right with her."

Browning shook his head. "Thanks, Harry. I'm really tempted — working for you would be a treat. But it's time to move on." He looked through the open doorway — Harry's doorway — and into the newsroom. "There are too many associations for me here. Too much of the old Bliss." A soft smile formed, giving his face a faraway look. "I found something essential in Greece, Harry. Something missing here. That's where I belong."

"I understand, Bliss. But how will you live?"

"Don't worry about me, Harry. I've got some money saved up. It's not hard when you're single with a decent job and only a few vices. That will tide me over till I can establish myself as a freelance travel writer." He laughed out loud. "Imagine Harry, after all those years of reading about it, I'm finally going to see the world."

Howard fiddled with a pencil on his desk. "What about your friend, what's her name again?"

"Matina."

"Yes, Matina."

"Matina," Browning began, pronouncing her name reverently, as if it were holy, "is very special. Her life has been a succession of cruel blows, yet she is undefeated. Someday I hope she'll agree to be my wife." Howard was watching him closely. "But there's no rush. I can wait."

THE DAY before Browning was due to return to Greece, an aging man who looked vaguely familiar accosted him on a downtown street. "Mitchell!" he cried.

The name jarred Browning's memory of his encounter with a booze-breathed bum on Sparks Street, and the $20 donation he'd coughed up to be rid of him. But this was not the Joseph Louis Bergeron he remembered. The bum's limp had mysteriously vanished. His shabby clothes had been replaced by a neat if nondescript suit and tie.

His cheeks were stubble-free. Bearhugging Browning, Bergeron explained what had happened since their last meeting.

"You don't know what you do when you give dat $20," he began. "You change ma vie, for sure. I was a bum, let's face it, un alcoolique. Dat story about ma jambe mauvais, I make dat up."

Browning arched his eyebrows. "No kidding," he said dryly. "I never guessed."

But Bergeron was oblivious to irony. "When you give me dat $20, I can't believe ma bonne chance. Most times, people give a quarter, maybe a loonie, but $20! C'est incroyable! I start right away tinking about buying a bottle, but then, all at once, j'arrete. No, Joseph Louis, I say, dis is un sign. Maybe from God, I dunno. Dis is ma chance to make something of ma vie mauvaise. Redeem myself. Get out of de goddamn gutter.

"So I put your $20 dans ma poche. Le jour suivant, I go to de Sally Ann and buy de best suit I can. I wear it now." Bergeron stopped and modeled the grey pinstriped garment. "Very smart," Browning said.

"Anyway," Bergeron continued, "I put on de suit and start looking for a job. De very next day, I get one! Okay, it's selling coupon books door to door, pas un bon travail, mais Mitchell, c'est un travail! Turns out I'm good at it too, Tabernacle. Must have learned something from tous les ans as a bum. I already make plus de mille dollars," he said proudly.

"Tremendous," murmured Browning, who in truth was astonished by Bergeron's transformation.

"All I need was une chance," Bergeron said, "and dat, you give it to me, mon ami, avec ton $20. Oh," he exclaimed, "dat remind me." Bergeron pulled a wallet fat with $20 bills from his breast pocket and peeled one off. "I tell you I pay it back," he said, thrusting the bill in Browning's direction. "No," Browning protested, "you don't have to do that. The way you used that money has rewarded me many times over."

"S'il vous plait," Bergeron insisted. "I took dis money under, um, false pretensions. I tank God you give it to me, but I now must give it back. S'il vous plait. S’il vous plait."

Browning looked at the reclaimed man before him. He thought of life's astonishing quirkiness. The differences that divide us. The similarities that connect us. "I understand," he said, accepting the bill. "Thank you."

"No," said Bergeron. "I tank you, Mitchell."

"The name is Bliss Browning," said the former Mitchell, extending his right hand, "and I'm honoured to make your acquaintance."

FROM THE AUTHOR

Thank you for reading *A Life of Bliss*. I hope you enjoyed it. Please take a moment to give it a review on Amazon.

Sincerely, Don Butler.

ABOUT THE AUTHOR

Don Butler is an award-winning journalist, who spent more than four decades at the Ottawa Citizen, including six years as executive editor. He lives in Ottawa, Canada, is married to fellow journalist Christina Spencer and has two grown children, Sean Butler and Meagan Zucco. He has been to Greece four times and may even have had some of the travel experiences recounted in this book. *A Life of Bliss* is his first novel.

Manufactured by Amazon.ca
Bolton, ON

27308682R00173